WHAT WE FOUND INSTEAD

WHAT WE FOUND INSTEAD

A novel

HEIDI REIMER

LAKE UNION PUBLISHING

This is a work of fiction. Names, characters, organizations, places, events, and incidents are either products of the author's imagination or are used fictitiously. Otherwise, any resemblance to actual persons, living or dead, is purely coincidental.

Published by Lake Union Publishing, Seattle
www.apub.com

EU product safety contact:
Amazon Media EU S. à r.l.
38, avenue John F. Kennedy, L-1855 Luxembourg
amazonpublishing-gpsr@amazon.com

ISBN-13: 9781662539923 (paperback)
ISBN-13: 9781662539930 (digital)

Cover design by Kathleen Lynch/Black Kat Design
Cover image: © Rebecca Aldernet

Printed in the United States of America

For Anena

PART 1

May

Chapter 1

Maggie

Maggie Dunn hacked into her boyfriend's phone and an unknown female voice joined her in the room. The passcode took only a couple of guesses: his birth year, their anniversary, and finally—more lighthearted stab than serious guess—the four digits that spelled out his name. *Really, Karl?* she thought. *And you work in a bank?*

The battery was at fifteen percent and she'd meant only to plug the phone in, having discovered the cold lump of it under her naked thigh on his unmade bed shortly after he kissed her goodbye. He couldn't have made it far. She'd shoved aside her laptop, got out of bed, and thrust her arms into the sleeves of his grey flannel bathrobe. The ceiling of his airy attic studio sloped, and she ducked under it and opened the door in time to see his blond head swallowed into the throng of morning commuters. With one hand clutching his phone and the other grasping the railing, she yelled, "Karl!"

It was Friday, the day he traveled north after work to help at his parents' lakeside home—repair docks for his aging father, spoon broth into his ailing mother, and whatever else he did without her every weekend.

"Karl!" she called again, creeping gingerly down the wooden steps in her bare feet. The spring sun was warm on her face, and for a moment she was distracted by the unexpected sensory pleasure. "Karl!" He didn't turn around.

She'd have to drop it at the bank for him on her way to work. She turned back inside to caffeinate her brain and start tackling one of the thousand tasks awaiting her. Well, one task: completely rewriting the dissertation her supervisor had just informed her would not pass. *Here are eight thousand revisions you must make, I've taken the liberty of canceling your dissertation defense, sorry, I know you've only been working on this for eleven years.*

That's when she saw it: Karl had a new voicemail.

Her finger hovered above the screen. *Turn it off, Maggie.*

It could be urgent. His mother, her cancer—

The code got her into the phone, then the voicemail. She set the audio to speaker and placed the phone on the bed, as though physically distancing herself from it minimized her transgression. The woman's voice was clear and unhurried. Solid, substantial. The pitch deep for a woman.

"Hey, baby, it's me," said the voice. "I was trying to catch you before you left for work. I just had a thought—remember how you broke that sandal last summer? The weather's warming up this weekend, so if you get this in time, bring it and I'll fix it while you're here. That's it. Love you! See you tonight."

Maggie, standing beside the bed, began to tremble. She reached for the phone but gripped the puffy white duvet instead, squeezing hard.

Baby.

Love.

Tonight.

Trying to steady her hand, she pressed play a second time, standing stock-still as the words entered her, alarming in their casualness.

Not smarmy or provocative, just practical and loving and serene. *I called to fix your sandal.*

Who was calling to fix Karl's sandal?

Maggie snatched up the phone and searched the missed calls list. Half an hour ago, someone named Eve.

Karl always kept his phone on silent. Half an hour ago, they were having sex.

She played the message again. The voice was calming, the tone easy, as though Eve didn't mind that Karl hadn't answered when she'd called. As though she knew without a doubt that he would be with her tonight. As though it wouldn't occur to her to worry, when she said *Love you*, whether he loved her back.

A woman who knew about the sandal that broke last summer as Maggie and Karl outran a rainstorm on College Street together, five hours after they met, thirty minutes before Maggie's desire erupted into romance.

Heart pounding, Maggie pulled up his texts and searched for the name Eve. Nothing. She scrolled his recent calls—Eve, no last name, appeared over and over—and then she swiped to his inbox, where she found hundreds of emails from an Eve Moretti. She spoke the full name out loud, then the email address too, trying to take in the existence of this woman. The most recent message was from Wednesday; Eve had forwarded an order confirmation from a pet store. A note at the top read Flora's new bed—pick up on your way home? xo E.

Holy hell, and who was Flora? Did Karl have a *kid*? No. It was a pet store. It was a dog bed. Karl had a dog. Or Eve Moretti had a dog, for whom Karl picked up purchases on his way home. Except his home was *here*. Maggie was standing in it.

She felt herself hyperventilating. Forcing herself to deepen her breath, Maggie searched for her own name. Apart from the texts they'd exchanged this week, she wasn't there. In Karl's phone, Maggie existed only from Sunday afternoon on.

Footsteps pounded on the stairs outside. Maggie dropped the phone to the bed and threw the duvet over it, turning around just as Karl came back through the door.

"Forgot my phone." Karl, always relaxed and upbeat, looked the slightest bit agitated.

She stared at him, frozen. He rummaged in the bedside drawer, then threw back the covers and grabbed the phone.

"My mom freaks out if she can't reach me," he said.

The mom he wouldn't let her meet.

She was spiraling, standing there in her bare feet beside the man she loved, who suddenly looked like a man she did not know. She had yet to say a word.

He kissed her on the mouth, hurriedly. "Everything okay, babe?" he asked.

She managed a nod.

"Gotta run, love you!" He dashed out, his overnight bag banging against his thigh.

Those trips—all those trips north—almost every single weekend! Cancer the ultimate argument ender, Maggie petty and selfish to even consider complaining. Karl's evasions when she asked if she could join him, if she might even help out: *My parents aren't very social, trust me, baby, it wouldn't be fun.* His protectiveness of his phone, the way he always kept it in his back pocket or tucked inside the nightstand. He must have been distracted this morning—by the knowledge that he'd be seeing Eve soon? By excitement at getting away from Maggie and being with *her*?

Maggie's fingers shook as she clutched her own phone and googled the name Eve Moretti. The first hit brought up the website for some place in Northern Ontario called Labelle's Cabins. At the bottom of the page, under the heading *Your Hosts,* were two photos: an older moustachioed man holding a fish, and a stunning woman in a canoe. She had short, disheveled hair against tanned skin, and her long legs were bare in ragged cutoffs. The caption under the photo read *Eve Moretti.*

Maggie navigated to the photo gallery and scrolled frantically through it. There amongst snapshots of little log cottages and kids leaping from docks was a photo of Karl, unmistakably Karl, lit by the flames of a bonfire. The date was last September, a month into Maggie and Karl's relationship. At the fireside Karl faced Eve Moretti, soft-eyed and open. Maggie sank to the bed, gut-punched by undeniable evidence. It was a look of adoration.

Her breath came in quick gasps as she dialed her mother, far away on sabbatical in Crete. But as she waited for connection, anticipating the soothing evenness of her voice, the thought of recounting another crisis to her mother felt too shameful—not now, on the heels of her academic failure. She ended the call and tried her best friend, Charmaine, choking back panic as the phone rang and rang.

Did Eve know that when the sole peeled from Karl's sandal, he tripped and slammed into her, and they clutched each other, gasping with hilarity and unacknowledged, unexplored electricity? Did she know they stumble-ran together, Karl hampered by his broken sandal, both of them drenched and laughing, and at Maggie's apartment she'd led him to the bathroom, turned on the shower, and stripped off her wet dress? He followed her in without stopping to remove his clothes.

Maggie's black lace negligee nestled against Karl's pale pressed shirts and dark pants. She plucked it from the closet, the hangers clinking against each other as they swayed. Her toothbrush on the bathroom sink, her spare clothes in the bottom drawer, the dried head of a rose on the dresser, left over from a bouquet she'd given him—she took them all. The message played over and over in her head while she zipped her dress, smeared on lipstick, stuffed her laptop into her bag.

As she descended the stairs to the street, she placed one hand over her heart. What she felt, beneath the mounting alarm, was something so much deeper and quieter that she did not identify it until she was on the streetcar, surging and stalling through the clogged street. It was resolve.

She would find Eve Moretti. She would uncover the truth. She would not be felled by this.

Chapter 2

Eve

Eve Moretti was still in her rubber boots and worn jeans, dragging her canoe ashore early Friday evening, when she recognized the rumbling muffler of Karl's Jeep Wrangler as he shifted for the gravel slope. Her chocolate lab, Flora, heard it too, bounding up the path and behind the house to greet him. Eve followed more slowly, savoring her own delight at her favorite moment of the week.

The car door opened and Karl's head sprang up beside it. He dropped to the ground and met Flora as she leapt. They tussled, Flora pretend-growling and Karl pretend-growling back.

"All right, you'll wreck your fancy bank shirt," Eve said at last, and Karl gave Flora a final push as she nipped at his shirttails, then rose to meet Eve, one hand to her waist and the other twined through her cropped curly hair.

"You smell good." Eve pressed her nose to his shoulder, laughing at herself. "Woodsmoke and sauna."

He grinned. "Hey, not bad. I'll take it."

She sniffed him again. "But also concrete and street meat and *city*."

He narrowed his eyes at her.

"And maybe a hint of climate-controlled corporate air."

He grinned with the easygoing self-confidence that had first won Eve over, and she kissed him.

"You made good time," she said.

"I left early." He released her to turn back to the Wrangler and retrieve a large paper bag from the back seat. "And I brought dinner, as promised."

She saw the logo on the bag. "From that trattoria that makes the excellent bolognese?"

"We'll just have to heat it."

"You are perfect."

"Aren't I? I picked up a few groceries too, but these are just from Larkin, so nothing special."

"You get my message about bringing your sandals?"

"What message?"

"I left you a voicemail. I thought I'd finally fix that sandal."

"Oh. No." He pulled his phone from his pocket. "No notification, sorry. Weird. But I'm pretty sure I tossed those sandals last year. I did get *this* for Flora, though." He pulled a red checkered dog bed from the back seat.

Eve took the bed and grasped the handle of a cloth grocery bag while Karl bundled the rest into his arms, and they climbed her sturdy steps side by side.

Indoors, Eve built up the fire in the glass-fronted wood stove while Karl heated dinner and opened a bottle of wine. She leaned back on her heels as she waited for the flame to spread, watching him in her kitchen. He moved fluidly between the knotted barnboard cupboards and her giant dining table—the only piece of her own she'd sent from New York, and it was huge, a solid slab of oak she could have sold for many thousands. It had practically cost that to ship it.

Karl sliced a loaf of ciabatta and set it on the table with plates and cutlery, crossed the floor to hand her a glass of red wine. The fire whooshed to life. She gave it one last blow, took a sip of the wine, and padded to the kitchen island to help him fix a salad. They sat down at the table together, and as they ate she told him about the rust-brick patio she was laying at Labelle's Cabins and listened to his work story of the forgery scam he'd narrowly averted, happening to glance at the check as the teller was putting it through. They'd called the police, and an investigation was underway.

"Good thing something's keeping your adrenaline up," she said. Teasing but not teasing, because in Karl's previous career with a travel expedition company, his official title had been Adventurer, and banking was definitely a step down in the thrills department.

"Are you going to your parents' tomorrow or Sunday?" she asked.

"Sunday, I think, on my way out."

"Bold choice. Putting your mother off till the very end."

Karl laughed and shook his head. "Poor Ma. She'll be fine."

"She misses her boy."

"How about you? You miss your boy?"

They both laughed at the clumsy segue, and Eve pushed her chair back and went around the table to straddle him.

"Sure did."

His fingers massaged her rib cage under her shirt, crept upward and cupped her breasts, and she kissed him until he pulled her shirt over her head and nudged her to the braided rug beside the wood stove. She shook her head and shoved him off, scuttled to the bathroom to yank open the bottom drawer.

The flap of the condom box wagged hollowly against the side as she shook it. She rooted in the drawer for a stray.

"Do you have a condom?" she called from the bathroom.

He was naked now, a muscled sculpture in her living room, waiting for her.

He grinned. "Risky sex is the only sex worth having, baby."

"Awfully flippant for a man who doesn't want kids."

"Do we really have to worry about that? How old are you now, almost fifty?"

"Ha. Forty-three, you asshole, a measly year older than you. Keep talking like that and no one's getting laid."

"You know you don't look a day over twenty-five. Give me a second."

She watched from the bathroom window as he scampered buck naked into the night. He opened the front door of the Wrangler and bent over to reach into the glove compartment, wagging his butt in the air for her benefit, and she laughed. Back inside, he deposited a jumble of silver-wrapped Trojans into her hands. She'd thought his emergency Wrangler stash was strange when they first met, like he was a horny teenager hoping for sex around every bend, but it had come to their rescue more than once. Usually after a hike, miles down a back road, both of them sweaty and exuberant and ready for more.

She dropped the extra condoms into the bathroom drawer and returned to the living room. They made out in front of the wood stove, Karl unzipping her jeans and slipping them down her hips as they kissed. She tore the condom wrapper open with her teeth. A full moon hung outside the kitchen's wall of windows, and as he moved inside her she stared over his shoulder at it, large and near, a third presence in the room. Afterward they went onto the deck to look at the moon and its reflection, two white orbs against black sky and black water. Both shivering, he bare-chested and she wearing only his button-down bank shirt.

Eve received the email on Monday, her first day back at work after Karl returned to the city. She was eating a chicken sandwich at the desk in the office, checking reservation inquiries, when she switched to her personal inbox. She had a new email from someone named Maggie Dunn. Subject line: Please Read. I'm Sorry.

It sounded like spam. She almost deleted the email, but the desperation of the subject line drew her in.

> Hi Eve,
>
> I'm crossing my fingers this reaches you. I have something important to discuss with you concerning Karl Tarvudd, and I'd like to meet you.

> There's no nice way to say this, so I'll come out with it: I think Karl is playing us both. I feel strongly that we need to speak about this face to face. I'll be at the Georgian Bay Travel Center on Thursday, May 11, at 2 p.m. I believe that is the halfway point between us. Please text or email to confirm this time works for you. I'll explain everything I know. I realize this is out of the blue and probably sounds crazy, but I'm hoping that despite this you'll trust me as one woman to another and will agree to meet.
>
> Karl doesn't know I'm contacting you. Please don't tell him. I'd prefer if we could try to get to the bottom of this together.
>
> If I sound calm, the truth is that I'm freaking out. Please meet me.
>
> Again, I'm very sorry.
>
> Maggie Dunn

At the bottom was a phone number.

Eve's first thoughts were logistical. She deliberately didn't own a cellphone, so she wouldn't be texting this person.

Her second impulse was to laugh. Karl had mentioned crazy ex-girlfriends before, usually in the context of his relief to be with someone as even-keeled as Eve. Clearly this was one of them. Georgian Bay was at least two hours away; she wasn't taking half a day off to go hear some deranged theory from a stranger who herself admitted that she was freaking out.

But all that day, the email nagged at her. Twice as the afternoon wore on, she picked up the phone in the office to dial Karl, to ask him who

Maggie was and why she thought Karl was playing them. Both times, instead, she hung up and stared vacantly out the window.

Please don't tell Karl.

Trust me as one woman to another.

She thought of the women she knew—her manipulative mother, her gossipy aunts, her exhaustingly sunny sister-in-law. Did she trust them just because they were women? Ha. No, she did not.

When she got home from work she took the canoe out. Flora perched at the bow, spine straight, eyes alert to water bugs and beavers. The next-door neighbor's fishing lodge slumped on the hill above her, two log buildings natural and modest as decaying trees on a forest floor. Windows peeped through slits of half-drawn blinds and plywood X's bolstering cracked glass. Eve dipped her paddle and the canoe skimmed closer.

Bernice, the woman who'd run the lodge in its heyday, shuffled down the staircase that cut into the slope between the lake and the lodge. Eve remembered her from childhood, old even then. Eve waved, but Bernice only stared, motionless, like a forest animal into whose territory Eve was trespassing.

Bernice definitely didn't trust Eve just because she was a woman.

Eve canoed on past the old lodge, then leaned back, her paddle resting across the gunwales, and dunked her fingers into the water. It was spring-cold and bracing. She shook off the wetness, tucked her tingling hand into her pocket, and let the canoe drift. Spring peepers were beginning their night song, and the sun had already set, the sky a deep grey-blue with leftover strands of pale pink.

This was why she'd moved here. Peace. Isolation. Desire to escape the type of stress Maggie Dunn had lobbed at her in this letter.

Playing her? Karl was not playing her.

She plunged her paddle in and J-stroked the canoe homeward. From the lake her house was almost invisible, cedar siding shingles an extension of earth and trees, tall windowpanes reflecting water. Karl was campaigning to borrow a chainsaw and let in more light, but it was the insulation she loved, the cool, protective darkness. Her house enclosed. Guarded. Safe.

Safe. She *was* safe. She was a grown-ass woman who'd built a life she loved and a relationship she loved, and she had no intention of inviting some stranger's drama into it.

For the first time since she'd moved here, she wished she had internet or a smartphone, just for the satisfaction of deleting that email. She had to wait till she was at work the next day, but as soon as she arrived, she marched straight to the office, sent Maggie Dunn's email to the trash, and emptied the bin.

Chapter 3

Maggie

With every dark-haired woman who pushed through the door of the Georgian Bay Travel Center, Maggie's heart accelerated and her legs braced to rise. Eve Moretti hadn't reached out to Maggie, hadn't texted or emailed or called or otherwise given any indication that she would show, yet here Maggie was, sitting in a mini-booth with a view of the entrance, two and a half hours north of the city. She'd borrowed Karl's car—he thought she was helping her roommates with a trip to IKEA—and she'd called in sick to Sukha, the bookstore-café and event space where she worked. On nothing but intuition, hope, and a desperate need to know, she'd driven into the wilderness to meet Eve.

She'd arrived early and her laptop was open to her dissertation, her belief that she might get work done in this state of mind a symbol of all her greater delusions. That she was in a solid relationship. That she was cherished. That her future was sunny. She switched to her web browser's history and brought up the search results for Eve Moretti. Apart from the cabin website, the links were mostly New York City-based, a bizarre assortment of design blogs and trade magazines, woodworking journals and culture sites. A mention in *Architectural Digest*, in a celebrity home tour, tasteful curve-legged wooden chairs and the caption *by NYC artisan Eve Moretti, founder of Stillcraft Designer Furniture.* And then the big one, a huge spread in *New York Magazine.* Close-cropped curly hair, brown-black eyes, a simple button-down. *"I work with wood so I can disappear,"* purred a pull quote, oxymoronically, above the giant close-up. In marginal insets, photos of a bookcase, a graceful desk with a dozen tiny drawers, an elaborate, whimsical birdhouse.

This was the woman she was hoping would walk through that door. This was, evidently, Karl's Eve, because those same dark curls and effortless style appeared in that campfire picture with Karl on the Labelle's Cabins site.

To the left of the door, canoe-emblazoned sweatshirts and racks of brochures welcomed Maggie to the north. In the other corner, the head of a moose was pinioned on a board, its eyes arrested in wide, startled dismay.

Was it possible Eve already knew about Maggie? Maybe she didn't care. Maybe Karl was with Eve first but they had an open relationship—one he'd neglected to mention. Maybe he was with Maggie first and he'd told Eve about her, but Eve was the kind of emotionally secure, morally bankrupt person who could be like, *No problem.*

Maggie hadn't seen Karl in the six days since she'd discovered Eve on his voicemail. Confronting Karl would have been the obvious choice—definitely less logistically complicated—but she'd spent the past six days questioning every word he'd ever spoken and every action he'd ever taken, and the last person she trusted to give her the truth was Karl. She wanted to look into the eyes of the one other woman in the same position as her, and she wanted to arrive at the full truth together. All week she'd begged off seeing Karl with excuses of failed-dissertation overwhelm and work at Sukha and general exhaustion. She *was* exhausted. Turned out that discovering your life was not your life was mentally, emotionally, and physically decimating.

She was a generally cheerful person, and she could usually bright-side life's bumps; just look at her with this dissertation—*of course, I can totally rework this, no biggie!* But she was having trouble summoning optimism about being cheated on. The only person she'd told, other than Eve herself, was Charmaine, who worried that driving all this way to meet Eve could backfire in all sorts of ways. Surely if Eve was going to come, she'd have messaged by now; if she did come, there was no guarantee she would be gracious. Maggie had told Eve in an email, a decision she'd second-guessed a hundred times since. She'd tried not to spill everything, while still giving enough detail to convince Eve to meet. *You and I are in a relationship with the same man*—though she'd more than implied it—seemed like information more respectful to deliver in person, where Maggie could convey through body language and tone of voice that she wasn't a threat.

But she was beginning to worry that Eve might turn out to be one.

Maggie and Karl had met in the most old-fashioned of ways: at a party. She loved that it wasn't on the apps—so authentic, so romantic! She'd been on a dozen first dates in the previous month with no trace of spark, and she was staring down a future of soulless connections with maladjusted man-children while her ovaries shriveled and she died of loneliness. And then she showed up at her friend Jasmine's housewarming party, and Karl opened the door when she rang the bell, and Maggie took one look and thought, *Who* is *that?*

An acquaintance of Jasmine's husband's, it turned out; they'd met at the gym and had started playing squash together, and he'd invited Karl spontaneously just that morning. Karl was vital and funny and thoughtful, as she discovered over the course of three hours, trying not to be over-obvious in her desire to talk with no one but him. He laughed at her jokes and made eye contact like he was really seeing her, and by the end of the night she was entirely smitten. They left the party at the same time and were both headed west, so getting on the same streetcar was natural. At her stop she proposed they get a drink, and after that his sandal broke as they ran in the rain.

Come on, Maggie, she thought, *find your center.* She pressed both hands over her heart, closed her eyes, and forced herself to breathe deeply.

When she looked again at the door, there on the other side, pulling the handle, was the woman from the campfire photo. She wore jeans torn at the knee and a long-sleeved white shirt, bright against tanned skin, and she was striding forward into the building.

Maggie wobbled to her feet and held her body as tall as it could go. Eve Moretti walked briskly between tables, scanning faces, progressing rapidly in Maggie's direction.

Maggie reached out her hand as Eve was about to pass her. "Eve."

Eve stopped abruptly beside Maggie's table. She stared at Maggie, brow furrowed. "Why is Karl's car here?" she asked.

"Oh. I borrowed it."

"Does he know?"

"Yeah, of course."

Eve had not taken her hand, and Maggie retracted it to fiddle with the belt on her skirt.

"I'm Maggie," she said. "The weirdo who sent you that email?" She laughed nervously. "I guess that's obvious."

"Please tell me what's going on," Eve said.

She definitely didn't know about Maggie. She definitely cared.

"Do you want a coffee? Or tea or a muffin or a spoonful of sugar to, you know, help the medicine go down?"

"I'm fine."

Okay, then. Not a Mary Poppins fan. No pleasantries. Straight in.

"Will you please sit, at least? I'd love for this to be an actual conversation."

Eve dropped into the seat opposite Maggie's, straight-backed and regal, her stare leveled at Maggie.

"You think Karl is playing us both," Eve said before Maggie could sink back into her own seat, before she could land on the right tone for what she needed to say to the person Eve Moretti had turned out to be. Not the warm, laid-back earth mother who fixed sandals instead of buying new ones, but this suspicious, sharp-edged woman who would clearly have no qualms about disappearing Maggie through a crater in the floor.

Maggie gripped the table as she sat.

"What I want to know," Eve said, "is why you say that. I'd like some facts."

Maggie felt like she was defending her dissertation after all. This interaction was progressing far more aggressively than she'd hoped for, and she was not in control of it. She'd imagined easing in. She'd wanted to get Eve to like her before she dropped the bomb—or to be positively inclined toward her, at least. Which had clearly always been a far-fetched expectation.

"Karl lives in Toronto," Maggie said, launching into Exhibit A. "He's only up north on weekends."

"He lives up north," said Eve. "He's only in Toronto for his job during the week."

"Right. Okay." Maggie was startled by this alternate perspective. "Either way—two places, two homes, two . . . lives, right?"

Eve squeezed her hands together on the table between them. "What are you trying to imply?"

Maggie hesitated for a moment. She couldn't say it. "Can I ask how long you've been together?" she asked instead.

"Two years."

For one brief moment Maggie covered her face with her hands and closed her eyes. Karl was not, then, cheating on Maggie with Eve. He was cheating on Eve with Maggie.

"We've been together nine months." Maggie blurted the words.

Eve laughed, a derisive, incredulous spurt of sound. "No, you haven't."

Maggie opened her eyes. "Yes. We have."

Chapter 4

Eve

Eve took in the swooping bangs and the dirty-blond bob that fell with a slight wave to Maggie's shoulders. Open face, lips stained bold red, eyes enlarged with the right brush strokes, and an earnest wonder.

"Do you have a phone?" Eve asked.

"Of course."

"Can I borrow it?"

Maggie looked uncertain, but Eve held out her hand and Maggie slid her iPhone across the table.

"What are you doing?" Maggie asked.

"Calling Karl."

"No, please!" Maggie snatched the phone back. "I really wanted just to talk, the two of us—woman to woman. To get at the truth together without whatever excuses or lies Karl might give us."

"It makes you seem more unhinged, you know, the fact that you don't want me to ask Karl about you. Because then I'd uncover *your* lies?" Eve stood. She was grasping at any means of invalidating Maggie's claim, but she could feel her body starting to shake, just a little.

"Then why are you here?" Maggie rose, her voice hitching toward desperation. "Why did you drive all this way?"

Eve turned away from Maggie and stared into the parking lot at the black pavement and bright-yellow lines, at Karl's metallic-blue Wrangler.

She hadn't planned to come. She'd tried to put the email out of her mind, but by this morning she'd had to admit that her inability to focus—or to think about anything else at all—meant she was not succeeding.

She'd never thought Karl was evasive or withholding—no more than she was, at least; she didn't *want* a partnership of constant analysis or forced sharing. They were comfortable together. They weren't demanding. She'd even thought of their long-distance relationship as ideal, the solitude she craved with weekly forays into intimacy that prevented her from hardening up.

But apart from the office party invites he knew she'd decline, he'd never suggested she come for a weekend in Toronto. He seemed edgy whenever she borrowed his phone, which she'd chalked up to digital addiction and had even smugly teased him about. And she'd once found an earring in the Wrangler, fallen between the passenger seat and the door. He said he'd given a co-worker a ride to work and it must be hers, but she knew he never drove to work because the bank was downtown and parking was a bitch. Why hadn't she asked him what he was doing driving to work?

She'd deleted Maggie's email before she could think through the implications, so she didn't have a phone number to call and demand an explanation. But she did remember the meeting place and time.

She would just get a look at Maggie, she told herself. Scope her out. If Maggie turned out to be a stalker, Eve should know who to watch out for.

The Wrangler, when Eve parked and walked toward the entrance, had alarmed her. She'd headed straight to it and peered through the windows. Karl's running shoes on the back seat. His kayaking sticker on the dash. A tube of lipstick in the tray.

Trust me as one woman to another.

Please don't tell Karl.

From the moment Eve read the email, part of her had feared that Maggie was telling the truth. Of course she'd feared that. Why else wouldn't she have asked Karl about her? Why else would she have driven for two fucking hours?

"Okay." Eve dropped back into her seat. "Okay. Tell me this again."

"Karl is my boyfriend," Maggie said. "He's been my boyfriend for nine months."

"Boyfriend."

"My partner. My *person.*"

"And you're telling me this because . . . ?"

"Because I might not know you, but I do know we're both women, and I do know it's looking a hell of a lot like we've both been betrayed by the same man."

"*Betrayed.*" Eve couldn't stop repeating the stunning words coming out of Maggie's mouth.

"Yes, *betrayed.* Screwed. However you want to put it. I told you—he's playing us both! Which puts us in the same position." She took a breath before continuing. "Maybe it's illogical, but you were the only person I wanted to talk to about it."

Maggie reached for Eve's arm, and Eve flinched and pulled away. She was only just willing to listen to this woman; she definitely wasn't ready to be touched by her.

"Starting by just telling you," Maggie said. "Until last Friday, I didn't know either, I swear. I found out last week, and I wrote to you."

"It's a bit presumptuous, you contacting me like that."

"You do mind that he's been with someone else for nine months and hiding it, don't you?"

"Of course I fucking *mind*!"

Heads turned. Eve looked away, setting her eyes again on Karl's Wrangler in the parking lot, the one familiar object in this bizarre, horrible show she'd stumbled into. There was the rust Karl kicked at, the gash in the paint where Eve had once scraped a tree, the back seat where they'd had sex after running empty on a back road. She wanted to steal into the passenger seat and kiss Karl at the wheel and drive away with him, home. She didn't want to know that Karl's Wrangler was here only because this woman drove it here, because Karl loaned it to her, because she was his girlfriend.

She may have reveled in their independence, the health and balance of their separate lives, but that didn't mean she wanted him to take up a separate life with a whole other partner.

"Why should I believe you?" Eve asked.

"I thought I could show you texts?"

Eve imagined pet names, sexting. *Please no.*

"Or pictures?" Maggie suggested. "Nothing explicit. I know it's kind of uncomfortable, but I can understand if you're having trouble processing this, and maybe you need to really see it? If you . . . if you want to."

"I damn well want to."

She did *not* want to, but she couldn't walk away from this encounter without definitive proof. Maggie unlocked her phone and turned it to face Eve. A photo filled the screen, but Eve could bear it only through lowered lids, forcing her gaze to the surrounding details. Grass and a blue sky. A stage, lights, a crowd of summer-dressed strangers at some kind of festival. Her eyes circled at last to the focal point: Karl and this woman in matching band T-shirts, Karl's arm around her. It was friendly. But it was more than friendly. It was—alive with something. Charged. Intimate.

Maggie flicked her finger across the phone. Had she created a special album? *Proof of Relationship with Karl for Doubting Sucker Girlfriend*?

Karl grinning at this woman in a kitchen, a wooden spoon in his hand and a pot on the stove. Karl behind her at a party, arms around her waist, chin resting on her head. Karl and Maggie on a ferry, his hand proprietary at her waist, Maggie's hair blowing against his shoulder. In this one he looked constrained, uncertain, as though at the moment of the flash he might have been thinking of Eve.

"When was this taken?" she asked. This could have been years ago. Maggie could still be a crazy ex-girlfriend.

Maggie pressed her finger to the screen. The date appeared, irrefutable. Last September.

"I want to see more," Eve said.

"You sure?"

"I said I did," Eve snapped. She had to be certain. Or maybe she was inoculating herself. Or maybe she was punishing herself.

Karl and Maggie enjoying a candlelit dinner. Karl and Maggie in theater seats. Karl and Maggie snuggling together in bed. Eve recognized the haircut she'd given him sometime in the fall, saw the passage of time as it grew out. In the restaurant picture Karl had mushrooms on his plate. Karl never ate mushrooms. These were photographs of a stranger, someone in another place with another life.

It was not casual. It was not sex or the occasional date. It was a relationship.

Eve waved the phone away, and Maggie returned it quietly to her bag. All Eve wanted was to flee. Back to her home, back to her dog. Back with Karl. She did not want to share her disgrace with the stranger who had partnered her boyfriend for nine months while she—what had she been doing?

Trusting.

Apparently she'd succeeded in transcending her emotional remove; apparently, with Karl, she'd managed to open her walled-off heart and *trust*.

Because would it hurt this much if she hadn't?

Wordlessly Eve gathered her keys and stalked to the exit. Travelers streamed through the door, held it for others, spoke in carefree tones. She looked back and saw Maggie with her head in her hands, hunched over the table with her phone, her evidence, her truth.

Chapter 5

Maggie

Maggie cried as she drove back to Toronto. Her disappointment was so huge that she only now realized how sky-high her expectations had been for this encounter with Eve Moretti, sandal-mender, furniture-maker, employee of Labelle's Cabins, girlfriend of her boyfriend. She'd wanted answers, explanations, some comparing of notes and dates to decode how this had unfolded, where Karl had been when they'd each thought he was someplace else, what truths had lain between them all this time. But more than that, she'd hoped for commiseration, some female solidarity even, some clinging together in their mutual pain. Maybe thanks for giving Eve the truth, for courageously facing her rival, for putting her own work on hold so that a woman she didn't know and should despise would be deceived no longer.

She was vaguely aware of silver-black rock rising on either side of the 400, of peeling white birch and glistening lakes. She'd fantasized about coming here with Karl, loading the Wrangler on a Friday afternoon, chatting and playing music over a shared bag of kettle chips, her hand on his thigh. She'd fantasized about meeting his parents, making them love her. She'd planned their engagement party. She'd daydreamed the faces of their future children. She'd *named* them.

She punched her earbuds in, driving one-handed. Charmaine had appointments all afternoon, so she called her mother. Her "Hello" in Maggie's ears was immediately calming.

"Go over to the house if you need to get away from your roommates," her mom said after Maggie had spilled the sad tale of Karl's duplicity. "Dad's at his office so much, it'll be almost like having the place to yourself."

"I *like* having people around me. And I can just imagine explaining this one to Dad. Can we please keep him in the dark on this particular disaster?"

"Oh, sweetie. Don't think of it like that. And I only meant that being in a quieter space for a while might be rejuvenating. Without roommates *or* boyfriends." No condolence, only a suggested path forward, compassionate but practical.

"I will never have a boyfriend again," Maggie said.

"A dubious proclamation, my dear."

Regret and longing twisted inside her. "If only I could be you."

Her mother clucked, and Maggie pictured her on the other end of the line, in her little Airbnb in Crete. Unruffled, self-contained Sophie Dunn, she of the measured personal life and the blip-free professional trajectory. Respected tenured professor, forty years married to Maggie's father in a partnership that Maggie would consider emotional starvation but her mother found grounding and steady. As opposed to Maggie, who was thirty-five and flailing between a never-ending Ph.D., a low-paying but nevertheless demanding job, and teaching the odd yoga class, which paid virtually nothing and would never become a career. Who'd thrown herself body and soul into one doomed relationship after another, Karl just the latest in the pileup.

"Do you have the impression that I want you to be me?" her mother said.

"I definitely wouldn't be driving my cheating boyfriend's car away from a meetup with his hostile *other* girlfriend if I were."

"You never know."

The image was so incongruous, it made Maggie laugh out loud. "Dad probably wouldn't even notice if you had someone on the side," she said.

Or maybe that wasn't funny—Maggie, after all, hadn't noticed either. Or wait—*Maggie* was the *someone on the side* in this scenario, and Eve was the one who hadn't noticed. *Maggie* was the other woman.

"Are you taking care of yourself?" her mother asked. "Remembering to eat? Don't let this get in the way of your work. I know that not defending this spring is a huge setback, but if you focus and take it seriously, I know you can do it. Maybe by fall?"

"Mom, I can't even—"

"Think about the money, then, if you need extra motivation."

Maggie groaned.

"It might seem like a crass incentive, especially when you're heartbroken, but getting that money will give you options and help you move forward and create your own life."

"I do have my own life." One she'd wanted nothing more than to merge with Karl's.

"All I'm saying is the money will make a big difference for you. You're so close."

The money was in a trust arranged by her father on the day she was born, when Maggie thought maybe he ought to have been at her mother's side in the hospital room, gazing into the face of his newborn. It had started as one thousand dollars, and it had grown to a sum so astronomical Maggie could barely wrap her mind around it. Maggie also didn't *have* this money, because in his zeal for ensuring her well-being in life, coupled with his belief that money should be earned, her dad had repeatedly moved the goalposts: first, she would get it when she turned twenty-one; then, only if she'd graduated university; then, he decided a Ph.D. was crucial. The more the investment grew, the higher the stakes became. Her parents were comfortable but not wealthy; neither of them had come from money, and they'd both worked hard for their comfort. Her father didn't want financial ease handed to his only child through no effort of her own, and he wanted her to have a stable career. And while her mother had initially questioned academia as the right fit even as Maggie embraced it, the closer Maggie got to completion, the more her mother seemed to want it for her too. Both her parents worried that, left to her own devices, she'd end up careerless and penniless, endlessly adrift and struggling. No matter that it was no longer 1980, when both of Maggie's parents had walked their freshly minted doctorates directly into cushy jobs-for-life.

Though perhaps that *didn't* matter, because once Maggie got the money, she could afford to teach yoga and work in bookstore-cafés and raise a family and do whatever else she most wanted if she inevitably failed to land a non-existent job in some university's English department. She did enjoy reading, and she loved mentoring young people and fostering vibrant discussion inside a classroom. She was great at the parts of academia that involved people skills. The parts that required holing up with towering tomes and the thoughts of her own brain, producing clear arguments? Not so much.

"Listen," her mother said. "You're going to be all right. Let yourself grieve, but understand that knowing the truth now instead of further down the road is so much better."

"It just hurts, you know? I feel manipulated and disposable. And like such an idiot. Why didn't I suspect anything?"

"Your gut must have been telling you something. You wouldn't have checked his phone if it weren't."

"In my next relationship, I'll demand daily phone checks."

"Perhaps an ankle monitor."

"No, I'll keep it to location sharing. Maybe one surveillance drone."

Her mother chuckled. Love for her crested in Maggie's chest and swelled into tears. She ended the call, bereft.

She should have called her mom earlier to tell her about Karl's other girlfriend. But she was getting tired of her lifelong routine of running to her mother for consolation, of baring her missteps to her mother's calm inspection. She was also getting tired—so far beyond tired—of relationships that sapped her vitality and left her a discarded husk in the end.

Before Karl there was Judd, the man to whom she gave ages twenty-nine to thirty-four, but he put off moving in together and wasn't sure he believed in marriage and took a job in Vancouver without asking her to come with him.

Preceded by Greg, aloof and alluring until the constant chase became too painful.

Darren, who proposed when Maggie was twenty-seven, but by then she was already thinking of leaving, realizing that she loved the way he loved her, but perhaps didn't quite love *him*. She accepted the ring—they wanted the same things, she didn't want to hurt him, she could make this work!—but two months later she gave it back.

Aaron, the most passionate and tumultuous of her relationships, fights that left her exhausted, intimacy that made her high, more fights, until after a year—just before her twenty-fourth birthday—the relationship exploded like a brilliant star that couldn't contain its energy.

Jason, kind and self-deprecating and funny but also possessive and insecure and stifling; they were together all through her undergrad.

Amir, Jeremiah, Felix. Intimacy that made her feel seen and known; sex that made her feel adored and chosen; connection that was almost all she could ever want—except when they withdrew, when they criticized her, when they failed to live up to basic standards or decided she was too needy or too much. All the way back to Luke at age fifteen, her first real boyfriend, a musician who wrote her songs and showed her how deeply she could feel, how irrevocably bonded to another person she could become. Sex and romance, her heart to his, her essence to his, his body inside hers. It was impossible to get any closer to another human being. Eureka. She had found it.

Maggie had never been this far north and was relieved to be pointed south again, back toward the city. Near Barrie the traffic picked up, the rock cuts ended, cultivated fields and then box stores and industrial complexes replaced trees and water. The shift happened with one curve of the road: in the north, then not in the north. She drove thirty kilometers over the speed limit, feeling rooted and solidified to see the city unfurled in high rises and fast-flowing roads, in exits to street names she recognized.

The sun was still high enough to cast warm, gold-tinged light as Maggie crept up Major Street. Facing Karl this evening was impossible; the Wrangler could go back tomorrow. He'd need it to travel north to Eve, but what did she care if he had it on time or not. Obviously Maggie would be breaking up with him—there was no other self-respecting choice—but she wanted to do it from a place of strength, and she didn't trust herself to see him right now and not fall apart. She was too tired and too sad. A few blocks from her apartment, she slipped into a parking spot. It required an overnight permit; the possibility of towage pleased her.

Two missed calls from Karl waited on her phone.

The sidewalk was dirty and unyielding under her feet, the air several degrees warmer, even in evening, than it had been up north. She climbed the steps to the house and unlocked the front entrance. From behind her apartment door came laughter and the smells of tomato and beer.

"Maggie's home!" her roommates cheered when she walked in.

There were three of them, and they were gathered at the stove and sprawled on the sagging couch along with a couple of boyfriends and a guy she remembered from a party.

Sarita held out a red-tipped spoon, Gina at her elbow, picking leaves off a sprig of cilantro. "You're just in time for chili!"

Maggie smiled wanly. She was the de facto house mother, the eldest by ten years, but also, under normal circumstances, an excellent confidante and nurturer who liked nothing better than to be the hub of a warm, close circle. She was the one who'd taught them this chili recipe.

"You okay?" From her boyfriend's lap, ponytailed and chipper, Natalie folded her face into a concerned furrow.

Maggie sat down on the other end of the couch and said, "How'd your exam go today? Don't you have another one tomorrow?"

"Yup. Wanna tell me why you're avoiding my question?"

"It hasn't been my best day, but I'll be all right. Just a couple of setbacks lately."

"Want a beer?" asked the guy from the party.

Mason, she remembered, a drummer, a friend of Natalie's, and possibly only five years younger than Maggie. He wore his long hair gathered back with a rubber band, a brown leather jacket that looked buttery soft. The urge to rub it between her fingers was irrational and compelling. At the party they'd talked about his band and her studies. Mason was attentive. Mason was hot. Maybe Mason could love her?

She almost sobbed. She was pathetic. She shook her head at the beer Mason held out.

"Come on, what's going on?" Natalie asked, her head tilted in sympathy.

"I have to leave Karl," Maggie said, to Natalie and to the room. Apparently she was telling people now.

"No!" Natalie cried. "No, no, no. We love Karl! *You* love Karl!"

Sarita squeezed onto the couch beside Maggie, handed her a bowl of chili, and wrapped her arms around her. "What happened?"

"Cheating," Maggie said.

The room erupted in boos and gasps. She wished she hadn't spoken. She'd once shared this apartment with her closest girlfriends, all of them twentysomethings working crappy jobs and going to school and going dancing and dating people who were sometimes great and sometimes left them crying at one in the morning, and the girlfriends would rally for a cuddle pile on this very couch, hours of relationship dissection and building each other back up. Now most of those women were siloed off in homes of their own, and the tears they soothed belonged to their children, and their partners were more likely to support them in their struggles than cause them. Maggie missed Charmaine especially, with whom she'd dragged this couch six blocks after they found it on the curb the day they moved in. Who was now so consumed by her career and her family and her overfull flourishing life that Maggie expected her to be available for only one out of ten phone calls and even fewer coffee dates. While Maggie was still living with and being consoled by twentysomethings.

"I'll be okay," she said.

"Of course you will!"

"I think I'll take this to my room." Maggie hoisted herself and her chili from the couch. "I have a few things to deal with."

But once in her room, she felt way too alone and wished she'd stayed where there were people to distract her. She tried Charmaine and gave a cry of relief when she picked up.

"Good timing," Charmaine said. "I got home an hour ago, I've spent time with the hooligans, Sean's just taken them for baths. Tell me everything. Did she show? What happened?"

"*I'm* the affair," Maggie said. "Or the mistress. Or whatever. He was with her for over a year by the time we met." Speaking the words, she was horrified all over again.

"Fuck. That takes high-level strategy. Or compartmentalization or self-deception or complete assholery or *something*."

"I can't wrap my head around it. He could have told me he was unavailable. Or he could have decided I was worth it and ended his relationship with her. But instead he juggles us both in secret?"

"I hope you drove straight to his place and dumped him."

"Obviously I'm ending it. I just couldn't face it tonight after the drive and the ordeal with Eve."

"Was she awful?"

"She made it clear we are not allies."

"I guess that's understandable, but she didn't have to be mean about it. Was she mean?"

"Kinda."

"Is *she* dumping him?"

"I don't see how she could do anything else. Unless she forgives him and they go to counseling and end up stronger than before?"

"Yeah, you'd need a really good therapist for that."

"Do you think it's better to beat her to it? The dumping, I mean. I almost feel like—ugh, I hate this, but do I need to defer to her because she was the original girlfriend? Let her be the one to break the news to him?"

"Fuck that. *You* uncovered the truth. *You* went to crazy lengths to address the situation with some kind of integrity. Don't let her take over now."

Maggie flopped face down on her bed and groaned. "How have I done this? How have I invested so much in someone who was never going to love me and never going to stay with me? It's one thing to do that at nineteen. But I'm thirty-five years old! I'm supposed to be established in my life. Settled. With a partner and a career and enough experience to know what I want and notice when something's off."

"Don't have an existential crisis; there'll be enough time for that later. You just need to take care of yourself right now. Do your nervous system regulation stuff. Or have a massive glass of wine and cry a bunch. That's okay too." There was a crash and a wail on Charmaine's end, and she sighed. "That's my cue. I'll try to call again, but it's kind of the bedtime drill now for the next hour. Or three."

"Of course. No problem. I love you."

Maggie stared into her phone after Charmaine hung up, contemplating her options. She started a text to Karl: So, I met Eve today. That would be a nice shocker for him. She deleted it. Is anything you've ever said to me true? Delete. Did you ever love me, or were you always playing a game? Delete.

She wasn't ready to confront Karl tonight. But then again, maybe what she wasn't ready for was losing him. Speaking the truth out loud to Karl would make it final. She couldn't say *I know you've been deceiving me our entire relationship* and not follow it with *We're over.* And she didn't want to be over. What she wanted was to unknow the truth. That's what she wanted.

She texted him the location of the Wrangler. He sent a thumbs-up, then a question about IKEA and a hope that she wasn't working too hard. His last text said, I guess I'll see you Monday after I'm back? Dinner maybe? She didn't respond to any of it.

Not until the next morning, lying in bed, putting off rising to face her new broken life, did Maggie think of the pregnancy test. Along with weeping into frozen McCain cakes, a pregnancy test was her breakup ritual—her way of assuring herself that, regardless of how long her mind and emotions continued to cling, every last bit of the guy was gone from her body. She'd always thought the pregnancy test she'd take with Karl would feature the two of them side by side. A whoop, a kiss, happy phone calls to their families.

Natalie kept a stockpile of dollar store tests under the bathroom sink. She'd need to take another one in a few weeks to be sure, but she might as well get the ritual underway. Maggie hauled herself out of bed and down the hall.

Chapter 6

Eve

Long before New York City became unbearable to her, Eve had begun answering "Still Lake, Ontario" to the "Where are you from?" of new-acquaintance conversation. New Yorkers didn't know where Still Lake was any more than they knew where Kitchener was, so it didn't make a difference, except to Eve. She'd come every summer with her family, helping her dad's best friend, Sam Labelle, with his rental cabins and living for free on the lake. Every summer until age thirteen, the year of her alarming eruption of beauty and the resulting unwanted attention, the year she got her period and her breasts, lost her confidence and her self-esteem, the year her father gave up on her mother and took Eve's twin away from her. Still Lake was the watershed of her life: on this side, innocence; on the other . . . everything else.

Two years ago, at the age of forty-one, when she left New York and the business she'd built to a pinnacle of suffocating success, there was nowhere else she'd wanted to go.

"Have you forgotten how hard you worked to *get* to New York?" her twin brother, Daniel, asked, waiting with her in the disorderly line at Penn Station. "How it was all you wanted for years?"

No, all she'd wanted was to be near him, and New York happened to be where he was.

She could have flown, but she wanted to depart as she had arrived: on the train, alone, unburdened by more than a few possessions. Daniel's wife, mercifully, did not accompany them to the station. It felt like the first time in a decade that Eve got her twin to herself. She spent one night with her mother and stepfather in Kitchener, slept briefly and badly, and in the morning an online search turned up a truck listed for sale by a man who also happened to need a home for a one-year-old lab. Flora the perfect afterthought, an unrecognized need whose fulfillment she was desperate for as soon as she became aware of it. On hold with the insurance company, Eve caressed Flora's silky head as her mother gave the familiar litany. "This is what happens. You throw your whole self into this business, no husband, no kids, not even a boyfriend you ever told me about, and now what do you have? Nothing! A bit of money, which you're blowing on a house you've never seen. Blowing all your money to go back *there*."

"There's enough money," Eve told her, but her mother couldn't comprehend a woman with her own money and preferred the shame of impoverished spouselessness.

Then, as Eve and Flora were getting into the truck: "Don't go. I haven't seen you in all this time and then you come for just one night?"

The two-lane highway of her childhood had expanded into four divided lanes. She rolled down the window and breathed air thick with freshness, cool and crisp and cleaner than she'd breathed since she was thirteen years old. The thought astonished her, that she had not breathed fresh air since age thirteen. This was *her* air.

She drove the rest of the way laughing and crying in an emotionalism foreign to her. Beside her Flora seemed to smile, head out the window, wind whipping her ears. The new high-speed road funneled back into the two narrow lanes she remembered. Silver-black rock flanked each side of the road. Birch and maple trees quivered with buds. One river after another, one lake after another, appeared alongside the highway, a landscape painting around every bend. As one receded she strained ahead to the next, and there it would be, limitless beauty welcoming her home.

Past the French River Trading Post she pulled off the highway into the village of Larkin, squinting at the tall-spired Catholic church, the hockey arena, the library and grocery store of her memory. She stopped to buy gas and ask for directions, because her smartphone was among the things she'd left behind. A man crouched at the air pump, winding the hose with relaxed fluidity. He rose, turned. Khaki work pants, white T-shirt, sandy-blond hair grown an inch out of a buzz cut. His smile was easy. His eyes were a startling blue. It was like discovering a jaguar in a farmyard.

As Karl gestured rights and lefts, warned of loose gravel, potholes, oncoming ATVs driven recklessly by teenage boys, her urge to laugh out loud was in keeping with the heightened emotions of the day. He was a gas station Adonis, and she a worn-out urban exile, and her stomach was flipping on the first day of her reclamation of herself.

"It should take you half an hour," he said, then, "Hey—this might seem weird, but I'd be happy to show you the way. It'd be no problem."

No problem?

She'd spent the journey envisioning a triumphal entry into her New Life. Arriving alone at her simple house, found and purchased long-distance with the help of Sam Labelle, Eve's soon-to-be employer at the same rental cabins she'd loved as a kid, where her responsibilities would be varied and undemanding, and would leave room for perks like a personal life. Stripping to dive into the cold waters of the lake in a cleansing ritual that would wash away the last three decades. Peering across the watershed, searching for thirteen-year-old Eve somewhere in the flow.

The solitude was important. The freedom to regain her lost self, or discover a new one, alone.

No problem? If her flipping stomach was any indication, there was definitely a problem.

But there were downsides to giving up your smartphone. She didn't want to spend her first day getting lost on Vermillion Road.

Within a month he was spending the night. Within three months she'd stopped trying to kick him out in the morning because she realized she didn't want to. She kept turning reflexively to her usual evasions and defenses—clamming up when conversations got too personal, trying to end the whatever-it-was between them when it started demanding too much—and he'd call her out on it while simultaneously letting her off the hook with a "Hey, it's no big deal, we don't have to go there," which made her feel safer to go there. She wondered if she might be able to have the kind of soulmate love her brother had after all, if her insistence that she didn't want it was only defensive. She *liked* having Karl around, liked how capable he was, how gung-ho to pitch in with yard maintenance and house repairs, liked this feeling that the property was theirs and not just hers. His upbeat companionship made mundane tasks fun—painting the bedroom, running to the hardware store—and his thrill-seeking brought more adventure into her life. He took her on hikes and canoe trips she wouldn't have attempted on her own, convinced her to try bungee jumping and snowmobiling, and kept her from becoming a hermit by dragging her to backyard barbecues and introducing her to his high school friends, some of whom she even liked. And they had the kind of sexual chemistry that made just walking into a room exciting if he was in it.

By the sixth month he was staying at her place more than he wasn't, and they agreed to be exclusive. By the ninth month they decided they should declare themselves living together, and she was pretty sure she'd fallen in love. When he took the job in Toronto a year after they met, she hadn't minded his absence during the week—she still craved space and time to herself, and she understood his need to get ahead in the city. The separation only made the weekends together more special. And while they'd rarely talked about long-range plans, she did consider him her partner. She saw a future. She'd felt—oh, the humiliation—she'd felt secure.

The day after Eve met Maggie, she stayed at work late, making up for her earlier absence, putting off seeing Karl. The Wrangler was already in her driveway when she got home, and Karl himself was at the woodpile, splitting logs from the load they'd had delivered for next winter. Eve watched as Flora bounded from the truck to greet him. He stopped to wave at Eve and ruffle Flora's neck as she bit playfully at his pants leg, and they went through their whole roughhousing routine. Eve wheeled away before he could turn his full attention to her, slammed through the door, and pulled a pizza from the freezer.

She'd tried calling him last night after she got back from the rendezvous with Maggie. He didn't answer, and she didn't leave a message. Today it had rained, and she'd stayed indoors all morning, attacking the cluttered office of Labelle's Cabins and trying not to think, the anger and sadness colliding unexamined inside her. Receipts and invoices, flyers and government remittance forms—she sorted with mad focus as drops flowed down the window in a steady, pacifying stream. A fire burned in the lounge's big stone fireplace, and the few guests around in the off-season huddled close with books and newspapers but left her alone. From the doorway, Sam watched her with his crinkly eyes, inviting confidences she did not give.

When Karl entered the house ten minutes later, he walked over to her at the stove and kissed her, smiling.

"Hey, baby," he said, squeezing her around the waist.

Eve had been sure Maggie would drive the Wrangler straight back to Karl to confront him with the truth, but he didn't seem like a man guilty or chastened or caught. He seemed the same as always: happy to see her, enthusiastic about the weekend ahead. She allowed herself to be kissed, too numb to resist, but she couldn't bring herself to speak to him. She wished she had a script, something reliable to guide her forward. Biting words that would keep the grief at bay.

He moved to the pantry and pulled out the dog food bag, began scooping kibble into Flora's bowl. Eve watched him with mounting disbelief. How could he be acting normal? How could he have known all this time that they weren't what they seemed and still be so glibly, comfortably loving? When Flora sauntered toward him, Eve wanted to wrench her away by the collar. *How dare you touch my dog!*

"What do you think about going to Killarney tomorrow?" Karl asked. "Maybe hike the Crack?"

Was Eve his outdoor activity girlfriend and Maggie his urban culture girlfriend? Did Eve not exist in his mind when he was in Toronto, being City Karl? Did he manage to genuinely forget the fact of Maggie when he was here with Eve? The cognitive dissonance was overwhelming. She had so many questions, and she couldn't bear to hear the answers to any of them.

"Or we could stay put." Karl looked at her over the can of wet food he was adding to Flora's bowl. "There's plenty of spring cleanup to do around here."

How did he keep the lies straight? How had he even made time? An out-of-town job and ridiculously dependent parents, and he decided to add a second girlfriend to the mix?

"Eve?"

"What did you do this week?" she asked, an edge to her voice.

"The usual. Work. Went to a comedy show Wednesday night."

"Who with?"

"Raoul from work."

Was that true? How could she know? Wednesday was the day before she met Maggie. Had Maggie been the one he went with?

"Where was it?"

"Second City."

"Was it funny?" Her tone was too serious for the question, her grilling of him too abnormal. He was cocking his head at her now, mystified.

"It wasn't bad," he said slowly. "I laughed."

Eve just stared at him.

Karl pushed the bowl to Flora and started toward Eve, eyebrows drawn together in a perplexed furrow. "Eve? What's going on?"

She buried her face in the cupboard, reached for two plates. She said, "I don't even know why you come back here."

He waited until she was facing him again. "*Obviously*," he said, "I come back because you're my partner and here is where you are."

"And your parents."

"My parents too. But mostly you."

You have a girlfriend in Toronto. Her name is Maggie. I met her. I met her! Once she said the words, she couldn't unsay them. She would have to sit through his denials or justifications or apologies—she had no idea how he would play it—and her humiliation would be laid bare between them.

She opened the oven. The cheese was bubbling, green peppers brown at the edges. She pulled the tray out with an oven mitt, set it on the stovetop, and reached for a cutting board. With scissors she cut the pizza into four large slices.

"It isn't working," she said. "Us. Your job. The long-distance."

"Okay," he said, cautious but calm. He placed a hand on her hip, pulling her nearer and tilting her to face him. "I thought we were handling it pretty well."

She wriggled out of his grasp. "You're almost never here, and you expect our relationship to just absorb it. It's not fair to—to the relationship." *To me!*

"But—you like your own space. We have a good time on the weekends. We have a *great* time. Don't we?"

"It isn't enough for me anymore."

"This is coming out of nowhere," Karl said. "I had no idea you weren't happy."

"We need to split up."

"What?" He stared at her. He seemed genuinely shocked. Then his expression softened and he stepped toward her again, his voice soothing as he took her into his arms and asked, "What is this about?"

Her body sagged, leaning into him before she could stop it. For one second she wanted to be lulled back into complacency. She could let him reassure her. She could let herself be convinced that she'd believed Maggie out of insecurity or self-protection; nothing was actually wrong.

"Everything was perfectly fine last weekend," Karl said. "And now we're over? Come on, Eve. Talk to me."

She couldn't say it. She couldn't bear the shame of voicing the awful truth that she had given herself, had committed, had loved—and he'd gone looking elsewhere.

She'd been so naive.

She pulled away from him. "I'm done. It doesn't matter why."

He dropped into a chair at the dining table, watching her—bewildered, or maybe trying to calculate what she knew and how she'd found out.

"You've never let me in far, you know," he said. "And now you won't even tell me why you're breaking up with me?"

"I let you in further than I've ever let anyone in!"

"Well, how can we work through this if you won't tell me what's wrong?"

"Oh! Work through it?" She picked up the plates, then dropped them onto the countertop more forcefully than she meant to. "You want to work through it?"

"Yes! Isn't that what couples do?"

"I don't know, Karl, you tell me."

Both plates were cracked. Eve ripped off a length of paper towel—she didn't trust herself with more breakable dishes—and dumped a slice onto it. It was hot, and Karl fumbled as she handed it to him. The slice landed upside down in his lap. He grabbed the trailing end of the paper towel and blotted at the tomato sauce on his jeans.

When the sauce had seeped into a red stain on his thigh, he said, "I could see about getting transferred closer."

So Maggie did vanish from his mind when he was here. "You don't want to live here full-time," Eve said. "You never have. I'm not even sure you want your whole banker life in Toronto. I'm not sure any of this is enough for you."

"So you're deciding for me what I want, and you're ending us because of what *you* think that is?"

It had to be about the thrill. The intensity of balancing two women, keeping a secret that could blow up in his face—it was an adventure.

Dangerous. He didn't have any glacial gorges or Class V rapids; he had to create some kind of risk to keep his life exciting.

She wanted to smash the rest of the plates, every one in the cupboard. When she'd met Karl, he was in the middle of a reluctant pivot, restless but determined to make it work. He'd grown up here and left at eighteen to travel, attend university, and work as a climbing and rafting guide in the Rockies, a job that led to his real calling: a decade leading adventure tours in Patagonia, the Amazon, the Himalayas, until the cancer news brought him home. Two years later, when Eve met him, his mother had beaten her illness, but he was the only child of aging parents dependent on him for practical and emotional support, and disappearing to the other side of the world was no longer an option. Neither was doing what he loved regardless of the money. Northern Ontario ought to offer at least a tamer version of the wilderness work he excelled in, but he'd managed to land only dead-end jobs. He had a head for numbers, and when Eve met him he was already halfway through an online M.B.A.

He didn't want to be in Northern Ontario, then or now. He didn't want to work in a gas station—what he'd been doing when she met him—but he didn't want to work in a bank either. He also didn't, evidently, want to be with Eve. Or not *only* with Eve.

Ripples slanted diagonally across the lake. With a sudden, piercing ache, Eve wished for Daniel, her twin—his presence, his counsel, even his derision, for surely Daniel would deride Karl in this moment. After the horrible meeting with Maggie, she'd called him in New York, and his wife, Violet, had chirped on about their busy, happy lives, apologizing that Daniel was at the hospital, working the night shift. How was Eve getting on there in the woods? Why didn't she come visit sometime soon?

During the fifteen-year period in their teens and twenties when she and Daniel were separated, Eve had tried, unsuccessfully, to develop telepathic communication with him. She imagined she could hear him saying to her in this moment, *Don't be an idiot, Evie.* He would be calm and sure. *Karl's not invested. He's not worth it. Move on.*

The pizza crust was underdone, already turning sweaty in her palm. Her hands shook as she took hold of the garbage can and shoved the remaining pizza into it.

"I'd like you to leave now," she said.

"You're serious."

"Go stay with your parents. Go back to South America. Go figure out what you really want from your life."

When the crunch of his tires on gravel receded, Eve walked to the lake and undressed. In two long strides she waded to her shins. The cold hit, pain like a knife wound searing through her, and she plunged forward to her knees, howled as the water reached her pelvis. Then she was numb, and she kept going, Flora swimming gamely beside her. As the lake met each body part, it jolted her alive. She shrieked, but she kept going because the cold felt like the most real thing, the most purely her own, that she'd experienced in the two years since Karl Tarvudd had entered her life.

Chapter 7

Maggie

In the five days since Maggie had peed on that slender white just-a-formality stick, it was all she could think about, the questions and the worry and the what-will-I-do looming over everything. She was accomplishing the bare minimum at Sukha and couldn't concentrate on the dissertation at all. Every moment of every day, her thoughts were consumed by nothing but the trajectory of her relationship with Karl and the pregnancy test she was carrying around with her everywhere she went, its giant plus sign glowing from the bottom of her bag.

She felt like she was trying to complete a jigsaw puzzle with half the pieces missing. Two jigsaw puzzles. One that showed a picture of the past: how this had happened, how Karl had so thoroughly deceived her, not to mention how they had conceived when Maggie insisted on two forms of birth control nearly every time. And one that showed a picture of the future: Maggie with a baby. Maggie by herself with a baby. Maggie with *Karl* and a baby? Because she *wanted* kids—plural! By the time she extricated her heart from Karl, met someone new, established a strong enough relationship to be reasonably confident it would last, *then* started trying to conceive, she could be thirty-eight or older. Forty! She was already elderly in pregnancy terms, and there was no way she was not having this baby. She might never get another chance.

But single motherhood had never been the dream.

She was slumped, forehead against her palm, in a library carrel, pretending to work on her dissertation. So far all she'd done was read the same paragraph four times, at a loss to decide if it was incomprehensible because it made no sense or because she was incapable of comprehension.

The day after she took the test, Karl had called her. Apart from a few texts, they hadn't spoken since the morning she found out about Eve, eight days earlier.

"Hey!" he said. "I know you're slammed with work, but it's been a while—I hope you're okay?"

He sounded eager, surprised and happy she'd answered the call, but also distracted. Was he asking if she was okay because Eve had told him he was busted, or was he just wondering why Maggie was avoiding him? Before she could decide how to respond, he said, "I have something important I need to tell you."

He had something important to tell *her*?

The sound of his voice, the audacity of his lies, the truths she'd uncovered—the brand-new head-spinning truth on the pregnancy test—it was too much. Obviously Eve had told him she knew about the cheating, but maybe he didn't know that Maggie also knew, and he was heroically calling to come clean. Or maybe he knew everything and was calling with some convoluted web of explanations and excuses. Either way, she couldn't bear to hear it.

She'd hung up on him. He'd called back immediately, and she'd turned her phone off. Now she wished she hadn't, because in the four days since then, she'd been texting and calling him with mounting urgency, asking to meet up, asking him to at least call her, and he wasn't responding. She needed the closure of officially breaking up with him, but she also needed to tell him she was pregnant—that was only fair, no matter what kind of asshole he'd been—and to discuss what the future might look like, whether he might at least help support the baby, whether they could find their way to some kind of harmonious co-parenting future together.

She'd never admit this to Charmaine—the only person so far who knew about the pregnancy—but as the reality of single motherhood sank in, she even wondered if they might be able to stay together. She was heartbroken, she would insist on couples therapy, they would have to rebuild trust, but she *loved* him. They were going to be parents! She owed it to her child to act from faith and forgiveness, not woundedness and revenge.

But before she could figure any of this out, Karl needed to answer his phone.

Now Maggie scrolled to the top of her document and stared at her cover page. *The Politics of Personal Fulfillment and Collective Responsibility in the Marriage Plots of George Eliot, Elizabeth Gaskell, and Charlotte Brontë.* A topic she'd chosen at the age of twenty-four because she was spending so much of her time and energy trying to find love that she figured she might as well pour it into a professional credential; at least she was reasonably certain she wouldn't get sick of the subject four years in. But her topic now seemed a mockery: Not only had she failed at love, she'd failed at writing this dissertation about, among other things, love.

She slammed her laptop shut, gathered her bag, and plodded through wide double doors into open air, sliding onto the nearest bench as clusters of students emerged from buildings, flowing past her in indistinct shapes. For weeks she'd felt drained, she realized now, not quite in command of her usual energy. But there'd been no sign of morning sickness, at least not yet.

She groped in her bag for her phone. A series of supportive texts from Charmaine, but nothing from Karl. His name was there in her favorites, clear and concrete, as accessible as it had been twelve days ago—before she'd listened to Eve's voicemail, before she'd stumbled on the truth.

She knew him, didn't she? He couldn't have been faking everything the whole time—his feelings, his personality. He would want to take responsibility, wouldn't want her to be alone in this crisis.

She pressed his name. The call went to voicemail again. Impending fatherhood was not the kind of news you left in a voicemail. She kept trying, calling him over and over. Finally she tried calling Karl at the bank where he worked, but kept getting caught in a labyrinthine automated system. Then she texted her friend Jasmine to see if her husband had seen Karl at the gym this morning; he hadn't. She tried a few more mutual friends, with no luck.

And then she thought of Eve. She looked up the number for Eve's workplace, Labelle's Cabins. She put in her earbuds and dialed. A man with a warm drawl picked up.

"Sure," he said. "Hang on a sec, I'll get her."

Her heart raced as she waited, but it was only a moment and then the voice from Karl's phone was in her ear. "This is Eve."

Maggie clenched and unclenched her free hand. "Eve," she said. "It's Maggie Dunn."

There was a pause.

"You're very good at tracking me down, aren't you?"

"I'm sorry, but it's important. I need to reach Karl."

"I'd suggest trying *his* phone."

Maggie raised her hand to her forehead, the elbow anchored against her knee, and leaned her weight into it. She kept remembering the ease in Eve's voice on Karl's phone. She kept expecting her to turn into the serene woman her mind had conjured that day. "Obviously," Maggie said, "I did that before trying you."

"Text him or leave a message and he'll call you back. That's how it usually works."

"All I'm asking is if you know where he is."

"I didn't know where he was the entire time we were together. I'm not sure why you'd expect me to know now."

So she'd definitely broken up with him.

"I assume you told him we met," Maggie said.

"I didn't, actually."

"You didn't? Wow. Okay. Why not?"

"I don't think that's something I need to share with you."

"Right." Fine. Not allies. Got it. "I haven't told him either, mostly because I was refusing to speak with him, but now it's urgent that I do, and I'm desperate enough to call *you*, so if you have any leads at all, could you just—maybe his parents?"

Eve laughed abruptly. "Please don't call me again."

Maggie was about to slam her finger on the button that would end this call, but she stopped herself and said, "I'm a *person*, you know. I'm affected by this too."

"I'd prefer if we could be affected by it far away from each other," Eve said.

"You do know we could help each other, don't you?" Maggie said. "That we're the only ones who can fill each other in on what of the past nine months was real and what wasn't?"

"And you think we should try? The two of us side by side, figuring out how he pulled it off, what he said, what he didn't say?" Eve's words gathered speed and the angry bite of ridicule. "You think we can join *forces*?"

Maggie lurched upright. "Listen!" The fury bolted through her. "I didn't try to steal Karl from you. I didn't know there *was* a you. I just fell in love. With someone who gave every sign of also being in love with me. We built a relationship. We were *together*. Don't blame me just because I found out first. I've got as much right to be angry at you for being with him. When I heard your voice on that message, my first thought was that he was cheating on *me*."

"What message?"

Maggie stopped, momentarily bewildered. "On Karl's voicemail."

"On his phone?"

"Where else?"

"What were you doing with his phone?"

"He was my boyfriend. Sometimes I stayed at his apartment. It's something girlfriends do. And at his apartment, he left his phone."

"I didn't know that. How you found out."

"I guess we didn't get to that, did we."

"Fine. Tell me what happened."

Maggie drew a shaky breath. "He'd left for work. I was only planning to plug the phone in, but I . . . maybe I suspected something. Not consciously, but . . . I cracked his password and listened to his message. It was about fixing his sandal."

Eve chuckled, unexpectedly. "Karl's cover was blown because of a shoe?"

"Well, yes. Yes," Maggie said. "Because of a shoe."

For a split second, Maggie and Eve both laughed, and then the emotion tipped into despair and Maggie's tears pooled. What was she going to *do*?

"You sound like you're struggling," Eve said.

"Well, aren't you?"

Eve was silent. Maggie looked down at the chipped red of her toenails, bare in sandals.

"It hasn't been the best week of my life," Eve said.

Maggie was grateful for this simple admission. "Why did he do this?" she asked quietly.

"I have no idea. I'm trying not to overthink it."

"Overthinking is all I'm doing." Maggie dropped her head to her knees. "I feel stupid for not figuring it out sooner. It was such a thin excuse, a grown man driving all that way every single weekend to see his parents."

"That was partly true. He didn't always get to spend much time here."

"You mean his mother does have cancer?"

"It's in remission, but she's still pretty fragile."

"You know them?"

"They don't approve."

"So they're as strange and demanding as he says."

"They're pretty strange and demanding."

"And it's true he's their only child?"

"There'd be a lot less pressure on him if he weren't."

Maggie uncurled her body to sit straight on the bench. A cloud passed across the sun and she fastened the buttons on her jacket.

"It'll be fine," Eve said. "You'll be fine. We'll both be fine." She cleared her throat. "Have a good life, Maggie." The phone went silent. Eve was gone.

"But I'm pregnant," Maggie said out loud into the emptiness. "And I really do need to reach Karl."

Chapter 8

Eve

Eve stretched across a bed to snap the elasticized edge of a clean sheet over the mattress. The bed fit too snugly in its alcove, and she bruised her knuckles against the paneled wall as she worked the elastic. She lay there a moment, the springs groaning, and closed her eyes.

You've never let me in far replayed in her mind, a splinter she couldn't remove. A variation on the charges leveled at her since she was a girl: *Eve's so quiet. Such a hard one to read. Doesn't come out of her shell, that one.*

She forced herself to stand and unfurl a top sheet. It was Thursday, six days since she'd broken up with Karl and one day since Maggie had phoned, just to drill in Eve's humiliation. She'd worked every day since, grabbing at any distraction. "There's no reason for me to be home weekends anymore," she'd said to Sam, and he'd nodded and patted her shoulder. That was it, the only person apart from her brother whom she'd told about this sudden gulf in her life—the only person she *had* to tell, because she knew no one here except Karl's friends, and during her years in New York her work left no time to connect with people as more than colleagues or clients or acquaintances, and she had no lasting friendships from before then. Daniel was the only person she'd ever felt comfortable enough with to truly confide in anyway.

Daniel had liked Karl. He and Violet had visited last summer, the first time Eve had hung out with them as a member of a couple herself. She'd loved not being the third wheel. Loved showing Daniel the home and the life she'd built here. From the beginning of Eve's scheme to abandon the city and return to the lake she hadn't visited in almost three decades, Daniel had insisted she was only hiding from her talent and holing up in a misguided re-creation of a childhood she mythologized. Hiding, period. But he was enchanted by her place on the lake and thought Karl was great for her. He'd never been a fan of Eve's long stretches on her own or her no-strings-attached flings.

Had she been trying to prove something to Daniel when she dove into the relationship with Karl? *See, I'm still pushing the edges of my comfort zone. See, I can connect deeply and build a life with someone too.*

See, I don't need you.

It'd been a relief for Daniel, knowing she had someone. Someone other than him.

But the phone call yesterday, when she'd finally told him about Karl's cheating, hadn't been very satisfying. He'd fumed on her behalf, called Karl some choice names, then had to run to meet Violet for a charity gala.

She smoothed a quilt over the fresh sheets and backed away until she stood in the doorway, gazing in at Bushwhack Cabin. Making beds wasn't strictly in her job description—they had cleaners for that—but Sam didn't care much about defined roles, and she tended to do a bit of everything, from repairs and outdoor maintenance to updating the website and checking in guests, and she felt proprietary about this particular cabin. Two rooms joined by an archway, the bedroom an alcove fitted with a double bed and a bunk bed a foot apart, the main room holding a table and wardrobe, sink, propane fridge and stove, small stiff couch, and wood stove. Her mother had hated the cramped quarters.

"The point," said her father, weary under sagging eyebrows, "is to spend time outdoors."

"With the mosquitoes?" squawked her mother. "Do you think I'm crazy?"

As it turned out, he did.

Labelle's Cabins consisted of twenty rustic cabins tossed like dice along the lakeshore, tucked between trees and joined by little pathways. The main lodge was a log A-frame that housed the office, the laundry, the lounge with a fireplace, and the apartment where Sam lived. Families came year after year, usually in the summer, but the cabins were winterized and Sam had enough cross-country skiing and ice-fishing devotees to keep the place running year-round.

Sam's head bobbed along the path, and then his body appeared in the clearing in front of her. Flora was at his side. Eve always brought her to work, where the dog roamed at will—one of the thousand things Eve appreciated about her employment with Sam.

"Thought I'd find you at the Bushwhack," Sam said.

She smiled, strained.

"You could take a holiday, you know," he said.

"Maybe. Go visit Daniel, I guess."

"That'd do you good."

It *would* do her good. As long as they could get off on their own without Violet traipsing beside them, her hand in his back pocket, his in hers.

Danlet, she'd long ago dubbed them, but only to herself.

"I'm making ham sandwiches for lunch. With pickles. I'm forcing you to stop working and come sit. It's spring! We're having a picnic on the dock."

"It's not too buggy?"

"We're tough."

She nodded, tried to smile. This was Sam acknowledging her loss. This was Sam taking care of her.

The impromptu picnic, when Eve joined Sam on the dock ten minutes later, reminded her so strongly of the dock hangouts of her childhood that for a moment she was leveled by nostalgia. Legs dangling and fishing lines trailing, Eve, Daniel, their father, and Sam used to gather at this exact spot after the day's work was done. With the men, Eve had affinity, brotherhood—all of them against her mother, a related but separate species with her ineffectual power plays, her fluctuating moods and changeable laws. Eve was always casting furtive glances to ensure that her mother was not emerging to make her help with dishwashing or food. She felt secure on those sun-soaked evenings, sucking on her Coke straw next to her brother and listening to her father and Sam's easy conversation, because she knew she was hanging out with the rational ones, the reliable ones. It never occurred to Eve that she wasn't one of them.

She remembered vividly the day reality accosted her. A warm afternoon at Still Lake, red stains on the crotch of her yellow bathing suit. "You're a woman now," her mother crowed, and presented her with the thick cotton pad Eve was meant to put between her legs.

"How will I swim with this on?" Eve sputtered.

"You won't."

Being a woman meant going the final week of their Still Lake summer without swimming. It meant sitting on the shore while Daniel dove from the dock without her. It meant pain. She told her father she had a stomachache, then seethed with shame when her mother stage-whispered, "*Her period*."

Being a woman meant limitation, and no one had even warned her.

By September her father had announced his intent to divorce, and by January he'd moved back to his native New York State, taking Daniel with him. Men with the men, women with the women. This was not the original plan: Eve and Daniel were both supposed to go with him, returning to their mother for summers and holidays, but in a last-minute rethink, her father had decided he was not equipped to raise a teenage girl, that alarming, hormonal, physically blossoming thing Eve had suddenly become. There were no courts involved in the custody change, not even any freak-outs from Eve's mother; it was just "a girl needs her mother" and "I think you'll be better off with her" and Eve alone on the sidewalk, waving her brother and father off into another life.

That was the moment Eve knew for sure that being female was the worst of the things you could be. It was also when she shifted from looking up to and identifying with her father to shutting herself off from him. He had let her down in the gravest way, he had abandoned her, and he was never to be trusted again.

Daniel, though, was a similar victim of circumstances, wronged alongside her. She talked to him on the phone every Sunday and many weekday evenings. They sent each other apartment listings, laying out in intricate detail the home they would share and the life they would live once they became adults—they'd apply to the same colleges, move to the city together, get a two-bedroom. But though she knew he missed her, knew the separation was hard for him too—he told her this—he seemed to have no trouble building a new life. Making new friends, joining the basketball team at his new school, serving on the student council, the center of a vibrant circle. While Eve felt she was mostly on hold until she could be back with Daniel again.

She visited White Plains at Christmas and summer break, she went along on vacations, and for those brief periods she regained something of the belonging she'd once taken for granted. For those weeks, her new real life didn't exist, only games and jokes and movies and camaraderie with her brother and even her dad, whom she usually forgot to punish by about the third day. She entertained them with the plots of the soap operas her mother had taken to bingeing and the arguments of the Jehovah's Witnesses she hosted for entire evenings. She told Daniel, in whispers at night, about their mother's sleeping pills, the entire weekends spent in bed, the wedding photographs slashed with pinking shears and weepingly pieced back together. The first time she revealed the extent of their mother's loneliness and incapacity—she'd waited, wanting to tell Daniel in person and enlist him in persuading their father that Eve should live with them—Daniel told their father, who called their mother immediately. He asked probing questions that she answered with a performance of normalcy that stunned Eve, listening in with Daniel on the other line. Whenever Daniel visited after that, their mother was able to pose herself in a tableau of happy purposefulness for one-week stretches; when he left, she collapsed from the effort of holding herself together. Even when Daniel tried to help, even when he called regularly, it was Eve who was there for the day in and day out.

And then, two years after the divorce, her mother met someone and came alive again, reinforcing the message she'd always tried to impart: A woman really did need a man to be whole.

After lunch with Sam, Eve went to the office to answer booking inquiries and succumbed: into the search field went Maggie Dunn's name. There she was in plain sight, a face in an Instagram feed, the assistant manager on the website of a bookstore-café. Crowding her Instagram were the same pictures she'd shown Eve, not even privacy screened, available for everyone in the world to see.

Everyone but, until now, Eve, who was not the type to internet-stalk anyone, who possessed only the social media accounts created by her marketing director and now taken over by the people who'd bought her business.

Karl knew about her aversion to internet connectivity, social media, any media. He knew, too, that she didn't like to ask questions, to probe or be probed.

He knew and took advantage.

"Go home," said Sam from the doorway. "You were here all weekend. Also, I know you're not supposed to say this to a woman, but you do genuinely look tired."

She genuinely was tired. She nodded dully and closed the browser on Maggie Dunn's wide-eyed, radiant face.

When she got home, Eve sat by the lake, heavy and sad in her green Adirondack chair. Wrapped in an old blanket, staring, dozing, Flora a silent companion at her feet.

Karl's parents, at least, would be pleased by the breakup. On the first dutiful visit she and Karl had paid together, his mother fed them *pulla* and hard Finnish ginger cookies, and both parents wore unchanging expressions of bewilderment, as though resigned never to crack the mystery of their child's defection. They seemed to blame Eve for Karl's new city job and for his weekends split between their house and hers.

She closed her eyes and saw Maggie's sunshiny smile again, all that beaming into the camera for her Instagram followers. Winsome, with those big brown eyes—rather like Flora's, come to think of it—and always that huge smile. She was pretty. Cute-pretty, not gorgeous-pretty, not the kind of vixen you'd expect to steal your man. Eve hated herself for thinking it; so victim-ish, so catty and retrograde and female: *That vixen stole my man.*

"That's what I hate most about this," she whispered to Flora, who perked up her ears and cocked her head. How stereotypically female it made her, this discovery that she'd been cheated on, that she'd loved and been betrayed. ("Betrayed!" she'd scoffed to Maggie, but what other word was there?) How helpless and passive, her life happening to her instead of she herself driving her life. It was so—her mother. *That vixen stole my man*. Those were her mother's words when Eve's father remarried mere months after the divorce.

And that alone, Karl turning her into her mother, was enough to make her spitting mad—or it would be if she weren't too tired for such an aggressive emotion. Karl's rug-yanking had left her depleted, and she felt, horrifyingly, closer to tears than anything else.

Eve was nodding off in her Adirondack chair when there came the gruff, phlegmy clearing of a throat. A presence loomed. Eve paddled upward through layers of consciousness and opened her eyes.

A woman stood over her, brown-flecked skin hanging loose from jaw and cheekbones. Overlarge glasses slipped down her nose. Polyester slacks, a windbreaker with a stuffed front pocket.

Eve blinked, pulling herself up in her chair and leaning forward to check that the woman was a physical reality.

"You won't be sleeping outside once the blackfly come."

Eve shook her head, her brain thick and useless. "I'm sorry?"

"The blackfly. You don't know blackfly?"

"Yes. I know blackflies."

"No more long walks and lounging outside for you, once the blackfly come." She cackled. "I talked to Sam Labelle. He says I can trust you."

Bernice, the fishing lodge woman. Despite living next door for two years, Eve had seen her close up only a few times since childhood.

"Pardon me?"

"You ever have company stay overnight, you can use my lodge. Your house is so small you have nowhere to put them."

Eve blinked again. "I don't have much company."

Bernice eyed Eve's disheveled hair, her hands clenching the armrests. "I'm visiting my sister in New Brunswick for a couple of months. But I don't trust to leave the lodge sitting here that long with no one watching it. If I give you the keys, you can go round once in a while. I see you, you walk past it anyway. It's right next door, no trouble for you. You have the keys, you can use the rooms if you want."

"I don't have any use for a lodge."

"Okay, then, I'll pay you."

Eve shook her head. "You don't have to pay me."

"The buildings haven't been used for a few years, so they need fixing up. Probably squirrels get in. You can clean up if you need to use it."

Eve stared.

"Pick any room. Doesn't matter. I started paying the electric again because my sister was going to come stay, but now I'm going there instead and all that power is going to waste. You might as well use it and get my money's worth."

She handed Eve a key ring, grunted, and trudged along the lake toward the path between their properties. Eve watched her go, too bewildered to object.

If Eve hadn't seen Daniel's name on her call display later that night, she would not have thought it was him, his voice was so altered. Thin, strangled.

She was perched on the edge of her bed, one pajamaed leg on the floor, the other curled under her, nine o'clock and already climbing into bed.

"Violet," he said, and her body stiffened as she recognized anguish. Her twin could barely speak, and Eve knew before she knew that the reason for this was horrible.

"Daniel," Eve said. "What is happening?"

Flora's head surfaced from between her paws—an emotional lightning rod as usual—and she shambled toward Eve and pressed her snout into Eve's lap.

"Violet," Daniel said.

It was the only word, over and over, that he could get out.

In the end it was someone else, Daniel's friend Ivan, who was with him at the hospital, who told Eve. "Violet was riding her bike," Ivan said.

Daniel's wife got to and from her obstetrics practice that way, even deep into winter. Violet, with her confidence in the goodness of life, her cheer in the face of potholes and sewer grates, wind and rain, snow, ice, aggressive taxi drivers. Violet, in her perky yellow flowered helmet, a streak of sunshine in New York City traffic.

The sister-in-law Eve had tried, for Daniel's sake, to love.

But this wasn't winter, there was no ice, no poor visibility or hard-assed cabbie. Only a distracted mother with three kids in the back of her SUV, Ivan said, who hadn't seen the woman on the silver Flyer until it was too late.

It was that yellow flowered helmet Eve kept thinking of as she waited on hold with the airline, threw together T-shirts, underwear, a black pantsuit that Violet herself had helped Eve find. That yellow flowered helmet, that optimism, that insistence on joy.

She lay back on the bed once her suitcase was packed, staring at the ceiling with tears tight in her throat. Yearning for someone, anyone, beside her to turn to for comfort. Yearning—she couldn't help it—for Karl.

Chapter 9

Maggie

Maggie arrived for her shift at Sukha, swallowing back nausea. It had kicked in, along with some dizziness, just this morning. She'd spent the hour from five to six slumped in front of the toilet, trying to throw up.

Karl had not answered his phone in the six days since she'd hung up on him, the morning after she discovered she was pregnant, and she was now calling and texting multiple times a day asking him to call her. Please. Immediately. Urgently.

Her co-worker Jenna noticed Maggie leaning against the doorframe.

"You okay?" Jenna asked.

Maggie smiled wanly. "Nothing a bit of toxic positivity won't cure."

Jenna laughed.

Karl was wonderful during the one day every month when her period laid her low. He'd have insisted she stay home today. He'd have researched the right kind of tea for morning sickness, gone out to buy it, brought it to her steaming on a tray beside a plate of saltines. Pregnancy would have been a nine-month stint of coddling and care.

Except on the weekends when he was up north with Eve.

Maggie shuffled across the store, past the people slurping drinks and scrolling phones at the tiny tables and on the overstuffed couch, past the books piled ceiling-high, past the doorway to the event space/yoga studio and the office, where she had a desk. She propped herself behind the tin-plated counter.

"Okay if I take my break now?" Jenna asked.

Maggie nodded. "Is Daria here?" She glanced toward the closed office door.

Jenna looked at her watch. "You're probably good for another thirty minutes."

In direct contradiction to the Zen aesthetic she purported to espouse, their boss, Daria, was a coiled spring of stress and micromanagement, constantly moving goalposts and swooping in to suck the air out of interactions her employees were handling just fine. But when Daria *wasn't* around, Maggie often loved it here.

I love it here, she told herself as Jenna headed for the door. She loved her life. Even without Karl, even without a Ph.D., her life was good. Her life was good, her life was good, her life was good.

She'd worked at Sukha as an undergrad, then returned seven years ago after her supervisor informed her there were no more funded teaching positions available to her, those being reserved for the Ph.D. candidates still within the four-year window considered ample for completion. This was embarrassing but okay. She loved working at Sukha just as much as teaching, and way more than toiling over her dissertation. It drew on the same strengths that made her a good teacher and mentor: her passion for people, her talent for speaking, for listening, for intuiting needs. She could not sufficiently defend her ideas in the dissertation-that-still-was-not-passable, but she could meet people where they were, initiate difficult phone calls, ease visiting writers, press the right book into the hands of a struggling customer, convince sponsors to part with more money, plan the details of events and not forget that online listings should be posted and the speaker retrieved from the airport—and to be sure these things got done, she usually did them herself. Along the way she'd taken teacher training in the back yoga studio, looking for a healthy way to channel excess energy and connect with people without anxiously monologuing at them, and now she occasionally subbed there.

But she did not make enough at Sukha to support herself and a baby.

Jenna had been gone five minutes when Charmaine appeared in the entrance. Maggie gasped in joyful relief as her friend nipped behind the counter and accepted Maggie into a long-limbed hug.

Maggie clung. "I've *missed* you," she said. The fierceness in her voice felt too strong, even to her. She modulated it to a whisper as she continued, "I miss when we lived together and worked together and our lives were one big long conversation and we knew everything that was going on with each other."

Charmaine pulled back to look at her. "We still know what's going on, we just know it from texts and phone calls."

"Not the same," Maggie said. "How are you here? Isn't it too early for lunch?"

"Cancellation."

"Thank god for flaky patients. How are *you* doing? We've only been talking about me lately."

Charmaine laughed. "I can think of at least two giant reasons for that."

"But I feel bad."

"I'm fine. Still daily breaking the news to ten-year-olds that they have to start wearing glasses and to forty-five-year-olds that they have to start wearing progressive lenses. And to my two-year-old that he can't wear diapers forever. And to my husband that I'm way too fucking tired for sex, possibly for the next five years or maybe until the boys graduate high school. Who cares about that, how are *you* doing?"

Maggie and Charmaine had met working at Sukha as undergrads. Now Charmaine was a full-on adult, an optometrist with her own practice in an office building nearby, in addition to the house and husband and kids. Her ability to effortlessly become a grown-up still boggled Maggie's mind. She was so afraid Charmaine would realize they had little in common anymore and move on to some new best friend that she tried to make herself as indispensable as possible with free babysitting and private at-home yoga sessions and surprise deliveries of gluten-free black bean brownies that her sons didn't know better than to love.

"You look pretty washed out, actually," Charmaine said.

Maggie scanned the store. Some browsers, some loiterers, some nurse-a-chai-for-three-hours-ers, but no one needing her attention. She leaned her elbows on the counter, then her whole body. She was so tired.

"I feel terrible."

"That's normal. What about the whole emotional aspect?"

"Not awesome, but it'll definitely improve once I feel better physically."

"Why don't I make you a coffee and you pull up a chair, and we'll see if we can figure this out."

Maggie reached for a mug, then set it down and shook her head. "I feel pretty queasy. Maybe I shouldn't do coffee."

"Yeah, you're definitely pregnant."

Maggie dropped her head onto the counter. Charmaine rubbed Maggie's upper back, fingers kneading muscle.

"There's nothing to figure out," Maggie said. "I'm going to have the baby. I'm going to break up with Karl, if he ever answers his phone, and maybe also force him to commit to helping out, and I'm going to have the baby on my own and rewrite my dissertation and get my Ph.D. and fulfill my father's stupid requirements and get my stupid investment money so I can *afford* to have a baby on my own."

But she didn't want to have a baby on her own.

After Karl's sandal had broken and he'd followed her fully clothed into her shower, after the hot water had pounded down and they'd stripped off his wet clothes and stayed there for ages, hands everywhere, mouths everywhere, Maggie had slipped on a trail of spilled shampoo. Karl caught her just as her head hit the side of the tub, heaved her wet body into his arms, wrapped her into a towel, and carried her from the bathroom, still naked himself. He laid her on her bed, weak from the steam and the sex and the fall and the man. She was afraid to be alone, in case she had a concussion, so he stayed the night. They made love again, this time slowly and gently, Karl handling her like fragile treasure.

That was hers. That had happened. That was real, even if he'd had a girlfriend up north, expecting his Friday return.

"I don't actually want to break up with him," Maggie said quietly to Charmaine. "Am I a total doormat for thinking we could salvage this?"

"Oh, sweetie, this isn't the 1950s. Don't saddle yourself with a cheater just because you got knocked up."

Maggie turned her face a quarter inch so she could see Charmaine. "But what if I still love the cheater?"

She would have called him again right then—called him, berated him, punished him, railed and screamed, and then told him she loved him and they were having a baby so he had to fix whatever twisted wounding had caused his behavior, commit to healing and reconciliation, and then come be with her, *only* her—except the nausea was shifting inside her, tightening into a horrible pain in her stomach.

She hobble-ran out from behind the counter, through the office to the private employee bathroom. She heaved into the toilet but nothing came.

Charmaine had followed, her fingers gathering Maggie's hair away from her face. "Go home," Charmaine said.

Maggie slumped to the floor beside the toilet. "I'll just rest." She could barely get the words out. The pain—in her abdomen, her pelvis, her shoulder—was immense.

From the counter someone hollered, "Hello? Some service, maybe, please?"

"You stay here. I'm sure I can remember how to run the cash register." Charmaine raced out.

Maggie lay on the floor, the tile cold against her cheek.

A moment later, Daria's phone voice carried from the store entrance, quicksilvering between playful and appeasing, threatening and charming. The voice rose as Daria entered the office, and Maggie curled herself smaller on the floor, clutching her abdomen.

"You come up with something else for me, or heads'll be on the chopping block," Daria was saying, then, "Maggie? Where's Maggie? Charmaine, what the hell are you doing behind the counter? Did Maggie come in? Because I can't get through this day—" A rap on the bathroom door. "Maggie, is that you in there? You won't believe what I'm dealing with. You saw the pile on your desk? Mine's eight times higher, and I'm transferring more of it to you because—you won't believe this—we lost our sponsor for the Felicity Chong event."

The click of heels, another phone call. Maggie needed the toilet suddenly, desperately, but she couldn't drag herself onto it. Charmaine was with the neediest customer of all time.

She was going to shit her pants, right here on the floor.

And then, horribly, there was a gush inside her underwear, warm and gooey. She threw up at last, all over the floor and across her hands and arms. She was so tired. She could sleep here, and it would all be gone in her sleep. None of this would be happening. Perhaps she would die, and then nothing would matter. She writhed against the floor as another pain—more pain, the same pain, new pain, old pain, eternal pain—pummeled her stomach, her pelvis, her shoulder.

She woke to Charmaine slapping her face. Daria was shrieking into her phone, "Yes, I have an emergency, why the fuck else would I call you?"

"It's okay," Charmaine said. "The paramedics will be here soon. You're going to be safe."

"Call Karl," Maggie whimpered.

"Don't worry about Karl."

She was freezing. She was lying in pools of every kind of discharge that could come from a body, and she was doing it on the bathroom floor at work, and she didn't even care.

The pain exploded again. Hot pain, preposterous pain, unsurvivable pain. Maggie screamed, the noise in her ears like a horror film soundtrack.

"Call Karl!" she shrieked. It was all she could think: *I'm dying* and *Call Karl.*

Charmaine was sobbing, her eyes bugged out with terror. There was a frenzy of commotion and barked orders as blue-clad paramedics charged into the office. Maggie was whisked onto a gurney. Her final glimpse before she passed out was of Charmaine punching furiously at her phone, fulfilling Maggie's request.

Chapter 10

Eve

Eve had sensed the city enclosing her the moment she stepped out the sliding glass doors of LaGuardia and into the cab that was now carrying her westward toward it. She rolled down the window and focused on the green of trees in full leaf, on the blue of sky above the city, and not on the buildings rising like an invading army before her. Her sister-in-law had been dead for twenty-two hours.

She had the driver drop her a few blocks from Daniel and Violet's apartment. Broadway and West 75th was frantic with sight and sound, honking taxis, determined pedestrians, newspapers and handbags and pretzels and sunglasses and hot dogs for sale. Eve yanked her small suitcase from the trunk and backed into a woman rushing by on the sidewalk, then was nearly trampled by a man shouting into his phone. She turned, momentarily disoriented, and speed-walked toward the relative quiet of West 76th Street. She kept going until she reached the pale limestone and arched windows of Daniel and Violet's building near the park.

In the vestibule she pressed the buzzer. How many times had she come here? Hundreds? Thousands? A tenant came to the door with a bag of groceries, and Eve slipped through after him.

She'd pictured herself arriving to Daniel alone in a devastatingly empty apartment—waiting for her, needing her. But when she knocked and the door opened, she felt instantly foolish. Because it was Eve who would be alone in a situation like this, needing her twin; Daniel's apartment, of course, was full. Violet's parents and brothers sat on the couch opposite Eve's dad, half-empty takeout containers scattered on the coffee table between them. Hovering around the living room or bustling through from the kitchen, crying, talking in huddles, making phone calls, making arrangements, were all six of Daniel and Violet's closest friends, the three other couples who'd also met and paired off in med school, and who'd looked at Eve, with her industrial woodworking certificate, like she was a fascinating pet.

Violet's best friend, Renata, gave a cry when she saw Eve, opening her arms for a hug.

"He's in the bedroom," Renata said. "I made him try to nap. I don't think he's slept at all."

"How is he?" Eve asked.

"A wreck."

"How are you?" Eve asked.

"In shock. I think my brain's gone into organization mode to keep me from processing reality." She held up her phone and motioned Eve inside. "I'm about to call the funeral home."

The apartment was brimming with flowers. Eve sat on the couch beside her father, accepted his hug, said how awful it was, words ridiculous in their inadequacy.

She kept expecting Violet to emerge from the kitchen, proffering canapés, or from the bedroom, modeling the T-shirt she'd found on sale, and look, she got one for Eve too, wasn't it adorable? And it would be, and it would fit perfectly.

Instead, from the bathroom came Eve's mother—how had she managed to make it here already? Eve stood and her mother fell into her arms, weeping.

"A tragedy! It's such a tragedy! She was such a marvelous girl—they had such a great love—how *will* Daniel survive it? Eve, I don't think he'll survive it!" Then, "Where's Karl? Didn't Karl come with you? Oh no, you need your partner at a time like this! You need *support*! Eve, wouldn't you let him come?"

"He couldn't get away," Eve said.

"But he'll make it for the funeral," her mother insisted.

"Is George here?" Eve asked, looking around for her stepfather.

"Oh yes. We drove through the night as soon as we heard."

Eventually all the people left to eat or sleep or run funeral errands, and Eve was alone on the couch when her brother came out of the bedroom. She sprang to her feet and went to him. His eyes were bloodshot, hair longer than when she'd last seen him. Longer now than hers, curling around his ears. He clutched a glass, and she could smell the alcohol. She put out her hand. He gave her the glass, and she set it gently on the side table beside a notepad scribbled over in Violet's handwriting. Evidence, so recent, of life.

They moved into each other's arms and stood there silently, just holding each other.

"I'm so sorry," she whispered.

"Thank fuck you're here," he said. His arms gripped tight around her back, and they held each other.

For an hour they sat side by side on the couch. Eve's body felt heavy, like it was weighted down with sandbags. She'd never realized grief was a physical weight. She couldn't imagine how Daniel was staying upright. He told her more of the details of Violet's death, going over and over their last moments together, the rushed goodbye as Violet fastened her helmet at the door and Daniel waved from the bathroom, shaving cream on his face. Both of them running late, neither walking the five paces to meet the other for a kiss. Not knowing it was the end. He said he didn't want to sleep, because the one time he had, he'd awakened to three seconds of forgetting, then had to experience all over again the trauma of learning Violet was dead.

"It won't be like that every time," she said.

"It's horrific," he said. "Forgetting. Then remembering."

The fireplace mantel was crowded with framed photos. Daniel and Violet in goofy hats. Daniel and Violet in front of the Eiffel Tower. Daniel and Violet in tux and gown at their wedding—the wedding Eve had left the city just in time to miss. Violet's laugh burst into the camera, one preserved instant of pure delight.

"You loved her so much," Eve said.

"Jesus, you're already making it past tense?" Daniel said.

"No. Sorry. *Love.*"

The longing with which Eve had watched Daniel and Violet, once. Longing and incomprehension. She'd finally achieved her goal of returning to her brother—after high school, after trade school, after her industrial woodworking certificate, her apprenticeship, her journeyman's papers, her first years as a working carpenter, all completed close to home because, even though she had dual citizenship thanks to her American father, even though she'd planned to go straight to Daniel once she was old enough to make her own decisions, her connections and frames of reference were all in Canada and staying put was cheaper and logistically simpler. Or maybe, Eve hypothesized later, she'd had a premonition and was afraid of testing her reunion dream by making it reality. When she finally did, fourteen years after the divorce, fifteen years ago, how bewildered and envious she was. She'd always been with Daniel and their dad for vacations and special occasions, when they were all focused on each other, but now that she was joining them for real life she understood how thoroughly they'd both moved on, her father into his happy new marriage and Daniel into this ecstatic relationship with the woman he brought to Penn Station to meet Eve's train. Petite and beaming, springing into Eve's arms to cry, "I've always wanted a sister!" She was so small Eve could have boosted her onto a hip and carried her. Daniel had threaded his fingers through Violet's and grinned. "Eve, meet the love of my life."

Eve had never wanted a sister. She had wanted only her brother, and she had thought, when she boarded that train to Penn Station, that she was finally getting him.

On the couch now, Daniel's head on her shoulder and Violet's body somewhere in an Upper West Side funeral home, Eve pressed back an alarming sensation, an abhorrently selfish thought that was very like the feeling that had pulsed through her that entire train journey, moving to New York fifteen years ago: *I'm getting my brother back.*

She sprang from the couch so abruptly that Daniel cried, "What the hell?"

"Sorry," she said. "Are you hungry? You should eat. Even if you're not hungry."

"I feel like I've been hit by an asteroid."

"I'll make Mom's mac and cheese." Daniel's childhood favorite. Comfort food.

"There's loads to eat."

"I know, but . . ." It would give her a way to be useful. To take care of him. To atone for even dreaming of personal advantage resulting from the worst tragedy ever to befall the person she loved most in the world.

"Okay," he said. "That would be nice."

"I'll run out for cheese, then I'll cook," she said.

He motioned to his keys on the side table. She found a canvas shopping bag under the big white porcelain sink, then headed out to brave the city.

She wasn't going to—she had blocked the possibility from her mind, had not allowed herself to entertain it—but once on the street she found her feet carrying her west. On West 78th Street she crossed Amsterdam, then Broadway. Inexorably drawn. Up one block to West 79th. A Starbucks where the florist had been, a new restaurant next door. She stopped on the sidewalk across the street. There it was, tastefully understated script on a glass storefront: *Stillcraft Designer Furniture.*

She still yearned for the idyllic years when no one knew that name. When she was just Eve, a twin no longer needed by her other half, rescuing herself from bleak purposelessness in the relentless city with the simple act of making things. Three years of immersion in walnut and oak, in hand lathes and chisels, in the intricate, absolute attention they commanded. Three years, until she sold a chair to her first celebrity client and his home was featured in *Architectural Digest* and overnight Stillcraft became the coveted choice of anyone with an appreciation for craftsmanship and local artistry and the money to pay for it. A demand that would feel, all too quickly, like a consuming fire.

By the end she was spending the bulk of her days tending her brand, managing her staff, fielding the rich New Yorkers who bought her work. Her first acknowledgment of misery came when the marketing firm she'd hired declared her face the best feature of her business and twisted the whole enterprise to focus on *her*. "I work with wood so I can disappear," she said in an interview, and the magazine printed a full-page spread of her face and minimized her furniture to insets. Even the "I work with wood" was a sham; she could barely be said to do that anymore. She knew the quality was excellent, but she was embarrassed when her name became what people were buying, astonished at the prices they would pay. Horrified that the success of the work she loved had taken the work she loved from her.

Standing in front of her former shop now, she considered crossing the street to get a better look inside. But she was too fearful of running into someone she knew, of getting walloped by some painful emotion she had no capacity for, and instead she turned and skulked away.

For the next four days, Eve left the apartment only for the twenty minutes a day she could persuade Daniel to shuffle down the block and into the park for some fresh air. She prepared meals and snacks, tidied up after each wave of mourners, tried to keep Daniel from drinking too much, sat alone with him while he talked and while he didn't. He could shift from vulnerable to belligerent without notice, a volatility Eve had never seen in him before. More of Violet's family arrived, a keening mass of grandparents, aunts, cousins. Their own mother returned and made everything worse with her histrionics. The funeral home called with questions, and Eve relayed Daniel's answers or made decisions herself when he shrugged and said, "What the fuck does it matter." She tried to get him to sleep.

Their father came by on Saturday afternoon, just after Daniel had successfully drifted off, and Eve talked with him in whispers in the entryway. He asked how she was holding up, asked when her fellow was arriving for the funeral.

"We broke up," Eve said, and he patted her shoulder.

When Daniel emerged from his bed on the morning of the funeral, five days after Eve had arrived, she was hunched over the toilet, scrubbing. It wasn't dirty, but she'd run out of ways to be useful. He leaned in the bathroom doorway, dark-eyed and pale.

"Honestly, Eve, if you don't tell me where you put my bourbon . . ."

She put up her rubber-gloved hands. "Of course, no problem, give me a second."

He cracked the barest smile. "Life sucks."

"It does." She peeled off the gloves, left the toilet water foaming with all-natural cleaner, and rose from her knees to retrieve the bourbon from the top of the bookcase.

He poured himself a generous glass and raised the bottle to Eve. "Want some?"

"I'm okay."

"That's right, I forgot," he said. "*You're* not grieving."

"Daniel." She plopped down on the couch beside him. "Of course I am, just not in the same way you are."

"You know what I've been torturing myself with?" he asked.

Eve ran a hand along the back of his neck, but he leaned forward, elbows on spread knees, out of her reach.

"Every single time I failed her. Every situation where I didn't ease her pain."

"I'm sure there aren't many of those. Daniel, you were devoted to her."

"You know which one I can't get out of my head?" He didn't wait for her to guess. "You not liking her."

"What? Of course I liked Violet! Violet was—"

"I know, kind and compassionate and smart. Violet was a light. It's all anyone has said to me since she died."

Her throat was dry. She swallowed carefully. "She was never anything but friendly to me. Why wouldn't I like her?"

"I don't know, Eve. Why wouldn't you?"

The painting above the fireplace was askew, an abstract of black and red swirls overlaid with green cubes. Eve stood and straightened it, both arms extended across its length.

"You know I didn't believe her when she said you didn't like her?" Daniel said. "I thought she was paranoid. That it was twin mythology getting in her head, giving her this idea that you and I were fused and it would get in the way of what I could give her. I dismissed her intuition for *years*. I told her you always had your guard up, that you weren't particularly warm with anyone."

Eve forced herself to turn around and face Daniel again.

"You know what made me realize she was right and you just plain resented her?" he asked.

Eve shook her head, mutely horrified. The ugliest part of her had crept to the surface against her will, and she couldn't stuff it back. Not with Daniel. Daniel knew her too well.

"You leaving New York a month before our wedding," Daniel said. "Leaving and not coming back. It was a bit of a giveaway."

"You know how burnt out I was with Stillcraft," she said. "It had been building for years. And your wedding was a surprise—you practically eloped." This wasn't strictly true, but the timeline *was* short.

"So you couldn't hang out one more month, or, you know, buy a plane ticket back for a measly weekend?"

She could have. She was stressed and desperate for escape, but of course she could have. "It just came together that way," she said weakly.

"No, Eve. All of a sudden, one month before our wedding, it was *urgent* that you get out of here. You made it happen. Violet was still hurt about that. She looked for the best in people, but that was a hard one. You're my sister. You were supposed to be there."

"I'm sorry," Eve said. The words were inadequate even to her own ears.

"So what I want to hear is you admitting to me out loud why the hell you did that."

Carefully, Eve stepped closer, making herself uncross her arms, trying desperately not to look defensive.

In retrospect, Daniel and Violet *not* marrying for so many years had given Eve hope. Had made her believe their relationship was impermanent, that she just had to ride it out and one day they'd break up, and maybe Daniel would partner with someone he was less consumed by or maybe he'd partner with no one, and either way she could be a more central person in his life again.

"You sold your business and moved to the wilderness and refused to come back because you couldn't stand to see me get married," Daniel said.

She clenched her hands behind her back. "No! God, Daniel. It was Stillcraft, it was New York, it was what my life had become. It was lots of things, culminating, and I couldn't—I couldn't go on." This was all true!

"I know you've had a rough go of it. But I hope someday you'll get to experience what it's like to truly, deeply love someone."

"That's so patronizing."

"Sorry. But I mean it."

"Karl was different! I loved Karl."

"And I loved Violet, but you could never accept that and find a way to love her too. Violet, who was the most beautiful person anyone could hope to know, ever."

He opened his mouth and a gruff, eerie wailing burst from him, a depth of anguish so visceral that Eve began to weep too. She rushed to the couch and knelt in front of him. Her head dropped to his knees. His hands gripped her hair. For several minutes they wept together.

But when she raised herself to sit beside him, he pushed her gently away.

"Go," he said. His expression was unreadable.

"What?"

"Go, Eve. I love you, but I don't want you here right now. This is the worst thing that has ever happened to me, and it makes me sick to be around you because I'm convinced that a tiny part of you is glad about it."

"I'm not!" She tried to reach for his hand again, but he shook his head, pulling away.

"Prove it."

"What do you want me to do?"

"Forget it. Just please leave. I'm not joking."

"I'll go for a walk."

"No. I mean go home."

She stared at him, her mouth opening and closing.

"I can't be with someone right now who spent fifteen years wishing Violet wasn't in my life."

"I never said that."

"You didn't have to."

She swallowed. "But the funeral's in three hours."

He nodded. "Yeah. It is."

He rose and crossed to the study with the sofa bed she'd been sleeping on, began tossing her belongings into her suitcase. His hand did not touch hers as he passed it to her. He yanked her jacket from the closet. She heard and watched, sure that the next second—now, and then now, and then now—he would smile, slap an arm around her shoulder, apologize. He opened the door.

Chapter 11

Maggie

"Your mother should come back," Maggie's father said on the fifth day of her hospitalization. Five days since Maggie had woken in a fog of pain and morphine and the residue of a nightmare that Charmaine had to tenderly inform her was real. Her left fallopian tube had ruptured. She'd needed three blood transfusions. And she had lost the baby. The baby, steadily growing in her fallopian tube instead of her uterus, had never been viable, never a reality at all.

"I'll be okay," Maggie said into her pillow, squeezing her eyes shut to keep the tears in. She had never felt more destroyed—physically, mentally, emotionally, spiritually.

Her father's hand hovered just above her hair, as though he was daring himself to smooth it back. She could feel the malfunction alerts going off in his ordered brain. He couldn't correct or instruct her, not when she lay so wholly broken in a hospital bed, only narrowly not-dead, and he clearly didn't know what to say or where to look.

"I know her work is important and we both told her to stay in Crete," her father said, "but I wish she was here for you." Translation: *If your mother came back, I could hand the all-gone-wrongness over to her and step away with a clean conscience.*

Her entire life her mom had been there for her, and it was Maggie who'd persuaded her not to cut her research sabbatical short. Her father was the one in the room with her—couldn't *he* be there for her this once?

He pulled his hand away.

Next to Charmaine, he'd been her most frequent visitor, visibly uncomfortable every minute he spent at her bedside, but still Maggie held out hope, in her drugged-up and defenseless state, that *now* might be the time he'd find it in himself to muster empathy and comfort. She'd been seriously imperiled, he'd almost lost her, and surely even he would agree that Maggie was not, for once, being more emotional than the situation warranted.

"You'll be back to those dissertation revisions in no time," he said, apparently believing this to be encouraging.

If he mentioned the investment money she would scream.

"Soon it will be as though this unfortunate incident never happened."

Unfortunate incident. Like she'd slipped on the sidewalk and broken her leg.

She thought of her preteen self crying with joy when her favorite actress got engaged. (His response: *You do not even know this person.*) The time she full-on wept when the radio DJ announced a song she loved, then played a different one instead. *(For pity's sake, this was not the only opportunity to ever hear that song.)* The time she ran shrieking into the yard to cartwheel in the rain after weeks of a hot, dry summer. *(It's only precipitation.)* The time she locked herself in her room for an entire weekend upon discovering her first-ever boyfriend making out on a park bench with someone else. *(You're only fifteen, there will be other boys—lord help us.)*

"I can't deal with that right now," she said. Didn't he *see* her, here in this bed, strapped to monitors, *grieving*?

She knew he loved her. What horrified him about her current condition was the emotional messiness of it—the pregnancy that meant she'd had sex, the ruptured fallopian tube that meant she couldn't even do an illegitimate pregnancy properly, the tears that meant she was falling apart. Again. The absence of the man responsible for putting her here, which meant he was a deadbeat, yet another ill-advised choice. Maggie could just imagine his dismay if he knew the truth.

She still hadn't been able to reach Karl.

On the morning of the sixth day, a kind nurse wheeled Maggie to the taxi stand and waved her off. Maggie had promised over and over that even though she had no one escorting her home—no, there was nobody; her father was presenting a paper at a conference, Charmaine was at her older son's first-ever school play, Natalie was writing exams, and Maggie didn't want to further burden the other friends who'd been texting and visiting all week—she would go directly to her parents' house in the cab, and when her dad returned, he would bring her nourishing soups and extra pillows and she would not leave her bed for many days. Straight home.

"Actually," Maggie said, as they pulled away from the curb, "could you take me to Bay and Dundas?" This was not where her parents lived, but it *was* where Karl worked and where he would be at ten o'clock on a Monday morning.

She wasn't entirely certain she could walk. Natalie had brought her clean clothes, but it was all comfort wear, not exactly the glamorous look she'd choose for her reunion with Karl. She had on sweatpants and a long T-shirt; her jean jacket improved the outfit slightly. She asked the driver to wait.

Five slow steps across the sidewalk. A deep ache pulsed with every shift of her weight, and there was a tight, dragging pull at the site of her incision. Even the brush of fabric made her flinch.

A heavy glass door—she pressed the automatic opener—and then another one. Her legs were shaking by the time she stood inside the bank, scanning the faces of Karl's colleagues.

At the far end of the counter, a manager waved to her. She knew him from the Christmas party and her occasional drop-ins, and his face was a beacon from another life. Xavier, the bank manager, recognized her. She hadn't dreamt her relationship with Karl, hadn't invented her status as his acknowledged girlfriend. If the fetus she'd just had violently extracted from her wasn't proof enough, this man's recognition of her was.

Xavier would not, she wagered, recognize Eve.

She bypassed the queue of clients to edge between two teller stations. Xavier gave her a concerned look as she approached.

"Hi!" She tried for peppy, but it took everything. "I'm looking for Karl."

"You don't—you don't know?"

Her brain was so fuzzy. She leaned her elbows on the counter to hold herself up. "Have I just missed him?"

"More than just, but—hey, are you okay?"

In a plastic stand on the granite counter, a sheaf of leaflets offered a house, a baby, a smiling husband, and three months with zero percent interest.

"He's not here?" She felt stupid with incomprehension.

"He quit," said Xavier. "I don't think his heart was ever much in banking. Good guy, though. Kind of admire it. Takes balls to walk out on everything and go do whatever it is you really want to do." His voice dropped and he hunched closer, seeming to register Maggie's distress. "Uh, sorry. I didn't mean he should walk out on you. He didn't—did he?"

The pain in her belly throbbed. "Do you know where he is?" she asked.

"Do you maybe need to sit down?"

"I just need to find Karl."

"We're not in touch, but he was up north at his parents' when he called," Xavier said. "He had stuff to take care of there."

"When did this happen?" she asked.

"Over a week ago. Week and a half?"

She thanked him. She made her way unsteadily to the door, feeling even weaker than she had five minutes ago. Her taxi still idled at the curb, and she slid in, panting with the effort, trying not to panic. He'd *quit*?

"Meter's ticking," the driver said.

Across the street, the bus depot loomed like an answer.

She had his parents' address. Just a month ago, stopping in to see her at Sukha, Karl had bought a gardening book for his mother and Maggie offered to mail it. The address was still saved in her phone. Surely there were buses that delivered people somewhere close enough to the wilderness Karl hadn't let her near.

But just because Xavier from the bank thought he was up north didn't mean for certain that he was. Even if he'd quit, he could still be in the city. She gave the driver Karl's address. Her remaining energy was fading fast. When they arrived, she eyed the stairs and knew there was no way. She knocked instead on the downstairs apartment door, where his landlord lived, thinking she could ask him to go up and knock.

The landlord stared at her. Her boyfriend, he informed her, had broken his lease and moved out.

She made her way carefully back to the cab and considered Eve's number in her phone. But what would she say? *Karl quit his job! He broke his lease! He's gone missing!* And Maggie and Eve would mount a joint search party? Eve had just dumped him and probably didn't even want to hear his name right now. She sure wasn't going to go out looking for him.

Besides, he wasn't missing—according to Xavier, he was just at his parents' place.

"Where to now?" the cab driver asked.

Her parents' house, she thought dully. In a matter of minutes she'd be arriving at their front porch, moving back into her childhood bedroom, bearing her father's disappointment and his expectations for as long as her convalescence took. She recoiled at the thought. But she also didn't want to return to her overcrowded apartment. What she wanted, deeply, was to press pause on the fact of Karl's infidelity until she was strong enough to face it again. Just until she was no longer weak and weepy and sore and so, so in need of the person she'd hoped would be her companion and comfort for the rest of her life.

If he knew what had happened to her, he would be here. At her side, caring for her, for as long as she needed him.

And *then* she could go back to attempting strength and independence.

She asked the driver to take her back to the bus station. She needed Karl and she wanted him. Maybe that was desperate—she could already hear her mom and Charmaine's horrified objections—but so what. She *was* desperate.

In the cavernous station her brazenness disintegrated. What the fuck did she think she was doing? Panic clamoured in her chest, and she clutched the bag that contained her laptop and notebook, phone, chargers, wallet, a tube of lipstick, the clothes from Natalie, painkillers, and eight jumbo menstrual pads from the nurse, all she had with her in the world. Her body quivered and tears materialized as unavoidably as breath. Each person on the vinyl seats seemed to produce the noise of twenty. Each automated announcement was augmented a hundred decibels. Each pigeon loose in the rafters was a terror. This was stupid. This was possibly the stupidest thing she'd done in her life. She fumbled for one of the painkillers. She researched routes and stops on her phone and bought the ticket. She texted her father—Decided to go to a friend's, don't worry about me—and then, more guiltily, her mom: Going to Charmaine's. I'm okay.

Finally she was on the bus, no longer thinking of Karl at all, thinking only of a reclining seat and sleep.

She slept most of the four-hour trip, doubled over with her feet curled under her, her head against the window, bumping hard and damp with every jostle of the coach. She woke periodically to rocks and trees, a river, a lake, more rocks, more trees. She was cold, her abdomen ached at the site of her scar, and blood seeped steadily into her extra-large pad. Each time she woke, she changed the pad in the smelly rear bathroom, then stumbled back to her seat and back into sleep. The bus meandered off the highway into every two-house hamlet it could find. She didn't know where she was going, and she wouldn't recognize it when she arrived, and she'd conceived a baby and lost it, and she took more painkillers and slept.

The driver nudged her awake at her stop. She descended the steps, one foot at a time, like a child, her bag clutched against her body. "Thank you," she whispered.

She wasn't at a bus depot at all but at a gas station and convenience store. Making her way to the door—*Please let them have a bathroom*—she stepped inside to find five aisles of chocolate bars and chips and motor oil, two men watching a game on a small TV behind the counter. Her pad was full; she could feel the damp, sticky warmth of blood at her crotch.

She cleared her throat and both men looked up. There was no way she could walk the rest of the distance to the counter. Instead, she enlarged the address on her phone and held it up to them. "Is there a cab or an Uber that I can take to get here?"

She felt the lunacy of the question even as it left her mouth. Of course there was no cab or Uber. There was no anything. The men exchanged a glance and laughed, not unkindly.

"'Fraid not, miss," the older one said. "Not too many people down there year-round, but hang out for a bit and maybe someone'll be passing that way."

She asked for a bathroom. The toilet was spattered with yellow smears. Maggie laid toilet paper across the seat and peed, peeled off the gigantic blood-soaked pad, wrapped it in more toilet paper, and buried it deep inside the garbage can.

She had to grip the wall to stop herself from falling as she exited the bathroom. One of the men fetched her a dusty hard-back chair from a back room. Her stomach and her pelvis ached. She groaned, and the men shot her half-wary, half-sympathetic looks.

Her father had responded to her message about going to "a friend's." As long as you're all right and in good hands. Keep me posted. Translation: *I'm so relieved I don't have to be responsible for you.* She had warmer messages from her mother and Charmaine, and she texted them back to assure them she was fine and to convince Charmaine not to visit her tonight.

Then, for the thousandth time, she pressed Karl's name in her phone. She'd come here—been idiotic enough to come here—and if this wasn't where Karl was, she'd be at the mercy of the reportedly odd parents she'd never met, so Karl *had* to be here.

The call went straight to voicemail, and his mailbox was full.

"I'll take you," said the older man. "Only half an hour, nothing happening around here anyways."

She was about to say, *You don't have to*, but stopped herself and accepted his offer—she needed to arrive at somewhere with a bed very soon, regardless of who was or was not waiting upon her arrival. The man didn't seem like a serial killer—but then again, Karl hadn't seemed like a cheater, had he?

The man's maroon minivan drove endlessly along a dirt road with nothing but bushes and trees and a lonely string of hydro poles along its side. After the fourth bump she'd asked him to go more slowly, and now he steered with dramatic care around each pothole.

A glint of blue through trees, then another. Narrow lanes broke off into the bush and disappeared in the direction of the water. White numbers on green metal flags stood at attention beside each lane. "There it is," she said, and he swung the van to the right and they descended. The slope sharpened, then curved. "This'll be rough in winter," he said, and she wondered how Karl's elderly parents managed it. They rounded on a house, small and neat and many-windowed, with a deck wrapped halfway around it and a woodpile by the door. Karl's Wrangler was not in the driveway, but neither was any other car—there could be parking around the side? Beyond the house were a lake and a dock.

So maybe Karl hadn't been lying about repairing docks. Maybe he'd been telling the truth about something. She needed at least one truth.

She thanked the man and stepped onto the ground. He executed a three-point turn and drove back up the curving drive the way they had come. She stood until his tires on gravel receded and she was alone.

There was no human sound.

She crept up the four steps to the deck, pausing to clutch the banister and breathe through the pain. *Some pain is normal*, the doctor had said. *Even a lot of pain is normal.*

This was a lot of pain. It was normal.

She made it to the first door, wooden with three diamond-shaped panes. She knocked, tried the handle, peered in through a window. Spare, neat, absent of life. She dragged herself around to a patio door facing the lake, but could see no one through it either. It was also locked. There were no other doors to try.

She was not capable of taking one more step.

She lowered herself to the smooth wood of the deck, fumbled for another pill, and plunged into unconsciousness.

Chapter 12

Eve

A single wracking sob escaped Eve as she stepped through the front door of her house. She tore off her jacket, shoved her suitcase into a corner, and slid down the door to the floor. Flora, newly fetched from her five-day stay with Sam, nuzzled Eve's arm as Eve stroked her chocolate fur. Eve felt like a small woodland creature narrowly attaining its burrow. Safe, just barely, from the dangers of the night.

Violet was dead. Daniel despised her. Now there was grief to surpass the grief of Karl.

After Daniel banished her, she'd roamed the Upper West Side with her suitcase and finally took a cab to LaGuardia. She was able to get a flight almost right away. New York to Toronto, Toronto to Sudbury, where she collected her truck from airport parking, drove the hour to Sam's, and finally came home.

Flora took off with wagging tail to inspect the house, then stopped at the patio door and started barking urgently.

"What is it?" Eve asked.

Flora wouldn't stop barking. Eve pushed herself off the floor and crossed to the kitchen as Flora raced back and forth between Eve and the door.

"What is up with you, baby girl? You need to go out?"

A form—a *person*—lay sprawled across Eve's deck.

"Hey!" Adrenaline leapt and Eve wrenched open the door. "Hey, what do you think you're doing here?"

A drunk? A burglar? A *corpse*?

A woman, asleep. Her back was to Eve. Flora barked for an instant of guard dog usefulness, then proceeded to lick the cheek in welcome. The woman stirred, moaning. She turned toward Eve and opened her eyes.

What the fucking *fuck*. It was Maggie.

She looked wrung out, hair unbrushed, face pale and bloodless, and she stared up at Eve, blinking stupidly.

Eve grabbed Flora's collar and pulled the dog to her side.

"Are you for real?" Eve exclaimed. "It wasn't enough to harass me with emails and phone calls, now you're setting up camp on my doorstep?" Dear god, Maggie really was unhinged. She *was* a crazy stalker!

Maggie just lay there, staring. "*Eve?*" she said finally. "Why are you—are Karl's parents home?" With painful slowness she inched her body into a seated position.

"*Karl's parents?*" Fury surged through Eve. Maggie had a glazed look in her eyes—was she stoned? Eve wanted to slap her. Of all the shitshows to arrive on her deck on this day of all days. Eve thought *she* had taken Karl's betrayal hard, but Eve was thriving in comparison with this. Maggie was in worse shape than Daniel.

"What are you *doing* here?"

Maggie eased herself up the side of the deck railing until she was standing. She leaned back, facing Eve. "I need to find Karl."

"I already told you he isn't here. I haven't seen him in two weeks."

"At the bank, they said he quit. The bank. He left."

"That's why you're here? He wasn't at the bank, so he must be at my house?"

"*Your* house?" Maggie's voice shook. She looked around, steadying herself against the railing. "I thought this was his parents'. They live on a lake—don't they?" Her tone rose an octave as she spoke, landing finally in a shaky, desperate plea.

"*I* live on a lake," Eve said. "*Me*. Anything Karl told you about his weekends at a lake house, it was *mine*. I thought we clarified that."

"But you said he did also visit his parents on weekends?"

"They live in Larkin—it's a very small town about half an hour from here, back out that long dirt road you had to come down to get to my place," Eve said, expending great effort to modulate her voice into, if not a kind tone, at least a neutral one. "I will drive you—to a hotel or to Karl's parents' house, if that's really where you want to go, but FYI, they are not the welcoming sort."

Maggie was bending at the knees. "I don't know if I can . . . I'm sorry . . ."

And then she sank.

Eve lunged. Her hands landed under Maggie's armpits. Maggie's knees swayed just above the deck, her dead weight dragging Eve down. Eve shifted position so her arms encircled Maggie's waist, and Maggie yelped with what sounded like pain.

"Holy crap, you're bleeding," Eve said.

Maggie's pants were stained at the back, a patch the size of a lemon.

"It's normal. Supposed to be resting."

Shit fuck hell crap fuck. "What *happened* to you?"

"I need to talk to Karl."

"I'm taking you to the hospital."

"I was just there."

"And they discharged you like this?"

"I was all better. I'm really fine now."

"Let's get you inside, at least, while I figure this out." Damn it, Karl, now she had to bring this woman into her *house*? How had Maggie even got here?

Eve hoisted Maggie by the armpits and half carried, half dragged her across the threshold and into her sanctuary. Flora stood at concerned attention as Eve left Maggie in a heap inside the door. Eve rummaged in a bottom drawer for the plastic drop cloth she'd used when she painted the bedroom. She spread it over her burgundy couch, covered it with a clean sheet, and gathered spare blankets from the closet. Then she put Maggie's arm over her shoulder and dragged her toward the couch. She was not light.

"Listen, Maggie." Eve knelt on the floor beside the couch, speaking louder as Maggie's eyelids fluttered shut. "You have to tell me what's going on. You are not okay, and I need to know why, because I can't have you bleeding out on my watch."

"Do you have any pads?"

"*What happened?* You tell me now or I'm kicking you out into the bush." Eve's voice was ferocious, but under her anger she was terrified.

"I had a baby." Maggie spoke with her eyes closed. "Kind of. There was a fetus."

"What do you mean?"

"It died. It wasn't viable."

Whoa. Okay. Stay calm. "So—are you okay?" She obviously was not.

"It was ec-top-ic." Maggie emphasized each syllable. "It's gone. The baby's gone. They had to cut it out. My fallopian tube ruptured." Quietly, she began to cry.

Eve watched with mounting alarm. What was she supposed to say? What was she supposed to *do*? She extended one hand toward Maggie's shoulder but stopped short of touching her.

"Who knows you're here?" she asked as gently as she could.

"I was supposed to go to my parents' and stay in bed. For a couple of weeks."

Jesus. So she'd thought it would be a good idea to take a four-hour trip to the middle of nowhere?

Maggie mumbled something unintelligible. She was going slack.

"My brother's a doctor," Eve said. "I'm calling him."

But she couldn't call him, could she? She had alienated her brother with the same failure of empathy she was showing Maggie right now.

But Maggie was an idiot.

She called him anyway, inhaling deeply before she dialed. He did not, as expected, answer. No doubt he was back at the apartment with friends and family—*where Eve should be right now*—drowning himself in post-funeral alcohol. Briefly, she wished she had a cellphone; assuming he was even checking his phone, he might be more likely to read a text than answer a call. She tried Karl next, walking away from Maggie toward her bedroom. The call went straight to voicemail. The mailbox was full, but she hissed into the phone anyway. "Your little mistress is here, and she is bleeding and barely conscious, and I *need you* to come take care of this."

She walked back to the living room. Maggie's eyes flitted open.

"Where's your phone?" Eve asked.

Maggie's eyes closed again. Eve rifled through the enormous blue faux-leather handbag Maggie had come with: a laptop, makeup, a giant monster pad that probably needed to be put to use right now but no way was Eve playing intimate nursemaid to Karl's other so-called girlfriend, and in a side pocket, a phone. Locked. She held it up to Maggie's face and it sprang to life. Karl's iPhone got only a spotty signal here, but it could usually handle a text message. Here's hoping Maggie's could too. She punched Daniel's number in and hoped his life-saving instincts would eclipse how angry he was with her right now.

It's Eve. EMERGENCY. I'm sorry to bother you, especially today, but I have somebody in my house who recently had a fallopian tube rupture. I don't actually know how long ago, but it was an ectopic pregnancy and she's been in the hospital—I think she had surgery? But she took a 4-hour trip today and now she's bleeding and passed out. Does she need to go to the hospital?

First responders would take forever to get all the way down Vermillion Road. Eve should just put Maggie in the truck and bring her to Sudbury now, but the hospital was over an hour away, and Maggie did not look like she should be upright.

The seats in Karl's Wrangler folded down. *He* could take her.

She picked up her landline again. If there was one person to whom Karl had shown exemplary devotion, it was his demanding mother. If he wasn't with her, she would know where he was. And Eve would *make* him drive here and get Maggie. She would haul his ass over here herself.

His mother answered.

"Hello, Mrs. Tarvudd?" There were so many reasons to cringe right now—the parents never liking her in the first place, the parents probably knowing she'd kicked Karl out and hating her because their son must never be hurt—but she soldiered on. "It's Eve. I'm trying to get in touch with Karl."

"You are no longer Karl's girlfriend, according to him. This is true?"

"Yes, but—"

"I believe it is always better to move on, don't you? No contact. No getting pulled back into something you already decided was not right. Move forward, not backwards. You agree?"

"Generally, maybe, but this is an emergency. Trust me, I wouldn't be calling otherwise."

"I can pass a message."

"But he is there with you? It's urgent."

"I will pass the message on." The line clicked off.

Eve slammed the phone down. She dropped to the floor beside the couch, her head by Maggie's, and pulled her knees against her chest. Crying would feel great right now.

She'd picked up her phone again to dial 911 when Maggie's phone dinged.

How much bleeding?

Oh, thank goodness, Daniel.

She rose to her knees and gingerly nudged Maggie to her side.

Enough to show through but not spreading. It doesn't look fresh.

When was the rupture?

"Hey, Maggie." Eve slapped her face gently and Maggie groaned. "How long since this happened?"

"Friday," Maggie grunted.

Six days ago, including today.

Keep an eye but should be ok.
Hemorrhaging = call ambulance
but some bleeding normal.

How do I tell the difference?

Hemorrhaging doesn't stop.

Eve checked the blood spot again, dried to a crusty brown, not spreading.

I'm sorry, Daniel. I feel sick that I'm not there with you. I'm sorry. Please could we talk on the phone?

She didn't know what else to say. She pressed send, then stared at the numbers on Maggie's iPhone clock as they ticked up and she waited for Daniel's response.

It doesn't have to be now. I don't want to bother you but when you're ready would you please call me?

In the quiet room, on the floor beside Maggie, hugging her knees and staring at the phone screen, Eve waited for ten minutes, twenty, thirty. Daniel didn't text again. Eve scrolled through their messages. She didn't want Maggie finding them later. She deleted the texts, and it was as though she and Daniel had never spoken.

All night Eve watched over Maggie. She hadn't intended to, but she was so worried about Maggie dying on her couch that she dragged her blankets to the living room and set up a makeshift bed on the floor. Flora had chosen Maggie anyway and was already curled at Maggie's feet. Eve scrolled through the contacts in Maggie's phone, considering a mad rampage through the list, dialing every number and demanding, *Do you know the woman passed out on my couch? Are you close enough to her that you would drive however many hours it is between where I live and where you live to get her and make her your problem instead of mine? No? Well you're closer to her than I am, because I do not know her at all.*

Except she *was* close to Maggie, wasn't she? One degree of we-made-love-with-the-same-person separation—almost no separation at all.

Made love, made a life. All those weekends Karl was with Eve and going straight back to Maggie, Eve and Maggie had been side by side. Invisible to each other through the curtain of his deception, but right there nonetheless.

At dawn she thought of Bernice's lodge. Maggie was breathing normally and hadn't started bleeding again, but she didn't look nearly well enough to travel back to her own life and out of Eve's. The lodge would give Eve somewhere to put her, out of Eve's immediate sight but close enough to monitor. At least until she could find Karl or track down someone else to take responsibility.

She scrawled a note. *Be back soon, don't go anywhere.* But that was absurd; anywhere that wasn't here was exactly where she wanted Maggie to go. She tore the second part off and left only the first. She whistled for Flora, but Flora only looked at her and settled her head on Maggie's feet. "Traitor," Eve muttered. She gathered a broom and dustpan, a bucket and a handful of rags from beneath her kitchen sink, grabbed Bernice's keys, and pulled on rubber boots.

Mist rose, ghostlike, off the lake. Eve turned right, following the rutted path until roots and moss and wet brown piles of last year's leaves gave way to open shoreline. A dock sagging into the lake. A sauna, its silver chimney poking through the roof. And looming on a hill above her, the two log buildings of the former fishing lodge.

Eve took the stairs and circled the buildings. They were big—unlike Sam's private self-catering cabins, this lodge was designed for food service and communal gatherings, sleeping quarters housed under one roof. The place didn't look worse for the days she had failed to carry out her neighborly checking-in duties. She wriggled the first of the old woman's keys into the first door, braced her shoulder against it, and shoved.

She was in the dining hall. Faded fishing posters and disembodied antlers plastered the walls. The floor was a linoleum grey with dirt or age, the fissures snaking across it opening periodically into craters of rotting chipboard.

Her family used to canoe from Sam's to the lodge on special occasions—Eve and Daniel's birthday, their parents' anniversary—and eat at a wobbly table in this dining hall. Bernice balanced steaming plates of rib-eye and rainbow trout up her arm, thumped rowdy American fishermen on the back of the head, scrunching her nose in a series of rodent-like movements to nudge her glasses upward. In this room their parents had sung "Happy Birthday" to Eve and Daniel on their thirteenth birthday, the last birthday of their intact family life, the last of their Still Lake summers.

It had never occurred to anyone to give Eve and Daniel each their own rendition of the song, their own cake or candles. They were twins, united, one.

She walked to the bank of windows and blew at cobwebs stretched over the sill. The air was heavy with neglect. The strings of dust flailed and disbanded as she blew.

Sam said the lodge had been for sale for years. The realtor had given up. *Imagine taking over Bernice's fishing lodge*, she thought. Buying it and bringing it back to life. She could just hear Daniel's diagnosis if she did *that*. More romanticization of her lost past. More chasing what could never be again.

Across the path at the second building, the door stuck and then gave way, and she stumbled after it into a spacious common room under a cathedral ceiling. A rusted wood cookstove, a heavy picnic table, blanket-draped couches. Dead flies and mouse dirt carpeted the thick wooden windowsills. The second floor was suspended above her, the doors to more unused rooms hanging limply ajar.

She thumped a door open and gazed at bed frames with rusted springs and stained mattresses. A closet, wire hangers empty and expectant. A desk and bookshelf rimed with dust, pink insulation poking through holes in the walls, caulking peeling from a grimy bathtub.

She put her hand to a three-by-three square of dinged-up maple propped against the wall. She turned it over and saw that it was a painting on canvas in a crude maple frame.

A woman, naked to the waist. Over-large hands, arms thick and sinewy. Breasts like globes, continents of dark areolae. Behind her, deep blue and unruffled, a lake. At the bottom, two words in slanting cursive: *Truth Landing*.

Eve stared into the eyes of the woman in the painting. They stared back with an unsettling perception.

"Truth has landed, all right," Eve said out loud. She turned the painting back around.

Upstairs was better. She chose a lake-facing room—the view automatically cut the room's shabbiness in half—and threw the windows open while she swept and mopped and scrubbed and emptied bucket after bucket of blackened water. She turned the mattress on the bed. She cleared the desk of fishing magazines and a jumbled assortment of bolts and extension cords and batteries.

When she returned home for clean sheets and blankets, towels and pillows, a flashlight and candles, Maggie was still asleep. Flora dozed serenely at her feet. Eve took her load over to the lodge and stood in the doorway to assess the room. It was a lot homier, but it could use something extra. She rummaged through the common room until she found a toolbox. She lugged the *Truth Landing* painting up the stairs, heavy in its awkward bashed-up frame, and slammed a nail into the wall over the bed. There: decoration.

Then she headed back across the path to oust Maggie Dunn from her home.

Chapter 13

Maggie

"What's your dog's name?" Maggie asked.

When she'd woken on Eve's couch, the chocolate lab had been gazing at her with soulful eyes. Maggie had sat up and sunk her fingers into the soft fur, then buried her whole face in it. She wished she could do it again now, but she didn't dare with Eve assessing her from across the room.

"Flora," Eve said.

Flora of the new dog bed. Maggie turned her head and there it was, in a corner of the room, red and black checks with a fluffy white lining.

Eve eyed Maggie over the top of a ceramic mug and sighed. "She likes you."

Maggie smiled. One positive thing. One simple, happy, comforting thing. Also possibly the kindest words Eve had ever spoken to her.

"Can you walk?" Eve asked.

"I think so," Maggie said. She stood and tried a few cautious steps. She asked for the bathroom, and once inside she wiped carefully at the crusted blood on her inner thighs with a dampened length of toilet paper, twisting her sweatpants around to find a rusty brown stain across the back of them. Pulling them off, she maneuvered herself to standing, laid the pants in the sink, and ran cold water over the spot. Then she raised her eyes to her half-naked body in the mirror and slowly lifted her T-shirt.

Her abdomen was a mottled purple turning to yellow-green as the bruising traveled outward. The incision ran from just below her navel to the top of her pelvis, a rigid pink seam held shut by a line of staples and covered in translucent Steri-Strips. The skin around each staple was pink and puffy, the line tacky with dried fluid. They'd used dissolving staples—better for younger skin, the nurse had said, leaving fewer railroad track marks; better for *female* skin, she'd implied, because a woman, even one who'd nearly died, was supposed to care about how she looked in a swimsuit.

A gulf opened inside her, a great passage of absence and sorrow. Regardless of how she'd been closed up, she was now literally scarred for life. She crouched against the bathroom cabinet and leaned her forehead into her hands on the counter. *Don't cry, Maggie. You've humiliated yourself enough. Don't cry.*

She felt weak, body and soul. She couldn't imagine ever, ever being strong again.

You lost half your blood, sweetheart. Anybody would be weak after that. The words came to her in her mom's voice, and she squeezed her eyes shut against the tears. So stupid, such a misplaced attempt at independence, to insist her mom not come back from Crete. To lie to her about where she was! She needed someone caring for her who loved her. That was definitely not Eve. Maggie had just enough optimism left to believe that *maybe* it was Karl, that two opposing truths could coexist: He'd deceived and manipulated, but he'd also borne genuine affection for Maggie. Except Karl was no more present and available in this moment than her mother was.

A rap on the door. "Hand me your clothes and I'll wash them. I have something here for you to put on."

Slowly, Maggie uncrouched from the cabinet. She peeled off the rest of her clothing, unlocked the door, and held it out, accepting the T-shirt and jogging pants Eve gave her. She had more clothes of her own in her bag, but asking Eve to get those instead felt like a rejection of this small act of care and would also require energy.

She suspected the pants were capris on Eve, but they reached past Maggie's ankles. She put them on and stared at her bleary eyes in the mirror, splashing water on her face and dragging her fingers through her hair. She looked haggard and old and broken-hearted. A bath would feel excellent—they'd told her she could—but she didn't want to stretch Eve's generosity that far. Eve was doing Maggie's laundry, though, which meant she had at least a couple of hours before she had to figure out where to go next and how to get there.

Karl's parents were her only lead. And if Karl wasn't with them, if he wasn't up north at all, she'd have to call her father to come get her. He *was* a person who loved her—of course he did—but abstractly, distantly. Asking him to rescue her all the way up here was a thousand times worse than going home to him yesterday in the first place, but if Karl didn't magically arrive to take responsibility and give support, she wouldn't have much choice. Charmaine couldn't take a day off for her—she had a life, obligations, people other than Maggie relying on her. Such as her patients. Such as her children. She would also be pissed about Maggie lying to her and coming here—to *Eve's* house, which was worse than going to Karl's parents'. Maggie had other friends, but no one she felt comfortable asking such a huge favor of.

By this afternoon, hopefully, she'd be able to stand up without feeling like she was about to faint, and as soon as that happened, she would be out of here. One way or another.

Eve was waiting for her with a mug of tea and a slice of buttered toast at the large dining table. The plastic and blankets had been cleared off the couch. Maggie retrieved her phone from her bag and joined Eve at the table. She had five missed calls from Charmaine, more from her mom. Texts from both of them, texts from her dad, nothing from Karl.

"I can make you eggs," Eve said, "but I wasn't sure how much food you could stomach."

"This is fine."

From somewhere nearby a wash cycle churned.

"Karl isn't answering his phone," Eve said.

This was not news.

"I talked to his mother last night, though," Eve said.

The first cause for hope since she'd arrived. "And?"

"If he's there, she's not saying. She's stubborn and she didn't want to tell me, so she didn't tell me."

"So he *could* be there? I can't remember if I told you, but he moved out of his apartment."

"Then I wouldn't be surprised if he was at their place."

"Do you think maybe if I called her and explained—"

Eve's voice was hard. "She doesn't know you exist."

"How do you know? Karl might have told her."

"He was keeping a secret. Why would he tell his *mother*?"

"I don't know, maybe because I was important to him? Because he loved me? Because he was conflicted and trying to figure out what to do? We don't know."

Eve was staring at her. "Seriously?"

Maggie crunched into the toast. "Forget it. Thanks for calling his mom."

"My reasons weren't purely selfless."

Had Eve made a joke? There was a tiny smirk at her mouth, possibly even self-deprecating.

"Anything to get rid of me, right?" Maggie meant to be playful, but it came out accusatory. She lowered her eyes to her toast. *Just eat. Forget talking, just focus on the necessities of survival.*

Maggie looked out the patio door, away from Eve, across the tumble of grasses and rocks to the water. Karl, now that she was in the place he'd been disappearing to for their entire relationship, felt far away and unreal. Had he really sat at this table, gazing at these rocks and trees? Is this really what he'd been doing, stepping into this parallel life at this dining table every chance he got?

The crunch of each bite was thunderous in the room. The toast tasted like buttered cardboard.

"If you find him," Eve said, "what exactly is it you imagine Karl can do for you?"

Maggie gulped tea, tasting nothing.

He couldn't bring the baby back, could he? He couldn't change the fact that the rupture had happened. He couldn't make the pregnancy not ectopic. Eve was kind enough not to say it, but he probably wouldn't have wanted the baby. They'd talked about kids abstractly—he knew she wanted them, he said he expected he did too, eventually—but was that just more of him telling her what she wanted to hear? Because clearly he was in no place to start a family, and even he must have known that.

There was nothing Karl could do to help her, to fix any of this. Nothing except comfort her. Hold her. Make her feel safe. Safer. Safe-ish.

Not words she could say to Eve.

"Because it was pretty desperate, what you did," Eve said.

Eve, no doubt, had never wanted an unattainable thing, never carried out an irrational action, ever in her life.

"Getting on a bus in that state," Eve went on, "just to talk to the guy who's been cheating on you from the start."

Maggie was sick of being the stupid one in every interaction with this woman.

"He wasn't cheating on me," she said coldly. "He was cheating on you."

"Which makes him the stand-up guy you turn to in a crisis?"

"My insides just erupted, I feel like shit, I almost *died*, and I want the person who's been my partner for the last nine months. The person who's been comforting and supportive. Is that really so crazy? Because he *was* those things to me, even if he was also those things to you at the same time."

Eve stared at her. "But was any of it true?"

"It felt true."

"Cut your losses, Maggie. That's what you need to do."

"My losses?" Maggie widened her eyes. "Okay, that's what I'll do. I will cut my losses. Fetus—cut! Karl—cut! Sense of safety—cut! Thanks for that."

Eve regarded her silently. She said, "Whether Karl is around or not, I don't think you can go anywhere today. I'd drive you all the way back to Toronto right now, but frankly you look like if you don't lie down in the next five minutes you might become a medical emergency again."

"I'd hate to inconvenience you."

Eve pushed her chair from the table. "I have somewhere you can stay."

The silence stretched between them as they climbed into Eve's truck and drove up the steep driveway, Flora a genial buffer between them. Maggie felt shaky and unnerved. Was this the part where Eve left her in the forest to starve? Staged an accident with a wood-chopping axe?

They hadn't gone far before they turned into another gravel drive and a pair of log buildings appeared, birch and maple standing close, the lake below. The two buildings had a decrepit beauty, not elegant but also not ugly. Sad and old and past their prime, a beauty that felt experienced and truthful.

They looked like Maggie felt.

"This is my neighbor's fishing lodge," Eve said. "It hasn't been used in years, so most of the place is a mess, but there's one room that's pretty nice. It has an ensuite bathroom."

"You're leaving me here?"

Uncertainty flashed on Eve's face. "Just until you're well enough to travel? While I try to find Karl? I thought it was peaceful. I'll check in on you, I promise."

Living in an architectural manifestation of her psyche might not be terrible.

"It's just that my house is so small," Eve said. "I'm not set up for house guests."

"Especially ones you can't stand," Maggie said.

"*You* came *here*," Eve snapped. "I'm only trying to fix the mess you dropped in my lap."

Maggie leaned into Flora's side, holding back tears, and the dog turned toward her with what felt like genuine sympathy.

Eve parked and turned the engine off. "I'll go over to Karl's parents' place," she said in a tone clearly expressing her endeavour to stay measured. "I'll see if they'll give me a straight answer about where he is. If he's around and knows you're here, I'm sure he'll come." She didn't look at Maggie as she said this.

Maggie followed slowly behind Eve as she forced the door open with her hip, leading Maggie across a common room and up five painful steps to the landing, then five more to a ledge of hallway that looked down into the dusty sunlight on the first floor. A cathedral ceiling gave everything a spacious, almost majestic feel despite the dust. Eve pushed open a door.

"You're okay, right? Is this okay?"

Eve looked anxious for the first time since Maggie had known her. She almost wanted to reassure her. *Do not worry, Eve. My life and body and hopes and future have been blasted apart, but I am dandy.*

"I need to rest," Maggie said. "That's all I need."

The room *was* kind of peaceful. Maggie crawled onto the high double bed, pulling the patchwork quilt over her body. Her head dropped onto a pillow and the feathers squished aside to accommodate the heaviness of her skull.

"You sure you'll be okay?" Eve asked again.

Maggie's fingers clung to the quilt's homey knots and loose lengths of yarn. Her diaphragm was spasming; she wedged a cushion behind her back, and slowly it began to settle.

Flora stood sentinel at the foot of the bed, then circled and settled on the floor with her head on her paws.

"I think she wants to stay with you," Eve said. "Do you mind?"

Please, yes, Maggie thought, but she only nodded.

"I'll leave you my landline number," Eve said. "The reception here isn't usually good enough to make a call from a cellphone, but you can try. Texting works most of the time, so you can get in touch with whoever you need to that way. I don't have a cell, but I'm just next door. It's a two-minute walk. I only drove because—"

"I'm fine," Maggie whispered. "You can go."

Eve hovered for one more moment. Maggie waited, eyes closed, until she heard the door shut. Tears leaked out and ran into her ears. Her eyelids fluttered. She caught snapshots of a wooden ceiling, a series of wide windows, trees, and the deep, still blue of the lake. Through the screen door she glimpsed a balcony. Above her was a painting, but from her vantage point she saw only bright swaths of color. She patted the bed and Flora jumped up beside her. She reached for her phone.

Her mom: I talked to Charmaine and you aren't there! Maggie, where ARE you?

Charmaine: WTF you didn't go to your dad? You told your mom you were HERE? Where are you??!!!

Telling either of them she was looking for Karl and taking refuge with Eve was too complicated—she'd have to explain, answer too many follow-up questions—so she said she needed space, she'd checked into a lodge, she was resting and safe, doing okay.

She had a text from an unknown number: I don't know who I am anymore.

She said out loud, "Neither do I."

The air was not still, not quiet as she'd expected in the country. Instead, there was the cacophony of birdsong, crickets, bullfrogs, small unseen creatures rustling the underbrush. She was alone in this large rustic building, a fishing lodge of her own. Just what she'd always wanted.

Her phone buzzed again.

Charmaine: A lodge WHERE?!

The unknown number: It's hard to connect to much of anything I used to care about. Hard to connect to the stupid stuff everyone else focuses on. Everything feels pointless.

A wrong number. Or a scam, but this felt too authentic for a scam. Then again, wasn't that the point of a scam—to seem real? She didn't recognize the area code, and it didn't sound like anyone she knew.

Her eyelids drooped. Her body was heavy against the mattress.

I'm sorry, read the next text. You say and do irrational things when you're out of your mind with grief.

She texted back: I know exactly what you mean.

She let the phone fall. Her exhaustion, too complete to fight, was sweet. She surrendered at last to its conquering force.

PART 2

May–September

Chapter 14

Eve

How the fuck am I here, doing the bidding of my ex-boyfriend's mistress? Eve thought as she pulled into Karl's parents' driveway. They were both outside, his mother kneeling at the flower bed, his father raking at the edge of the yard. Eve stepped from her truck and they went still. Eve lifted her hand in a wan greeting, plastered a smile on her face, and walked toward them.

Maybe she should have brought Maggie. Maggie would have some awkward, just naive enough, just idealistic enough point of connection to open with, something like *You don't know me, but I just miscarried your grandchild!*

Karl's mother unfurled her body slowly, then shuffled toward Eve in steps that managed to be both shaky and purposeful.

"Hello," Eve said. "How are you doing?"

"You're not interested in how I'm doing," Karl's mother said calmly. She was small and bony, her hair so like the color of her face it seemed at first glance not to be there. "You're only interested in seeing Karl. Not so interested a couple of weeks ago, when you kicked him out, but now I guess is a different story?"

Civility was clearly going to get her nowhere. "I understand that I'm not your favorite person, but could you please just tell me where he is?"

"Not here," Karl's mother said.

Eve would search their house if she had to. She was not leaving without Karl himself or a firm knowledge of his whereabouts—and those whereabouts had better be nearby, because nursing Maggie through her recovery was, as any sensible person would agree, beyond Eve's duty. Maggie was safe and comfortable, and all that was now required of Eve was to find a more appropriate person onto whom she could transfer the responsibility. And that person was Karl.

"He's in Argentina," Karl's father said.

Eve stared. "What?"

"Or maybe Chile," he said. "Patagonia. It's a backcountry expedition. He'll be in both places."

No. No, no, no. This could not be true; Eve needed it to not be true.

Mrs. Tarvudd was shooting her husband a dirty look. "There you are," she said to Eve. "You have your information."

Argentina?

"He went back to his old job?"

"It shook him, what you did."

"What *I* did?"

"He came here after you ended things," his mother went on. "He contacted Vital Adventures. Turned out they needed a last-minute fill-in. So he quit the bank and went."

Daniel was the only person to whom Eve had revealed the humiliating fact of Karl's cheating, but she was just angry enough now to throw the truth at this woman, restrained only by the knowledge that she would surely find a way to spin it into Eve's fault.

"I'd like to see proof," Eve said, instead of *Your son is a lying cheater*.

Mrs. Tarvudd rolled her eyes, but Karl's father set down his rake and shambled wordlessly toward the house. Eve followed him inside and into the dining room, looking over his shoulder at the screen of an ancient desktop as he pulled up an email account and clicked to a photograph of Karl in front of a mountain, a sign in Spanish behind him. He wasn't exactly holding a dated newspaper, but the email was time-stamped a week ago.

Patagonia was not within drive-over-and-take-Maggie-off-my-hands distance.

"Is he contactable?" Eve asked.

"He's off-grid," Mr. Tarvudd said. "He might be able to check messages sometimes, but not reliably."

This was officially more words than the man had ever spoken to her before.

"Thanks," Eve said. "I appreciate you telling me."

She'd turned to leave when he gripped her arm. "I hope you are all right?" he said.

For a horrifying second, tears brimmed in Eve's eyes. The small gesture of kindness felt like more than she could bear. Was she all right? Well, she was trying damn hard to be. She nodded quickly, left the house, and drove off.

Maggie was asleep when Eve knocked on the lodge room door and pushed it open. From the foot of the bed, Flora raised her head and flopped her tail in greeting. Eve laid out a thermos of Lipton soup and a couple of slices of bread on the desk, then decided that might be too far away given Maggie's physical capacity and rearranged the meal on a nightstand.

She headed to work, late, and settled into the office to answer emails. Someone was asking about meal plans, which the website made clear did not exist, but as she responded she wondered what she'd eat for dinner tonight, and then, after barely twenty minutes' reprieve, she was back to thinking about Maggie. Because what was *Maggie* going to eat for dinner? Whatever it was, Eve was the person who'd have to bring it to her.

She stifled her irritation. Maggie was obviously suffering—she'd almost died, for god's sake. Or so she said, but could you get more melodramatic than claiming a near-death experience?

Maybe it *was* that bad. Eve hit send on the meal plan email and googled ectopic rupture. She read the medical explanations first: the fetus implants in the fallopian tube instead of the uterus; if undetected, the fallopian tube can rupture, endangering the woman's life. (So it was that bad.) In no cases can the fetus survive.

Then her search turned up a discussion forum for women sharing their first-hand accounts, one horrifying story after another of pain and panic and trauma, a string of empathetic comments after each post. It was appalling, and Eve couldn't look away. This was far more detail than anything Maggie had given her—had it been like *this*? No wonder Maggie was so fragile.

Eve redirected herself to the medical sites and looked up what she needed to know: Maggie was probably okay now. As long as she'd been closed up with dissolving stitches, she shouldn't even require follow-up care. She just needed to rest. A lot. Did she need to do it in Eve's lodge? Surely she'd be okay to travel in a few days. Eve could drive her. She'd be willing to do that. She picked up the phone and dialed Daniel to confirm that travel wasn't medically inadvisable—to get rid of Maggie she was even willing to risk Daniel's rejection—but he didn't answer.

Despite the reassurance of WebMD, Eve went home early, afraid she'd left Maggie too long—without internet or phone service, with only a dog to watch over her! Even as she worried, she resented the worry, because why should this be *her* worry?

She knocked on Maggie's door, then nudged it open. Nothing had changed—the same lumpen shape under tangled blankets, same spray of dark-blond hair across the pillow. Same closed eyes. From the foot of the bed, Flora thumped her tail, and Eve scratched behind her ears and whispered grudgingly, "You're a good nurse-dog. I guess."

She held her hand in front of Maggie's mouth. The puff of air across it was warm and steady. On the nightstand, the food Eve had left earlier was half gone—she was surprised how relieved she felt, seeing that—and beside the heel of loaf, something new. Eve picked up the scrap of ruled paper. *Thank you.*

When Eve returned to the room the next morning with breakfast, Maggie was groggy and disheveled but awake.

"Do you think you could help me to the bathroom?" Maggie asked.

Fuck. If Maggie couldn't stumble to the ensuite on her own, she definitely couldn't hop a bus back to Toronto, and maybe she couldn't even remain vertical in Eve's passenger seat. The shocks on the truck were not the best.

"Sure," Eve said. She stood beside the bed as Maggie grasped Eve's arm with one hand and pulled herself to a seated position, her other arm cradling her abdomen. She sat for a moment, then inched her legs over the side of the bed to the floor.

"You're not using the bathroom on your own?" Eve asked.

"I am," Maggie said. "I just feel shakier this morning. I'm sorry. I'm sorry to be so much trouble."

"Don't even . . ." Eve said. *Don't even think about it? Don't mention it? Don't acknowledge what an uncomfortable situation this is and how much time and energy I'm expending on you when I'm the last person who should have to?*

"I'm almost out of pads," Maggie said. "I'm so sorry."

"I have some at home," Eve said. "They're thin, but I'll bring them over and go to Larkin for bigger ones."

"I'm so sorry."

Maggie seemed on the verge of tears. Her vulnerability and contrition felt unbearable to witness.

"Come on, let's get you to the bathroom," Eve said.

Maggie went into the ensuite alone, and Eve waited outside the door. She couldn't tell Maggie about Argentina-or-maybe-Chile, not now, when she already seemed so broken. Finding Karl was the whole reason Maggie had come here—however stupidly—and it was all for nothing.

When Maggie finished in the bathroom, Eve helped her back to the bed, painfully conscious of their proximity as Maggie leaned against her. She offered her the smoothie she'd brought over. Maggie took a sip and set it on the nightstand. Eve stood by the door, poised to leave—surely Maggie didn't want Eve seeing her in this weakened state any more than Eve wanted to see it—but she found herself standing there, not moving. Finally she turned slightly to exit, and as she did, Maggie said, "I feel like my life has ended and I'm waiting for a new one." Her voice was quiet.

Eve turned back to face Maggie, pausing before saying, "You mean, like, as if you'd died?"

"Not exactly, but kind of."

"I guess you almost did?"

"I feel completely overwhelmed." Maggie again looked like she might cry. "I can't imagine how I ever accomplished anything or had motivation or hope ever in my life."

"I know I don't know you, not really," Eve said, "but you seem like the type who just has this energy that propels them? I'm sure that's still there."

Maggie nodded. She sipped the smoothie again. Eve left to get pads.

That evening, alone in her empty house, Flora with Maggie, Karl AWOL, Daniel impossible to reach out to, the truth of Eve's aloneness was visceral and excruciating. She barely restrained herself from driving back to Sam's and insisting she really had to fix the broken cabinet in Blueberry Cabin tonight or—worse—going over to check on Maggie, which she'd only just finished doing.

When the phone rang, she answered even though the call display warned that it was her mother. Who turned out to be calling to chastise her for leaving before Violet's funeral. What could possibly have been so urgent that she couldn't stay, her mother wondered; was her work really so important; where were her priorities? After they hung up, Eve thought that even this was better than being alone with the torture of her own thoughts.

Had Karl ever missed her, those weeknights in Toronto? Probably not. He had a whole city of distractions. He was hanging out with Maggie. He was going to parties and shows and restaurants with Maggie. He was *in bed* with Maggie.

Had Eve willfully ignored red flags? Accepted the long-distance too readily? Been stupid never to visit him in Toronto, to be so city-averse after her years in New York that she didn't even want to see his apartment or come for his branch's holiday party? A party that, let's face it, she would have hated, but still. How easily her introversion and her desire to retreat had played into Karl's hands.

Every time she thought of calling Daniel for some kind of comfort, she was stopped by the memory of his face as he sent her away, his harsh, certain need to have her gone. That and the fact that the things he'd said hadn't been entirely wrong.

In this moment she and Daniel were probably both the loneliest they'd ever been—twin symmetry at its worst—but they couldn't even reach out to each other.

"I have bad news," Eve said at last, three whole days after she'd found out about Patagonia.

Maggie had spent most of those days sleeping, or at least she was asleep almost every time Eve stopped by. When she wasn't, they talked about the weather, the scenery, and how Maggie was healing, which Maggie insisted was well, but Eve had seen her limping to the bathroom and thought she was overstating her progress. Thank goodness for Flora, who was an endless source of conversational inspiration on these visits to Maggie's room—how steady she was, how snuggly, how she seemed to understand everything you thought or felt, which was the closest they came to discussing what they thought or felt.

The screen door in Maggie's room swung both ways, out onto the wraparound balcony and from there the steps to the ground, so Flora could let herself in and out and barely seemed to need Eve anymore at all. Eve had given up trying to lure her home and had brought her bed over, along with her food and water dishes, and begun feeding her in Maggie's room.

Now it was seven p.m. on Sunday and Eve had just returned from work. She'd brought over homemade macaroni and cheese, baked in Sam's kitchen. She was officially becoming the world's worst employee, but she'd explained to Sam today that she had a friend staying while she recovered from surgery, and Sam seemed so delighted about this newly surfaced friend that Eve felt guilty for misrepresenting the situation and told him the truth. She was immediately appalled at her openness, her palms sweaty as she revealed Karl's cheating and her own gullibility, but she felt better when Sam called Karl a bastard and told Eve she was a good soul to be caring for Maggie like this.

Eve knew Maggie was waiting on information about Karl, but she hadn't asked and Eve had decided to wait until Maggie was stronger. Which apparently was now, because when Eve entered Maggie's room with the mac and cheese, Maggie was propped up in bed, smiling widely, looking positively cheerful to see her. It was the face from Maggie's photos—sunny, buoyant—a face Eve hadn't ever seen in person.

"That soup you left me for lunch was amazing!" Maggie said. "Carrot ginger, right?"

"Yeah," Eve said, surprised.

"There was a spice in it I've been trying to place," Maggie said. "Coriander?"

"There is coriander. And cumin."

"That must be it! Did your mom teach you to make it—or your grandma or your dad or whoever? Or are you an experiment-on-your-own kind of cook?"

"It's just from a cookbook," Eve said. She handed Maggie a fork and the glass container with the mac and cheese—something her mother *had* taught her to make.

Eve waited a minute, letting Maggie take a few bites. She was trying to be gentle—wasn't she?—as she introduced the bad news about Karl, but she heard the smallest hint of gloating in her voice. Urging herself to make her tone neutral, she said, "Karl went back to being an adventure guide. In Patagonia."

Maggie looked up at her from the mac and cheese, uncomprehending. "The store?"

"The geographical region," Eve said. "He's in Argentina. Or Chile."

Maggie blinked, keeping her eyes closed a fraction of a second before she opened them and said, "*Argentina?*"

"It could be Chile. I guess the expeditions straddle both, and he's mostly off-grid."

Maggie set the dish on the bed beside her and hugged her knees to her chest, then winced and eased them down on the mattress again. "When?"

"I guess shortly after I broke up with him, just before your . . . medical emergency. About when you were trying to reach him?"

"He moved to a whole other hemisphere without telling his girlfriend?"

"I ended it," Eve said. "I wasn't his girlfriend anymore."

"I meant me."

The words were a knife to the heart. "You aren't his girlfriend," Eve said, trying to keep her voice steady.

"Actually, we never technically broke up."

Eve's anger flared. It was too much. She could handle caring for Maggie if she thought of her as simply a fellow human being in need, but this—*I meant me; we never broke up*—was unfair.

"How could you fucking not?" Eve asked, in lieu of asking *Are you a fucking idiot?*

A wounded look crossed Maggie's face. "I know I should have done it immediately," she said, "but I was still processing, and probably punishing him by avoiding him. Then I found out I was pregnant and it got more complicated. I was trying to figure out what to do."

"Wasn't it obvious? He's completely untrustworthy. He's a liar and a cheater."

Maggie turned her head away.

"Well, he is!" Eve said. Why was Maggie unable to accept these facts? He *was* a liar and a cheater and not to be trusted; he wasn't even on the continent, he wasn't coming to Maggie's rescue, and he would not be helping her through the healing process or whatever it was Maggie wanted from him.

"He did call me," Maggie said. "A few days before the rupture. He said he had something important to talk about. I hung up on him."

"Good for you," Eve said.

"I'm just saying, he might have been calling about Patagonia. He didn't know that you and I knew. He didn't know that he and I were over. He still doesn't know."

"You think he believes he's still in a relationship with you when you haven't spoken or seen each other in weeks and the last time he called you hung up on him? You are not still together! You have a twisted idea of relationships if you think you are."

"*I* have a twisted idea? You didn't even tell him why you were breaking up with him."

There it was, the cattiness Eve had been waiting for since the moment she set eyes on Maggie in the Georgian Bay Travel Center. Maggie knew nothing about Eve, about her history, about what it meant for her to open herself up to Karl as wholly as she had. She knew nothing of the humiliation Eve had felt, finding out she was right all along and she'd have been much, much better off alone.

"I don't have to explain myself to you," Eve said. "We're not friends. I only came over to give you more of my food and to tell you why neither of us has been able to reach Karl. So now you know, and you also know there's nothing he's going to do to help you. So if you have everything you need to survive until morning, I'll be leaving now."

"Eve," Maggie said.

But Eve was done. She was desperate to have her space back, to rid herself of this burden, to return to her normal, calm life. She left before Maggie could say more.

Chapter 15

Maggie

I think I've just realized how deeply I was holding on to an illusion, Maggie texted her mystery friend after Eve got mad at her and left. She wanted to cry, but she was cried out. Something that never would have worked, but I was believing in the fairy tale anyway. I'm feeling stupid and devastated and stupid for feeling devastated.

It was the sort of thing they texted each other. Not frequently—only a few times since the morning Eve first brought her here—and never any specifics, just the meat of an inner reality. If these texts were a scam, Maggie would have to unravel *that* illusion when the time came, because they had been a lifeline this week, these missives of grief or regret or hope, this disembodied imaginary friend. Especially because the only human physically in her life was, though taking mind-bogglingly excellent care of her, not exactly a reliably warm or safe confidante. Maggie was staying in touch with her mom and Charmaine enough to keep them from tearing Northern Ontario apart in search of her, but when she'd finally told them the whole truth, she wished she hadn't. SERIOUSLY?! Charmaine's reply might as well have been written in flame. You and Eve have got one messy history, and she has not been kind to you. Even if Karl turns up, you KNOW you should not be re-engaging with him. I am worried about this!! After that, Maggie asked for space to rest and ignored or gave cursory replies to any text messages that weren't from the mystery stranger. The well-wishes and heart emojis and concerned inquiries, the requests for reassurance she was somehow expected to provide even though she was the one in pain. She didn't feel like explaining herself to people who were out there living their normal lives, undecimated.

For four days Maggie had lain in this bed. Even in the bathroom, just feet away, panic thrashed at her, flashbacks she couldn't stop. The open space was too uncontained, the air too fraught with possibility. It was as though, now that one catastrophe had occurred, anything, everything, had the potential to be life-threatening.

At first her mind refused to cycle around again to the true meaning of what had happened. She had fainted, ruptured her fallopian tube, required emergency surgery and three blood transfusions, her life saved by the accident of it occurring while she was with people instead of alone. All of this had happened. But the other layer of reality, the reason it had happened—*I had a fetus inside me. If it had implanted in the right place, I could have become a mother*—she could look at only from the side, tiny snatches of acknowledgment that were now too painful to dwell on.

Maybe she was focusing on the pain of Karl's betrayal instead of on the lost pregnancy because that was the easier pain. She was focusing on the fantasy that if only she could find him, tell him, have him here at her side, hear his story, and try to understand what complex psychology had caused his behavior, they could make everything right. But there was no making everything right. Karl was in South America. Karl wasn't her boyfriend. Karl wasn't a good person. Karl was a fantasy, and so was their baby.

The only thing that calmed her in the first few days was Flora. The dog was there almost every time Maggie woke, curled close but not too close on the bed. If she wasn't, Maggie's heart rate leapt and she flailed around looking for her, had to force herself to breathe deeply, talk herself down. She shifted her pillows to lie with her head at the foot of the bed so she could stare into the *Truth Landing* painting, and the woman in the painting seemed to say, *You are safe. You are resting. There is nothing wrong with you anymore. Flora will come back.*

Flora did come back.

The woman was naked by a lake, dark hair a mane down her back. Muscled arms. An expression peaceful and confident and also offhand, as though her strength of arm and spirit negated the vulnerability of her bareness. The woman understood so much more than Maggie did. The woman could handle it all.

Along with the dog, food appeared. In her early dazed state Maggie associated the food with the dog: Flora carried it over on her back and laid it out on the nightstand several times a day, then curled at Maggie's feet and waited for her to wake and eat it. At first she saw Eve only occasionally, and sometimes she dreamt her, the voice from Karl's phone talking to her as she slept.

Two days had passed after her arrival in the lodge before she read the next text from the mystery stranger.

How are you? the person had asked.

She'd responded with the truth: Devastated.

Me too, the stranger texted immediately. Complete wreck. Guess things can only get better from here.

The texts, like the dog and the food and the painting, felt like mysterious gifts sent to comfort her, and she was grateful. She was exhausted and rationing out the last of the painkillers, and intellectually she knew this was messing with her perception, but it still felt true: A dog brought her food; a woman in a painting transmitted her strength; a compassionate stranger sent messages to her phone, magically articulating her own experience.

The morning after Eve told her Karl was in Patagonia, Maggie woke to a wispy pink sky advancing to blue as the sun rose. She looked out through trees to water first inky dark, then glassy pale blue. A response pinged on her phone. I've got time for stupid. What's up?

She hadn't mentioned any details of what she was going through. No doubt this was where scams tightened the net—got you to name people and places and events of your reality, till they knew everything about you, including your passwords and your credit card number.

I recently found out my boyfriend was with someone else for our whole relationship.

Your WHOLE relationship? He's a jackass. You were right to leave him. Don't think twice.

I actually didn't leave him. Because something horrific happened to me before I could decide what to do about Karl, and it sort of eclipsed the Karl situation, and all I wanted afterward was him. For him to make it better. For us to work it out. I did something pretty dumb to try to force that, and yesterday I found out just how much it was never possible. I feel ridiculous but also crushed, which makes me feel even more pathetic because I shouldn't want him anymore.

The horrific thing being MY horrific thing.

Maggie was propped against the headboard, Flora's head snuggled on her lap, feeling the deep, yearned-for exhale of sharing the truth with a receptive listener. She reread what she'd written, looking for some connection between what she'd said about Karl and what they'd discussed earlier. *The horrific thing being MY horrific thing*—what did *that* mean? Before she could compose a response, another message came through.

The horrific thing that eclipsed Karl. You're talking about Violet.

Who the heck was Violet?

Three dots on her screen, and Maggie waited.

I'm sorry you weren't at the funeral. I really am.

Funeral? Maggie felt, belatedly, ridiculous.

I'm sorry I was such a shit. It felt wrong not having you there. I spent the whole thing feeling like Violet would be ashamed of me. I get that you've had your own stuff going on. And I know you're grieving Violet in your own way. I don't mean to diminish that. I'm just mad at everything. Including you. But maybe that's not your fault.

Maggie knew this was a wrong number. But the mysterious stranger sent to comfort her, evidently, did not.

I'm sorry. She used a chagrined emoji. I guess you thought I was someone else.

???

Hi. I'm Maggie.

There was a pause.

WTF?

Wrong number, I think?

I'm so confused. I don't know a Maggie.

What's your name?

Daniel.

Hi Daniel.

Who did you think you were talking to?

My guardian angel?

She included a rash of smiley faces in hopes of coming across cute and not deranged.

Fair enough.

Who did you think you were talking to?

My sister.

So you're more sane than I am.

Not necessarily. I am currently very not-sane.

No wonder we hit it off, then.

He told her that his wife had recently died, suddenly and tragically. Maggie said how sorry she was, how she couldn't imagine, tears brimming at the thought of it. She told him that in addition to discovering the two-timing boyfriend, she'd lost a pregnancy.

He checked their message history and reported that his sister had definitely messaged him from this number. On Maggie's phone, the thread began with the first mystery message.

Your pregnancy loss, he said. Did you suffer an ectopic rupture?

Eve, Maggie texted. Is your sister named Eve?

She was.

Maggie felt strangely deflated. Of course there was a logical explanation for these miracle messages to her soul. Of course they weren't magic. They were a plain old rational mistake whose origins could have been traced easily and immediately if Maggie weren't still believing in unicorns.

Worse, the person on the other end of the texts was, once again, not Maggie's at all. He was Eve's.

And so was Flora, and so was this peaceful lodge room and the *Truth Landing* painting. Every small comfort of her recovery was not hers at all but belonged to Eve, a woman she was pretty sure—despite the smoothies and the tea and the homemade mac and cheese left over on the nightstand—despised her.

I'm so sorry for your loss, Daniel said. And sorry to have bothered you with those messages. Now I feel stupid.

Don't. It felt like they were meant for me. I guess that's why I didn't say anything. I didn't want them to stop.

You ok now? Healing well?

I guess so? The emotional part feels harder.

Of course. It IS hard. And on top of the cheating too. I guess you and Eve have a lot in common.

Well, we have the man in common at least.

?? Seriously?

Seriously.

RIGHT! Karl!!

Yup. Karl.

So, are you and Eve actually friends?

I wouldn't say that. She doesn't like me much.

Eve doesn't trust easily. Karl being such a dick will only reinforce that, I'm betting.

She's taking incredibly good care of me. Way above and beyond the call of duty. But she can also be . . . sorry if this sounds harsh, but sometimes she's downright mean. Makes it hard to know which is the real her—the hostility or the caring actions.

I like to believe the hostility is just self-protective. But if your whole personality becomes self-protective hostility, at what point is that just who you are?

Ouch. Are you two not close?

Maybe too close. It's complicated.

Maggie was composing a response when Eve's knock sounded on her door. She stuffed her phone under the covers just as Eve's face appeared in the doorway.

"Morning!" Maggie cried. Too cheery. Too false. Like she was trying to cover up a minor crime, which she supposed she was. Because if Eve had a close, complicated relationship with her brother—who had just basically been siding with Maggie against Eve—Maggie wasn't sure Eve would be thrilled to know about their correspondence.

At the door Eve shifted her weight from one foot to the other. Maggie was keenly aware of the silence between them, the haunting call of a loon, the croaking of frogs at the lakeside.

"You seem to be feeling all right today," Eve said. Her tone was stilted; it had some of last night's fight still in it.

"I'm pretty good," Maggie said. She watched as Eve set out her breakfast. It was oatmeal today, with what looked like sliced apples and cinnamon, the usual travel mug of tea, yet another painfully generous instance of caretaking.

"Listen," Maggie said. "I know what an inconvenience I've been. I'm not sure I've totally acknowledged that. There's no way to thank you enough. But now that we know Karl isn't here, I'll be getting out of your hair. Maybe I can pay you to stay a few more days, until I feel stronger. Then I'll go."

Eve's look was scornful. "You're not paying me."

"I think I should. I don't want to be in your debt. It'll be cleaner if I pay you for your time and your food and—"

"Oh Jesus, I'm not that inhumane. Just—take the time you need, and then I'll drive you wherever you need to go."

"I appreciate everything you've done. I know you didn't have to."

"I kind of did. Imagine if I let you die behind my house."

"Think of the paperwork," Maggie said.

Eve cracked a smile. She couldn't be *too* mad—she'd actually smiled!

"I'll call my dad as soon as I can stomach the thought of a car ride," Maggie said. "He'll come get me."

"If that's what you want."

"Isn't it what you want?"

"Well—sure. Of course," Eve said. "I do need to get back to my life."

"And you'd probably like your dog to live with you again."

"I do miss her."

They were being unbearably polite. Maggie wasn't sure this was better than the antagonism. At least that was honest.

"I'm sorry for what I said yesterday," Maggie said, as another message from Eve's brother vibrated under her thigh. "The unhealthy relationship thing."

"I said it first, so . . . only fair."

"None of this is fair, though," Maggie said. "Is it?"

Eve blinked rapidly, her eyes moving away from Maggie and then back again. Maggie sensed she was trying not to cry, and her own emotion welled in response. For that one moment, it was like Eve's armor had slipped and Maggie was seeing the real her, the one the hostility was protecting. And Maggie could tell that this real Eve was only hurt, probably humiliated, and just wanted to keep herself from being wounded again.

"You don't have to go," Eve said, looking out the window instead of at Maggie.

"I don't?"

"Unless you need to. Or want to. But the lodge owner isn't home for another month or so. It's not like you can go back to work yet or do much except rest, right?"

Was Eve . . . *pitching* Maggie on staying?

Maggie was stunned. But—what if she *did* stay? What if she got to remain here in this cocoon of safety and care, far from her real life and the obligations waiting to be reshouldered, snuggling with Flora and imbibing the lake view and accepting nourishing meals from Eve until she felt resourced and whole again?

"This room is saving me," Maggie said.

Eve looked at Maggie with surprise and the hint of another smile, her eyebrows raised.

"That's what it feels like, anyway," Maggie said, and now Eve smiled fully, her whole face transforming with it.

"Then you should stay," Eve said. "Obviously it's been a bit disruptive, having you here—and definitely weird—but I don't mind. That's what I'm trying to say."

"I can't stay if you hate me, though," Maggie said.
"If I hated you, would I invite you to stay?"

After Eve left, Maggie checked her phone. Daniel had asked her not to tell Eve they were in touch, to let him be the one to do it.

We're in the middle of a fight, and I thought I was extending an olive branch by messaging with her. Not sure I have the energy to have that convo again now that I know I haven't actually had it. Just going to give myself some time.

Of course. But I do think Eve has a good heart. Don't take too much time!

Chapter 16

Eve

Eve woke the next morning crying—actual wetness on her face and actual noise from her mouth. She'd been dreaming of Violet, alive and effervescent, teasing Eve good-naturedly, trying to make her laugh. Then Violet was plowed down by an SUV. The driver was Eve.

Thanks, subconscious, Eve thought. *Laying it on a bit thick.*

She reached for Flora on the bed, but Flora wasn't there.

It was almost June now, the first June of Violet's non-existence. She'd been so present in the dream, so real. How could she be dead?

Eve got out of bed, put the kettle on for tea, dumped fruit and yogurt into the blender for smoothies. The tears were just another instance of a new, weird emotionality. Ever since her relationship with Karl imploded, or ever since Violet died, or ever since Daniel banished her, or ever since Maggie showed up on her deck—one of those events or all of them combined had turned her into a raw, vulnerable, needy desirer of *something*. Connection. Belonging. *More.*

She'd invited Maggie to stay!

Had she actually done that? She had.

She crossed the path to the lodge, swatting ineffectually at blackflies, two smoothies nestled awkwardly in the crook of her arm and a travel mug of tea in each hand.

Maggie was sitting out on the wraparound balcony with a quilt around her shoulders.

"You're up!" Eve cried from the ground, and Maggie waved to her and called down, "But the bugs are terrible! I'm going back in." Eve laughed and joined Maggie in her room, handed over the tea and the smoothie, and dragged two chairs to the open screen door.

"Now you can appreciate the view without being eaten," Eve said.

"Thank you," Maggie said as they both sat down.

"No problem."

They sat for a few minutes, the silence not exactly awkward but not entirely comfortable either, until Maggie said, "I'm pretty sure it is."

"What?"

"Everything about me is a problem for you."

"Please," Eve said. "We settled this. I invited you to stay, I said I didn't hate you, it's fine."

Maggie nodded and sipped the smoothie, scratching behind Flora's ears with her free hand. "But why did you?" she asked. "Invite me to stay."

"This lodge is just sitting empty," Eve said. "It's a practical solution."

"We could have found another practical solution," Maggie said.

Eve stood and looked out between the balcony railings. The view was different here, a higher vantage point than her house, a more expansive stretch of blue.

"My dad really would come get me if I asked him," Maggie said. "I think in a day I could handle the car ride."

"Of course you can go if you want to," Eve said.

"I don't, actually," Maggie said. "It's so peaceful here. Getting more breathing space before I go back to my real life feels like such a gift."

"Like I said, it was vacant. Might as well be used."

"And I guess it's emptier around here than it used to be," Maggie said.

"For sure," Eve said. "This fishing lodge was hopping back in the day." She stepped outside and began sweeping twigs and pine needles from the balcony with her feet.

"No, I mean . . . emptier since Karl left," Maggie said through the screen door. "For you."

"Oh," Eve said. She picked up a fallen maple branch and turned it over in her hands.

"Do you know what's nuts?" Maggie said. "Karl *gave me* your address."

"What?" Eve took the branch back inside with her, sitting down next to Maggie again. "*That's* how you got it?"

"He said it was his parents'. He gave it to me so I could mail his mother a book—or mail you a book? You wouldn't happen to have received *A Guide to Gardening with Intention* from a bookstore in Toronto?"

"That came from *you*?"

"Well, he bought it for his mom—I thought—and I offered to mail it."

"And he actually took you up on that."

"He maybe hesitated for a second? But yeah. He did."

"He was getting cocky."

"Maybe he thought it was hot. The two of us getting so close to each other but not."

"Ugh."

"I almost added a note telling his mom I was looking forward to meeting her one day."

"Wow. He could have been busted so much sooner."

"Probably a million ways he could have been busted, if we were paying more attention." Maggie slurped thoughtfully at her smoothie. "Do you still think about him?" she asked.

"Sometimes," Eve said.

"Not a lot?"

"I try not to." Eve fished her Swiss Army knife from her jeans and began peeling away the bark from the branch, exposing the naked wood.

"My brain knows all the facts and recognizes that I should want nothing to do with him," Maggie said. "It knows I need to let him go.

But the rest of me is having a harder time catching up. It's not like you can flip a switch, you know? Or maybe some people can—is that what you've done?"

Eve shook her head. "No. Not totally."

"I've been using this thought technique. Every time I feel love or desire for Karl, or every time I indulge in some fantasy about him turning into the great guy I thought he was, I visualize placing the thought or feeling onto a flaming arrow, and then I shoot it into the lake."

"This lake?"

"Yup."

"So Still Lake is choked with flaming arrows."

"You can't see them?"

Eve leaned forward and pretended to look. "Yeah, there's definitely a couple over there."

Maggie beamed.

"So does it work?" Eve asked.

"I can't figure out if I'm letting go or if I'm just repressing feelings that'll come back to bite me in the ass later. But it does make me feel better."

For the first time, Eve felt a sliver of understanding. The reason Maggie had written Eve instead of confronting Karl was because Eve was the one other person in the same situation. The only person in the world experiencing the exact same pain, inflicted by the exact same man, whom they had both known and—yes—loved. Of all the human beings in the world, this woman she'd wanted nothing to do with, wanted nowhere near her, was the one person who got it.

And maybe the real reason Eve hadn't wanted Maggie anywhere near her wasn't because she despised her or scorned her but because with this mirror of her own pain constantly reflecting her back to herself, she couldn't deny the pain, bury it in overwork, pretend it away. With Maggie here, Eve had to feel it.

Eve dug the knife into the maple, beginning to whittle small indentations along its edge.

"Maggie," she said, keeping her eyes on the wood, hearing the hesitation in her voice as she spoke. "When Karl met you, did he immediately . . . I mean, did he go after you right away?"

"It was pretty quick."

"How quick?"

Maggie paused. "We hooked up the night we met. I'm sorry."

Eve nodded. "So, sudden irresistible passion?"

"That's what I thought at the time. Maybe he expected it to be a one-night stand—still a betrayal, but not a whole relationship—until I glommed onto him with all my feelings and turned it into a real thing."

"Or maybe this is what he'd been doing all along in Toronto. Maybe there was a whole series of affairs, and he knew exactly what he was doing."

Maggie looked stricken. "Oh. Please don't say that. I don't want to be that . . . unspecial."

"Doesn't feel so great, does it?"

Maggie exhaled a stream of breath. "Nope, sure doesn't." Suddenly she leaned forward, placing her hand on the arm of Eve's chair. "Oh my god, you could be right. Because his colleagues knew I was his girlfriend, so they can't have known about you. He worked there long before he met me. Why would he keep you a secret if he wasn't already planning to cheat?"

"Or already cheating."

"Or at least leaving the door open." Maggie moaned. "I hate this. I way prefer the version where he was overcome by desire for me and it short-circuited his judgment and he couldn't help himself and got in too deep."

"The version where he loved you."

"*And* he loved you. I can wrap my head around that, sort of. But a premeditated thing—a *habit*—it's that much more . . . gross."

"Well, none of it's great."

"Yeah."

They sat in silence for a while. A path forked in front of Eve: She could keep deflecting Maggie's attempts at connection, or she could share something real.

"It's been a weird time for me," Eve said. "I don't feel much like myself, to be honest. Maybe that's part of why I invited you to stay."

The branch was starting to resemble a face. A long one—maybe a deer's? She bent over it, notching something like eyes.

"I get that," Maggie said. "I haven't been my normal self for one second that you've known me."

"What's your normal self, then?"

"Cheerier than this. Chattier than this. More useful. Not sleeping all the time."

"Understandable."

"What are you making?" Maggie asked.

Eve held up the lopsided sort-of face. "A forest creature? Possibly an imaginary one?"

"I like it," Maggie said. "Wow, you are good with your hands."

Pleasure made her flush unexpectedly. Eve *was* good with her hands, obviously; she'd made her living with them, and she'd been recognized for her skill by people more knowledgeable than Maggie, but something in Maggie's admiration made her feel acknowledged in a new way.

"So are you not yourself because of Karl's assholery?" Maggie asked. "And because of me landing here and messing with your life?"

"Not only that." Eve paused to measure whether she could say it out loud. Carefully, she began working on some kind of body for the creature. "I also just lost my sister-in-law. Her funeral was the day you got here. Only I wasn't at the funeral because—" Eve's voice caught. She swallowed. "—Because I'm cold and unfeeling, basically."

Maggie opened her mouth, her face strained and unreadable. She did not say *You aren't cold and unfeeling*.

"She was a very nice person," Eve said. "Never anything but sweet. I just couldn't connect with her, though she really tried and I guess I didn't, and my brother could see how I felt about her. And now she's gone and my brother's grieving, and I only make his pain worse."

"Eve, I'm so sorry. That sounds complicated."

"Yeah."

"And this led to you inviting me to stay?"

"I don't know. I thought . . . maybe it explains why I'm not myself."

"Because if you were yourself, you'd have kicked me to the curb on the first day."

"You were in no shape to be turned out by anyone but a monster."

A blue jay landed on the balcony railing, and they both watched it until it flew away.

"So . . . do you think I'm a stand-in for your sister-in-law?" Maggie asked. "I'm someone you should actively dislike, who you can instead choose to be kind to because it's too late to be kind to her?"

"God, are you a shrink? I don't know. Maybe? But also, I think I . . ." Was she really going to admit this? "I think I must like having you around."

Maggie laughed, then doubled over, moaning. "Guess I can't laugh yet," she said.

"I'll try not to say anything funny ever again."

"I don't get the impression you're much of a comedian, so we should be okay."

"Clearly the two of us liking each other is a bit of a joke."

"*You* liking *me* is hilarious. I always liked you."

"Liar."

"Well." Maggie smiled. "I liked you until I met you."

Now it was Eve's turn to laugh.

"Seriously," Maggie said. "I pictured us as allies. Kicking down Karl's door together, telling him he couldn't fuck us over. Then I met you and you were pretty scary, and it got harder to imagine us teaming up."

"God, I *would* like to kick down his door with you. I'd love to see the look on his face."

Maggie mustered a weak little kick and put on a menacing voice. "The jig's up, Karl. We know your dirty little secrets."

Eve laughed again.

Over the next three weeks, Eve started bringing her own meals to the lodge and eating with Maggie. As the weather warmed and Maggie healed, they spent more time on the balcony outside her room, and Maggie had even begun hobbling down the stairs to the lake, where she waded to her shins, threw sticks in the water for Flora to fetch, or sat in a lounge chair in the sun. Eve brought her to Sam's lodge to use the internet, though afterward Maggie declared that she'd hated returning to the real world and wanted to stay unplugged as long as she could. Or semi-unplugged, because Eve knew she could send and receive texts from the lodge and had been in touch with family and friends that way.

Eve had now whittled a forest's worth of animals—a rudimentary moose, a bear, a wolf, a loon, a beaver, and a porcupine—while Maggie read or dozed or listened to audiobooks beside her. But more often now, what Maggie did was talk. She'd told Eve about her childhood, her parents, her friends, the "marginally woo-woo" bookstore-café/yoga studio/event space where she worked, and—though she was relishing the break while she recovered—the Ph.D. she still needed to complete. She drew Eve out with innocuous questions that grew deeper almost without Eve noticing, asking where Eve had gone to school, then if her dad had taught her woodwork, which led to Eve admitting she hadn't really grown up with her dad beyond age thirteen, and not until three questions later did Eve realize she'd divulged more than she'd ever told anyone.

Eve could barely remember the feeling of working with wood for no purpose but the pleasure of forming an object with her own hands. She could not remember the feeling of such rambling, open-ended female conversation, because she was pretty sure she'd never had it.

Maggie didn't need watching over anymore, so there was no pretense left—Eve was sitting with her because she wanted to.

Eve had also started a new swim routine, every morning before she brought Maggie breakfast. Ten minutes breaststroking toward the middle of the lake in the bracing cold—summer hadn't yet officially arrived when she started—then ten minutes back to her own shore. She'd been so exhausted since Violet died and Daniel cast her out, since she'd decided to give him space and let him choose when they would speak again. Her grief was a tangible heaviness inside her, and she'd hoped the swimming would both calm her and give her energy. On the outbound trip her mind was cluttered—anxiety about the past and the future, about Daniel and Karl—but by the return swim, her mind felt clearer, jolted awake by the cold water, soothed by the meditative task of one stroke after another. She didn't have answers or direction exactly, but she had something like peace.

She hadn't spent this much time *in* the lake instead of on or beside it since she was a kid here with her brother, the two of them making up water games for hours, cannonballing off the dock, diving for treasure, perfecting their underwater communication system until they could carry out full conversations. Sometimes Eve revealed her deepest secrets this way—the boy she liked at school, the lies girls had spread about her after she went from gangly to gorgeous—and Daniel always understood.

"This place feels like summer camp," Maggie said one morning on her balcony, when she'd been in Bernice's lodge for three weeks. "It must have been awesome as a kid. Did you ever bring friends here with you?"

"Uh, no," Eve said. "Although my twin brother was my best friend, so I guess I kind of did."

Maggie straightened in her Adirondack chair, her face brightening. "You're twins!"

"Guess I haven't mentioned that," Eve said. "How about you? I bet you had loads of best friends."

"I had one. Andrea. We told each other everything. We were in a group with two other best friends, and the four of us talked and giggled non-stop. I'm sure everyone thought we were annoying, but we had the best time together. Till we all went to different high schools and then Andrea moved to Vancouver."

The sort of normal girlhood friendship Eve had felt excluded from.

"It sounds amazing to have a best-friend twin, though," Maggie said. "I always wanted a sibling. At least then no one moves away."

"Actually, he did. When we were thirteen. When my parents divorced."

"They *split you up*?" Maggie looked so shocked that for one visceral moment Eve felt the horror of that long-ago decision all over again.

"Yes," she said simply.

"That's fucked up," Maggie said.

"Thanks. I thought so too," Eve said. "It's why I hate that Daniel's cut me out now."

"He hasn't cut you out, though—has he? Just asked for some space?"

"I left the ball in his court, and it's been almost a month and he hasn't contacted me."

The look on Maggie's face was uncomfortably pitying. "Maybe you should try him again. Making the first move might be more than he can handle. Deep grief is debilitating. Responding can be easier than taking the initiative."

"Yeah, but he *didn't* respond. And I don't want to force him to talk to me if he doesn't want to."

Maggie placed one hand on Eve's arm. "Grief does funny things to people."

"So don't take it personally?"

"Well . . . that sounds dismissive, but—maybe?"

Eve nodded. Just expressing the anxieties helped; imagine that.

Chapter 17

Maggie

Maggie texted Daniel as soon as Eve left for work: You have to call Eve!! She thinks you're still upset with her and she is SUFFERING.

He responded immediately: I AM still upset with her.

You're not as upset as you used to be. You reached out to apologize almost a month ago.

I was still upset then too, but I was desperate for someone to talk to. Then I found this faceless texting friend I have no history with.

I'm serious. She keeps talking about you. And she's worried. It's getting uncomfortable for me.

Guess I'm putting it off. It's not straightforward with me and Eve.

I know you asked me not to tell her we're in contact, but I WILL tell her if you don't.

Yes, ma'am.

Sorry. I just feel strongly about this.

Hey. Remember our rule. No apologies.

No apologies. What a relief to show up to a friendship with a rule like that. She and Daniel were real with each other, they spoke the truth of what was, they didn't sugarcoat or pretend, and they didn't say they were sorry. This was probably easier because they didn't know each other in real life. Maggie suspected Daniel kept talking to her long after he knew she wasn't Eve because without any past or any context, without even a voice or a face, Maggie was a safer and easier place to entrust the complexity of his experience. It was the same for her, texting her heart out to this almost-imaginary friend day after day. And if that wasn't real, it was having real, undeniable effects.

Where are you on the grief scale today? Daniel asked.

5, Maggie replied. You?

7, came the response.

Maggie was keeping in touch with her mom and Charmaine, Jasmine and Natalie, and a few other friends. She talked to Eve daily, but no one but Daniel had a lived experience of the kind of life-shattering crisis she'd been through. No one else was free of opinions on how she should be or what she should do. Even Charmaine, so bothered by Maggie's indefinite vacation with her former rival, so insistent that her only concern was Maggie's mental and physical health, had blurted out when Maggie FaceTimed her from Eve's work, "Are you *ever* coming back? What about my kids? They miss you. What about *me*? *I* miss you!" Which was gratifying in one sense—she loved Charmaine's boys and her standing Thursday night babysitting gig, and of course she loved Charmaine and wouldn't want her indifferent to Maggie's absence—but this outburst was more pressure than she needed. Now she felt guilty for abandoning the boys and for being too overwhelmed by her own situation to be the good friend she wanted to be. "I'm sorry." Charmaine backpedaled immediately. "That was selfish. Of course I just want you to be happy." But even that felt like pressure. Maggie *wasn't* happy. Or not purely, uncomplicatedly happy.

Thus the grief scale. She and Daniel had started it after the night a couple of weeks ago when Maggie asked him, *Can you grieve the loss of something you've never had?* Because now that the physical danger to her was past, now that she no longer feared peril around every corner, she found a deeper grief surfacing. She'd lost a baby. An almost-baby. She'd yearned for a child, and for so short a time she'd believed there would be one—there was the beginning of one, however doomed—and now there wasn't. She'd yearned to be a mother, and for so short a time she'd believed she would be—she *was*, because her body was already nurturing a fetus inside her, however incompetently—and now she wasn't. *Can you grieve the loss of something you've never had?* She posed the question hesitantly, conscious that Daniel was grieving the loss of a person and a life and a self he'd very much had, nothing nebulous about it. His response was immediate: *Yes.* Just the one word, but inside it was permission, affirmation, a witness. You are grieving. Your grief is legitimate. You have the right to feel what you feel.

But she also, increasingly, felt brought back to life. As though she had dissolved to goo, incubated, and was now hatching from this room, a changed version of herself. Not a mother, no. But something new—she had yet to discover what.

"I don't suppose you feel up to catching some dinner?" Eve asked when she came over one afternoon two weeks later.

Maggie was folded over in wide-legged child's pose on the balcony, about as strenuous as her practice got these days. She'd bought the yoga mat the day before on a momentous excursion into the real world, the two-hour round trip to Sudbury with Eve, where she'd also bought Eve a thank-you picnic basket and shored up her wardrobe with sundresses, skirts, tank tops, and a floppy straw sunhat. It was the first week of July and she'd been at Still Lake for six weeks now. Natalie had arranged a subletter for her room—only for one month, but with the option to extend—so her meager savings were no longer draining into oblivion, especially since her expenses at Still Lake were almost zero. She was feeling more and more normal. She no longer looked like she'd been pummeled in the stomach. Her period was back. She'd even opened her dissertation a few days ago. She'd immediately recoiled and closed it again, her revulsion bone-deep, but at least she'd opened it.

Maggie looked up over her left shoulder. "There's a restaurant around here?"

"No, I meant literally. Do you like fishing?"

Maggie laughed. She could laugh now. "I have no idea."

"Maybe too much physical activity."

"Can I just sit and watch? Maybe my new self likes fishing." She rooted under the bed for her flip-flops.

Every time Maggie left the bed, she was aware of her incision, her cut muscles, her raised scar, like they were a vulnerable being she had to care for—a kitten, maybe, or even a baby. She followed Eve slowly along the path to her house, put on the life jacket Eve handed her, and stepped gingerly into a yellow canoe while Eve held it steady. Flora jumped in after her, and Maggie gasped as the canoe rocked side to side, clinging tightly as she sat down. Eve tossed a second life jacket into the bottom of the canoe and pushed off with one foot, the canoe lurching as she swung herself inside and they glided forward.

When they left the shore, the air felt instantly different—fresher, purer, a sensation of leaving earthly tethers behind. Maggie breathed it in. Eve paddled steadily. After a few quiet minutes, she propped her paddle across the canoe, opened a container, and affixed a worm to the hook on her line.

"Please tell me I don't have to do that," Maggie said.

Eve laughed. "You're just watching, right?"

"Right."

Eve flung the line far into the lake and languidly, her wrist barely moving, reeled it back toward her. Flora let out one cheerful bark and then sighed contentedly, settling her body low in the center between Maggie and Eve. A breeze skimmed the surface of the water. The canoe drifted. Eve cast and reeled.

"I've never been in a canoe," Maggie said.

"Are you serious?" From behind Maggie, Eve's voice was startled and deep. "Karl used to say he was most himself in a canoe."

Maggie twisted round to scan Eve's expression. Is this what they were doing now? Comparing knowledge of Karl?

"Well, preferably a canoe shooting rapids," Eve added quickly.

Jealousy reared inside Maggie, sudden and unexpected—that Eve had known the canoeing Karl, the breakfast in bed and afternoon sex and leisurely play at the lake Karl, while Maggie had been given only frenetic workweeks truncated by that Friday drive north.

Maggie turned around to face forward again. She didn't smile as she said, "Actually, I've never fished before either. Can I try it?"

Eve gave the rod over and Maggie fumbled with the handle, mutely following Eve's instructions. Her abdomen ached as she cast, and on her second attempt she opted for dropping the line over the side of the canoe. Eve did not tell her this was the wrong way to do it.

"Sorry," Eve said. The canoe rocked as she shifted. "I don't know why I said that. About Karl."

"I'm sure there are plenty of places where he was most himself in Toronto," Maggie said. *With me*, she didn't say. She wished she could think of one. The bank where his co-workers knew her name? His attic studio, where they had sex in his bed and he left her for Eve? And if they were talking tokens to prove who had been the holder of an authentic piece of Karl, how about the fetus that had exploded her insides?

She and Eve were doing so well. Why did Eve feel the need to introduce some Who-Knew-Karl-Best contest? And why did Maggie care? She was healed! She was over him! She was a butterfly newly hatched, new, new, new!

The rod jerked in Maggie's hand. She yelped and lurched forward, steeling herself too late against the pain at her belly. Something grey-green glinted in the churning water.

"What do I do?" Maggie squealed.

"Start reeling!"

The rod bent and the line danced taut and slack in the air.

"Not too fast!" Eve cried.

The rod pulled against her. Maggie half rose, trying to see, then slipped when the canoe rocked under her shifting weight.

"Careful!" Eve reached for her.

Maggie fell hard against the side of the canoe. Pain bloomed. Oh god, what the heck was she doing *fishing* in a *canoe* six weeks post-surgery? The fish jerked on Maggie's rod, and for a moment the canoe tipped far to one side. Then, as Eve leaned toward Maggie and Flora scrabbled for purchase, Maggie's foot caught in the strap of the second life jacket. She tripped and the canoe gave in to its unbalanced load and spilled them all into the lake.

Water engulfed her, the cold hitting with breathtaking force. Maggie surfaced quickly, gasping and stunned. The life jacket held her, thank god; she leaned back into it, floating helplessly. Eve bobbed several meters away. Flora woofed, swimming merrily toward Maggie. Maggie blinked the water out of her eyes, staring at Eve as Eve stared back at her.

"Fuck, I am so, so sorry." In a few quick strokes Eve swam toward Maggie. "This is all my fault. I shouldn't have brought you out in the canoe, and I should have taught you some basic safety, and I should have worn that stupid life jacket so you wouldn't have tripped. I'm an idiot. I just thought it would be nice for you to get out on the water. I shouldn't have—"

Maggie's giggles started somewhere in the middle of Eve's speech. She was pretty sure she hadn't done any real damage to herself. Her wound was closed; no danger of lake water contamination. Her healing muscles weren't strong enough for swimming, but the life jacket was handling that. And Eve was babbling with more fervor than Maggie had ever seen from her—Maggie would never have imagined Eve *babbling*—and it struck her as hilarious.

"City girl goes fishing!" Maggie cried.

Eve gaped at her. "And the fish pulls her in?"

"And the boat capsizes!" Maggie crowed.

"And the fish gets away," Eve added. But the rod was floating nearby and Eve lunged for it, calling, "It's still here!" Doggy-paddling, Eve reeled the line in. A green-spotted fish flopped at the end of it, gills pulsing.

"A bass," Eve said. "It must be twenty inches!"

"That's great," Maggie said, "but now I need to get to dry land before I drown."

They weren't far from the lodge beach. Eve nudged Maggie toward the shore, the rod in one hand, until their feet touched bottom and they could walk. Eve placed the fish in the sand while Maggie collapsed onto the beach and wrapped both arms around her poor aching body. She lifted her shirt to inspect her abdomen, half expecting her long-dissolved staples to have opened, her scar reverted to a gaping wound.

"Are you okay?" Eve asked.

"No!" Maggie said, but she was smiling. "I can't believe that just happened! Were you trying to kill me?"

"I'm so sorry." Eve dropped beside Maggie on the sand. She looked distraught. Maggie swatted her, and then they were both laughing.

"I hated the way you brought up Karl like that, though," Maggie said. "Can we have a rule that we don't mention Karl?"

"Maybe we need a Karl jar."

"Like a swear jar?"

"Exactly."

"And when it's full we can use the money to go to a really great restaurant and never need to fish again."

"No restaurant today, though." Eve flung her arm back for the fish and held it aloft. "He's gorgeous, Maggie."

"He'd better be, considering what we went through to get him."

"This was such a bad idea. You're really okay?"

She was more than okay. She was *laughing*. She was enjoying a normal, lighthearted moment. Not normal. Bizarre. A bizarre, lighthearted moment—with Eve.

Maggie pointed. "Shouldn't you go rescue your canoe?"

"Oh shit." And Eve was back in the cold water while Maggie laughed from the shore, and as Eve dragged the upturned canoe awkwardly behind her, neither of them could stop laughing.

Chapter 18

Eve

"So, is that sauna in working condition?" Maggie asked Eve after they'd rescued themselves from the lake.

"Doubtful," Eve said, but she opened the door and peered in at smooth rocks on a cast iron stove. It *looked* functional.

"We have to turn it on!" Maggie said.

"You mean fetch kindling and firewood and matches and build a fire and wait an hour for it to get hot enough?"

"Is that how you do it?"

"That's how you do it."

"Well—want to?"

"Are you sure you're up for a sauna?"

"I need to get warm after that freezing water you somehow swim in every morning."

"You don't even have a bathing suit here."

"I bought one in Sudbury yesterday." Maggie grinned. "But aren't saunas better naked anyway?"

"Seriously?" Eve said. "What could possibly be awkward about you and me naked together?"

"What in our entire relationship *hasn't* been awkward?"

So Eve built a fire in the stove and walked back home to peel off her clothes, the absence of their clinging wetness a relief. She eyed her bathing suit, hanging from the towel rack in her bathroom, but what the hell, Maggie was right: saunas *were* better naked.

She gutted and filleted Maggie's fish, lit the barbecue, and wrapped potatoes in foil, feeling free, unfettered. She'd seen Maggie through what was surely her worst. They'd been dumped into the lake. Maggie had, improbably, caught a fish.

She and Maggie ate together at Bernice's picnic table near the beach. In the small sauna change room afterward, Eve kept her eyes averted as they both stripped down. She clutched her towel around her and pulled open the sauna door. Dry heat and woodsmoke pinched her nostrils, and her pulse quickened as she climbed to the bench. Maggie followed with little gasping noises, squealing, "This is ten times hotter than any spa sauna!" She settled a few feet from Eve, her towel folded across her lap. Eve scooped water into a ladle and tossed it onto the rocks. It hit with an eruption of steam, and a second later the heat landed like a physical thing at her throat. Eve leaned forward into it. Beside her, Maggie covered her face with her hands and breathed in slow, heavy breaths.

"You can get down on the floor if it's too hot," Eve told her.

"I can feel the toxins dripping off me. I'm staying here."

They were quiet for a few minutes, and in the silence, Eve turned and looked at Maggie. Her body was shorter and more voluptuous, none of the intimidating length and hard angles of Eve's. She could imagine a man—Karl—wanting the small, the engulfable. The body he could feel robust beside, the body he could hoist against a wall, carry over a threshold, piggyback without tiring. Karl had, conceivably, done any number of those things to the body beside her on the bench.

She closed her eyes, then opened them again just as Maggie shifted position. Her towel gaped and the scar was revealed, a pink gash that began at her belly button, still bright and new. Maggie's gaze caught hers and Eve looked away, then back at Maggie's face.

"Does it hurt?" Eve asked.

"It's tender. But it doesn't hurt. Not anymore."

Eve didn't know what to say. She tossed another dipperful of water onto the rocks and breathed into the steam.

"You're officially the first person who's seen that," Maggie said. "Apart from medical people."

"Is that okay?" Eve asked.

"Hey, I'm the one who suggested a naked sauna."

Eve couldn't tell if Maggie really was breezy about it—about the scar and the reason for the scar; about Eve seeing it—or just putting on a good face.

"You don't have to make light of it to me," Eve said. "I know that scar represents something horrible."

A bead of sweat traced down the side of Maggie's neck. Her shoulders rose with each shallow breath. "Thanks," she said. "You're right."

"Just—in case you felt like you had to give it a positive spin."

"I do have a habit of compulsive positivity."

"I've noticed."

Maggie laughed, then turned to Eve with a serious expression. "I actually only looked at the scar for the first time without crying, like, yesterday. To tell the truth." She lifted the hair off her neck, tilting her head back against the cedar slats. "I see it and wonder if I'll ever feel comfortable in a bikini again. I imagine having sex with a new person for the first time and worry they'll be turned off. But mostly it's a reminder of the terrifying thing that happened. And of what I lost."

"I'm really sorry," Eve said.

"I *would* like to stop putting a positive spin on the fact that I'm dying in this heat, though," Maggie said. "Can we please go cool off now?"

"Absolutely."

Eve climbed down from the bench and threw open the door. An enormous cloud hovered the width of the lake, and the air was cool and moist as they made for the water. Flora followed them in. Eve closed her eyes and floated on her back, the lake a silk robe on her naked skin. Rain pattered in the distance. When she opened her eyes, she saw it falling in grey sheets into the trees on the opposite side of the lake. Maggie was standing, the water to her shoulders, looking out at the wind as it ruffled the trees where the rain fell. The wind swarmed in a circle around the bay until they were surrounded, its evidence in rippling water and shaking leaves, the two of them calm in the eye of it.

Beyond the cloud, in the pale, darkening sky, a full moon was just visible. Eve raised her arm and saluted it.

The circle of wind encroached. The deluge opened, all at once, on top of them. Eve laughed and reached for the rain as it pummeled darts into the cold black water and into her skin, ricocheting off the lake so that the water appeared to be swarming, dancing, alive. At the first strike of lightning, they scrambled to the sauna for their towels and clothes, clutching them close as they stumbled barefoot up the hillside stairs to the lodge.

Maggie's room was pleasantly clammy, warm and insular in the storm. Eve tried the light switch. Nothing. She lit candles as Maggie spread their soaked clothing on the desk, and they both huddled at the window in wet towels while the rain lashed the earth and lightning flared. Flora whimpered, her head slinking low between her paws. Eve ran her hand across her back, murmuring comfort.

"Think the lodge owner keeps clothes here?" Maggie asked. "All my new thrift store clothes are over at your place, waiting to be washed. Everything else I have is drenched."

"I kind of doubt Bernice's clothes will be your style."

"Maybe my new self has a new style."

"Your new self, huh? You keep mentioning this person."

Maggie shrugged. "It's something I've been thinking about. I'm pretty sure this is a dividing line in my life. I don't think I'm going back to the person I was before all this."

"If your new self adopts Bernice's style, you will have to seriously rethink this new self."

Maggie pointed to the *Truth Landing* painting. "I was thinking of going for *her* style."

Eve raised her eyebrows. "Well, then. You're all set."

"Not the nude part."

"The piercing gaze?"

"The self-assuredness. I think that's what it is."

Every time Eve had entered Maggie's room in the last six weeks, the *Truth Landing* woman had gazed at her over her muscled shoulder, leaning into her large, strong hand. Taunting with her ownership of herself, her easy vulnerability, her eyes that said *I know who I am*. Eve understood what Maggie meant.

Eve took a flashlight to investigate the upstairs rooms, the floor gritty under her bare feet. The light cast shadows across stripped bed frames and skeletal dressers, windows stippled with fly marks and rain. She rummaged among boxes of bolts and washers, mosquito repellent, expired sunscreen. In a closet in the common room downstairs, she unearthed a box of plaid shirts and baggy sweatpants, and next to them a wooden case stacked with wine bottles. Jackpot.

Back in Maggie's room, Eve tossed Maggie a set of clothes and they each pulled on a shirt and a pair of pants.

Maggie spread her arms wide and twirled. "I've officially turned into a lumberjack," she said. "A comfortable sweatpants-wearing one."

Eve held the unlabeled bottle aloft. "Does the comfortable lumberjack want to get tipsy?"

"Is that *homemade*?"

"I'm afraid it might be."

"Every activity you've suggested today has turned into a mini-trauma, so I'm sure mystery wine is also an awesome idea."

But Maggie was smiling, and Eve fished her Swiss Army knife from the pocket of her wet jeans and uncorked the bottle. She sniffed and shrugged. "I forgot to look for glasses. I don't mind if you don't." She sat cross-legged on the bed and held the lip of the bottle to her mouth. "It's drinkable," she pronounced.

"Good enough for me."

Flora walked circles around the room, then curled up on the floor beside the bed. Rain pounded, a jar of nails emptied onto the roof.

"It seems like we have some time to kill," Maggie said, settling on the bed beside Eve. "*So* . . . how are you doing?"

Eve raised the bottle. "Great."

"I don't mean now that you have gross wine to drink. I mean for real."

"Uh-oh, is this an interrogation?"

"*No.* It's a conversation," Maggie said.

"I'm moving on. I'm moving forward."

Maggie laughed. "Wow. Really baring your soul here, Eve."

"Well, how about you?"

"I'm getting through it, but there've been a lot of feelings to feel," Maggie said. "I've been grieving the death of the relationship I thought I was in, but also the loss of my pregnancy." Maggie chugged from the bottle, looking seriously at Eve. "I don't know if I've said this to you, but I wanted that baby. Even though I'm not in a great place to bring a child into the world, and even though it couldn't have worked out with Karl. You probably think that's crazy."

Wow. Yes. Yes, she did. Completely delusional. Masochistic, even.

"I'm sure having the baby would've been challenging," Eve said. "But that doesn't mean you're crazy to want it."

"It's just that I've always wanted to be a mother. And it's such a cliché, but the clock is ticking, especially now, with a busted fallopian tube. But going into a new relationship assessing the guy for fatherhood potential is not an attractive look."

"You still have time, though—don't you? You're only thirty-five."

"You know what they call thirty-five in the maternity world? *Geriatric.*"

Eve considered and discarded platitudes. She landed finally on "That's shitty."

"A term coined by men, for sure. But it's your turn now. How are your feelings doing?"

"Oh. Well. I don't know what I feel half the time."

Maggie raised her eyebrows.

"I try not to know, maybe," Eve offered.

"That feels safer?"

"I guess. Probably." Eve reached for the wine bottle and sipped from it, wincing. It really was not great. "My brother calls me the queen of self-protection, and he's usually right about me, so yes. Not feeling feels safer." But of course she didn't not feel. She felt all the fucking time.

Maggie's face wore the same distressed, over-earnest look that came over her whenever Eve mentioned Daniel or their rift.

"It's okay," Eve said. "It's fine. He'll come around."

"Definitely," Maggie said, shifting her gaze to her hands for a moment. "And I don't think shutting down feelings is any unhealthier than running around looking for love from everything that moves, just FYI."

"That's what you do, is it?"

"Daddy issues, and yes I have had therapy, thanks. I'm trying to get the love I didn't feel from my father, blah blah blah. I've thought about it a lot, actually, while lying in this bed in this room. I expect the people I love to be incapable of loving me back the way I want to be loved. And then they are. It's always been like that. And Karl was the ultimate experience of a person who couldn't commit to loving me, wasn't he? Because he already had you."

Lightning flared and for one instant Maggie's face was clearly visible before the room settled again into candlelit shadows. Eve pushed herself up the bed and reclined on a pillow against the headboard, loose-limbed and weightless. She was definitely a bit drunk now. "My dad wasn't exactly there for me either, but I think I responded by going the opposite way, and I'm not sure that's any better."

"Self-protection."

"Exactly." The rain picked up speed, louder and harder. Eve's next words came out like breath held too long. "I thought my relationship with Karl was *progress*. I thought it was me finally opening up to something healthy and real."

"It can still count as progress even if he wasn't keeping up his end of the bargain."

"You think?" Eve asked.

"I don't know. I'm still running irrational scenarios in my head where I carry the baby to term and Karl chooses to make a life with me. I'm not the authority on healthy and real. But I'm trying."

"I'm really sorry that happened to you."

Maggie flopped backwards to lie down on the bed. "You know what? I am long overdue for some commitment to *me*. I've never been alone as an adult, you know that? My first real boyfriend was at age fifteen, and I haven't been on my own for more than a couple of months since. I need time to be myself, to figure out what I can provide myself, without some dude I'm expecting to rescue me and make my dreams come true."

"You've never been alone and I've been too alone," Eve said.

"Put us together and we make the perfect woman."

"Hey, Karl was on to something."

"Not such an idiot after all!"

"Oh, he's definitely an idiot."

"A jerk, at least."

"A scumbag."

"An asshole."

"A motherfucker."

"We're going to owe the Karl jar so much money." Maggie sat up and took the bottle from Eve, nearly empty now, and raised it in the air. "Cheers to Karl the Motherfucker, who is horrible but brought us together!" She sipped and thrust the bottle back at Eve to complete the toast, smiling as she watched her. Then she drew a pillow into her lap, hugging it as she said, "Okay, so let's think about this. You've been too guarded and independent, I've been too trusting and codependent. You need to develop your—what do you need to develop?"

Eve laughed. "I need more wine for this." She knelt on the end of the bed and reached across the gap for the second bottle on the desk. "Trust? Interdependence?"

"And I need to develop—well, self-love. I need to stop looking to other people—i.e., men—to make me feel like I'm good enough or lovable enough. A year. *That's* what I need." She smiled and raised a palm. "I hereby promise myself one year of singleness. A year to put myself first. To fall in love with myself. To be kind and loving to *me*."

"You're serious?"

"A little drunk on this terrible wine, but yeah. Dead serious. And while we're at it, I think we should vow to each other that we'll never take Karl back," Maggie said.

"Of course we'll never take Karl back. That would require stooping to deep levels of self-deception."

"The kind of self-deception we are never stooping to again."

"Ever."

Maggie gestured at Eve, then back at herself. "This right here," she said, "is the best revenge, don't you think?"

"Us together?"

"Us together, thriving. Can you imagine the look on Karl's face if he could see us right now?" Maggie giggled, and she looked so delighted that Eve couldn't help but laugh too.

Then they each raised their right palms and made their promises to each other, laughing.

They stayed in the room all through the storm. Later, Eve didn't remember falling asleep, remembered only the thrashing of the rain, the spreading warmth of red wine, the peaceful, lulling rest of talking with Maggie. Talking and talking. She did fall asleep at some point, because she woke to votive candles sputtering in melted pools of wax, to herself propped against the headboard, neck askew, to two empty bottles on the nightstand. To Maggie asleep on the other side of the bed, sprawled on top of the quilt.

She folded her side of the quilt over Maggie, patted Flora's head, and slipped out.

The rain had stopped, and the air was fresh and new. A flock of clouds obscured and unveiled the light, gliding across the face of the full moon like migrating geese intent on their direction. She stopped on the path to look at it, resting against a tree, its bark saturated, spongy at her fingers.

A full moon. That final time she'd slept with Karl, that full-moon-lit night, that stash of condoms from the Wrangler—it was two months ago.

When was her last period?

Before that.

It had crossed her mind, all these days of Maggie's recovery from a pregnancy gone awry, but Eve's cycle was erratic. When she ran Stillcraft, she could go months between periods and always thought it good riddance. And now she was squarely in the age of perimenopause—wasn't it normal for your cycles to get longer? (Or was it shorter?) The pill gave her migraines, and she'd gone off it years ago. But she and Karl used condoms faithfully. Never once had they skipped the condom. Condoms were ninety-eight percent effective with perfect use; even with imperfect use, she could live with the odds.

She'd had no symptoms . . . had she? No nausea. Definitely some fatigue—she'd been bowled over by exhaustion after Violet died, but she'd chalked that up to grief. Her breasts had felt sensitive tonight in the sauna. And she'd been undeniably more emotional. Was *that* what this was about? Did she feel so fragile and open because she was pumped full of pregnancy hormones?

Her steps quickened on the path, and she raced along it and through the door to her house.

She could not be pregnant. The odds would be stupid. It was way too coincidental, that it would happen to both her and Maggie.

She went straight for the bathroom and hauled open the bottom drawer. The condoms from Karl's emergency stash glinted in their silver wrappings like faux pirate treasure. She picked one up and peered at the lettering pressed into the foil.

The expiry date was three years ago.

Chapter 19

Maggie

When Maggie woke the morning after the storm, Eve was gone. She reached for her phone and texted Daniel: I am telling Eve TODAY if you don't!

Eve was her friend now. Maggie couldn't sit under the piercing gaze of the *Truth Landing* woman much longer without coming clean.

Another truth had been feeling increasingly undeniable too, and Maggie left her room and made for Eve's house to act on that realization. She'd been coming here more and more, starting to do her own laundry, sometimes cooking a simple meal to share with Eve when she returned from Sam's. The house was empty now—Eve would be at work—but Maggie found the cordless phone on the kitchen island and called Sukha. She'd been on leave since the hospital, and now she made it official. When Daria answered, Maggie quit her job.

"But what will you *do*?" Daria sputtered.

"I'm on a kind of retreat," Maggie said. "I'm going to stay on my retreat, and I'll figure out my next step from here."

Then she called her mom to tell her what she'd done, promising she would use the time to focus on her dissertation. She left a message for her supervisor, letting her know she was recovered and ready to resume her work. She called Natalie to say she wouldn't be home for at least a couple of weeks—good news for the subletter, who wanted to stay.

She saved Charmaine for last. She expected celebration—for years Charmaine had been lobbying her to move on from her position as Daria's minion—but Charmaine's tone was anxious as she said, "You are coming back to Toronto, though, aren't you? Like, soon?"

"I'm remaining open to the nudges of the universe," Maggie said.

"Maggie. Come on."

Maggie braced herself, recognizing Charmaine's "time to be the adult and rein Maggie in" voice.

"You experiencing so many traumas on top of each other and then deciding to stay with your ex's other girlfriend *and* quitting your job at the same time? How is this not a cry for help?"

"This place is good for me, Char," Maggie said. "Eve and I are good for each other."

"Really? I feel like I should be contacting cult rescue teams."

Maggie laughed, though she knew Charmaine was only half joking. "Trust me on this."

"That's what people in cults tell their concerned friends."

"I miss you too, if that's what's going on here."

Charmaine sighed. "Yes, I miss you, but I am also genuinely worried. Just promise you'll keep talking to me."

"Of course I will, but maybe you could promise to consider not questioning every one of my decisions?"

"I will when you stop making decisions I disagree with," Charmaine said, but Maggie heard the smile in her voice, and they ended the call laughing together.

Maggie wandered back to the lodge on a disorienting sensation of freedom. She felt she could do anything, be anywhere, become anyone. She was in this beautiful, unexpected location. There were no markers to hold her in place, no schedules directing her actions for the coming days or months or years. The dissertation still needed rewriting, and that was a giant drag, but at least her work schedule could be her own now. She was pretty sure her new self didn't even want a job in academia—she'd probably never had much chance of landing one anyway, even back when she'd thought she wanted to—but the Ph.D. would get finished, the trust money would come through, and her life would be wholly her own to create.

Stepping over the threshold into the lodge, Maggie wandered around the common room, her fingers trailing along each piece of furniture, each wall, each wide wood windowsill. She entered the first bedroom off the common room, a dirtier version of her own, and continued through every room in turn, pausing to consider the view out each window, letting her hand skim the walls, standing in the center and rotating to take it in. Upstairs, she drifted through the rooms, one by one. Each featured huge windows overlooking the lake and doors opening onto the wraparound balcony.

When she arrived at her own room, she held her hands over her heart and thanked her room for the haven it had been as she put herself back together. From the hallway, she entered each room again, listening, thinking.

Sagging doorframes, dead flies, mouse dirt.

Airy, woodsy space, cushions and quilts and yoga mats, writing desks, views of lake and sky.

A sanctuary. A place for sleep and resurrection. A place to come for what was needed, whatever that might be. A place for truth to land.

I'm on a retreat, she'd said to Daria.

Across the path in the dining hall, she peeked into the kitchen, with its industrial stoves, walk-in cooler, smooth stainless steel countertops. She saw the plastic tables in the dining room replaced with pine, women clustered, talking, reading, writing, sketching, dancing, meditating, saluting the sun. She heard laughter. She saw life.

She had to rub her eyes to bring back the abandoned fishing lodge.

That evening Maggie cooked a stir-fry in Eve's kitchen and had it ready when Eve returned from work. She waited as they ate together on Eve's deck, making herself chat about other things—the plot of *Adam Bede*, which she was revisiting for her dissertation, took up a good fifteen minutes—until they'd finished eating and Maggie announced at last that she had something important to show Eve. She led Eve to the lodge and through the same tour of the buildings she'd taken herself that afternoon, ending up at last in her own room, the room that held the proof of what the whole place could be.

"I'm not sure what you're showing me here," Eve said.

Maggie smiled, motioning for Eve to sit in the armchair. "You've owned a business," she said. "I've been managing one for years. You know everything there is to know about fixing up this place. I know tons of people through Sukha and the university and yoga circles. Energy healers and movement coaches and writers and activists and artists, people who could lead such beautiful retreats, not to mention people desperately in need of a restorative escape. You grew up helping to run a lodge, and you're doing it again now. Running a lodge on a lake is in your blood. Building community and facilitating gathering space is in mine."

"Okay," Eve said.

"You have all kinds of skills I don't have, and I think I've got some that you don't. Right? Karl was on to something? Put us together and we make the perfect woman! Or—the perfect partners."

"What are you saying?"

"Together we could open a kick-ass retreat center." Maggie caught her own reflection in the mirror through the open bathroom door as she said this, and her face was transformed, lit from within. "Women only, and obviously an inclusive safe space for trans and gender-diverse folks too. I mean, how perfect is it? Honestly! Can you imagine a more ideal melding of our strengths and interests?"

And then she stopped short, noticing at last the tautness in Eve's expression.

"What?" Maggie asked.

Eve picked up a knife and a block of wood from the basket she kept under the chair and started whittling, not even looking at Maggie.

"You think it's silly," Maggie said. Her deflation was sudden and thorough. "You think it's impractical. Pie in the sky."

Eve was silent. This was not the Eve of last night, honest and open and compassionate. This was hostile Eve, back after so many weeks that Maggie had become convinced she wasn't real.

"It's too fast," Maggie said. "We barely know each other. That's what you're thinking, right?"

"There is that," Eve said. Her voice was tight.

"That's me, I guess, gung-ho to dive headfirst into a new passion. At least it's not a relationship." Maggie laughed uneasily. What the hell? Was Eve vulnerability-hungover from last night, or actually hungover, or genuinely scornful of Maggie's idea?

"Do you have any capital?" Eve asked.

"You mean—"

"Money. Do you have money?"

"Actually, I do have money coming to me once I finish my Ph.D."

"The one you've been almost finished for a decade?"

Maggie flushed. "I'm *close*, okay? I'll be defending this year."

"Since when does finishing a Ph.D. mean getting a bunch of money?"

"It doesn't, that's just the condition my dad put on releasing some investments he made for me."

Eve stared at her for a second. "That's the reason you've been working toward this? Read and write an insane amount of words and your dad rewards you with money?"

"Okay, it sounds ridiculous when you put it like that, but I actually did want the Ph.D. Or I convinced myself I did. Both my parents are profs and it felt like a natural path, back before I knew myself better. My dad was always just trying to make sure I'd be well set up in life."

"It seems a bit . . . manipulative?"

"It's more complicated than that, but yeah—you're not wrong. It's manipulation or it's extreme hands-on care for my welfare, but either way I've been working toward it, and the point is, I will have money.

There are also grants and loans to look into. I have experience with grant-writing. We could see about setting up as a not-for-profit, maybe?"

"Even a non-profit needs money to run. And a shit-ton of time and energy investment."

"Obviously I haven't thought through all the details yet. The idea is four hours old."

Eve tossed the wood back into the basket, shoved it under the chair, and stood. "You're making a lot of assumptions about my strengths and interests," she said.

"Oh." Now Maggie felt not just deflated but reprimanded. "I'm sorry. You're right." She *was* right. "I just got excited."

"I'm exhausted," Eve said. "I'm going home now, if that's okay. Thanks for dinner."

Eve opened the door. Her steps echoed on the stairs. Maggie watched her go, bewildered. She had definitely made some big leaps in her enthusiasm, but wasn't that required in big-dream brainstorming? She stood and followed Eve uneasily, stopping midway down the staircase and gripping the railing.

At the door Eve turned. They looked at each other a moment, and then Eve said, "Don't you have to go back to Toronto?"

The question sliced through Maggie. She heard: *You have to go back to Toronto.*

"Eventually, yes. I guess so."

"Or are you hiding out here indefinitely? Walking out on your life and making a new one here?"

"No. But I . . ." This might not be the best time to share her celebratory news. "I did quit my job today."

"*What?*" Eve's hand moved from the doorknob to her hip, and she stood there, staring up at Maggie on the stairs. "*Why?* To move here and open a retreat center?"

"I need to make changes. I can't even imagine going back. I knew it was a leap I had to take, and I took it."

"You're only barely recovered. Of course you can't imagine going back. But this is not a good time for making life decisions."

"I think it's actually a great time. I have a perspective I couldn't have had before my life exploded. I can see what matters. And I look around me and see this retreat center like it already exists."

"I look around me and see a dump. It needs so much work. You have no idea. If we're lucky, the work is only cosmetic, but even that's huge. More likely, the buildings aren't structurally sound. Why do you think there's been no buyer in all this time? We'd probably have to demolish everything and start over."

"These are questions we'd have to answer. I appreciate you being the voice of practicality, but—"

"I've owned a business," Eve said. "I spent the last two years recovering from owning a business."

"Okay, but this isn't New York City."

"It would be stressful. Still Lake is mine, Maggie. My refuge. It took me almost thirty years to get back here. You've been here a month and a half, and you want to turn my refuge into a business."

"Right." The reality of Eve's anger began to penetrate. Maggie was a house guest who had overstayed her welcome, and she'd been extremely presumptuous. "I didn't mean to barge in on your territory," she said.

"Do you even have any idea what it takes to start a business?"

This conversation felt so much like the first time they met that Maggie slumped down on the stairs in bafflement.

"It's just that I can't take on more responsibility right now," Eve said.

"Of course. But if it's because of the responsibility you took on in caring for me, I'm doing so much better now, and you really don't need to—"

"Not everything is about you!" Eve cried.

Maggie blinked.

"I'm sorry," Eve said. "Ignore me. I'm tired and—I think I just need to go home and crash."

Long after Eve left, Maggie sat on the stairs replaying the conversation, trying to figure out exactly where she'd gone wrong.

Chapter 20

Eve

"Will you come keep me company?" Eve asked as she stood in Maggie's doorway the next morning. "I'm going to clean up the dining hall."

From her desk, Maggie eyed Eve warily.

"*Not* because I think we should buy it," Eve said. "I have today off and I thought it would be a nice gesture for Bernice when she gets back, that's all." And she felt bad for lashing out at Maggie yesterday and wanted to offer some kind of concession. *And* she was looking for a distraction—any distraction.

For two nights and a day now, Eve had kept her suspicion a silent flame inside her. *I could be pregnant; it is possible.* The more logical day-off activity would be buying a pregnancy test, except she couldn't quite convince herself that was necessary. It was nothing but a late period, a baseless hunch. But the suspicion still scrolled non-stop through her brain, and wasn't that the real reason Maggie's retreat center scheme had upset Eve last night? Not because she hated the idea of buying Bernice's property and restoring it to beauty and function—not in theory, anyway. She felt its specialness too, and she actually had money thanks to the business she'd built from nothing and sold at a profit. And not because she hated the idea of doing this with Maggie either; preposterous as it might be, Maggie was rapidly becoming the closest friend she'd ever had. Also not because of the ridiculous revelation that Maggie's share of the capital would come through writing a paper no one needed, to gain another paper she didn't even want, all to impress her dad so he'd award her an amount of cash most people couldn't dream of. And she wasn't even all that angry that Maggie was bounding in like a big fucking golden retriever slobbering on everything Eve most wanted to protect, asking to turn Eve's haven into a giant resource-sucking responsibility.

The real reason Eve had been upset last night was because Maggie wanted to do this while Eve was facing the possibility of a whole other giant resource-sucking responsibility. A life-altering one.

Not that Maggie knew about that.

In the dining hall, Eve dragged tables to one end and started filling oversized black bags with garbage. Maggie was on a chair in a corner, sorting boxes of junk into potentially useful objects and definite trash.

"I wasn't trying to force you into something," Maggie said. "I was just excited. I got carried away."

"I know," Eve said. "I overreacted."

"But you know what I realized last night? The way you've taken care of me here is part of what inspired this idea."

"All I did was bring you food and do some laundry."

"You did a lot more than that. I needed support and rest and a safe space. This place gave them to me. The lake, my room, but you especially. You gave those to me."

"Jesus," Eve said. "You make me sound like a nurse, a priest, and a therapist rolled into one."

"Oh, just take the gratitude. I'm grateful and I'm acknowledging it, and you can just accept it!"

Eve laughed. She was wielding a large broom across the fissured linoleum, leaving hills of wood chips and crusted mud in her wake. "So this retreat center would be a place for people who need support and rest," she said. "Basically a Victorian convalescent home?"

"No! Well . . . maybe kind of? I wasn't thinking medical recovery, more like . . . life recovery? It could also be a place for artists to work and be inspired and learn from each other—musicians or painters or writers. Maybe potters? Woodworkers? But mostly just regular people who need space to pause and breathe and recharge from whatever life's thrown at them. Maybe there could be guided retreats—yoga or meditation retreats, self-development workshops, forest bathing—"

"Excuse me, what?"

"It's a thing."

"If you say so."

"But also self-guided stays, people booking to come on their own for a week or a month to reset and reflect and recreate themselves and—whatever they need. Like I did. A place of supportive community and healing."

It sounded pretty damn nice, to be honest.

A chunk of linoleum peeled off in Eve's hand, and she held it up and surveyed its grubby surface, then tossed it like a Frisbee. She pounded her fist into the rotting plywood subfloor she'd uncovered, then reached for her hammer. Maggie crossed the floor and squatted beside her, and with two quick thumps Eve broke through the plywood.

"Oops," Maggie said.

Eve clawed at decaying wood. "Might be a leaky pipe somewhere."

"So, not promising for whoever buys the place."

Eve shrugged. "Fix the leak, put in a new floor." She pounded again and the head of the hammer broke through with one swing. The hole was now the size of a small watermelon.

"You've got business ownership trauma," Maggie said. "I get that."

"Yeah, maybe. That's part of it anyway." Also abject fear of the future if she was indeed pregnant. Inability to see beyond that one prospect. The constant imaginative effort going on in her mind as she tried to picture herself as a mother.

Eve had raised the hammer again when a door behind them creaked open on rusted hinges. Eve and Maggie scrambled to stand. Like children caught misbehaving, they arranged themselves side by side in front of the hole in the floor.

In the doorway stood Bernice, squinting at them through the pale frames of oversized glasses. Maggie shot Eve a look. Eve stood in front of the hole with legs spread, the hammer dangling between two fingers. Bernice's stare pierced: Eve, Maggie, the hammer. The hole in the floor.

"You fixing my lodge or wrecking it?"

"We were just checking . . ." Eve trailed off, uncertain what exactly she'd been doing.

"Needs a new floor," Bernice said.

"It does," said Eve.

"Twenty years ago I'd have shot myself before I let it get like this." Bernice sidestepped piles of garbage, stopped to stroke a mounted fish. "I used to love fixing this place up. Keeping it beautiful. Maybe you remember?"

"I used to come here as a kid," Eve said.

"I wish I'd seen it then," Maggie said. She stepped toward Bernice, one hand extended.

"Maggie's a friend of mine," Eve explained.

Maggie turned to Eve, her smile bright and quick. "I've been staying here," she said to Bernice. "I hope that's okay. Because I have to tell you, I'm starting to think this place has healing powers."

"Is that so?" Bernice said. "And how long are you here?"

"Not much longer," Maggie said. "I'm not sure there's a need for me to be here anymore."

"Don't leave on my account. You can keep cleaning up if you feel like it. In return for staying."

"Just don't bash too many more holes into floors?" Maggie asked.

"If you can help it," Bernice said. And then she laughed. Laughed! This woman Eve had known her whole life without ever getting past the crotchety exterior—thirty seconds into knowing her, Maggie had made her laugh.

"I'm interested in uncovering the potential here," Maggie said. "Eve tells me you've had trouble selling?"

"Can't imagine why," Bernice said, and laughed again.

"If you don't mind my asking, why didn't you have it fixed up before you put it on the market?" Maggie asked. She was shameless.

"No energy. No money. Why? You interested?"

"We really aren't," Eve said.

"Maybe," Maggie said.

Bernice nodded like this contradiction was reasonable. "You want to know my asking price?"

"That would be helpful," said Maggie.

"Let me think about it. I'll get back to you."

"Great!" Maggie's smile might as well have glitter and rainbows in it. "I do have one more question, now that you're here. I've been wondering since I got here."

"Sure."

"The painting of the woman by the lake," Maggie said. "Why is it called *Truth Landing*?"

"That's the name of the spot where it was painted." Bernice gestured vaguely. "Just the other side, used to be a place where the boats put in. It was called Truth Landing."

"Why Truth?" Maggie asked.

Bernice shrugged. She hefted the door open. "Because fishermen are liars?"

She walked out the door and it slammed behind her.

Maggie sighed. "So much for all the deeper meaning I've been reading into that name."

"Her asking price? Jesus, Maggie, it's a nice thought experiment. And it's not like buying this property hasn't occurred to me too, but—"

"See, it's a good idea! You do think it's a good idea!"

"I don't. Do you have any clue what a project of this scale would require?"

"A lot."

"I can't do it," Eve said. "I can't even think about doing it."

"I realize there are a lot of steps between here and there. And maybe most people would think it was nuts for us to team up, given our history. But don't you think we've surmounted a lot already? Don't you think *this* would be the ultimate revenge on Karl?"

"Yeah, I'm not motivated enough by revenge to risk my life's savings for it."

"Why don't we make a list of all the complications and considerations. We can do some research—"

"It's not just that!" Eve exclaimed. God, Maggie was relentless. "I mean it is, but there's also a whole other thing, and I can't even remotely entertain this right now because I'm—I think I might be—" Her voice caught and she swallowed. She couldn't speak the word out loud. She especially couldn't speak it to Maggie—not until she knew for sure. "I'm just going through a lot," Eve finished. "That's all. Daniel and Violet and . . . everything."

But Maggie was looking at Eve now with suspicion bordering on fear. She'd seen something in Eve's face, heard it in her evasion. "You think you might be what?"

"Overextended."

"You said 'because I'm—' and then you changed it to 'I think I might be.' Might be what, Eve?"

"Nothing. Nothing!"

Maggie sank to the dirty floor, sitting cross-legged beside the hole. Her shoulders were trembling. "Pregnant?" Maggie asked. "You think you might be pregnant?"

"No! No, not at all—I mean, I don't know. I'm *not.*" Eve knelt beside Maggie. "I'm just—worried I am."

"You are," Maggie whispered. "Of course you are."

"It's not a *good* thing for me, Maggie. Not like this."

Maggie was silent a moment, and then a deep, gravelly sound emerged from her. Eve needed a second to realize what it was: laughter. Harsh, angry laughter.

"What the hell was I imagining?" Maggie said. "That I could *move* here? Live and work and create a future here? Happily ever after with the woman Karl loved the whole time he claimed to love me? I'm such an idiot. The whole premise of this stupid retreat center idea—it's ridiculous. It's bullshit."

"Maggie. I haven't even taken a test."

From her cross-legged position, Maggie rolled forward onto her hands and knees, then sprang to her feet. Eve waited for a hug, a squeeze of the hand, some empathic Maggie-esque outreach that would enfold them in we're-in-this-together-ness despite the complicated reality.

Maggie said, "Of course you're pregnant! Probably with a totally healthy, normal baby. Because you were in the *real* relationship, weren't you? You were the *real* girlfriend."

For one second Eve stared at Maggie, taking in her accusing tone, uncomprehending. Then she reared to her full height, Amazonian beside Maggie, suddenly furious. Eve was facing a crisis, she'd confided in Maggie, and now Maggie was expecting Eve to deal with Maggie's emotions about Eve's crisis?

"We were both fucking real, okay? But if I am pregnant, it has nothing to do with you. I had sex with my partner, and as far as I knew at the time, you didn't exist. Karl's stash of expired condoms from the Wrangler sure did, though."

Maggie's head snapped up. "What?"

"In the glove compartment? I don't suppose you're familiar with it?"

"You're kidding me."

"No, *Maggie*, I am not kidding you." Eve bit off Maggie's name like it was a bitter weed. "And my possible pregnancy is my business, not yours."

Maggie's eyes filled with tears. She nodded and walked to the door, yanking it open. She stepped through and then turned back to Eve. "Now I get why Daniel doesn't want to talk to you," she said. "I've been trying to convince him he needs to reach out to you, that you're hurt and sorry and not heartless. But clearly he knows you better than I do."

Eve felt like she'd been slapped. "How the *fuck* are you in touch with my brother?" At the small, satisfied curl of Maggie's mouth, she decided she couldn't stand breathing the same air as her for one second longer. "You know what, I can't deal with this right now. I don't want to know." Eve shoved past Maggie on her way out the door, knocking into her shoulder as she went.

"We've been talking for six weeks now," Maggie shouted at Eve's back. "Every day. We've gotten very close. Turns out Daniel and I click."

Eve marched home with one hand on Flora's collar, her anger a pure light propelling her, her legs long and righteous on the path. She reached her house and sprinted up the steps, closed the patio door and flicked the lock. Her home, her safe, small haven, her fortress. She moved to the front door and locked that too, then closed and locked all the windows and sat down on the couch, huddling there with her knees drawn to her chin and her arms around her legs.

She'd been right to be wary of Maggie early on. The intimacy of these last few weeks felt embarrassing, horrifically exposing, dangerous. The things Eve had told her! And Maggie, in turn, had *not* been transparent; when Maggie had said things like "You've been going through your own stuff too," she hadn't meant just the Karl mess—she must have known about Violet's death before Eve told her, known about the rift with Daniel, known and said nothing. *How*? Could it really be true that all these weeks, as Eve soldiered through alone, desperate for connection with her brother, he'd been supporting *Maggie*?

Eve's desire to fold herself up, a drawbridge denying further admittance, was palpable.

She patted the couch to invite Flora up beside her. Flora nuzzled her head into Eve's lap and Eve stroked her behind the ears.

"I've missed you over here, baby girl," she whispered.

She'd given Maggie her *dog*! First Karl, then Flora, then her brother, and now Still Lake itself—Maggie planned to horn in on all of it.

She and Flora stayed hunched on the couch together while the room grew darker and cooler. Her phone rang. She ignored it, but on the fourth ring the hope of Daniel on the other end sent her scrambling from the couch to peer at the call display.

Holy fuck: Karl.

She threw the phone away from her and it bounced onto the couch. Striding to the base, she yanked the plug from the wall.

In the kitchen, Eve turned on a burner and opened a can of chicken soup, her hands shaking as she worked the can opener. She sniffed—did the smell make her nauseated? Possibly.

She didn't know what Maggie would eat tonight, but she'd taken enough care of Maggie. Maggie could take care of herself.

Chapter 21

Maggie

Maggie's overwhelming urge after Eve stormed from the dining hall was to text Daniel. *Eve thinks she's PREGNANT! I can't handle this! I can't stay!* But she couldn't text Daniel, because he was Eve's brother and this wasn't Maggie's news to share—she had that much perspective, at least. She texted the words to Charmaine instead, stuffed her laptop and essentials into her bag, applied lipstick, and went for a walk on Vermillion Road in the direction she thought the village lay. She didn't know if she was planning to just walk or if she was heading back to Toronto—and if she wasn't heading back to Toronto, why had she brought so much of her stuff? The idyll was over and she couldn't stay, not with this angry Eve who was possibly carrying a baby she'd made with Karl. Not with this Eve who wanted her gone.

And why wouldn't Eve want Maggie gone? Maggie's attack had been deliberate. *Your beloved brother who won't speak to you? He's been speaking to me all along.* She'd known this would hurt Eve, and in that moment, Maggie had wanted to hurt her.

She'd never seen a look of such hatred directed at her in her life. She'd felt briefly triumphant—she'd wounded Eve more than Eve had wounded her!—and then completely, utterly, horrible.

She was trudging along the road in the heat when her phone rang with Charmaine's ringtone. The sound was startling, a balm after so long with spotty service—the road must be a higher elevation than the lodge—and she lifted the phone to her ear with relief.

"I don't actually *want* to still be pregnant," she said after she'd filled Charmaine in. "Do I? Not without a partner. Not with my life so chaotic."

"Of course you do," Charmaine said. "There was no part of you that wanted what happened to you."

"So do you think I have a little bit of a right not to be ecstatic if someone else has what I lost?"

"Maggie. This is allowed to be complicated for you." Charmaine spoke the words with so much compassion that Maggie felt tears welling. "Pregnancy is primal," Charmaine said, "and you've always wanted to be a mom. Plus, I'm not sure there's a deeper way to tie yourself to another person—and you and Eve had the same person."

Maggie took a breath. Her shoulder bag was already too heavy for this walk. Charmaine was right. Maggie wasn't just upset because Eve might be pregnant. She was upset because Eve might be pregnant *with Karl's baby.*

Because what but a child could so solidly signify that you had mattered? That you would continue to matter? That you could never be entirely left behind? If Eve had made a baby with Karl, if Eve gave birth to an infant that was both hers and his, Maggie and Eve would not be on equal footing as the women Karl had lied to. Eve would be, forever, the mother of his child, Maggie just the woman he'd banged on the side.

"Eve was deceived too, remember," Charmaine said.

"Now you're on *Eve's* side?"

"You know I'm always on your side. But Eve's in the exact terrifying position you were in when you found out you were pregnant, trying to figure out the same stuff. You don't have to be happy for her, but maybe realizing that could help you find some empathy?"

Maggie stifled a sob. *Empathy?* She was all about empathy. But how was she supposed to empathize with *this*?

"From what you've told me, Eve seems to have no one," Charmaine went on. "At least you've got me to reach out to. And your mom, and other people who care about you. Including Eve's own brother."

She had *not* told Charmaine about throwing that information in Eve's face. The reminder made her feel even worse.

"I'm pretty sure I'm not the person Eve wants to be turning to in this situation," Maggie said, "even if *I* could handle it. Which I can't. I was so horrible to her, Char. I was awful." And then Maggie's phone lost reception and dropped the call, and she was alone on the side of the gravel road.

She hadn't made it far and she was already exhausted. She dropped into a crouch at the edge of the road. When a pickup truck pulled up alongside her a few minutes later and a man rolled down the window and she recognized the bushy moustache of Eve's employer, she actually did cry.

"I'm headed to the grocery store," Sam said. "Need a lift?"

In her rustic bathroom, Maggie's lip color had felt garish, but it started making more sense the further out of the bush they drove.

Sam made easy small talk. As they pulled into the parking lot of the Larkin store, he said, "You know I haven't seen Eve this happy in years? She might not ever tell you that she likes having you here, so I thought I'd better. You're good for her."

Maggie stared at him for one guilt-stricken moment, thanked him, and climbed from the truck. She filled her basket with cookies, ice cream, three kinds of chocolate. In the small pharmacy aisle, the pink swirls on the boxes of pregnancy tests read *First Response*, like they contained paramedics rushing to an emergency. She grabbed a package of condoms while she was at it, carefully checking the expiry date (three years from now)—because, fuck it, she might not be having sex again for a year, but when she did, she would be ready, *she* would be taking control, and she sure as hell would not be relying on the man for birth control.

While she waited for Sam to finish his shopping, she took advantage of cellphone reception and checked her email. There was a message from her supervisor urging her not to delay any longer with the revisions, wanting to schedule a call to discuss Maggie's new ideas. (Had Maggie claimed to have new ideas?) There was a plea from Daria—*This place is falling apart without you; I'll give you a raise and promote you to manager*—and Maggie didn't find it entirely unappealing. There was an email from her father letting her know he'd accepted a semester-long guest teaching post at Columbia; would she be back in Toronto before he left in August? Maybe she would. Maybe she'd be back tomorrow.

And then, while she was sitting there on the bench outside the store, a new email came through. Maggie physically recoiled at the name. It was from Karl.

> I only just got all the texts and voicemails you left in May. I'm sorry it's taken me so long to get back to you. I was off-grid so I wasn't receiving messages, but I'm back in civilization again. It sounded like an emergency. Can you call again? I've tried your phone but it goes straight to voicemail and your mailbox is full. Please let me know you're okay.

Well, Karl. I'd be better if you weren't a cheating liar. I'd be better if you'd been there for me when I was almost dying. I'd be better if you hadn't impregnated your other girlfriend. I'd be better if you had just freaking loved me.

She put her phone away and breathed deeply into her belly, held the breath, let it out through her mouth in a long, measured stream. She did it again, and again, and again, until her heart rate slowed and the turmoil eased just a little.

She couldn't stay in this resentment and anger and envy. It wasn't her. She was a good person, a loving person—or at least she wanted to be. These feelings didn't serve her. These feelings would eat her alive.

If Eve was pregnant, the crisis, the decisions, the right to support, belonged to Eve. Eve, who had supported Maggie when she was in crisis. Maybe Maggie couldn't help the panicky reminders of what had happened to her. Maybe she couldn't stop the grief or the blow to her self-worth. But she could keep them from gaining dominance. She could try.

She pictured a flaming arrow. She created a mental image of resentment, then of anger, then of envy—they were cartoonish lumps of red and purple, small and impotent—and she placed them on the arrow, one by one, and watched them sail across the parking lot, through the air, away from her.

Maggie asked Sam to drop her at Eve's house. She'd bought the treats for herself, but when Eve opened the door, stiff and unsmiling, Maggie pocketed the condoms and handed the rest of the bag over.

"I thought you might want to know for sure," Maggie said.

Eve accepted the bag like it might be a bomb. Warily, she reached in and pulled out the First Response box. "Where did you get this?"

"I needed a walk."

"There's no way you walked to Larkin and back."

"I ran into Sam. He gave me a ride."

"Did you tell him what you were buying?"

"Of course not."

They stood in silence on either side of Eve's patio door.

"The other stuff in there is just for, you know, eating your emotions," Maggie said. "If you want. Also an apology. I'm sorry I didn't tell you earlier that Daniel and I were in touch. He asked me not to, and I was trying to respect his wishes."

"And saving it up for when it would hurt me most."

"I wasn't. I'm sorry that's how it happened. It just came out that way because—because I felt so hurt. But there's no excuse. I was mean. I'm sorry."

Eve fidgeted with the paper bag. "I have a lot of questions about how the hell the two of you got to know each other, but I guess that's not the most urgent thing going on right now."

"You used my phone to contact him. Back at the beginning."

"Ah. Right. Fuck."

"I'm sorry."

Eve rifled through the bag, not looking at Maggie. "I was mean too."

"For the most accurate results you're supposed to take the test in the morning," Maggie said. She turned and shuffled the length of the deck. At the top step she looked back. "Karl's condoms. They were really expired?"

"By three years."

"Well. That explains that."

Eve nodded. "Yeah." She held out the package of cookies. "Here. Keep a little emotion-eating for yourself."

In the morning Maggie walked back to Eve's house. Flora stood at the door, tail wagging in anticipation of company.

"I didn't know if you'd already be at work," Maggie said when Eve opened the door.

"I'm slow this morning. Didn't have the best sleep."

"Me neither."

Eve pulled the kettle from the stove, dumped it, filled its mouth with clean water. "You can come in."

The door clicked closed. Maggie stood just inside.

"I never asked you," Eve said. "Are you a coffee drinker? Because I haven't got any."

"It's okay. I'm through withdrawals by now."

On the stove the kettle thrummed and gurgled.

"This big fight and we don't even know if I'm pregnant," Eve said. "We should have saved getting mad until we knew for sure."

"So you haven't taken it yet?"

"I don't particularly want to." Eve took a box of Earl Grey down from her cupboard. "It's ridiculous. And unfair. You're the one who's always known for sure that you want to be a mother. You've gone through this terrible loss."

So Eve *wasn't* sure she wanted to be a mother. Was possibly not even going to keep this maybe-baby. Maggie spoke the words she'd been reminding herself of for the past eighteen hours. "It's not your fault."

"Wouldn't Karl be thrilled to know how virile he is."

"How virile he *might* be."

"I shouldn't have told you anything yesterday. It was insensitive."

"You didn't tell me. I guessed." Maggie pressed one toe into the heel of the opposite shoe, kicked it off, did the same with the other. She moved to the stove. "You go take the test. I'll make the tea."

"You know I'd rather make the tea," Eve said. "And have no test to take at all."

Maggie took the tea bag from Eve's hand. "If that test is positive, you have options. You won't become a mother today. Or tomorrow, or next month, or ever, if you don't want to. At this moment you are nothing but a woman standing in her kitchen."

"About to take a pregnancy test."

"About to take a pregnancy test."

"Alone. A single woman alone, about to take a pregnancy test."

"If you hadn't noticed," Maggie said, "I'm here. Unless you'd rather I left?"

"No," Eve said. "I'm glad you're here. Really."

She didn't look at Maggie as she passed through the kitchen to the bathroom. Maggie busied herself searching the cupboards, choosing the prettiest from Eve's selection of mugs, waiting for the shriek of the kettle.

By the time the tea had steeped, they would know whether Eve was pregnant.

Maggie's whole body was charged with tension. *Please let it be negative. Please, universe.* Eve didn't want this, she was pretty sure. Maggie didn't want this. The test needed to be negative.

The bathroom door opened and Eve walked out, the stick in her right hand. Wordlessly she handed it over to Maggie. The two lines were strong, almost fuchsia in their depth and brilliance. Fuchsia and undeniable.

Chapter 22

Eve

"Do you want to talk about it?" Maggie asked. Then, more quietly, "Do you want me to leave?"

Eve was sitting on her deck, a cup of tea and the positive pregnancy test in front of her, staring blankly between both. She'd called Sam to let him know she wouldn't be coming to work. That task completed, she didn't seem capable of action or coherent thought.

"Not unless you want to leave," Eve said. "If you do, I won't blame you."

Maggie sat down across from her. "I'm staying if you want me to stay."

"I think I'm in shock," Eve said. "I suspected, but I didn't really believe my suspicion."

"Give yourself time."

"Do I have time, though? I must be at least two months along!"

"Or more," Maggie said apologetically. "Because of the way gestation is calculated."

Eve stared at her blankly.

"At the moment of conception, you're actually already two weeks pregnant."

"What? How does that make any sense?"

"I know. They count pregnancy from the date of your last period. Even though you're not actually pregnant yet." Maggie pulled out her phone. "We can figure it out if you want, though. Facts are grounding, right? Do you know when your last period was?"

"Uh . . ." Eve had already tried to pinpoint that date, but she hadn't been tracking. "I do know when I last had sex."

"Okay. That helps."

"Come on, Maggie. This is too much. You don't have to do this. I can figure it out on my own." Or maybe she couldn't, because she'd had no idea you were two weeks pregnant the second you conceived.

"But you don't have to. Unless you want to."

If there was one thing Eve knew, it was that she did not want to be on her own with this.

"It was the Friday before I got your email," Eve said. "The weekend before I broke up with him."

"And you haven't been with anyone since Karl?"

"No, Doctor Dunn, I have not. Where would I find someone to sleep with around here?"

Maggie smiled. "Guest at Sam's? Some strapping fisherman?"

"If only."

"Hey." Maggie reached across the table and wrapped one hand around Eve's. "It's going to be okay."

That was not something Maggie could possibly know—look what had happened to *her*—but Eve still felt comforted.

They figured out that Eve was roughly eleven weeks pregnant, nearing the end of her first trimester, due in January.

How had she been so disconnected from her body? How had she not known?

All day and into the next, the words looped endlessly through Eve's brain. *Pregnant. I'm pregnant.*

I'm having a baby was incomprehensible. It was also, possibly, untrue. The number to call to make it untrue was on a notepad by her bed. For now, *I'm pregnant* was astounding enough.

She wasn't nauseated, only tired, with a heightened awareness of the food she put into her mouth, of the air she breathed, of herself as incubator, vessel, home of more than her own self. A bizarre and fearsome reality.

I'm pregnant.

She tried on scenarios. *I call the number on the notepad. I drive to Sudbury, I attend an appointment, I return home. Life continues exactly as before.*

Soon. She had to do this soon. Like, yesterday. But the prospect did not entirely fill her with relief. What was "before"? From the moment she received Maggie's email, her life had been upended. Apart from her safe, low-stress job, she wasn't even sure what her life was anymore—or what she wanted it to be.

Scenario two: She called a different number. She booked a different appointment. She listened to a heartbeat, watched her belly grow, became unrecognizable to herself. In a matter of months, a human being emerged from her body and Eve became wholly responsible for a life that was not her own.

This scenario was terrifying. But she was starting to wonder if it could be terrifying in a good way. Terrifying the way growth was terrifying. Terrifying the way leaving a comfort zone was terrifying.

Twice more Karl's name had appeared on her call display, and Eve had watched it there for as long as the phone continued to ring. She hadn't mentioned the calls to Maggie—Maggie, who'd practically risked her life in hopes of talking to Karl, and now here he was and Eve wasn't giving him to her.

She remembered clearly her one conversation with Karl about parenthood. They'd just made it through a run of whitewater, and he'd raised his paddle and whooped, leaned toward her in the bow, and declared, "This, right here, is the reason I never want to have kids."

She'd laughed. "Whitewater?"

He said, "Freedom."

She didn't tell him that she sometimes wondered what it would be like, that depth of belonging and care, another human being who came from you, to whom you were inextricably bound. Sometimes when she pictured it she felt a quiet tug of desire; other times she couldn't even imagine choosing the actions required to make that picture real. She'd never landed on a firm decision, never before been in a relationship solid enough (so she thought) to consider it. Though even in her relationship with Karl she wasn't facing the question head-on—she was already past forty when they met, and she didn't crave motherhood enough to undergo whatever invasive fertility treatment would probably be required. And yet she still wondered what if; she still entertained fantasies. She'd been a loner for so much of her life—what would it be like to devote herself to the care and well-being of a person she loved more deeply than she'd ever loved before?

And now she was pregnant and Karl was calling, like he had some sixth sense for the havoc he'd wreaked and was circling back to survey the damage. Or the blessing, depending on how you looked at it.

She had to figure out what she wanted with the pregnancy before she brought Karl into it. *If* she brought Karl into it. Because—*could* he be part of this hypothetical child's life? Would he even want to be, if Eve decided that allowing him near a child wouldn't be completely negligent and that she was willing to interact with him for the next eighteen years? She couldn't see him shouldering this responsibility or imagine how she'd co-parent with a person she couldn't trust, but she needed to at least tell him. Didn't she? When? Not until she was sure she was having it, which she wasn't.

The questions overwhelmed her, looping back to where they'd started. She couldn't decide about Karl until she'd decided about the baby. She couldn't decide about the baby without considering Karl.

When the phone rang, Eve let it ring.

The day after the test, as Eve was dressing for work, Maggie knocked on the door and announced that she was here to cook her the most delicious omelette Eve had ever tasted.

"I'll leave if you say the word," Maggie said, cracking eggs into a porcelain bowl.

"Are you kidding?" Eve said. "I've been cooking for you for two months; I am definitely not refusing breakfast."

"No, I mean leave Still Lake."

Eve was surprised how disappointed she felt. More than disappointed—distressed. "Really?"

"I'm pretty much recovered, and there's honestly no reason for me to be at Still Lake anymore," Maggie said. "Obviously the whole situation between us is messy, and I know I might just complicate things for you. My friend Charmaine is convinced we're in some kind of codependent trauma-bond two-person cult, and maybe she has a point? It's . . . not exactly straightforward."

"Do you really think that?" Eve didn't even know how to name what she was feeling. It might be panic—at the rejection looming in Maggie's words, at the prospect of being alone with this massive decision.

"No," Maggie said, and Eve's relief was palpable. "But we should get a couple of things out in the open. Such as, I feel like maybe you might have a hard time trusting me because of the whole Daniel thing."

"Oh," Eve said. "No. I mean, yeah, I was upset about that, but I get that you were trying to respect his wishes."

"I hated keeping it from you," Maggie said. "I need you to know that. Given the state Daniel was in and the fact that he's your brother, I thought I needed to let him take the lead on when to tell you. But I feel shitty about how it went down."

This did still rankle, especially because Eve herself had yet to speak to Daniel, did not even know for herself what state he was in.

But she could objectively see that Maggie hadn't kept their friendship from her out of malice—the secret had been ill-advised, maybe, but not ill-intentioned, and she didn't want this to be a new wedge between them.

"I appreciate that," Eve said.

"If you need your space and you want to just deal with the pregnancy on your own, I'll understand," Maggie said. "I do need to restart my life sometime. As you've pointed out."

"Forget I said that."

"Well, it's true."

"I don't hate it, you know," Eve said. "The thought of you moving here and us going into business together."

"You don't?" Maggie paused mid-whisk. "Because you did a pretty good impression of a person who hates it."

"I know. It's just a lot of change to consider at once. I need a minute."

"It's definitely not the priority right now."

"Do *you* hate it now? Because I would understand if you wanted to leave now that . . . you know."

"Look at us being all mutually understanding," Maggie said. "We should get a friendship medal."

A friendship medal! Because she and Maggie were *friends*. Eve leaned on the island beside Maggie, watching as she tipped her egg mixture into a frying pan. She felt surprisingly emotional.

"If I'd been through what you've been through," Eve said, "I'd want nothing to do with me right now."

"That'd be pretty petty, wouldn't it?"

"It would be human."

They were quiet as Maggie finished cooking the omelette. She motioned Eve to the table and set it in front of her, huge and fluffy, thick with mushrooms and tomatoes.

"I've accepted it," Maggie said. "I want to be here for you, if you want me to."

"Please stay," Eve said. "At least for a bit. I'd rather not be alone right now."

Maggie smiled. "You got it."

It was the best omelette Eve had ever tasted.

Before she left for work, Eve walked the path to the lodge and gazed up at the depressed log buildings, unused, waiting. The thought of going into business again had always caused a clenching around her heart; all she'd been able to see was herself lost in inauthentic PR, buried under paperwork and the demands of stressed-out people. It was what she had escaped, along with the city and Danlet. But who said it had to be that way? With a partner, with the benefit of experience, with the conscious intention to create balance and to approach the work on her own terms, couldn't she create a different outcome?

She knew she could make the lodge beautiful. She could design new furniture, build it for herself, for the joy and satisfaction of creating a useful and lovely object. Maggie could network with collaborators, design their offerings, create an atmosphere of welcome and ease. This could be a place for community, for healing, for renewal and unlikely alliances.

And there could be a child at the center of it all. At Eve's side, welcoming guests. Playing with Flora, inventing underwater languages in the lake, sitting in a bucket of cold water in the sauna until she could stand the heat full strength. Pestering or enchanting the guests with her curiosity and joie de vivre—because her mind's eye had already conjured a little girl, a pixie with Eve's dark hair in two braids down her back but, somehow, Maggie's personality. Talkative and trusting and large-hearted, a person Eve already found herself wanting to know, to care for, to nurture into the fullness of all she could become.

Eve filled the next few days with two areas of research: what she could expect in the coming months of pregnancy, birth, and life with a newborn; and what she could expect financially and practically in the next several years if she became the co-owner of a derelict lakeside lodge and took on the burden of transforming it into something new. Eve was keeping her lodge considerations quiet for now—she didn't want to get Maggie's hopes up or be overly influenced by her enthusiasm—but with the pregnancy, Maggie was being unfailingly, astonishingly supportive. Which was part of the reason Eve could see them as business partners: because Eve had some inkling of what it was costing Maggie to be this close to her pregnancy, and still she was showing up for her. Eve already knew that owning a business was a huge challenge she didn't want to undertake alone; now she also knew that Maggie was a caring and responsible person who would set aside her own feelings to be there through a challenge.

The pregnancy and the retreat center were beginning to feel linked in her mind. Two keystones of the purpose-filled life Eve could step into if she chose.

Because if she had a kid of her own, what kind of example did she want to set? Did she want to be someone who walled herself off and played it safe? Or someone who was willing to take risks and let people in to build a meaningful livelihood and a meaningful life?

Four days after the pregnancy test, Daniel called.

"I should have contacted you long before now," he said. "I'm sorry."

"*I'm* sorry. I'm *really* sorry." Eve was so shocked and relieved to hear his voice that *sorry* was all she could say, over and over. "About Violet. About not being there for you."

"Maggie told me she spilled the beans about us texting. And she told me you needed me. I finally got over myself and picked up the phone."

"Wow. Well . . . thank you, Maggie."

"I was still pretty mad when I reached out to you ages ago. But I was desperate to talk to someone who really knew me . . . and then talking with Maggie helped, and things still felt fucked up between you and me, and I was putting off having this conversation I thought I'd already had. I've been in survival mode, but still—I put it off too long. I'm sorry I didn't tell you I was talking to Maggie. And that I made her keep it from you. That really was my fault."

Eve slid the patio door open and settled into a chair on the deck. "I guess it's good you've got, you know, whatever support you can get."

He laughed. "You hate it."

"It's just weird!"

"So you forgive me?"

"Yes. I just want us to be okay. Are we okay?"

"Yeah. We're okay." He paused. "I hated not having you at the funeral. I've hated feeling cut off from you. But I hate everything in my life right now, so it all blended together. But I miss you."

"Are you all right?"

"I have my coping strategies. I give myself half an hour every day to cry and yell. I listen to podcasts when I get tired of the inside of my own head. I work a lot."

"And you text Maggie."

"I just lost a wife. She just lost a baby. There's a certain wavelength, I guess."

Eve couldn't help it; she felt dismayed. "You do know who she is, right?"

"I know she's your other woman."

"*Karl's* other woman. Who didn't lose a baby, by the way, she lost a nonviable fetus." She kicked herself for the harsh phrasing—she was only just getting Daniel back; she could try harder to prove that she was becoming more open-hearted. (Wasn't she?)

"That often makes no difference. Emotionally."

"Of course. I know. She's been through a lot. I'm just saying, her situation is not on par with your wife's sudden tragic death."

"You can't judge somebody's grief, Eve. There isn't a hierarchy. Christ."

She slumped back into her Adirondack chair. Was she destined to be a terrible, uncaring mother? Would Daniel even give a damn that *she* was pregnant if he was so fixated on Maggie's loss and his grief support group of two? Would she never stop comparing herself and her situation to Maggie's?

"Has Maggie told you anything about what's going on with me?" Eve asked.

"She says you've been a lifesaver."

"Anything else?"

"You've become real friends," Daniel said.

"Anything else?"

"She did say you needed me, so how about you go ahead and tell me what's on your mind?"

A great blue heron took off from Still Lake, its enormous wings commanding the air, a trail of disturbed water rippling behind it. Eve watched until it was gone. She said, "Do you think I could be a good mom?"

"Holy shit, what are you saying?"

"I'm just asking. Do you think I have it in me?"

"Absolutely. You're one of the most competent people I know."

"But I'm not a nurturer. I could fuck a kid up. Don't you think?"

"As far as I can tell, that's basically what parents *do*. You'd try your best."

"That does not inspire confidence."

Daniel laughed. "Are these questions theoretical, or is this how you're letting me know I'm becoming an uncle?"

"I'm serious. I need to know this answer from you."

"Are you worried you'll be like Mom? Overwhelmed or depressed or overly dependent on your kids or naggy and bitter or all of the above?"

"I don't know. Maybe."

"You have awareness. If any of that happened, you'd get support. Right?"

"I guess. Yes."

"You're a thoughtful and conscientious person. You're practical and capable. If you want to be a mother, you'll be a good one."

"You mean that?"

"I do. Any kid would be lucky to have you."

Eve couldn't stop the smile from creeping across her face. "I'm pregnant," she said.

"For real?"

"Does that change your answer?"

"No! Evie, I think that's amazing."

"You do?"

"Yes!"

"There's no father in the picture—or at least, that part's complicated."

"It's Karl?" Daniel asked.

"Unfortunately."

"Damn."

"I'm still trying to figure out the me-as-mother part, so maybe we could not talk about him for now."

"It really sounds like you want this baby. Right? Who cares about Karl—do *you* want it?"

And it struck her as astounding. That faithless Karl had impregnated both her *and* Maggie. That Maggie was her friend. That Maggie was Daniel's friend. That Eve, who'd accepted that she was probably never having a baby, was having a baby. Because she was pretty sure she'd decided to have the baby.

"Yeah," she said. "I think I do. I do want it."

He whooped. "I should come congratulate you in person!" he said. "I've just taken a lot of time off, so I couldn't get away for long, but I could swing a weekend getaway. You know of any lodges on any lakes anywhere?"

Chapter 23

Maggie

"We should call for an initial appointment as soon as possible," Maggie said, her arms around Eve, five seconds after Eve told her she was keeping the baby. Maggie sprang from the hug and stood on tiptoes to reach the old phone book on the top of Eve's fridge, took it to the dining table, and began leafing through it. "Have you given any thought to what kind of practitioner you want? I know you said you don't have a doctor here yet, but you can call a midwifery clinic directly if you want to go that route. Everyone else with your due date will have booked a couple of months ago already, so we might need to call around. In the meantime, I can find out what prenatal vitamin Charmaine used—I know she did a bunch of research—and if you want, I can show you some easy prenatal yoga poses?"

Eve laughed. "Wow. You are *ready* for this."

"Sorry," Maggie said. She did feel a bit manic, but whether she was just excited or overcompensating for her less pure, more complicated emotions, she wasn't sure.

"And also"—Eve smiled—"*we*? You keep saying *we*."

Maggie pushed the phone book toward Eve. "*You*. Obviously, you'll be calling."

"Please," Eve said. "You have no idea how relieved I am that I don't have to figure all this stuff out on my own. But I do have to tell you something."

Maggie eyed Eve warily. What else could there possibly be?

"Karl's been calling me," Eve said.

Ohhh. *Him.*

"I didn't tell you because I didn't want to make things weird between us again when it's finally a little less weird," Eve said, smiling slightly. "But he's called three times. I haven't talked to him."

"He emailed me," Maggie said. "And I didn't tell you because—same reason, I guess."

"Wow. Think he's back and trying to pick up where he left off?"

"We could have some fun with that. String him along for a while."

Eve laughed. "Then twist the knife just when he's confident he's getting away with it again."

"Not sure how I'd explain the fact that I basically live up here now, though."

Eve sat down beside Maggie at the dining table. "I feel like I have to talk to him sometime," she said. "But—do I? Can I just not tell him till after the baby's born? Because honestly, even if I'm already three months along, anything could still happen. If *you're* geriatric for pregnancy, that must make me ancient. So we don't actually know that everything's going to work out here."

Maggie shook her head. "You have to believe it will. But for sure you could wait. This is a big deal for you, and it's your body. Adding Karl into the mix will make everything more complicated."

"How about if I never tell him about the baby, ever?"

"I mean—you could," Maggie said. "Until they both decide to get genetic testing just for fun."

"Yeah, probably not the most ethical approach."

"Keeping it from him would serve him right, though."

"But would it be best for the kid?" Eve asked.

"Yeah, it maybe would. You want *Karl* influencing your child's values?"

Through the open patio door, the summer breeze wafted fresh off the lake, and Maggie shot a quick flaming arrow into the water. Of course a conversation about talking to Karl needed to prioritize Eve's baby—he was the baby's father. Eve had real issues to consider, and Maggie's dismay that they could no longer trash-talk him on equal terms was indefensible. Maggie was here for Eve, she *was* excited about this baby—she really was—and she could make herself exceedingly helpful with all things pregnancy-related. She could and she would. Even if this baby shared DNA with *her* baby. Even if part of her wished it actually were her baby.

She turned briskly back to the Yellow Pages. "You need to think about getting internet here, but unless this info has changed since"—she inspected the front cover—"2010, there are two midwifery practices in Sudbury."

Eve peered over Maggie's shoulder. "And what are the reasons to choose a midwife versus a doctor?"

"If you're not high-risk—and you're already older and it's your first, so it's possible—but if you're not, and you want a natural birth and a lot of autonomy over your choices, I'd go with a midwife."

"How do you know this stuff?"

"Charmaine's pregnancies. Also, I've been known to lurk on pregnancy Reddit. Even before."

Eve shook her head. "You and I are very different people."

"Yes." Maggie reached for Eve's cordless phone and started dialing. "I think we've confirmed that."

Over the next week, with some gentle nudging, Eve took Maggie up on almost everything she offered. Maggie ordered the prenatal vitamins, took over laundry duty, and borrowed the truck for the weekly grocery shop, long on saltines and ginger ale. She had noticed Eve scratching, and Eve admitted when Maggie asked that her skin had recently become dry and itchy, and Maggie added organic fragrance-free lotion to the list.

When Maggie returned with the groceries and found Eve collapsed on the couch, staring at the ceiling, she fed her the saltines and then insisted on the one form of assistance Eve was still resisting: yoga.

Eve glared at her. "I'm too tired to *stand*."

"This will help."

"How weird is it that I've been exhausted for months but managed to push myself to do all kinds of things, and now that I know *why* I'm exhausted I can barely move?"

"I think that makes some psychological sense. Like you have official permission to rest now. It's kind of your job."

"So can I just do that?"

"Of course. From what I hear, the exhaustion will lift once you're in the second trimester, but if you do want to try some yoga now, I promise it'll be super gentle."

Eve groaned. "Fine."

Maggie ran to the lodge for her yoga mat, used a cushion for a makeshift bolster, and took Eve through supported bridge, cat-cow, and a modified pigeon, gently adjusting her into alignment as Eve's grumbles turned into laughter and finally silence. At the end Eve lay in savasana on her living room floor, and Maggie thought she'd fallen asleep until she opened her eyes and looked up at Maggie with a serious expression.

"I'm a little scared of how much I'm already relying on you," she said.

"Don't be scared," Maggie said. "I'm here as long as you want me."

"It's just so much," Eve said, closing her eyes again. "All of it."

"You mean what I'm doing? Or what you're doing?"

"Both."

"I think it's normal to feel overwhelmed," Maggie said. "And it's definitely normal to need support."

"It just makes me feel—vulnerable, you know?"

"You are a bit," Maggie said. "You're incubating a human. It's a delicate process."

Maggie's voice caught on her last word, and Eve stretched out a hand to her. Maggie took it, then pulled away to go to her bag, retrieving a pair of tiny socks and a notebook.

"I got you a couple of other things," she said, handing them over as Eve sat up on the mat. "The socks are so you can start envisioning the little person who's on their way. Maybe I'm jumping the gun on clothes shopping, but I wanted you to have one small thing. And the notebook is for if you need a place to sort through your thoughts or record milestones or write to the baby or—you know. Anything."

She didn't know if this was something Eve would do, but she knew it was what she, Maggie, would do, if she were still having a baby.

Eve accepted the socks and the notebook, staring down at them in her hands. "How is it possible for feet to be this tiny?" she asked. "Are you sure these aren't for a doll?"

"Genuine baby socks," Maggie said.

"You're remarkable, you know that?" Eve said. "Thank you."

The next day, Maggie went with Eve to her first midwife appointment. They were waiting together on two upholstered chairs in the clinic's waiting room. A whiteboard on an easel listed names, birthdates, and birth weights of recent arrivals. The woman across from Maggie had an enormous belly and a man at her side. He turned her hand in his, the diamond on her finger reflecting light.

Eve slouched to bring her mouth to Maggie's ear. "So this money you have coming to you," she said.

Maggie turned in her chair, crossing her legs under her so her whole body faced Eve. "Yes?"

"I have a couple of questions. How much are we talking about exactly, and when do you get it, and are you serious about sinking it into Bernice's lodge?"

"When have you had the bandwidth to even consider this?"

"I've been thinking about the future, for obvious reasons," Eve said. "Keeping my life as stable as possible right now might be more logical, but I won't quit my job tomorrow. We can hire a contractor to do most of the work, and by the time we're ready to open the retreat center, the baby will be a couple of years old anyway. But it wouldn't happen without you. And I don't mean just financially."

"The money is contingent on me completing my Ph.D., which I've been spectacularly failing to do."

"But you *are* doing it?"

"Definitely. I need to buckle down and focus, but once I do, I might only need a few months. Four or five? I could be done by the time the baby's here. But to be clear, I don't have anything to contribute now."

"That's okay. I have money invested from selling Stillcraft, so I can handle things for a while, just not forever. We'd have to sit down and look at numbers, and we'd have to talk to Bernice."

"You're serious about this."

"I am. So I need to know—are you? Because the main thing I've figured out is that this will be a money pit. First we have to buy it, then the renovation will be huge, and then we'll need to fund daily operations until it gets on its feet and starts making money—if it starts making money—and all of that will take years."

"I've been thinking about it too," Maggie said. "I didn't want to push you, because obviously you've got a lot going on right now, but I've found a couple of gorgeous retreat centers online and they've sparked so many ideas. I contacted the owner of one to see if she'd be willing to speak with me about her experience."

"Look at you, sneaking around behind my back."

A bell above the door jangled and a woman entered with an infant strapped to her chest. The baby opened its mouth in a rosebud yawn. The mother cupped her palm against its fuzzy skull as she bent to greet the receptionist. That was going to be Eve. In a matter of months, Eve would be that woman.

"And you're sure you're up for this whole thing?" Eve was looking at the mother and baby too.

Maggie had meditated. She'd shot her flaming arrows. "I'm sure," she said. "Are *you* sure? About the retreat center and—me?"

"What I know is that I honestly want to try this," Eve said.

A door opened and they could see through it to a bed, an armchair, a basket of plush toys, a bulbous Venus of Willendorf on a shelf.

A woman came into the waiting room. "Eve?"

Eve stood and the woman offered her hand.

"I'm Abby. Will you come with me?"

"I'll wait here," Maggie said.

Eve started to follow Abby, then turned and strode back to Maggie, stopping and speaking quietly just to her. "So far you're the closest this baby's got to a second parent," she said. "You might as well come the rest of the way."

Maggie took one more look at the cozy, maternal room beyond Eve, superimposing onto it an alternate reality in which she was the one crossing that threshold, shaking that midwife's hand, settling onto that bed to begin her new life.

Then she rose and placed an arm across Eve's back, and they entered the room together.

On a thorough inspection with Sam Labelle a few days after the first midwife appointment, they discovered a pipe that had leaked long enough to cause substantial rot, and Eve decided the dining hall would be the place to start renovations. They also learned why the lodge had remained unsold for so long: Due to the condition of the property, it was unmortgageable. No lender would take it on, and any buyer had to be in a position to pay cash. Fortunately, Eve was. Money for renovations would be tight until Maggie could buy her half, so Eve decided to hold off on hiring a contractor, but there was enough cleanup and repair they could tackle on their own before then. They spoke with Bernice. Eve contacted a real estate lawyer and her investment advisor. After a flurry of logistics and paperwork, the lodge was theirs.

The day of the signing, Maggie and Eve went to the dining hall for a ceremonial groundbreaking in the form of destroying the floor.

"Karl!" Maggie yelled with her first smash of rotting wood.

"Cheaters!" Eve picked up the chant.

"Deadbeats!"

Ever since Maggie had caught that fish, this back-and-forth chorus was a bit they liked to incorporate whenever they found the chance. It was surprisingly satisfying, a new reality they were creating—or an old one they were dismantling—by raising their voices together. Hacking out the dining hall floor was more gratifying than anything Maggie had ever done—a real-life rage room. She propped her phone on a windowsill to record it. She'd already made a retreat center Instagram account and planned to document the entire renovation, growing a community and building excitement about what they were creating so they'd have a fan base well before they were ready for guests.

Eve had found a trio of restless teens staying the month at Labelle's Cabins and eager to earn money, and they came daily to clean up the buildings. Maggie filmed that too. With each room scrubbed fresh, each soggy cardboard box or stack of outdated fishing magazines dragged to the dumpster, the retreat center Maggie had seen in her mind's eye was becoming more and more real.

Maggie convinced Eve to install internet, and in the second week of ownership they set up command central in the common room, where Maggie was throwing herself wholeheartedly into research and development, covering pages with ideas on their focus and branding and the programs they should offer, growing the Insta account, reaching out to introduce herself and Eve to people she'd identified as possible collaborators. Sometime soon Maggie would return to Toronto to clear out her belongings. She would keep living in her room at the lodge, the on-site host when they began receiving guests. They planned a grand opening two summers from now, giving them almost two years to complete the renovation and set up the business. By the time they opened, Eve's baby would be a toddler.

But all of this depended on Maggie finishing her dissertation. Because, technically, it was only Eve who had bought Bernice's lodge, only Eve's name on the deed, and Maggie's funds would be required before they could finalize any of these plans. So she was also dedicating three hours every day to working on her dissertation. This was hardly enough time, especially when she spent the first of those hours shaking off the film of failure and shame that coated the project, then meditating to quiet her resistance. She'd taken the entire dissertation apart and it was now in more messy fragments than the lodge. She was antsy with every moment spent staring at a computer instead of working on the retreat center, moving words around in a document that felt increasingly pointless.

"Are you sure?" Charmaine had asked Maggie so many times, in one form or another—about not even trying to use her degree, about leaving Toronto permanently, about moving up north, about partnering with Eve, about being around for the birth and growth and life of Karl's kid—that Maggie finally had to get her on a FaceTime and say, gently but firmly, that yes, she was sure about all of it.

"Even this baby?" Charmaine asked, her eyes narrowing in concern.

Maggie had just gone with Eve to her second trimester ultrasound, her heart pounding as she watched the grainy image, the rounded skull and tiny nose, the mouth opening and closing right there in front of them. "Do you want to know the sex?" the technician had asked, and Eve, unsure beforehand, looked at Maggie and back at the technician and said, "Yes." The baby was female. Female, healthy, safely nestled inside Eve's uterus, where she belonged.

Afterward Maggie had to retreat to the bathroom to cry. But she was feeling and releasing the grief. She was moving forward despite it.

To Charmaine she said emphatically, "*Yes*. Even this baby."

Charmaine nodded slowly. "Okay. I believe you."

Now, halfway through September, one month into their ownership of a future retreat center, five months into Eve's pregnancy,

Maggie sat back on her heels to survey the hardwood boards that stretched nearly to the center of the dining hall. She spread her whole body out on the smooth new surface, floating her arms along the hardwood as though making snow angels. She couldn't believe that an object as tangible and practical as a surface to walk across had resulted from the labor of her own hands. Compared to the endless mental toil of a dissertation that nobody needed, building a floor was so *useful.*

"We should bring the *Truth Landing* painting in here so she can bless our efforts," Maggie said toward the ceiling.

"Or judge them," Eve said.

"She doesn't judge, she only challenges you in the direction you need to go. Plus, maybe she'll give us some of her arm strength for all this hammering."

Together they wrangled her down the stairs and set her up next to the Karl jar. Maggie had finally made one, a large Mason jar wrapped in strips from Karl's neon-orange moisture-wicking hiking shirt—one that both she and Eve, it turned out, had loathed on sight. Eve had found it under her bed and suggested a bonfire; instead, Maggie had gleefully shredded it. Eve had thrown her head back in a full-body laugh when Maggie presented the jar to her.

They'd hoped to finish the dining hall floor today, but half done would have to do, because tomorrow they were receiving their first guest: Eve's brother, Daniel. Maggie's safe, beautiful, magically unreal relationship with the text stranger who understood her soul was soon to become flesh and blood, and Maggie was as anxious about that as she was excited.

"Can I borrow your truck tomorrow afternoon?" Maggie asked as they surveyed the painting in its new home. "I thought I'd go to the Larkin library and work on this grant I found."

"You can't hide at the library for Daniel's entire visit."

"I'm not hiding! But you'll want time alone with him. I don't want to be in the way."

"Thanks," Eve said. "I could insist that's not true, but we'll definitely need some space to reconnect."

"It's not too weird, me being here?"

"Maybe it will be at first. Would you rather I introduce you, or would you rather I'm not even there when you meet?"

"See, just the fact that we have to consider that means it's weird."

Eve opened her mouth to respond, then froze, surprise flickering across her face.

Maggie stepped closer. "What is it? Are you okay?"

"Yes!" Eve laughed. "The baby's kicking again. Here."

Eve took Maggie's hand and placed it on her bump. They'd tried this before, ever since Eve started feeling movement a couple of weeks ago, but none of it had been strong enough to detect from the outside. As she pressed her hand to Eve's belly, Maggie couldn't explain the yearning inside her—to feel what Eve was feeling, to get as close as possible to the center of this experience—because the desire was becoming more complicated than "I wish this were me." She was growing attached to *this* baby, this being the size of a large banana (according to the app Maggie had downloaded)—her taste buds now developed, her cartilage turning to bone, her arrival expected at the end of December or beginning of January.

"Did you feel that?" Eve asked.

There was not so much as a twitch. Eve lifted her T-shirt and repositioned Maggie's hand on her bare skin. And then, as Maggie waited, it happened: the gentlest of flutters.

Maggie gasped, her whole being flooded with awe. She pressed her face close. "Hello, baby. Hello, little love! I'm so excited to meet you."

There was one more ripple, and Maggie could have sworn it was a hello in response. She waited a moment more, then pulled away and gazed at Eve. This time, she knew the tears in her eyes were joy.

That evening Maggie met Eve on the path to the lodge, and they walked the rest of the way to the waterfront together. Bernice was laying out food on a picnic table for her own goodbye dinner—tomorrow, she'd be moving to her sister's. The sun hung low and warm. The trees were mostly still green, spots of red and yellow only just beginning to appear. Maggie sat down across from Eve.

Bernice stood at the head of the table, peeling foil from dishes, motioning to a bottle of her homemade wine. "You can have some," she told Eve. "Everyone used to."

Eve brought a water bottle to her lips. "I've already put enough of your wine into this baby."

Bernice stacked corn on the cob and fresh roasted potatoes onto their plates, thick slabs of steak, buttered green beans. She waved aside their poised forks, their polite wait for her to begin, muttering, "Eat, eat."

"I have a question," Maggie said as Bernice sat down. "The *Truth Landing* painting. Do you know who painted it?"

Bernice eyed Maggie with suspicion. "You're really interested in that painting, aren't you?" She licked her fingers before continuing. "She was an American artist who stayed at the lodge. Can't recall her name."

"What about the woman in the painting? Was she a real person?" Maggie asked.

Bernice forked potato into her mouth. Eve glanced sidelong at Maggie and they both waited while she chewed. Bernice said nothing.

"Bernice!" Maggie crowed. "She's not you, is she?"

"Naked like that? Don't be silly."

"Come on! She's smoking! Is it you? You can admit it."

"She is Truth Landing. That's what it says on the painting, isn't it?"

"You told us that was the name of the place, not the woman."

Bernice gestured behind her. "It's that way. Overgrown now."

Bernice's look was both ornery and proud. Maggie and Eve both laughed. Goddamn, the naked power woman in the painting was none other than Bernice.

"Whoever she is," Maggie said, "she's now officially our mascot. We love her."

"Except when we hate her," Eve said.

Bernice watched them. “You two will do well.”

Maggie grinned and raised her glass. “To the retreat center and to our partnership.”

Eve lifted her water bottle. Bernice reached for her glass of wine.

“You are good friends,” Bernice said. “I can tell you’ve known each other a long time.”

“Not that long, actually,” Eve said.

Bernice waved her hand. “You have. I think you have.”

Maggie and Eve exchanged a glance.

Eve said, “We’ve packed a lot in.”

Chapter 24

Eve

Daniel stepped out of a rental car onto Eve's driveway just after two o'clock on the second Friday of September. His smile inched across his face, and he dropped his bag and held out both arms for her. In four months he had visibly aged, new, careworn lines on his face, a deeper expression behind his eyes.

"Daniel," Eve said. "You look—"

"Like shit?"

"Like you need three months at Still Lake, not three days."

"*You*, on the other hand, look great," he said. "About twenty years old."

"I do not. I'm a pregnant forty-three-year-old woman. I look forty-three."

He nodded, solemn. "But you seem different."

She'd dressed for Daniel's arrival in a teal tank top and a flowing grey skirt Maggie had convinced her to buy on a thrifting trip. Eve needed these new clothes because she was burgeoning—her breasts abundant, her belly protesting the limits of every pair of pants she owned. She was tall enough that she had lots of space for her new weight to be distributed—and according to Abby, she was carrying high, which made the bump less visible—so even now, at twenty-one weeks, the pregnancy wasn't obvious if she wore loose clothing. But to Eve, the changes were written all over her body.

"It happens more than you'd expect," Abby had reassured her two months ago when Eve's first ultrasound confirmed that she was twelve weeks pregnant and had spent most of those weeks with no idea. But Eve was done with things happening to her without her knowledge, and she was trying to make up for her unawareness by paying extra attention to the developments in her body and her baby now. She still didn't know what to do with the fact that, come winter, a living person would emerge from her and expect her to meet its every need, but she was becoming less anxious and more excited about it. A baby had made eye contact with her in a store the other day, and Eve had experienced a sudden upwelling of joyful anticipation for the day her own baby would look at her like that.

Daniel held his hand above her belly. "May I?"

She took his hand and placed it there.

"You know how excited Mom is about this baby, right?" Daniel asked.

"Oh yes. She's calling to give unsolicited advice and ask for updates daily."

"Sorry."

"I think even Dad's pretty thrilled about becoming a grandpa. He called me the other day to talk on the phone. I don't even remember the last time he called."

"Dad's good with young kids."

"Older ones, on the other hand . . ."

Daniel gave her a sympathetic look.

"It's fine," Eve said. "I'm due to let go of some grudges."

"So when are you telling the jackass who did this to you?"

She laughed. "Soon. But honestly, with Maggie here, I barely feel like a single mother. She comes with me to every appointment. She thinks of everything I could possibly need before I know I need it."

He nodded. "Good. So you're feeling okay generally?"

"The hormones are wild," she said. "I cried more this summer than in my entire life combined."

"So did I. Now we can do it together."

They walked to the house, arms slung across each other's shoulders, their paces matched. She could feel his surreptitious glances as she showed him around, his expectation that Maggie might materialize through the trees at any moment, and she sighed and punched him on the arm. "She's gone to Larkin."

"Okay," he said. "That's fine."

"She told me you two aren't in contact as much as you were." Eve had been relieved—their relationship made her uncomfortable in a way that felt petty to admit; the feeling of replacement was all too familiar, and the sooner they ceased to be mini deities to each other, the better.

"I guess we're both getting busy, getting on with life," he said. "I can't wait to see this retreat center you're making together."

"You're staying in it. Come on, I'll bring you over now. It doesn't look like much yet, but it will."

Eve walked him through the dining hall first, showing him the half-finished floor and the views through the wide windows, then took him to get settled in the room beside Maggie's. After he unpacked, they went back to Eve's house, swam, cooked dinner together, then sat on her deck until the sun sank behind the trees on the other side of the lake. Talking, not talking. He seemed both familiar and alien, the same easy manner and quick turns toward seriousness that she'd grown up beside, but deepened and altered into a man she didn't entirely know. A grieving man.

I am not losing you again, she said to him in her head. He reached between their chairs and grasped her hand. Maybe the twin telepathy was finally kicking in.

The next morning Eve rose early to prepare breakfast. Paper-thin crepes, strawberries and bananas, whipped cream, maple syrup. Bacon, slices of cantaloupe, tea and freshly squeezed orange juice. She sang along to oldies on the radio as pink wisps in the sky stretched taut and disappeared, her joy palpable at all the goodness she'd made from all the wreckage.

She was setting the table on the deck when she heard murmurs and laughter in the distance and Daniel and Maggie appeared from the path through the trees. So they'd met—of course they had; Eve had sent Daniel back to the lodge on his own the night before, and their rooms were side by side. Eve watched them as they walked toward her, Maggie radiant and animated, chattering away, Daniel tall and beaming beside her.

Daniel bounded up the steps and hugged Eve. She waved them inside, pressed plates and cutlery into Daniel's hands while Maggie moved to fill mugs. Eve knelt at the fridge for the dishes of fruit, and when she returned to the deck, Daniel danced her around while she clung to the dishes and swatted him off.

"I guess someone had a good sleep," she said when he released her.

His smile was wide and sheepish. "I had a fantastic night," he said.

She caught the glance between him and Maggie. The energy buzzing between them was undeniable. So was Maggie's too-careful avoidance of him, Daniel's too-wild delight. Delight that had nothing to do with Eve, it was suddenly clear, and everything to do with her friend, who sat now at the table on Eve's deck, hands pointlessly smoothing the tablecloth, in front of Eve's lavish breakfast.

Eve was aware of motioning toward food, of Daniel heaping crepes and fruit and bacon onto his plate, of Maggie's studious focus on the mug clasped in her fingers. Eve stabbed several crepes onto her plate and slathered them in maple syrup. If her brother and her friend were getting on particularly well, she knew she should be pleased, but the current flowing across the table did not include her, and she felt only dismayed.

"This food looks amazing," Maggie said. "Look at all this! You went to so much effort!"

"Shouldn't I have?" The words came out more aggressive than Eve intended.

Maggie's eyes were wide and guilty. "No, of course," Maggie said. "It's amazing."

Fantastic. Amazing.

"I thought we could visit Sam Labelle today," Daniel said. "Sound good, Eve?"

Eve could only nod mutely. Did he think she was an idiot? Did he think she couldn't tell? *Maggie* knew that Eve knew, which was why she could barely look at Eve, but Daniel wasn't sparing her an ounce of his exclusionary joy. He prattled on for the rest of the meal, raving about how great Still Lake was and how great the retreat center would be and how great he felt being here again. After breakfast, Eve put away leftovers while Maggie and Daniel washed dishes side by side, his face bent to hers, her body inclined toward him. Eve retreated outdoors and lingered on the deck to wipe down the table, taking as long as she could away from them. Wondering if she could close her eyes and they would both just disappear.

"That was so good, Eve." Maggie stood in the doorway. "I need to work on some things this morning, and I know you two still have a ton of catching up to do, so I'm going back to the lodge now."

From inside the house, Daniel protested. Maggie gave him a quick head shake, the flash in her eye a message meant only for him. An intimate shorthand unbearable to witness.

How natural intimacy was to Maggie. Eve saw it in a blink, the attraction Maggie must have held for Karl, coping with Eve's arm's-length relating, her gladness at his weekly absences. Maggie must have opened her arms and her heart, and Karl, effortlessly, dove in.

Maggie stepped toward Eve, trying to catch her gaze. Eve turned away until Maggie crossed the deck and started down the path to the lodge.

When she'd disappeared, Daniel threw his arm across Eve's shoulders and exhaled a long, low whistle. "She's gorgeous, Eve," he said. "In every way."

"Really? Overnight, four months after your wife died, you're in love?"

"That's a bit of a jump to a conclusion, but—"

"But I'm not wrong."

"Come on, Eve. Look at me. I've been through hell. Let me have a little joy here."

"Your wife has been dead *four months*."

"One hundred and twenty-three days, to be exact. You think I don't know that?"

"You cannot do this. You can't do it to yourself, because you're not ready. And you can't do it to Maggie, because she's been through too much to have you use her for your rebound."

"And I can't do it to you either, is that what you're saying?"

"That's right."

He retrieved his arm and turned, leaning back against the rail of the deck. "You have to let me live my life. We aren't kids anymore."

"I'm aware of that, Daniel."

"You know Violet used to say I was your emotional crutch?"

Eve shifted her eyes away from him.

"You used me to fill the void, that's what she said. But also you didn't *want* a real partner in your life, because then you'd have to do the work of opening yourself up. Instead of just relying on the one default attachment handed to you at birth."

She stalked down the steps and stooped to yank weeds from her beds of rosemary, basil, thyme. "You're talking to a pregnant woman," she said. She was trembling. "That required some attachment—to a man I'm still getting over, in case you somehow missed *that*."

Her hands pulled at foliage indiscriminately. He crossed the deck and sat down on the steps near her. She refused to look at him.

"I guess you have been doing some changing these last couple years. I'm sorry."

She shrugged. "You're not wrong."

"About what?"

She straightened and wiped her hands on her thighs. "Everything."

How easy it had been for Daniel. Coming out of the divorce with the victorious parent, the one who went on living and thriving and loving instead of falling gradually to pieces in what Eve could see now was undiagnosed depression but at thirteen could interpret only as an alarming descent into passivity, surrender, despair.

Daniel had never had the same desperate need to get back to Eve. He'd done okay without her all along.

"I'm thinking of offering Maggie a lift back to Toronto," Daniel said. "She told me she's been needing to go sort things there."

"What? You're *flying* through Toronto, you're not driving. You got the rental car at the Sudbury airport."

"I can arrange to drop it in Toronto. Catch my connecting flight there."

"Daniel, please."

"I'm leaving the day after tomorrow. Not much can happen."

"Lots can happen."

"You want me to promise nothing'll happen?"

"Think what you're doing, Daniel. Four months!"

He pressed his fingers into his closed eyelids. He did look older now. She didn't think they looked the same age now at all.

"Violet," he said, "is dead." His eyes were still closed, his hands tented around them. "And every single day without her has been torture. Four months might not seem like long, but when they're four months of hell, they're very, very long. Hearing from Maggie, having Maggie to reach out to day or night, that was my one bright spot. And meeting her in person has given me my first hope that I might be able to feel happiness again. Maybe even love. If it's too soon for hope, I'm sorry, but that's what I'm feeling."

"She wants to stay single."

His eyes opened. "Forever?"

"For a year."

"I can wait a year. Realistically, I probably need to."

"I wanted you to myself for a couple of days. Just a couple of days. Is that too much to ask?"

He exhaled. "Of course not. So let's get on with the day, yeah?" His voice was heavy with disappointment and the effort to rally. "Is Sam's close enough to canoe?"

Eve was not, she knew, the person he most desired to canoe with.

"Go to Sam's without me," she said.

"Come on, Evie. Don't be like that."

"I get tired. I'll lie down for a bit, and when you're back we can hang out here."

"Eve. We only have three days together, and you just said you wanted to spend time with me."

"If I canoe to Sam's, that'll be my energy gone for the day."

"We'll drive."

"I'm there all the time."

"Not with me."

"Take Maggie with you," Eve said.

He stared her down.

She said, "Just go."

Chapter 25

Maggie

Maggie studied the prow of Eve's yellow canoe as she and Daniel glided forward on the lake toward Sam's. She had witnessed at breakfast the moment of Eve's understanding, saw it like a wreck unfolding before her. She'd tried to act normal, to disguise the fact that her body was on fire and her mind was consumed and all she could feel was the electricity between her and Daniel, but she was like a drunk person trying to hide their inebriation—*totally speaking rationally here, totally able to walk in a straight line, nothing noteworthy about me!*

But she hadn't *done* anything, she wanted to explain to Eve. They'd only talked, that was all!

The day before, she'd stayed at the library till it closed. She'd made herself a sandwich for dinner, then closed herself in her room to work. Her desk overlooked the lake, the path from Eve's house, and the hillside stairs from the beach. She'd almost convinced herself that her motives for positioning herself there were practical, professional, pure—if her desk overlooked the route Daniel would take, it was still her desk; where else was she going to work? It was after nine, nearly dark, when the sensor light at the bottom of the stairs came on, and there he was, illuminated beneath her.

She'd seen pictures of him at Eve's—matching little-kid smiles, their arms around each other in bathing suits at the lake, more recent images of an undeniably attractive man Maggie had tried not to let Eve see her checking out.

In the beam of light his face wore an openness of expression and a battle-scarred raggedness, his bearing confident but reserved. He looked gentle. He looked humble. He looked strong. From her position above him, Maggie saw him, and the tempest gathered force in her gut and she thought, *Oh no.*

She turned off her desk lamp so she could see him better. A thrill careened through her, and she clung to her mantras like inadequate life preservers: *I need time on my own. I need to find my worth inside myself. I need to not fall back into the same patterns.*

Also: *His wife just died.*

She watched his progress up the stairs until the sensor light flicked off, then closed her notebook and capped her pen, hooking it into the spiral coils. A quick rake of her fingers through her hair, a tug to straighten the belt on her sundress, and she stepped into the hallway just as Daniel crested the stairs.

He had Eve's eyes, big and almost black. Untamed curls, angular face. He smiled and she could see the widening of his brown-black eyes and feel the undercurrent as she extended her hand and it locked into his like an electrical plug into a socket.

"It's you," he said.

His smile engulfed her and she could do nothing but fall into it.

"I can't believe it's you," he said. His voice was light and low.

"I'm so glad it's you," she said.

They were just looking at each other, smiling.

From the lake, the bullfrogs began their night song, a booming call nearby, a chorus of response farther away.

He was still holding her hand, and he pulled her to him and enveloped her in a hug. "How are you feeling, really?" he asked. "Is this okay, meeting each other?"

"It's way more than okay."

"Good."

"I was nervous, though," she said into his shoulder.

He pulled back to look at her. "And now?"

"Still a bit nervous."

They exchanged a look that was deep and stirring.

"Are *you* okay?" she asked.

"You have no idea how much I've been looking forward to this."

They stepped out of the hug and stood side by side in the hallway, the silence sparking as their shoulders nearly touched.

"I'm interrupting your work," he said, looking beyond her to the desk in her room.

"Trust me, I'm happy to be interrupted. I'm trying to write a mission statement for the retreat center—you know, a pithy guiding principle." She laughed. "So far it's terrible."

"Maybe the guidance only comes with the process."

"You mean you have to start doing it before you can figure out what you're doing?"

"I don't know. I'm just trying to sound intelligent."

"You're a doctor. I'm already convinced you're intelligent."

"Phew." He widened his eyes in a parody of relief, and she laughed.

She led him to the common room and they took seats on a couch a respectable distance away from each other. They talked—about his work and hers, his journey back to Still Lake, her physical recovery, his grief recovery. Their conversation was free and easy, playful without feeling frivolous, rooted in all they knew about each other and all they'd already shared, electrified by everything still to be discovered. He was forthright and sincere. Partway through the night she was aware of their knees touching; she was pretty sure he hadn't moved, that it was her body that had migrated toward him of its own accord, but it wasn't the desperate storm she was used to. More a steady magnetic pull, a *we belong together*, a scientific fact.

He was Eve's brother. He was here for Eve. His wife had died four months ago. Maggie was staying single. He was wonderful.

Once, long past midnight, long past when Maggie had decided she'd never need to sleep or eat or drink again, they looked at each other and laughed. Saying nothing, just looking, laughing.

Sam reclined on his dock, pipe gripped between thumb and forefinger. Daniel pulled the canoe alongside and bounded from it, and he and Sam gripped each other in a bear hug.

"I'm so sorry, buddy," Sam said, and Daniel nodded wordlessly.

Maggie watched from the canoe and imagined knowing this man intimately, being more than a brand-new acquaintance observing a reunion from the outside. Daniel extended one arm toward her, and she settled her hand into his and he helped her securely onto the dock.

They trailed Sam across the property, Daniel noting changes since his last visit, Sam rambling on about weather and the vagaries of business. The vibe was altogether too sedate for the riot inside Maggie's body, her whole self thrumming, alive, uncontainable. She forced her steps to slow, trying to still herself, ground herself, and at the same time trying to accept what was so: *I am feeling these feelings. Hello, feelings.*

"So, what'll it take to convince you to move here too?" Sam was asking Daniel. "Still Lake's seduced Eve and now Maggie. Could be contagious."

Daniel was ahead of Maggie on the path and she couldn't see his face.

"I won't rule anything out," he said.

"Because I'm losing my full-time help, you know. Maggie here is poaching Eve for the competition."

"We aren't competition!" Maggie exclaimed. "Completely different demographic."

Sam winked. "All I'm saying is, I might have a job opening for you, Daniel."

"I'll polish my resumé."

"Pretty sure we've got a doctor shortage in Northern Ontario too. Pretty sure the government could finagle some incentives for you to move here."

"It's possible I wouldn't need incentives." This time, Daniel looked at Maggie, halting on the path so that she almost slammed into him. She felt his body as heat.

"That's right," Sam said. "You've got a sister here, and you've got a niece coming."

When Sam turned back to check in new arrivals, Daniel led Maggie to the cabin where he and Eve had spent their childhood summers. She stood in the center of the room, surrounded by log walls and rough-hewn furniture, the artifacts of Eve and Daniel's past that Maggie knew Eve, not Maggie, should be sharing with her brother. Daniel stepped closer to her and the heat thickened and vibrated.

"Let me take you to Toronto on Monday," he said.

If she put her hand out, she would be electrocuted.

"It should be Eve," she managed. She was certain they both knew they weren't discussing just a ride to Toronto. "She needs more time with you."

"But she doesn't need a ride to Toronto."

If I leave Still Lake with you, she thought, *Eve will feel I've hijacked your visit. If I spend four hours in close proximity in a car with you, I will fall in love with you. If I fall in love with you, I'll betray my commitments to myself.*

He held her gaze and she saw everything that would happen in the car on that drive to Toronto. They would touch. They would kiss. They would lose access to rational thought. There would be no going back.

Yes, she wanted to say. "I'll think about it," she said.

On the return trip the wind formed small whitecaps on the lake, pushing against them so that at times they were only maintaining their position rather than moving forward. Maggie dug her paddle in and focused all her strength into each heave. Halfway back, she was spent. She was relieved when Daniel pointed to a mound of rock and pine jutting from the water. "Need a break?" he asked.

He guided the canoe into a recess in the rock and looped the rope over a branch. In flip-flops, they scrambled up the side of the island, thorns and twigs scratching their bare legs.

"There used to be a blueberry patch here," Daniel said. "I think they're past their peak, but maybe we could find a few. Bring some back and appease Eve with a pie."

"She's upset," Maggie said.

More statement than question, but Daniel nodded confirmation.

"We should get back as soon as we can," he said. "I'll spend the rest of the day with her."

Low, small-leaved bushes ran wild across the top of the rock island. Daniel let out a triumphant cry as he pointed to a cluster of late-season berries. They squatted to pick them into Daniel's baseball cap, shuffling forward as they exhausted each section of bush, the hat a buffer between them. They didn't speak.

When the nest of berries had risen to the top of the cap, he reached across it and traced his forefinger along her jawbone until each fine hair stood on end. In the reflection from his sunglasses, she was wide-eyed and longing and scared.

With a backwards leap-frog motion she hurtled herself away from him. "We have to get back."

He took her hand and they inched down the rock. She held his cap close against her chest, a meager peace offering. *I took your brother. But here! I brought you some berries.* Her hand burned in his.

When they reached the water, the canoe was gone.

For the next hour Maggie and Daniel waved and shouted at every boat that passed. The drivers of the boats cheerfully waved and shouted back, then sped on by. Neither of them had brought their phone. By the fourth boat, Maggie and Daniel were both laughing. After the fifth boat, Maggie gave up and sat cross-legged on the rock, next to the spot where their canoe had been.

"The only other time I've canoed was with Eve, and I tipped us," she said. "I'm two for two on canoeing disasters."

He sat down beside her. "First off, this was totally my fault. And second, is this a disaster?"

"We have no way home. We have no food or supplies. We have no way to contact anyone. The delay is definitely not going to make Eve less mad at us. So . . . maybe?"

"Someone'll stop eventually," he said.

"You're very calm in a crisis."

"If we're calling this a crisis."

"You must see crises every day at work. That's why you're so calm."

"You're why I'm so calm." He looked straight at her and her stomach gave a lurch. "It's a beautiful day and we're in a beautiful place," he said. "Not exactly a miserable time."

She shifted closer to him, just short of their thighs touching.

"I'm miserable," she said.

"I can tell."

She felt sure that if she tipped her face toward him, he would kiss her.

"So . . . how are you doing for real?" she asked. Alluding to his recently dead wife should dampen the mood enough to prevent her from breaking her detachment-from-men vow.

"I'm pretty good," he said. "I mean, in this moment? Maybe even really good."

The butterflies stirred in her stomach. "You are? In all these weeks, I don't think you've ever been *good*."

"Don't you yogis live in the present?"

"Yoginis."

"What?"

"Female practitioners of yoga."

"I'm glad you get your own word."

She laughed, and he laughed—it wasn't even funny, but in Daniel's presence her whole being was flooded with good feeling and everything was funny or totally wonderful, including being stranded on an island with only blueberries to eat and no means of calling for help.

"Tell me your life story," she said. "Fill in all the gaps I don't know."

"All of them?"

"Everything. Cuz, you know"—she waved in the direction of a distant boat, not even bothering to try flagging it down—"I feel like we have time."

And he did, and she did in return, exchanging childhoods and teen years and young adulthoods, trading stories up to the day they discovered each other on their phones, then to today stranded on this island. When a pontoon boat finally puttered toward them and they climbed aboard and began heading toward Eve and whatever ire awaited them, Maggie wished they could have stayed unrescued, possibly forever.

Chapter 26

Eve

The air through Eve's open patio door smelled of evening, of other people's campfires, of hours and hours since Daniel and Maggie had left for a quick visit to Labelle's Cabins.

We'll be back by noon, Daniel had promised her. She dialed Sam.

"It was still morning when they left," he said. "Maybe eleven thirty?"

Six hours ago. Whitecaps whorled the surface of the lake, and for the first time all day Eve felt not annoyed and abandoned but genuinely alarmed. Had they capsized? Had they *drowned*? Neither of them was an experienced canoeist—Daniel had been once, but he wasn't anymore.

"The wind picked up this afternoon," Sam said. "Maybe you better go look for them."

"*They* have my canoe!"

"Want me to go out in the boat?"

"Could you have a look? I'm sure it's nothing. I'm sure they're just—taking their time."

All afternoon, as it became clear Maggie and Daniel were in no rush to get back to include her in the day, Eve had felt both furious and forlorn. Now she was scared too.

From the stack of burgers she'd made earlier, she took a single patty out of the fridge for her dinner.

Footsteps sounded on the stairs outside. A knock, hesitant, on her front door.

She rinsed her hands and dried them on a towel as she strode to the door, intent on letting both of them have it. *Daniel's only here for three days! This is a vulnerable and important time in my life, and you both head off for an* entire day, *thinking only of yourselves and your fucking ill-advised love affair!*

Through the diamond-shaped window, filling the frame, eyes earnest, shoulders back. Shock of blond across his eyes.

Karl.

Eve tripped backwards, her hand with the towel rising to her abdomen. He knocked again. His hair was shaggy, uncut since she'd last seen it, his face in shadow. They locked eyes through the diamond pane.

You hate him, her brain said. *You want nothing to do with him.* But looking at him here on her doorstep, all she felt was *Karl.* Her Karl, her partner, her love. The father of her baby. The hormonal tears pooled.

Eve kept the towel in front of her belly, a shield across the bump that she was pretty sure no one but she and Maggie could detect. Still, it was there. She was wearing a long, loose linen shirt over jeans with the top button undone.

Grasping the doorknob, she pulled the door open, and they faced each other across the threshold.

He held her gaze so long she had to look away.

"I came to say I'm sorry," he said.

Flora had been dozing under the dining table. At the sound of Karl's voice she woofed one shocked, joyful woof, then skittered across the floor to him. He laughed and dropped to his knees in the open doorway, rubbing her all over while she yapped and nipped at his sleeves, then rolled onto her back to accept every inch of his attention, howling.

Watching Karl with Flora put a lump in her throat. Playful, warm, present—is this how Karl might be as a dad?

"Who's my girl, who's my girl?" he crooned, and "Did you miss me?"

She'd forgotten the exquisite presence of him, the charm whose source she couldn't place.

Charm was deceptive. Charm was how he got away with what he did.

She backed away from the door, moving behind the kitchen island and forcing a steely edge into her voice. "You're *sorry*?"

What did he expect her to believe he was apologizing for if he'd never admitted to the giant betrayal at the core of their relationship, if he didn't even know he'd knocked her up?

Karl sobered immediately. He gave Flora a final pat and rose to his feet, shutting the door and crossing the floor to stand on the other side of the island.

"I didn't invite you in," she said.

"I wasn't a good boyfriend," he said. "I was a worse boyfriend than you even knew."

"Don't you think I broke up with you because I knew you were a bad boyfriend?"

He ducked his head, then raised it again to look into her eyes. "Yes, but . . . it was so sudden. We barely talked about it, so I wasn't sure why exactly it was happening."

Did you find out about Maggie? Was that what he was after? She held the information like a secret weapon. Eve, from whom Karl had kept such a destructive secret, had a secret from him. Two secrets: She was pregnant with his child; she and Maggie were friends and business partners. Eve held this weapon, and she could conceal it or fire it as she chose.

"You wanted me to hand you a list on your way out?" Eve asked. This was better—she was accessing anger, some protective snark. She was almost enjoying this. "Here are all the ways you've been terrible?"

He didn't take the bait. "You breaking up with me so unexpectedly—it got to me. I felt how much I'd taken you for granted. I know it's a cliché, but I didn't realize what I had until I lost it."

Eve appraised him. He seemed sincere, but he'd seemed sincere before too. Karl's sincerity was all in service of getting whatever it was he wanted.

"So, did you come for a big, honest conversation? Is that what's happening right now? Or are you here for something else?"

"I hoped we could talk. That's all."

Was he actually going to confess? Part of her was curious to know what might come out of his mouth if she invited him to join her for dinner, take his usual place at her table. The other part felt the danger, little explosives going off in her body: *He's not trustworthy, he hurt you, you're feeling too abandoned and emotional right now to go anywhere near Karl. Stay away, stay away!*

"I was making dinner," she said. "Join me?"

He nodded. She turned to the fridge to take out another hamburger.

Karl said, "Can I light the barbecue?"

She watched him through the patio door as he opened the lid, turned on the propane, reached for the lighter. He knew where she kept it. He knew the ignition switch on her barbecue didn't work and that he would need the lighter. For one surreal second, she forgot he'd ever left.

She pulled out lettuce and cucumbers and green peppers and ran water over them, shredded them into tiny bits for a salad. She gave him the burgers to drop onto the barbecue. When he came back inside, he sat down on the couch and looked at her. Every time she snuck a peek, his gaze was on her, steady and unnerving. When she couldn't find any more vegetables to focus on, she wiped her hands and crossed the floor to join him on the couch.

She brought a cushion to her lap, just in case. He looked at her face, and she looked away and back again.

"I—" They spoke together, one word colliding and tangling and stopping them.

"So, you've been in South America?" Eve asked, finally.

He nodded. "Your last words to me, you might remember, were to figure out what I wanted from my life. It took me about ten seconds to realize the bank had to go."

"I saw your parents and they seemed weirdly supportive of your move. Unless they were just trying to get under my skin."

"They're not thrilled. I found somebody to check in on them regularly. They can still take care of themselves, they just have a lot of anxiety about it."

"So, is Patagonia over? Are you back here now?"

"The first contract was a last-minute fill-in, but it's turning permanent. I'm here to get some stuff and sort out arrangements for my folks."

Conflicting emotions rushed at her, colliding. Disappointment—so he wasn't here to try to get back together—followed quickly by irritation at herself, because why would she want that, except for the satisfaction of rejecting him? Then anger at Karl, because *of course* he was only here to immediately disappear again.

"A few things have changed since you left," Eve said. *Such as I'm building a life with the other girlfriend you still haven't copped to*, she wanted to say. "I bought the lodge next door, for one."

"No way! Eve, that's awesome!"

"Also—I'm pregnant." The words flowed out unadorned.

He drew back. On his face, incomprehension unfurled into shock, alarm. Denial.

"You should know that your stash of condoms has expired," Eve said. "You're definitely going to want to chuck those."

"Oh my god." He focused his gaze on the coffee table before looking her in the eye. "You must want to punch me in the face."

"I've considered it."

"Are you . . . keeping it?"

"I told you a lot had changed."

"God, Eve. Parenthood. I need time to think about that one."

"I'm not asking you for anything."

"I'd never forgive myself if I bailed on you and my kid. It's my responsibility too."

She laughed. *Now* he was Mr. Responsibility? "I made the choice to have the baby," she said. "I want the baby. I'll raise her."

"*Her?*"

She grinned, delighted all over again that her hunch had been correct. "Yup. Her."

"Wow. A *daughter*," he whispered. "I'm sorry for my stupid reaction. I think I'm in shock. A bit overwhelmed."

"Imagine how I feel. Someone is growing inside me."

His face was so close to hers. For all she'd told herself in these last months that Karl didn't matter, that she was better off without him, that she could do this on her own, sitting beside him with their baby inside her felt shockingly intimate and also more meaningful than she had imagined it could. For one brief instant, she wanted to stroke his cheek.

"I meant what I said earlier," he said. "I had a lot of time to think while I was away. About all the ways I failed you. About how fucked up I was. Am."

She pulled away to turn a lamp on, and the room leapt into focus. "Are you?"

"I got away with some unforgivable things," he said. "Things I shouldn't have got away with. And I don't want to tell you, because I know they're unforgivable, but I also think if I have any hope of ever not being a complete asshole, I have to own up."

She was as unsettled by his eyes as on the day she met him. She had no idea where Maggie and Daniel were, no idea if Maggie was leaving with Daniel on Monday. Despite everything, she did not hate Karl, even though she wanted to and knew he deserved it. She was lonely and she was responsible for this baby all on her own, and the weight of the responsibility was massive and disorienting, and here he was, owning up. Maybe starting to become something like the man she'd once thought he was.

Except—he *wasn't* owning up. He was talking around his betrayal, expecting her to fill in the pieces, which was no apology at all. Was *she* going to have to blurt it out? *Maggie. Nine months. Almost half our relationship.*

In one swift movement she pulled away from him. "Oh shit, our burgers."

Outside, the sky was streaked pink. A black crust covered one side of the burgers. Eve looked out over the lid of the barbecue, and Maggie and Daniel were walking across her yard from the lake. They reached the bottom step and stopped there. Behind Eve, the patio door opened and Karl came out onto the deck.

Horror shot across Maggie's face. Karl backed up toward the house, catching himself and leaning with one hand against the door.

"I was just about to mention." Eve closed the lid and turned to Karl. "Maggie's here."

Chapter 27

Maggie

Maggie sensed and looked and saw in one instant, so that she couldn't be sure whether the sensing or the seeing came first, Karl's blond head emerging from Eve's house. Her stomach heaved and her knees buckled, and she did not trust her legs to carry her forward.

Karl? Karl. Karl was here at Still Lake—tan and untended, his hair grown, his body leaner, but still Karl, standing on Eve's deck, right in front of Maggie after all these months.

He was staring at Maggie, saying, "What? What . . . what?" It seemed to be the only word he could get out, one shocked and strangled sound as he looked from Maggie back to Eve, then at Maggie again.

How many times had Maggie daydreamed this! A sweet retaliation, Karl returning to discover Maggie and Eve—surprise!—together. Happy, connected, thriving. They'd be side by side at the beautifully renovated retreat center, a cute little girl playing at their feet. They'd be leaning over a computer or relaxing after a good day's work, laughing at a shared joke. Always in the daydream they were laughing, alight with shared purpose and joy. They'd glance up, mid-laughter, and spot him. *Oh, why, look*, Maggie and Eve would say. *Isn't that what's-his-name?*

Instead, Eve stood with Karl, her gaze on Maggie pure condemnation. Maggie stood with Daniel, sucker-punched by this unexpected proximity to the man she'd once loved, separated from Eve by the gulf of her own disloyalty. But also, apparently, Eve's, because *what the hell was Eve doing with Karl?*

Beside Maggie, Daniel tensed, and his hand moved to the small of her back. She blinked at the touch, gripping tightly to the railing.

Karl stared again between Maggie and Eve. "You two—you two *know* each other?" he stammered.

He was, as in Maggie's daydream, stunned and ill at ease. Unlike the daydream, so was she.

Daniel was bristling beside her. "What's going on?" he said to Karl. "Why are you here?"

Karl looked like he might vomit. He cast pleading eyes on Eve. "I did come to tell you the truth," he said.

"You mean you came to soothe your guilty conscience by burdening Eve with facts that would just make her feel like shit," Daniel said.

Eve looked simultaneously amused and furious. "You're going all brotherly protective on me *now*?" she said to Daniel. "Where the fuck have you been? You seemed to think I didn't need you all fucking day—or most of my life, for that matter—so I don't know why you're trying to be a white knight now." She arranged two buns on the grill and closed the lid, standing there with her fist tight around the handle. "Or maybe you're showing off for Maggie?"

"Am I supposed to play nice with the man who screwed you *both* over?" Daniel asked. "I don't think anyone who knew what he did would want to see you letting him waltz back in, expecting supper."

"I'm only here because I thought Eve had a right to know the truth," Karl said.

"Oh, and I didn't?" Maggie said.

"Karl's not expecting anything," Eve said. "I asked him to stay. Because, I don't know, I was feeling a little *alone* for some reason."

"We're sorry about today," Daniel said. "We got stranded on Blueberry Island. I didn't tie the canoe well enough."

"The first rule of canoeing." Eve's tone was icy.

"So you're rolling out the red carpet for Karl to get back at me and Daniel for being late?" Maggie said.

Eve looked pointedly at Maggie. "Six hours is a bit more than *late*. It's more like *absent*. And we both know there's more to it than just *Oops, didn't tie up the canoe*."

Holy crap, she *was* cozying up to Karl in retaliation. Maggie held Eve's gaze, trying desperately to convey all the reminders of who they were to each other, until she couldn't bear the accusation and had to look away.

Eve opened the lid again, scraped the charred layer off two burgers, and levered them onto buns. Maggie pulled herself up the steps to the deck. She was acutely aware of her hands, which she didn't know what to do with, and her feet, which were in the way. Karl stood an arm's length from her. His stare shifted between Maggie and Eve, forehead furrowed, lips parted as though uncertain which question to choose first.

"I'm sorry," he said, "but can somebody tell me—can you explain why Maggie is *here*?"

"Or," Daniel said, "you could just ask Maggie. Seeing as she *is* here."

So Daniel had also noticed that Karl hadn't yet spoken a direct word to her.

"Maggie came here looking for you," Eve said to Karl.

"Okay, but—"

"That was a while ago," Eve said. "A few months."

"*Months?*"

"Four."

"Then why—how—what's she still doing here?"

Like Maggie was fucking *trash* rotting at the curb?

"We're actually business partners now," Eve said, finally sticking up for her. "Maggie and I."

"Business partners?" Karl looked like he needed to lie down. "How—?"

"I'm not sure you're owed an explanation," Daniel said.

"Okay, relax, Daniel," Eve said. "Karl's a piece of shit, we all know he's a piece of shit, he's admitted he's a piece of shit, he's trying to make amends, and I think we can all agree it took guts for him to come here."

"Not as much as it would've taken if he'd known you'd both be here," Daniel said. "It's one thing to sweet-talk you each separately, but how's he going to pull that off now?"

"Daniel, stop," Eve said. She sat down at the table set for two and gestured at Karl to take the seat beside her. Then she turned to Maggie and Daniel. "I made dinner for all of us, so you need to go get the rest of the burgers from the fridge and cook them, and then you need to sit down and eat."

Maggie and Daniel exchanged glances—were they really going to eat with Eve and Karl like this?—and seemed to come to the same conclusion, which was that they'd better do whatever the hell Eve told them to do. Maggie followed Daniel inside.

In the kitchen, Daniel closed the door and turned to her. "Are you okay?"

She shook her head, numb. "I have no idea. He's not here for me—he hasn't said a word to me—and I don't . . . of course I don't *love* him anymore, but—"

"He's got a lot of fucking nerve coming here."

"Eve's pissed at us."

"She should be pissed at Karl."

"She is! We've talked about it *a lot*. I don't understand what she's doing."

She couldn't put into words the terrible foreboding she'd felt when Eve turned on Daniel, her anger at him and Maggie palpable. The calm with which Eve had said, *I asked him to stay.*

Eve had *asked Karl to stay?*

Eve and Karl were together on the deck, shoulder to shoulder as they ate, talking. Eve looked perturbed, but not perturbed enough as far as Maggie was concerned.

Daniel palmed a raw hamburger in each hand. Maggie got plates and silverware.

"Deep breath in," Daniel said, and together they returned to the deck.

As Maggie lifted the lid of the barbecue and Daniel dropped the burgers onto the grill, she yearned with visceral longing to be stranded still on Blueberry Island, alone with Daniel and away from whatever was happening here.

Maggie lowered herself to the edge of a chair across from Eve while Daniel stayed with the burgers. The deck was silent apart from the creak of the barbecue lid. Maggie imagined she could feel Karl staring at her, though she tried to stay focused on Eve, who was eating with quiet determination and not looking at her. But maybe Karl was, because he finally spoke to her.

"I tried to contact you," he said.

Maggie had so much to say to him, so much she had tried so hard to tell him, so many imagined conversations she'd desperately wanted to make real. Now her voice came out squeaky and bitter, the voice of a sulking teenager. "Oh, so I was next on your apology tour?" Immediately, she wished she hadn't spoken.

"I know I have no excuse and I'm a hundred percent in the wrong, okay? I didn't come for understanding or forgiveness. I just came to say I'm sorry and you deserved better."

"You came to say *Eve* deserved better."

"Obviously you both did. I was hoping to see you next, but you didn't answer my email."

She forced herself to look at his face. "So inconsiderate of me."

"Maggie," Eve said mildly. "He didn't have to come. He's trying to take responsibility and repair some of the damage."

Oh my god, Eve really was siding with him.

"You *know* what he did to us!" Maggie cried.

"Yeah, but I'm also trying to believe in growth and change. Which you believe in too, by the way. Like it or not, Karl is my daughter's father, and he's going to be in my life. We all might as well start getting used to it."

Maggie stared at Eve, fighting tears. So she'd told him about the baby. *And* she'd decided to let Karl be involved.

Maggie felt like such an idiot. She'd been acting like she was this baby's second parent. She'd been *getting attached* like she was this baby's second parent. But she wasn't. Karl was.

On the tabletop Karl's fingers closed briefly around Eve's. The tendons shifted as he squeezed, and Eve did not pull away. Maggie watched like it was a close-up on a screen she couldn't look away from, and then she stumbled to her feet and fled to the lodge.

An hour later Maggie listened to the murmur of sounds as the door to Daniel's room opened and closed, as Eve showed Karl to the room on the other side of Maggie's. (*She's letting him stay in the lodge!*) When Eve left, Maggie sat cross-legged on her bed in the sanctuary of her room, flanked by the men, their presence in the building large and electric.

This was why they were creating a *women's* retreat center. For true retreat, true self-knowledge and rejuvenation, women needed a break from men. She and Eve had been doing *great*. A single day since a man arrived on the premises, and all their equilibrium was upended.

She rolled out her mat and took herself through a yoga flow, trying to calm herself. Muffled noises carried from both rooms, a chair scraping, a squeaky floorboard. As quiet gradually descended, Maggie crept out, down the stairs and away from the men, across the path to Eve's house.

Through the glass of the patio door, Eve was a motionless silhouette on the couch. Maggie raised her fist and knocked. Flora, on the couch beside Eve, whined and leapt down, wagging her tail. Eve didn't move. Maggie eased the door open and passed through it, standing just inside.

"Eve," she whispered. "We have to talk."

Eve stared straight ahead, not looking at Maggie. Methodically she raised a mug to her lips and sipped.

"Are you—you're not seriously thinking about allowing Karl back into your life." Maggie's heartbreak was like a physical object. "Are you?"

"He'll have parental rights, you know," Eve said.

"Yeah, but that doesn't mean you need to have a relationship with him. You don't even need to let him see her unless a court orders it."

"I know what an asshole Karl's been," Eve said. "To both of us. I know how much harm he caused and how hard it's been for both of us to get to a place where we're okay again. I don't need a lecture from you."

"I didn't come to give you one." Maggie tiptoed across the floor. She lowered herself to the other end of the couch and sat, unspeaking. At length she whispered, "I really, honestly, just need to know—what is going on?"

Outside the open windows, the whippoorwills began to call their own names.

"When you and Daniel were gone today," Eve said, "I felt how alone I am. How completely I'm on my own—with this baby and maybe even this lodge, because you haven't signed anything or put any money down. I'm tied to the baby and I'm tied to the lodge, and there's nothing to prevent you from walking away."

"There's my *promise*. My vision. My deep desire to be here. My love for this baby! There's our friendship!"

"Is there, though? Because today felt like the truth: All of that is precarious and can blow away with a gust of wind. Or with the first guy who comes along and shows you a little attention."

"The canoe washed away! We couldn't get back!"

"You two are all over each other. I'm not stupid. I can feel it. Anyway, Daniel told me."

At the mention of his name, Maggie's whole body turned into a puddle. "He did?"

"My point is that I feel alone. Even my own twin can't focus on me for a measly weekend, and he lives in another country—he won't be here when the baby comes. Karl's the only other person who's bound to this baby even close to as much as I am."

"You can't be serious. He didn't even know about the baby till today. Fathers walk out all the time! Especially cheating liars."

"I'm not saying we're getting back together. He's heading to South America again anyway. I'm just saying I don't think I should shut him out. I might need him."

Maggie pulled her legs up, wrapping her arms around them. "Do you still have feelings for him?"

Eve shrugged. "Feelings? I'm not eighteen." She looked away, out the window. "But, you know. Yeah. Maybe."

Maggie's tears were just on the edge, and she put all her concentration into staving them off. "I get that a good relationship with him is better for the baby. But if he were to come back here—if he did that instead of South America—Eve, I couldn't live next door to you and Karl. I couldn't stay and run the retreat center while you raise your happy little family together. I couldn't do it."

Eve was still staring off into the darkness beyond the lamp's pool of light. "You're set to run off with my brother anyway, so that shouldn't be a problem."

"Eve—I'm not."

"Did he ask you to drive back to Toronto with him?"

"He offered."

"You should go. You've needed to get back for weeks."

"It would only be to sort out my belongings so I can come straight back here. Daniel would be just . . ."

"Transportation?"

"Eve. Nothing has happened between us."

"It didn't feel like nothing this morning at breakfast. Or tonight at dinner. Or all day long, while I waited for you to come home."

"We would have been back by noon, Eve. We would have."

"It feels like confirmation that there really was a bigger reason you kept your relationship with Daniel a secret for so long. Like something weird was going on then and it's going on now, and you don't want me to know."

"No! Eve, none of this was premeditated."

"It's amazing." Eve laughed, a mirthless sound. "You weren't joking when you told me about your pattern with men. You really are incapable of passing up the chance for any male attention."

"I haven't done anything!"

"Getting involved with Daniel is a terrible idea. He lives in another country. He's been widowed for four months! Why am I the only one who thinks this can only end in disaster? I promise you, he is not over Violet. Whether he's conscious of it or not, he's just using you to numb the pain for a few days."

"He's not. He's genuine."

"So you'll admit there's something between you."

Maggie flushed. "Okay, yes. I'm attracted to your brother, but if you want to punish me for attraction, and for an accident with the damn canoe that was out of our control—"

"I'm not punishing you. I'm just asking you. If all you want is a fling, can you please save it for someone who is not my brother?"

Maggie's throat burned. She stroked Flora's head, over and over, until Flora squirmed and pulled away.

"It was excruciating for me tonight," Maggie said. "Seeing Karl look at you. Touch you. Choose you. Like he's obliterated me. Like I never happened."

"You have Daniel. Why should that matter?"

"Karl was my partner! I loved him. Being attracted to Daniel doesn't mean I don't care that Karl's acting like I never mattered."

"Ah, two at once. That sounds familiar."

Maggie stood.

"You want to be single," Eve said. "Focus on yourself. Remember?"

"And you want to never give away your power to Karl again. We vowed to each other that we would never, ever take him back, no matter what."

"I didn't say I'm taking him back."

"You're talking like you might want to."

Eve's voice was hard. "He's the father of my unborn child. He's a person I have a lot of history with." She turned, and their eyes met at last. For one moment, Eve's face was unguarded in the dim light. "I don't want to be alone again, Maggie. I don't want to face motherhood unsupported."

"You aren't. *I'm* here! Eve, you have *me.*"

"Not today I didn't."

"That was one day. You think *Karl* will be more reliable for the long haul than me?"

"When we were together, he was actually very reliable."

"Maybe with practical stuff, but he's not *emotionally* reliable. He's not honest."

"He's trying."

"I wouldn't know about that. I'm not the one he talked to."

"You were barely civil to him."

"After what I went through? He still doesn't even *know*, and now here you are with your healthy, normal pregnancy, upstaging everything."

"Oh, Maggie." Eve's voice softened. "It's not a competition."

Eve's house was shadowy and indistinct in the darkness. The table was a hulking ship. The fridge could be a bear.

"Isn't it?" Maggie asked.

"I thought we'd done a lot to make it not be."

If Maggie were still pregnant, would *she* be the one Karl was talking to, touching, tending? If Maggie and Eve were both pregnant, which one of them would he choose?

"Do you have any idea how hard it's been for me all this time, watching you?" Maggie asked. "Watching you pregnant—and with my ex-boyfriend's kid?"

Eve's face in profile was immobile, betraying no emotion.

"Do you have any idea," Maggie continued, "how many times I wanted to run away?"

"No," Eve said, "I don't. Because you haven't said any of that, not since that day in the dining hall when I told you I thought I might be pregnant. You've been so excited about this baby that sometimes it felt more like yours than mine."

"I *am* excited about this baby."

"But you also resent me for it?"

"No!" Maybe. Maybe she did. Maybe she hadn't processed and released her feelings, maybe she'd only put them away, because *something* was rising up in her now, some new layer of grief at seeing Eve and Karl and their future baby together, knowing what she'd lost.

"I will be here, Eve." She breathed deeply to regulate her tone, the tears sticking in her throat. "If you are raising your baby without Karl, I'll be right next door at the retreat center. I'm committed to us." She crossed the floor and slid into her flip-flops.

Eve's face was weary. "We've caused each other so much pain, Maggie. I thought the pain was over, but maybe it's not. Maybe it just goes on and on."

"That's just defeatist! It's not true."

"Listen to what you just said, though. Maybe it's time to accept that we've been trying to make something work that's always been impossible to make work."

Outside Daniel's door, Maggie didn't hesitate. She didn't even knock. She turned the knob and slid the door open and slipped inside. Warm candlelight dotted the windowsills. Daniel was in bed, sitting up against the headboard, a magazine in his hand. She stepped forward and he dropped the magazine and reached for her, his hands gripping her hip bones through her thin cotton skirt. With one heave, he pulled her up to straddle him on the bed. Even before their lips collided, she could feel him hard underneath her. She kissed him like his tongue in her mouth and her tongue in his was every true and necessary thing.

He rolled her onto her back and hovered above her, kissing her eyes, her neck, the tops of her breasts coming unmoored in her tank top. She'd landed on the magazine, and she swatted it out from under her. It cascaded to the floor with a whirr of pages. The sound of her heart falling.

With one hand he pinned her arm above her head while the other stroked her leg, climbing incrementally. Her skirt was already floating around her waist. Any moment now he would reveal her scar, and her heart pounded with each inch of flesh exposed.

"This isn't your favorite underwear is it?" he whispered.

She didn't remember which ones she had on. In one tug he tore them straight down the side seam.

She laughed. "So smooth."

He pushed the elastic of her skirt away from her waist, slid the skirt down her legs, pushed her tank top up, and the scar was unveiled. She felt it like it was all of her, enormous and pulsing. He looked into her eyes as his palm cupped the raised ridge of her skin, trailing gently from belly button to pelvis.

"Is this okay?" he asked.

"They said after six weeks—"

"But is it okay? For *you*."

She might break open, but she was willing to break open.

"As long as we double-check the expiry on the condom," she said. Her tone was as flirtatious as she could make it, until her voice broke and he wrapped his arms around her and nodded solemnly.

"Wait for me a second?" she asked. She wrapped her skirt around herself like a towel and hurried to her room, grabbing the condom she'd tucked into her bag on the day she made her symbolic purchase. As she scurried back to Daniel half dressed, hyper-aware of Karl two doors down—there was no way he wasn't hearing them—she decided she *wanted* Karl to hear. *Because fuck you, Karl. Fuck you once and for all.*

Then she was with Daniel again and thinking of no one but him. When he entered her, his face wore a look of longing so defenseless it was painful to gaze on. Afterward he held her and her tears flowed, the balm so soothing, the remedy for heartache so simple and so rare. She fell asleep in his bed with his arms locked around her, almost too tight for her to breathe, though she barely cared. She had love. Who needed breath?

Chapter 28

Eve

"Should you be doing that?"

Eve was alone the next morning, hunched over a broom, when the sound of Karl's voice startled her. She turned around and saw him, hands in his pockets, expression earnest, and she couldn't help it—her breath still caught at the sight of him.

"I mean physical activity," Karl said. "Is it okay for you to be—?"

"Karl. It's sweeping."

He grinned then and she found herself smiling back, crossing the floor to join him in the doorway. She was in the large shed on the lodge property that she planned to turn into her workshop. She'd woken early, her mind whirring with what-ifs and anxieties, looping thoughts of Karl, Maggie, Daniel, and the debacle of this weekend, and she'd come here to give her brain and body a calming, purposeful occupation.

"I was hoping to find you alone," Karl said.

"Oh yeah? Why's that?" She meant the words to sound suspicious, guarded, but they carried a tinge of flirtation. She took a step back, just in case she did something stupid. Like touch him.

"I've made a decision," Karl said.

"That's a big deal for you. Usually you just string things along on multiple trajectories at once."

He cast her an injured look, then nodded, raising his hands in surrender. "Fair. I deserve that."

"You're just lucky I didn't gang up on you with Daniel and Maggie last night."

"Why didn't you?"

"I was mad at them."

"Madder at them than at me?"

"The anger at you has had lots of time to fester. The anger at them was fresher. So, what's the decision?"

He looked at her for a beat—assessing, she thought, the depth and severity of her bad feelings about him. Then he said, "I need to move back."

"Karl."

"I know, but hear me out. I get that you're not asking anything of me, and maybe you don't want my help at all. Maybe you don't want the kid to even know me. But if that *isn't* the case—is that the case?"

He looked so boyish and vulnerable in his uncertainty. Eve was higher than him, standing on the threshold while his feet were still on the ground, a step down. She stepped forward, still up high but closer, shaking her head. "I can separate who you were as a partner from who you might be as a father."

"You mean that?"

"I think so."

"I guess I'm trying to redeem myself here."

"By being superdad?"

"Well, but also, I *want* to. I would quit Vital Adventures. I would move back here. Not *here*, but nearby. Near enough to do my share. To be in our daughter's life."

Our daughter—the words sent a warm, disorienting thrum through her body, a melting she wasn't prepared for.

"You don't even want kids," she said, "and you'd give up everything?"

"I didn't *think* I wanted kids. But this is real now. It wasn't real before. Don't you think I have a responsibility to help raise her? And if that's more than you want, I could just take the burden off you once in a while. Babysit or—something?"

"It's not called babysitting when it's your own kid."

"That would be what it's called if you don't want to co-parent with me."

"You wouldn't want that, Karl. You couldn't even handle staying faithful to one woman. Kids limit your freedom a lot more than girlfriends do."

"What I'm trying to say is that's not the man I want to be."

"It's the man you are. You've already proven that."

"I'd like the chance to prove I'm not. Or at least that I can change. That I *have* changed."

"Because of a few months of backcountry hiking?"

"I know there's no reason for you to care about my experience—believe me, I know that—but I do think I've changed. You dumping me like that, so suddenly, and then Maggie ghosting me—I figured one or both of you suspected something. But I didn't know for sure, so I convinced myself I got away with it. And it kind of freaked me out that I got away with it. I couldn't believe what I'd let myself become. Because, you might not believe this, but I did love you. I *do* love you."

She regarded him somberly. If Maggie told her Karl had said this to her, Eve was certain she'd be yelling, *Do not be taken in by this sad-eyed act!*

"Then why did you do it?" she asked. "Have you come to any conclusions about that?"

"I have, actually. I think I felt stuck. With my job at the bank. With my parents. My life."

"With me."

"No. No, it was more the whole picture of needing to conform to corporate capitalist, responsible, normal bullshit when I just wanted to shoot rapids and climb rocks. I didn't plan it, but when I met Maggie, she made me feel something that was completely different from my normal life and all the obligations. Freedom, I guess. Like I was my own person again. And I pursued that."

"Even though we had the most hands-off relationship ever. Even though you were only here on weekends! That's a really minimal amount of tying down."

"I didn't say *you* tied me down. It was everything else. And I think I justified my relationship with Maggie as harmless as long as it didn't infringe on our time together, which I know isn't true, but I was caught up in it and lying to myself, so—see? It's messed up."

"I don't buy it."

"It just happened, Eve. With Maggie. It wasn't conscious."

"So why didn't your co-workers and your Toronto friends know about me?"

"They did."

"They can't have or there'd have been a lot of raised eyebrows when you started parading Maggie around. She told me you met at a party where you had mutual friends, so you must have kept me a secret long before you met Maggie."

He was opening his mouth to argue, but Eve pressed firmly forward. "That's not unconscious, Karl. That's *calculated.* You don't hide the existence of your partner unless you're keeping yourself free to fool around."

"I didn't! I wasn't."

"Were there other hookups? Other *relationships*? Do you have a whole harem?"

"No! Eve, there was no one else. There was no calculation."

"Bullshit."

"People knew about you. They knew why I came north on the weekends. I just—well, after I met Maggie, I told everyone you and I had broken up."

For one second, Eve felt like she'd been elbowed in the gut. "Oh. Fabulous. That makes it all okay, then."

She moved abruptly away from him. She couldn't believe she was letting him explain himself at all. Then again, if they'd communicated more openly during their relationship, maybe they wouldn't have landed here in the first place.

"You helping your parents had nothing to do with me, and *I* got punished for it," she said. "And if this is true—if the explanation you're going with is that fulfilling your duty as a son and a wage-earning member of society made you so desperate for freedom that you had to cheat just to feel like your own person—how is giving up your freedom for fatherhood not going to end in disaster too? It sounds like another version of the same thing. Only this time, when you lie or take off or whatever you end up doing, there'll be a child you're hurting."

"I can make different choices."

"You treated me like trash." Her voice faltered as she said it, all the pain she hadn't allowed herself to feel flooding in now. She took a moment to compose herself, then said, "I felt so humiliated I couldn't even admit to you that I knew about Maggie. It was awful, finding that out. And I had to find it out from her."

"Oh, Eve. I'll never forgive myself."

"I don't need you to be a martyr about it. I just need you to . . ."

What? What *did* she need from Karl?

"Anything," he said. "Tell me."

"Do better," she finished weakly.

"That's what I'm telling you I'm trying to do."

Eve and Karl had never spoken like this with each other. Theirs had been a relationship of companionable, active doing, not one of communicating how they felt or analyzing who they were to each other. Even in ending the relationship, she hadn't told him the reason why.

Cautiously she placed a hand on his head. His arms wrapped around her waist, his touch so concrete it startled her. A physical presence after months of fury and sadness and creating a demon of him in her mind.

Was it possible she still *loved* him, even after everything?

He buried his face against her stomach and she tangled her fingers in his hair. The weight of their history—their inadequacies and fulfillments, the love they had made, the baby they had made—these pulsed in the familiar shape of his head under her hand, in the pressure of his arms.

Was it possible for him to do better? Was it possible for her to?

He stepped up to join her in the workshop, still with his arms around her.

"We're only talking about me letting you into the baby's life," Eve said.

"But?"

"But nothing."

"Eve," he said. "It could be more."

She pulled away. "You would hate it here again," she said.

"It would be different."

"I don't know why it would be."

"Because of my experience. I messed up with you, which makes me not worth taking back, but it also makes me a guy who knows a lot more than he knew before."

Eve shook her head and lowered herself to the threshold, her legs dangling. Karl stepped down to the ground and started poking at the scrap pile in the driveway, broken chairs and old boards she and Maggie and the boys from Sam's had cleared from the lodge. She knew that gesture, had seen it when they picked out bathroom fittings at the hardware store, when he pointed out a loon or a moose on a canoe trip. The constriction in her throat grew. His expressions, his moods, his body—she knew them. Maybe this knowing, combined with the future she carried inside her, was more important than the mistakes he had made.

"This wood will make a great bonfire," Karl said. He was circling it, looking at her, pulling out pieces for inspection. Looking at her. His gaze cut straight through her, and she had to look away.

Daniel was coming out of the lodge. She waved to him and he headed toward them.

"Let me get this wood out of here for you," Karl said. "I'll haul it to the beach. We could light it tonight." He stopped in front of her. "Unless you're kicking me out before then."

Daniel's face was crumpled from sleep, new lines imprinted overnight. He nodded to Eve and ignored Karl, and the snub made Eve smile.

"You know what?" Eve said to Karl. "You have fun with the woodpile. This weekend was supposed to be about me and my brother, and so far we've barely seen each other, so I'm going to spend some time with him now."

"You still have your wheelbarrow?"

"You know where it is."

Karl disappeared around the corner of the dining hall, and Eve patted the spot beside her. "You were irritating last night," she said to Daniel.

"Was I?"

"You know you were."

He looked beyond her into the workshop, stepping closer to peer inside. "Well, I was irritated."

"Let's not do this," she said. "Please."

He turned to her and relaxed into the Daniel he'd been on his arrival—calm and weary, accepting, smiling.

"I'm sorry about disappearing yesterday," he said. He sat down beside her. "You must have felt like it was Violet all over again."

"Is it?"

He shook his head. "I'm a mess."

"Of course you're a mess. Your wife just died." She studied him, his face set away from her, muscles working in his jaw.

"Every day," he said, "I wake up and I'm stunned that I'm living my life without her. We were going to grow old together, you know? We had a whole life planned. And since she died, I feel . . . lost. Like, what the hell is the plan *now*?"

"You'll figure it out. Eventually." She swallowed. "And—it's awfully quick, and I know I've been super against it, but maybe this is it. With Maggie, I mean."

He was quiet.

"Something happened," she said.

Maggie had rejected him. Eve saw it in the turn of Daniel's head, the purposeful missing of her gaze. Maggie had lured and promised and retreated. Of course she had. Maggie was wounded herself; of course she had wounded newly bereaved, already injured Daniel. And now their bond was proving as destructive as Eve had told them from the start that it would.

Eve vaulted to the ground. "Let's go borrow a boat from Sam." Her voice was low and determined. She glimpsed Karl near the dining hall, pushing her wheelbarrow. "Let's forget about Maggie and Karl and go find my canoe. Let's pack a lunch."

Daniel accepted her arm across his back. "Let's take all day," he said.

Chapter 29

Maggie

Daniel's room was like Maggie's. The desk, the windows open to the lake, the white cotton sheets. There was a depression in the pillow beside her where Daniel's head had been. Daniel was not there anymore.

Maggie sat up and pulled the covers to her neck. She leaned forward to check the ensuite bathroom, but the space was empty of presence, and she knew before looking that he wasn't there.

Her skirt and tank top, bra and ripped underwear lay folded in a stack on the desk. Maggie took heart at this evidence of care—surely Daniel had so neatly arranged the proof of last night's abandon out of consideration for her and not from any desire to erase it.

The memory was already tainted with doubt. She'd become involved with a man, and here was her punishment, this anxiety and unease, this precarious entrusting of her happiness into another's hands. And he wasn't here to assure her that her happiness was secure.

Why wasn't he here?

She craned her neck out the window, but the lakefront was empty. She wriggled into her skirt, fastened her bra. The reverse process of last night, with reverse emotions. She was sure he'd held her all night. She'd woken several times to confirm it.

When she was dressed, she smoothed the sheets and pulled up the quilt. She sat at the desk for a few minutes—maybe he was getting coffee?

There was nothing to do with her underwear but wad it into her fist and carry it.

She left the room. Her hand was still on his door, closing it behind her, when footsteps pounded on the stairs. She turned, smiling, feeling a gust of relief.

It was Karl.

Her fingers curled around her wrecked underwear. She felt the vulnerability of her bareness under her lightweight skirt.

"Hey." Karl looked flushed and energetic, vital, like he'd just returned from a run. "Eve and Daniel went out to look for the canoe."

He spoke like she was someone he'd met the day before. She stood with one hand on Daniel's doorknob and the other clutching her underwear. She was shaking, her whole body revolting against Karl and his lying, cheating presence.

"You two are doing a great job with this place." Karl smiled, already recovered from yesterday's shock, free and breezy, at ease in the world. He stepped around her toward his door. "Guess I'll see you around?"

The rage surged from deep inside her. It roared, and it stunned her. She could throw him down the stairs with the power of it.

"Don't you have any *feelings*? About *us*?" She was shouting.

He stepped back. One hand ran through his shaggy hair. "Yes . . . I'm sorry, Maggie."

"That's it? *Sorry*? Sorry you ever met me? Or sorry you got caught?"

"Sorry it's been so painful."

"What am I supposed to do with that?"

"It might help you move on."

"I wasn't supposed to need to move on."

"I didn't do this to be hurtful," Karl said. "I know that was the result. But when I did it—when I fell for you—it was because I fell for you. Please believe that, if it helps."

"Oh, why, thank you!" She flung her arm out in a gesture of mock gratitude; her ripped underwear came loose from her fist, and she waved it like a white and purple striped flag. Karl eyed it quizzically, and she didn't even care. "I'll just sit over here in my little corner, nursing my little *at least he fell for me once* while you start your happy family with your *other* girlfriend."

"I had no idea you'd be here."

"Aren't you even a little curious about *why* I came here? Don't you think it must have been something pretty significant to send me all this way trying to find you?"

"You were really worked up in your messages. But, Maggie, a lot of things were a big deal to you."

At these words, Maggie screamed—one guttural howl of rage—and stabbed her finger at his chest. "I was *worked up*, was I? Was I maybe *hysterical*, Karl, is that what you're trying to say?" She pushed into him and he took one strong step back, then stumbled as she kept pace with him. "You have no idea how I suffered because of you! You have no idea the agony and trauma you caused, you horrible, insensitive prick."

He took her hands and pressed them down to her sides. "I think I have some idea," he said. "And I know it sounds empty, but I *am* really sorry. I've been—"

"No. Just shut up. You don't know. You have no fucking clue." She flicked her wrists out of his grasp. Now. Now was the time to tell him they'd conceived a baby and lost it in the most horrific of ways.

"I assumed you'd found out about Eve somehow," he said. "And you were calling to tell me off. Or break up, or get back together. But it was a couple of months before I heard those messages. I figured if it was still important and still something I could help with, you'd have reached out again. I emailed you months ago."

She stared at him. His lips parted—there was his row of perfect teeth. So much handsome blandness. So much deceit.

"You know what?" she said. "You don't deserve to know. I am not going to tell you. You are so beneath even hearing the truth. Because you are a cheating liar."

She balled the underwear into her fist and wheeled toward her room.

"We were winding to an end anyway," Karl called after her. "With or without Eve, we wouldn't have lasted."

In the relationship *Maggie* had been in, they were headed for marriage. They had been in two completely different relationships.

"Fuck you, Karl," she said. She shut the door in his face.

In the safety of her room, Maggie sat on the bed, shaking, forcing deep breaths, determined not to cry. She would not shed one more tear for Karl Tarvudd. And she would never let him know the truth of what had happened to her.

Pulling on clean underwear, she composed texts to Daniel. Hey, I miss you! Delete. How could you disappear like that, don't you know how my mind is torturing me right now? Delete. Please marry me and have babies with me and love me forever. Delete, delete, delete. She'd never before needed to labor over the wording of a message to Daniel. She settled on what she hoped was a light and unperturbed I seem to have lost you!! She pressed send, but the *ding* of the message arriving in his empty room sounded a second later. She checked his room again, under the covers, under the bed, for a note she might have missed. She went for a walk. Back in her own room, she packed up her notebook and laptop and a few clothes, enough for a quick trip back to Toronto to close up her life there before she moved permanently to Still Lake.

By late afternoon, Daniel still hadn't returned and Maggie was exhausted from the mental and emotional turmoil of replaying their every interaction for signs of his feelings for her, for proof she wasn't deluded. She sent Charmaine a series of messages, asking to talk, then begging to talk, but Charmaine must have been off on some weekend adventure with her family, because the messages stayed unread. Eventually, Maggie passed out on the bed beside her packed bags.

When she woke, it was dark out. A shout and then laughter crescendoed toward her, the splash of water, more laughter. She peered through the window at a column of flame on the beach below, three dark forms in the firelight. She grabbed a sweater and stepped into her flip-flops.

Their voices reached her, as she descended the staircase, in muffled sounds and louder, almost decipherable bursts of words. Below her, Daniel, Karl, and Eve sat on a log, fire orange-red in front of them, earth and sky and water black behind them. Karl was telling a story. A cougar, a mountain. His hands folded dough around hot dogs as he talked, Flora at his feet. Eve whittled the end of a stick with a pocket knife, smiling. Daniel's white hoodie cut a swath in the night. He poked the fire and sparks exploded into the air. A burst of light leapt across his face, craggy and brooding, or perhaps only pensive, or perhaps only in shadow.

Maggie was a tightly wound spring, each coil made of something worse than the last: desire, insecurity, panic, desperation. She stepped off the last stair and her feet sank into sand.

All three faces turned to her. She couldn't smile; her muscles wouldn't form the necessary adjustments. Karl stopped his story mid-sentence. Eve looked at Maggie with hard eyes, a judge choosing between a low score and a lower one. Daniel was not looking at her at all.

"Hot dog?" asked Karl.

Maggie scanned the log for a space she might squeeze herself into. There was room next to Daniel if they snuggled, but snuggling was evidently, horribly, not on the agenda. Why wouldn't he look at her? Karl scooted closer to Eve and patted the spot on the other side of him. Maggie wanted to shove him into the fire, not gaze into it beside him, but she lowered herself to the log. He threaded a stick through the hot dog in his hands, moulded dough around it, and handed it to Maggie.

"So, the cougar kept leaving, you know, gifts by the cabin door," Karl said.

Maggie stuck her hot dog into the flame.

"Carcasses. Rabbit, deer." Karl's hand reached across Maggie and pressed on the stick, guiding it downward to a recessed bed of coals.

"Gifts or threats?" asked Eve.

"We're invading his territory, so probably threats. It's only fair."

The wind changed and smoke stung Maggie's eyes. She leaned away, backwards, and behind Karl's and Eve's backs, her glance caught Daniel's, one piercing second, one jolt of exchanged consciousness.

"How was your day?" she mouthed.

"We found the canoe," he said.

She smiled.

"If a cougar pounces," Karl said, "the only warning you'll get is an eight-hundred-pound weight on your back and a set of jaws around your neck."

Maggie pulled her hot dog from the fire and blew on it. When she bit into it, the dough was crusty on the outside, warm and gooey in the center. She forced it down like medicine. She stood and walked around the fire to Daniel's side.

"I'm going swimming," she said. "Does anyone want to come?"

Eve shook her head. Daniel's face was masked, unreadable. Maggie's heart pounded down the seconds to his answer.

Daniel held up his stick with its terrible hot dog. "A bit cold for nighttime swimming. Think I'll stay put."

She pretended the words weren't acid in her face. *Why?* she wanted to scream. *Could you please tell me what's going on?* Did he not want to swim, or did he not want to swim with Maggie? And if he was falling in love with her, shouldn't he want to eat thumbtacks if it allowed him to be near her?

I'll be naked! We had sex! Come with me, damn you.

Daniel's refusal hung leaden and obvious in the air.

"Swimming's a great idea," Karl said. "I could light the sauna?"

Kindness infused his words, and pity, and this was as gutting as Daniel's rejection. Was she so pathetic as to need rescue from a man who'd already made it clear he didn't want her?

"I don't want to wait." Maggie shuffled in the sand to the other side of the dock, stopping when she thought she could no longer be seen and peeling off her clothes. Swimming wasn't what she wanted—being alone with Daniel was what she wanted—but she'd said she would swim, so she would swim.

She waded in. The day had been hot, but it was the middle of September and, as Daniel had so cruelly observed, cold for nighttime swimming. She sucked in her breath, trying not to gasp audibly. When the water reached her shoulders, she put her face in. The underwater world was still and silent, a comfort. She swam submerged for as long as she could bear to hold her breath.

When she surfaced, the dark outline of a person waited for her at the end of the dock. The figure stooped forward, then crouched. Maggie dipped low, shivering, so the water came to her chin. She couldn't make out the face in the dark.

"You need to stay away from my brother," Eve said. "Please trust me that I'm saying this for your sake as much as his. He's not ready for any kind of relationship."

Maggie ducked lower. The water lapped against her ears. "I think he can make that choice for himself," she said.

"He has. We've been talking today. Believe me, getting involved with him would be a disaster."

"Well, thank you, but I can make my own choices too."

"You did make a choice, and that was to stay single. You also made a choice to live at Still Lake and go into business with me. *And* you made a choice to invest your money, which you might have by now if you hadn't been so self-sabotaging with your degree. So I'm starting to think maybe your choices don't hold a lot of weight."

Maggie's throat was blocked. This was her *friend*, throwing all this in her face?

"You know I'm working on the dissertation—I'm juggling it every single day with retreat center work. And if I get a ride back to Toronto with Daniel, it's only to pack up so I can move here. If you want to talk about choices, you're the one rolling out the welcome mat for the most unethical person we know."

"I told you my reasons for that. I think they're valid."

"You're afraid to be alone and you're probably worried no one else can love you, because Karl's the only person you've ever allowed close enough for that, and you suddenly think I'm unreliable just because I got stranded on an island. But trust me, you don't need Karl."

"Says the woman who's never been single and can't stay away from a man she barely knows just because he offered a crumb of romantic attention."

"This isn't fair. You can't shut me out and take Karl back because I like your brother."

"I don't know, Maggie. Right now I'm doubting why I ever thought a partnership between the two of us would work in the first place."

Maggie stayed in the water until well after Eve had turned and walked away, until her teeth chattered and her thighs were numb. On the shore she yanked her dry clothes over her wet skin. Voices carried from the fireside twelve meters away. Daniel's place was empty, and Karl and Eve sat alone at the fire, their faces illuminated. It was the image from the website, the first picture Maggie had ever seen of Eve—this long-legged, gorgeous woman, Karl goggle-eyed in adoration.

And then, as Maggie watched, Eve scootched closer to Karl and leaned her head on his shoulder.

Maggie scrambled up the side of the hill instead of taking the stairs, grasping at shrubs and weeds in the darkness. In the common room she found a box of black garbage bags, and she carried one to her room and packed everything she owned, all the sundresses and skirts she'd bought on thrifting trips with Eve, the throw pillow, the yoga mat. She left her folders and notes for the retreat center. Without her belongings, the room felt stripped, a ghost of itself, a blank slate for someone else to write on. Because it wasn't going to be Maggie—not anymore.

There was no way she could stay if Eve and Karl were getting back together, if they were making a family in Eve's house next door, if Eve was choosing to go backwards to Karl instead of forward to their dream.

It was over.

Vermillion Road was dark and gloomy, the setting for every cabin-in-the-woods horror film. Tree branches rose like supplicating arms, and the stars were in brilliant high definition. Maggie carried her bulging shoulder bag and alternated lugging the plastic sack across the gravel and hugging it in her arms. She didn't have a free hand for swatting the mosquitoes that buzzed around her, and she gave up caring.

If her dad could see her now. *Look at you, pushing forty, dragging your belongings behind you in a garbage bag, fleeing another romantic disaster. Get it together, Maggie. (Two romantic disasters, Dad. TWO!)*

She'd thought she was creating a new life for herself here? It had never been her life. All along she'd only been borrowing Eve's, making herself indispensable in decisions, places, experiences that didn't belong to her. Eve's lake, Eve's lodge, Eve's baby. Maggie had thrown herself into that pregnancy like the baby was her baby, just as Eve had said.

Eve's baby *wasn't* her baby.

If she kept walking in this direction, Labelle's Cabins would eventually loom in the darkness. Sam would give her a couch for the night and a ride to the bus in the morning. She could go to Charmaine's, sleep in her guest room for a week or two, be lavished with comfort and hopefully only a small amount of *Don't say I didn't warn you.* Her mom was coming back soon, so she could even go home and regress all the way to her teenage self, crying over a boy in her mother's arms.

The impulse to reach for her phone and text Daniel brought a sob to her throat—Daniel, the savior and companion of her recovery, no longer existed.

An engine rumbled and headlights flooded the road. She moved toward the ditch and kept walking, leaden steps forward, even as the car slowed and pulled over beside her.

An automatic window whirred down.

"Maggie," said Daniel.

She kept walking. She had been walking so long she wasn't sure she could stop now. The car inched along beside her.

"Maggie, I'm sorry."

Only when he threw the car into park and left it running to come out and take her shoulders between his hands did she stop moving.

"Maggie."

Tears were snaking down her cheeks. Daniel's hands squeezed her shoulders, rubbed up and down her arms.

"You're freezing."

"I'm still wet."

"Where are you going?"

"Away."

"I've been driving up and down this road, looking for you."

The beam of the headlights caught little bugs in its glow. The garbage bag was terribly heavy.

"Please," Daniel said. "Come sit in the car and warm up."

"I'm not going back. I can't be there anymore."

"We won't drive anywhere, we'll just sit."

She allowed herself to be led to the passenger door. Daniel set her garbage bag on the back seat. She was shivering, and he turned the heat on and they sat there silently, with only the sound of the air through the vents.

"I couldn't let you go," Daniel said. "I heard you leave your room, and I knew you were leaving, you weren't just going back to the fire. I had to stop you."

"Why have you avoided me all day?" She was out of unneedy ways to ask this question.

He was quiet a long time. "Meeting you," he said finally, "was like stumbling on a member of your own species when you've been lost on a foreign planet. That's what it felt like, a ping of recognition, almost from our first messages."

"In our first messages you thought I was Eve."

"Exactly. It was like I knew you, even though I didn't. And you recognized me too. You saw me. It's scary being seen like that, especially when so much of what there is to see is ugly. It's scary opening up to that. Not backing down from that."

"And you backed down, is that what you're saying?"

"Yeah. Yes. Yes, I did."

"You disappeared. No explanation. Then you wouldn't even *look* at me."

He bowed his head. "I'm sorry. It was the first time I've been with someone since Violet. I guess it brought up a lot."

"Is that going to keep happening?"

His gaze was frank. "Probably."

"Eve said you told her you don't want there to be anything between us."

"If I implied that, it was this morning, when I was freaked out and feeling stuck in my grief and like I'll never be able to move on. Which isn't the truth."

"She told me to stay away from you."

"She doesn't want you to hurt me. She probably thinks you already have."

"She's right, though, isn't she?" Maggie felt strong and sure, in control for the first time that day. "You're not ready to get involved with anyone, and honestly, neither am I. We were impulsive, and maybe we thought there was more between us because of the texting, but we barely know each other."

"Eve's wrong." He turned, facing her, and grasped both her hands in his. His touch jolted through her. "We have something, Maggie, and it's rare. I was sitting there by the fire, thinking about you and Violet and these last horrible months and this grief that feels impossible to pull myself out of, and I could barely stand myself. Then later, when I heard you leaving, I felt like, *fuck it*—I have to choose happiness, don't I? I have to take a path forward."

"I'm the *fuck it*?"

"You're the path forward."

"I'm *fuck it* and I'm a path."

"Okay, that's not very romantic. I'm trying to be honest with you. We're *us*. We're the ones who can say exactly what we're feeling in the middle of the night and know it'll be received. No expectations, no right or wrong. I'm trying to do that now, even though you're sitting in front of me and you're really intimidating me with how steely you're being, you know?"

"Am I?"

"Kinda."

"Is Eve taking Karl back?"

"She's thinking about it. It's looking that way."

"And how do you feel about that?"

"I want to drown him in the lake. I think he needs to suffer a lot more for what he did to both of you, and I'm sure he's just going to betray her in some other way. But I've said my piece and I can't control her actions."

"If you and I got together, I'm not sure Eve would ever forgive me."

"If she wants us to accept Karl in her life, then it goes both ways. She doesn't get to control our relationship either. This isn't about Eve. This is about us."

She wanted to tether his hands to her, keep this warm strength always on her body.

"I can't be jerked around," she said. "I can't be second-best. I can't be somebody's second choice. I promised myself I wouldn't be that again."

"I'm here now. On this godforsaken road in the dark. Wanting *you*." His hand caressed her neck and pulled her close.

"What does the path forward look like?" she asked.

They were nose to nose, millimeters apart.

"We'll create it together," he said.

Kissing him required the barest of movements. Her face inclined toward his and he met her, and she could have wept with the release and relief.

When they pulled apart, he said, "Come back with me."

"To Toronto?"

"To New York."

She laughed. "Are you serious?"

"If I've learned anything, it's that life really is short. So yeah. I'm serious."

"Where would I live?"

"With me."

"I guess I could work on my dissertation just as well there as anywhere else."

"I don't want to go back to text messages. I don't want to go back to the life I had before I met you."

Still Lake was over. If she had an opportunity to shoot for happiness with her own partner, create her own love and belonging and home—maybe even have a child of her own eventually—shouldn't she take it?

Going to New York with Daniel was no more preposterous than anything else that had happened this year. Maybe it was the wisest choice she could make.

"I've got all my stuff," she said. "Can we go right now?"

PART 3

December–January

Chapter 30

Eve

The snow fell to earth, gentle but determined. The trees were already covered, their bare branches bowing under the weight, and the frozen lake was an unbroken expanse of white. Eve stood in the open doorway of the dining hall. Christmas was a week away, and for more than four months now she had owned this dining hall, the land the snow fell on, the sauna and the beach, the bedrooms and wraparound balcony and roof of the main lodge. A roof that she had recently learned would have to be replaced if she didn't want this snow also falling on her guests in their beds—provided she ever had guests in their beds, because she was discovering by the day exactly how much she couldn't afford this place and its massive drain on the resources she'd depleted by buying it in the first place.

Especially because, yesterday, her one remaining hope had disintegrated: The business loan she'd applied for had been unequivocally denied.

She and Flora had spent the night here, on the smooth finished half of the dining hall floor. Preposterous accommodation for a woman in her thirty-sixth week of pregnancy, but most nights she was wide awake for hours anyway, and she'd had a blanket and an air mattress and a pillow, and she hadn't wanted to leave the property, this place where she'd devoted so much effort and desire. She'd returned from her humiliating appointment at the bank and come straight here to lay down a few boards with quick, hard flings of her hammer. The floor so solid and dark and hers. She hadn't touched this floor since September, since Maggie, and it felt like the right place to let out her frustration.

And then she'd wanted to stay. To camp out alone on the floor she had made with her own hands.

Well, not only her own hands. There had been other hands.

Now it was morning and the snow was falling on her land and her roof, and she stepped into it and let it fall on her too, because why not? Everything else was.

She went back inside, shaking snowflakes from her hair, and dragged her mattress over to the biggest window, sitting cross-legged and wrapping the blanket around her shoulders to watch the snowfall.

"Hey, baby, what are we gonna do?" she whispered, pressing her hand to her belly. It was a hackneyed move but she couldn't stop doing it, still awed by the mound that had taken over her body. "How are we going to save this place?" And how was Eve going to be ready for birth and a baby if she didn't figure this out in the three or four weeks she had left before she'd be talking to the baby without the barrier of a uterine wall?

The birth was a cliff she was hurtling toward, one she couldn't swerve away from, and though she'd surprised herself by loving pregnancy and was looking forward to caring for her baby, almost everything on the other side of that cliff was unknown. Once she was airborne, once she crash-landed on whatever uncharted terrain awaited her, she would be responsible for the survival and flourishing of a fragile human life. And she did not want to hit that cliff unprepared.

Pinpointing where everything had fallen apart was no challenge. First she'd had to buy the lodge outright, then sink more into lumber, wiring, an electrician, and a plumber. Reasoning, in the beginning, that they would get solid financially as soon as Maggie's money was flowing into the business. Reasoning, more recently, that a business loan would save her until she could start generating revenue.

Because when she'd committed to the retreat center, she had a business partner with funds to invest. And she no longer had this partner.

She closed her eyes, inhaled deeply, and held the breath for a count of four, exhaling through her mouth—a breath pattern Maggie had taught her, dammit, but it still infused her with a sense of calm and well-being. Inside her, the baby unleashed a volley of kicks. Eve smiled. Who cared what one stuffy banker had to say about her business prospects? She was growing a human! She was gigantic and amazing, powerful and primeval and connected to the laden trees and the frozen lake and the aggressive snow and to every woman through the ages who had created life and spread her legs to birth life onto the earth. If she could do that, she could find a solution for herself and her lodge and her baby.

She opened her eyes and looked up. Framed in the doorway—tool belt strapped around him, a stainless steel mug in each hand—stood Karl.

He darted inside, hunched under a snow-covered hood. His steps in his steel-toed boots were heavy as he walked toward her and handed her a mug. "You didn't think I'd worry you'd been eaten by wolves when you didn't come home last night?" He leaned over and kissed her forehead.

"Did you?"

"Not really. I was going to head over to check on you, but then I fell asleep on the couch." They'd both been working hard, trying to get as much done on the lodge as possible before the birth. Eve was down to part-time hours at Sam's for the winter season, but Karl had been picking up work in a friend's construction company, exhausted by the time he arrived home to put in a second shift at the lodge.

His tool belt clunked to the floor in front of the painting of Bernice at Truth Landing. "We have got to do something about this painting," he said. "Can't she go in a bedroom where I don't have to see her?"

"She's my inspiration." *Our* inspiration, she almost said, meaning hers and Maggie's, but there was no point mentioning her.

"She's mannish. Look at those arms. Those are brawny arms."

"I like her," she said. She'd already quietly stuffed the Karl jar inside a cupboard after he returned; she was not getting rid of Bernice too.

"You're not working today?" she asked.

"No, there's a delay with some supplies, so I thought I'd use the time to get stuff done here."

Eve nodded, feeling the suspicion that had been creeping in lately, tainting everything: Was this fact true, was that story real, or was it one he'd made up? The questioning came to her even about things that didn't matter. Had he really bought those headphones at Best Buy, or was it Staples? Had he invented his childhood shame over his dad being the school janitor; had his dad actually been the principal? *Was* Karl working construction, or was he off spending the days with a different girlfriend?

So far she'd resisted the urge to check his phone.

"The baby can't wait to get out," Eve said. "She's doing jumping jacks in here." She gazed upward at him. "Want to feel?"

He pressed his hand briefly into her belly and stepped away.

"Karl," she said.

"What?"

She knew the adjustment was huge for him. From international backcountry trekker to father-to-be settling down around the corner from where he grew up, preparing for an eighteen-year commitment. He'd come with her to a couple of midwife appointments, he listened patiently through her baby name indecision and threw out his own mostly joking suggestions (Lake, Rowan, or Paddler were his current favorites), and he was as useful with crib set-up and car seat research as he'd always been with any household chore. He'd even enlisted the help of a friend's wife and thrown Eve a surprise baby shower. But there was a slight hesitation, a carefulness around her and the pregnancy, that she couldn't read. He'd started using phrases like "your delicate condition," as though her pregnancy had turned him into a Victorian minister. It made her nervous, when on her own she felt quite powerful. *Was* she as vulnerable as he seemed to think? What if sperm quality contributed more to the health of a fetus than she'd realized? Her pregnancy and Maggie's had come from the same seed, and that was a fact she hadn't been able to get out of her mind recently. Her pregnancy wasn't ectopic, but all kinds of complications could still make themselves known at this stage. Was there such a thing as cursed sperm?

"Nothing," she said.

They'd agreed to start fresh. If they were going to be together, they had to trust each other, and if they didn't—if Eve, specifically, did not trust Karl—they shouldn't be together. But the hurt recurred in cycles. She was fine when they were busy, their same companionable, active selves side by side, but when she stopped moving long enough to realize what she felt, what she felt was unsafe. He'd cheated once; wasn't it only a matter of time before he did it again?

They'd discussed the terms of their new relationship: mutual respect for each other's needs, open communication, the airing of concerns as they arose. They weren't doing any of it. Eve, for example, had yet to tell him that her loan had been denied, and neither was she asking him the questions that rose unbidden. *Are your parents actually excited about the baby or are you making that up? Would you ever have come clean about Maggie if you weren't busted?* And, more to the point: *Do you want to be this baby's father?*

Once, in his jocular minister voice, he'd called her "Mother," and she'd thrown a shoe at him. "I'm not *your* mother," she said. "I'm your lover. Your horny lover, by the way." Her reconciliation with Karl had coincided with her second-trimester libido surge, and they'd spent energetic days and nights in her bedroom, shirking every responsibility to have sex three or four times in twenty-four hours. She'd always liked sex—even at the height of Stillcraft, when she hadn't made space for relationships, she'd had time for sex—but now she loved it. Her orgasms came quick and strong, one following another. She loved not worrying about birth control. She was permanently lubricated, had only to look at him to be ready for him. Sometimes, she had only to look at herself.

She wanted to use this body. She wanted to swim with it across the lake, build a table and a chair, dance naked in the bush, draw another body into hers and fuck and make love and fuck and sweat and lick and fill orifices and touch every inch and satisfy and be satisfied until she was depleted and full. She wanted to fuck like she was a dancer and a boxer and a swimmer and a carpenter and a woman so powerful she could create new life.

But they were accustomed to each other now, and busy renovating the lodge, and, astoundingly, she thought two weeks might have passed since they last had sex. Possibly three.

He wasn't touching her. He didn't want to feel the baby kick. They were definitely both keeping things from each other.

That evening Karl's friend Scott came over. Eve had spent the day penduluming between optimistic lodge-saving solutions and increasingly dire mental forecasts of her future, and she didn't feel like being social. She sat with Karl and Scott in the living room for thirty minutes, listening to them reminisce about high school, then excused herself to the bedroom.

If it had been *Karl's* name on the loan paperwork, she thought, lying on her back on the bed, would the application have been turned down? If she'd brought Karl into the meeting, Karl with his M.B.A. and his male genitalia and the absence of glaringly obvious maternal responsibility on the front of his body, would the loan officer have handed over a check?

That wasn't fair, though. Eve could see that she'd been sloppy, and that's what she was really mad about. First she had trusted Maggie too quickly, had accepted a good-faith agreement with nothing in writing to hold anyone to anything: the height of stupidity. Then she'd been so caught up in her growing body and her baby preparations and the sex-infused rekindling of her relationship that she'd put together a lazy application and just believed everything would—what? *Work out?* The Stillcraft Eve Moretti would not have been so careless, so confident without cause.

She should have involved Karl. At least had him look the application over. He'd offered. He had an M.B.A. He'd worked in a bank!

She got up to use the bathroom.

"An outdoor adventure center?" Scott was saying from the living room. "Wow, man, okay, I can totally see it now. *Now* it makes sense."

Eve stood stock-still by the bathroom door.

"How far along are you into making this happen?" Scott asked.

Eve unfroze and strode over to join them. "I'm sorry, making what happen?" she asked.

Karl reached for her hand. "I've been telling Scott about the lodge," he said.

He shot her a look she couldn't read. *Just go with it? I'll explain later?*

"There's a lot of work left to do—Eve originally had a contractor lined up, but we decided we could do most of the renovation ourselves and just hire people occasionally, so that's taking longer, but I'm hoping we might be able to start taking some canoe trips out by summer. Right, Eve?"

She stared at him. Adventure center? "Sure," she said. "Canoe trips." She did like canoeing.

"I'd give anything to have that be my life." Scott sighed.

Karl grinned. "We'll keep you in mind once we're looking for staff."

They were lying on her bed—their bed—after Scott left, gorging on the tub of Häagen-Dazs that Eve had made Karl drive to Larkin for. Karl was letting her eat most of it, or maybe Eve had commandeered it. She was behaving a little aggressively with her spoon.

"So, tell me about this *outdoor adventure* center," Eve said.

"Oh, you know," Karl said. "It's one possibility."

"It's a retreat center."

"Right, but theoretically at this point it could become anything, so I didn't see the harm in making it an outdoor adventure center for the night. Honestly, I was just making up something to get Scott off my back. He was suggesting I was in some kind of ball-and-chain situation, ribbing me pretty hard about losing my freedom. I just said that to throw him off the scent."

"The *scent*?"

"He knows I didn't want to live in Northern Ontario and that I didn't want to be a father. That's not a secret—you knew it too."

"Great. Comforting."

"Ignore this, okay?" He ran his hand along her forearm. "It doesn't mean anything."

Eve flopped back onto the bed. Flora scrambled up and sank her sixty pounds across Eve's legs.

"What if there was no lodge?" Eve said into the ice cream carton.

"How do you mean?"

"Well, if I—say I'd never bought it. You came back here, no lodge. Just me and baby. Would you still be here?"

"There is a lodge."

"But if there wasn't."

What she couldn't ask him: *If Maggie hadn't lost her baby, would you be with her instead?* Because Karl didn't know about Maggie's pregnancy. Early on, he'd asked Eve why Maggie had come to Still Lake; Maggie, apparently, had told him he didn't deserve to know.

"You know how dramatic she gets," Karl said. "Did she come just to confront me or get information out of you, or to try to make up with me or—?"

Eve had stumbled over her response. If Maggie had chosen not to tell Karl about her pregnancy, it wasn't Eve's secret to reveal. She was angry with Maggie, but she still felt loyal toward her too.

"All of those things," she said.

Which seemed to satisfy Karl, who Eve suspected didn't want to probe too deeply into the fallout of his transgressions anyway.

"Eve," he said now. "I know the lodge is a ton of work. I'm sure a few freak-outs are normal on the path to starting a business, but we're making it happen."

"I'm not freaking out."

"You're talking about having no lodge."

Her spoon painted swirls into the brown residue as she scraped up the last of the chocolate.

"Maybe it would help," he said.

"What?"

"Making the lodge something more active. Catering to a specific crowd."

"We *are* catering to a specific crowd. It's just not your crowd."

"I guess I thought the retreat center idea was more, you know . . . Maggie's idea."

Eve pulled her legs out from under Flora and swung them off the side of the bed so she was facing the window. Eve thought of Maggie constantly, but since that conversation about why she'd come to Still Lake, she and Karl had successfully avoided talking about her. Maggie was, in every respect, a disaster they both needed to move on from, and Karl was breaking the unspoken pact.

"Then call it the one good thing to come from knowing Maggie," Eve said.

"You *could* ask if she still wants to invest, even if she's not on-site," said Karl. "In case you don't get the business loan."

"I didn't get the business loan."

"What?"

"The appointment was yesterday. At the bank. They denied it."

"Fuck. Okay. So we need a plan B."

That was it? That was his reaction to her calamity?

"What if you did contact Maggie?" Karl asked.

Dear god, did Karl want Maggie to come back? Did *he* miss her? Was he thinking about her as much as Eve was?

"She screwed me over, Karl. I wouldn't be in this mess if she hadn't pulled out of our agreement."

"Yes, but to be fair to her, you did pretty much tell her to fuck off."

"I did not."

Did she? Karl had heard an earful from Eve about Maggie and Daniel in that first week, but all Eve had said to Maggie before she left was *Stay away from my brother.* Mostly all.

"She wouldn't have to be involved in running the place," Karl said. "She could just invest some money. She must have it by now. Go after her and find out. You know where she is."

"I don't want to do business with someone who's so . . ." *Untrustworthy*, she was going to say, but that wasn't a word she wanted hanging in the air between her and Karl. "Flighty," she finished.

She wasn't entirely sure he *would* stick around if she lost the lodge.

He laid his palm on her back. "Why don't we make a clean break?" he said. "No money from Maggie, none of Maggie's ideas. *We're* renovating this place, she has nothing to do with it anymore. Let's make it something new."

It wasn't a terrible idea, an outdoor adventure center. Specifically, it wasn't a terrible idea to create an environment where Karl could thrive. A fact that was in itself dispiriting. As though she had a toddler already and needed to devise diversions to keep it from getting bored, wandering off, falling into the lake.

Eve turned around slowly. Karl kept his hand where it was, and it skimmed her body as she moved, shoulder blade to bicep to chest, warm through her shirt. Heat pulsed between her legs and she thought of directing his hand down to her elastic-paneled pants. Was it possible they hadn't had sex in *four* weeks?

She grasped his hand where it rested at her heart and held it there.

"I'm doing *this* for you," he said gently. "Could you give just a little?"

She said, "Doing what for me?"

He waved his arm across her torso.

In a single motion she propelled her body off the bed, away from him.

"No one's holding a gun to your head. I can do this on my own."

She could *not* do it on her own. Care for a baby twenty-four seven while working to build a business and keep afloat financially? Handle whatever physical, mental, or emotional complications arose? What if she had postpartum depression? What if there were medical complications? What if something truly terrible happened, like with Maggie's pregnancy? She'd never before felt how much of a front her drive for independence was: bluster, self-preservation, covering a fear of being let down and left. She pre-emptively told herself she preferred being alone so she wouldn't feel the pain of abandonment when it happened.

But she needed Karl to *want* to be here.

"I know you can do it on your own," he said. "I don't think you should have to."

"If you're only with me because of your sense of duty, this won't work."

He crossed the bed on his knees. She waited, pulse quickening, looking down at him from where she stood beside the bed. When he reached her, he took her hands and looked straight into her eyes.

"Can we acknowledge," Karl said, "that this is a challenging transition for me without it meaning I don't want to be here?"

Eve let out her breath, slow like a deflating tire. "I have doubts too," she said.

"About parenthood?"

"About all of it. How I'm going to handle it. Whether I'll fuck it up. Whether I'll fuck the kid up."

"Do you have doubts about us?"

He asked it so directly. The frankness they'd agreed to and hadn't followed through with.

"Sometimes." All the time.

He nodded. "That's natural, given . . . everything."

"I just need you to be honest with me."

"I am being honest with you."

In a matter of minutes he'd fallen asleep. Eve lay awake for what felt like hours, thinking about Maggie.

In the first hours of Maggie and Daniel's disappearance, before Eve realized it *was* a disappearance, she'd been relieved that neither of them was around. The last thing she wanted, that night of the bonfire and the morning that followed, was for Daniel or Maggie to walk in. She'd let Karl kiss her at the fire, and that led them back to Eve's house and a solid twelve hours naked together, dozing and eating only in quick breaks from having sex and talking and having more sex. It was a relief to revel in the regeneration of their relationship without tiptoeing around Maggie's feelings or Daniel's judgments. She was still mad at Maggie for taking up with her bereaved brother, then toying with and—she thought—discarding him, and she didn't care if Maggie hid out in her room for a week. If she pulled up stakes and went back to Toronto for the rest of the month, even better—it would give them both time to cool off.

Eve might have been a bit brutal in her anger, she might have spoken some harsh words, but she hadn't wanted Maggie to *vanish*. Not forever.

But when Eve, throbbing and glowing and invincible, surfaced from the reconciliation sex binge to knock on Daniel's door the next morning, the emptiness was puzzling, then quickly panic-inducing. Because he was nowhere—nowhere along the water or on any of the hiking trails, nowhere in the outbuildings, nowhere at Sam Labelle's. His rental car was gone, but clothes were still tossed across the chair in his room, a New York Public Library book open on the nightstand—clearly he hadn't intended to leave for good, and something catastrophic had happened.

Maggie's room *was* cleared out. Clothes, laptop, jumble of toiletries in the bathroom—gone.

Eve dialed both their numbers over and over until one of them answered, a full week later.

"*Where the hell are you?*" she screamed at Maggie. By that point she was screaming.

There was a pause. "New York."

The words were a punch to Eve's gut.

"With Daniel," Maggie continued. Her tone was defensive but proud, a child announcing a stunt she knew she shouldn't have attempted but was nevertheless thrilled to have pulled off.

Maggie's next words, as Eve tried and failed to regain speech, were still seared on Eve's brain.

"We got married."

That was almost three months ago, and Eve had spoken to neither of them since.

Chapter 31

Maggie

How long after a partner's death should you start a new relationship? How long does it take to move past the loss of a spouse? Is it possible to EVER move past the loss of a spouse?

Four months before, Maggie had been researching website platforms and marketing strategies, copywriting, self-guided versus directed retreats. Her browser history had devolved to this.

She was hunched at her laptop on Daniel's couch (their couch), discarded coffee cups balanced on the table in front of her amidst notes for her green card application. She was supposed to be reading the instructions for the next interminable form in the lineup, not distracting herself with widowhood subreddits and wife-of-widower newsletters.

Maybe she should start a wife-of-widower Instagram. Maybe that could be her new life purpose. In addition to her languishing dissertation and this godawful application.

She picked up her phone and switched to her other compulsive distraction: the app where she'd been tracking the growth of Eve's baby since that first midwife appointment. This week, the baby was the size of a honeydew melon.

From the bedroom, feet thumped on hardwood. Maggie dropped the phone and scrambled to close the windows on her laptop, switching to the official US government immigration website. Daniel appeared in the doorway from the bedroom, shirtless and boxer-shorted, curls tousled in a way she'd have called sex-induced if she didn't know better.

She put on a smile. "Sleep well?"

"What time is it?"

She checked the clock on her screen. "Eleven thirty."

He nodded. "Is there coffee?"

"I just made some fresh." She set her laptop on the couch. "Let me get you some."

But he was already making his way to the kitchen, and she sat back into the couch and raked her fingers through her hair, scrabbled in her bag for a tube of lipstick. It was almost empty, and she had to dig her fingernail into the canister to pull up a clump of red. Funds available to replace this lipstick: zero. She smeared it on her lips and checked the result with her phone camera. Following Daniel into the kitchen, she became acutely aware of the silky silver negligee she still wore—sultry or slovenly? Hard to say. At the coffee maker, she took up a position behind him, close but not too close. One hand hovered at his shoulder: Touch? Don't touch? He stepped back and his shoulder smacked against her forehead, and he side-stepped away from her to the sink.

Don't touch.

From the cupboard she pulled down his favorite mug, ventured close enough to hand it to him.

"We have a logistical problem," she said. When in doubt, stick to practicalities.

"Yeah?"

"We're supposed to have letters from friends and family vouching for our relationship."

He set the mug on the counter, ran the tap, cupped water in his hands, and splashed it on his face.

"People who've known us as a couple, spent time with us together," she said. "People who can say we're legit."

He leaned back against the sink. "And the problem is, we're not legit?"

"*No*, the problem is, the only person who knows both of us is Eve."

"I'm sure she'd be *thrilled* to write up a rave review."

She wasn't ready to joke about the rift with his sister. The rift with his sister, when she allowed herself to think about it, brought a feeling of genuine illness to Maggie's stomach.

"I was thinking more along the lines of maybe it's time you introduce me to your friends."

He moved to the coffee maker, his back to her as he poured. She beat him to the fridge and poured his cream, one quick *splurt*.

He still wasn't looking at her when he said, "There is this thing tomorrow night."

Almost hesitantly. Almost like he was confiding something. Her radar pinged. A thing! A thing he was opening up about.

"Oh?" She leaned one elbow casually against the counter. *Sultry, please. Not slovenly. Do not mess this up.*

"It's a stupid thing. I wasn't planning to go."

"Stupid how?"

"A dinner party."

"With your friends?"

"Yes."

"*The* friends?"

He'd told her about these people on the flight to New York, in that mystical period when they'd talked non-stop. How they'd all met in med school and paired off early, four men and four women, best girl friends and best guy friends, Violet the dynamic social center of them all. Violet, who never forgot a birthday; Violet, who would pick you up and get you home no matter the hour or the depth of your inebriation, accompany you to your father's funeral, be your date to your ex's wedding. Violet the Great.

"Yes."

"I'd love to meet them." She was terrified to meet them, but surely his bringing up the possibility was a good sign.

"I don't know if I want to go."

"It'd probably be good, no? To see your friends?"

"Don't patronize me."

"I just mean . . . wouldn't it?"

"Not necessarily."

He stalked from the room and she was left there in her stupid, pointless negligee, blinking rapidly. These curveballs came, she should know to expect them, but they took her by surprise every time. Maybe she *was* being patronizing. She'd meant to be supportive.

What did he want? If he'd only talk to her and tell her, she would become it.

And *that* thought was so old and so familiar, she felt perfect dismay in the face of it. Hadn't she grown at all? All those enlightened post-Karl intentions, those grand pronouncements about loving and showing up for herself; how was she now inside this relationship—this *marriage*!—feeling yet again like a little girl trying to win her father's unwinnable affection?

A cry came from the living room, half growl, half wail. "What did you do with them!"

Maggie flew to the doorway. Daniel was standing at the mantel.

Oh. Right. The photos.

"They're nice, aren't they?" She tried for bright but not patronizing.

"The pictures of Violet—where are they?"

"I was going through photos of us for the application. I decided to print some and put them around the apartment."

He held a framed image of the two of them on the Brooklyn Bridge, on their second day in New York City.

"But what did you do with the photos of Violet?"

"They're in the guest room," she said.

She rushed there now, pulling frames off the shelves and piling them into her arms. Violet beamed up at her, and Daniel beamed alongside her. She'd done this late last night, waiting for Daniel to come home from work. She'd bought new frames—she wasn't so tone-deaf as to remove Violet and place her own image in the same frames—and then she'd put Violet in a room she didn't have to walk across a hundred times a day.

She wasn't deliberately trying to provoke him. Or maybe she was—trying to assert herself, at least—because goddamn it, *something* had to change.

"You can't erase her," he said, pulling the pictures from her arms.

"I don't want to erase her," she said. "I just want to create a little room for me."

He set the frames on the mantel, and for one moment he looked at her like he used to. Openly, tenderly. "I'm sorry," he said. "Of course. You deserve that."

She crossed her arms. "Daniel," she said carefully. "We are not okay. *You* are not okay."

"I promise I'll try harder. I love you. You know I love you. It's just . . . not as simple as I thought it would be."

He planted a kiss on her forehead and she allowed herself to lean into it, to believe it could all be good again.

"Give me some time," he said. "Please?"

"Of course," she said.

He held her tight and then let her go.

The marriage hadn't been her idea. They'd left Still Lake together, driving away from Eve and Karl and their clear wish to have Maggie out of their lives. Daniel had chased her down on that desolate road, he had abandoned his clothes, his suitcase—"I've got others," he said—and Maggie had never in her life felt so desired, so cherished, so chosen. He was leaving his sister behind for her! His twin sister, who would be furious. Who already was furious. He had come after her, he had pursued her, and they were driving together through the dark, his hand on her thigh, her head on his shoulder, and never mind the center console digging into her hip.

They drove to Toronto through the night, both of them wired and wide awake, talking the whole time. By three a.m. they'd checked into a downtown hotel. He changed his flight and booked her on it. In the morning she messaged Natalie and fetched her passport, a suitcase, and her most fondly missed outfits from her apartment, and they headed to the airport.

He loved her, he wanted to be with her, he didn't want to live without her.

Her first sensation, when she'd stepped out of the cab with him on 76th Street, had been of humidity and darkness. The air was heavy with moisture trapped between asphalt streets and concrete buildings, and the sun had already set. At Still Lake she hadn't noticed the days being light and long, but in New York she was startled by the earlier night.

New York. She had left Toronto behind, she had left Still Lake behind, and once again she was creating her life anew.

It was all exciting in the first week. The spontaneity, the boldness of what they'd done. Sneaking off, flying in the face of all the rules. The *you haven't known each other long enough* rule. The *his wife hasn't been dead long enough* rule. Screw that. They needed each other, they wanted each other, they had each pulled the other through a raw and terrible time, and from the beginning they'd skipped the shallows and plunged straight for the depths. Their relationship was young, but it had an old soul.

They married in that first week. He'd taken extra time off work and given her a whirlwind tour of his city—MoMA and Central Park, The Met and the ballet, the Cloisters and the Museum of Sex, a different restaurant every night and brunch on the mornings they could drag themselves from their lovemaking. It was a dream. They talked about everything. There was nothing she didn't love in him then, even his grief. Especially his grief. So sensitive. So deep-feeling. So pure. When he said, over mimosas on a garden patio in the East Village, "We should get married," she'd hesitated briefly—wasn't that just slightly nuts?—but it felt so *meant*. Maybe *this* was the purpose all along, the reason everything happened with Karl and Eve. To bring her to her husband.

They went to City Hall the next day for a marriage license, and they went back the day after that for a marriage ceremony.

He did not want to live without her.

She should have paid more attention to the subtext in that declaration, Maggie thought, sitting alone in his—their—apartment on West 76th Street after the debacle of the mantel photos, the coffee table in front of her strewn with the pictures and cards and over-wordy sentences she was trying to turn into convincing evidence for the US government on the validity of her fledgling marriage.

He did not want to live without her.

But more and more now, it seemed the person he didn't want to live without was Violet.

For the billionth time, she allowed her finger to hover over Eve's name in her phone. But she'd already had the ensuing conversation with Eve in her head, the one featuring many lordly *I-told-you-so*'s—and that was when Eve didn't hang up on her and refuse to have an imaginary conversation at all.

Now, three months since her arrival, that first week in New York *was* a dream. And so was Still Lake—one she caught remnants of in her peripheral vision, flashes of memory and impressions, but nothing solid that she could return to.

Daniel had gone out. He kissed her and held her before he went, but he didn't tell her where he was going or ask her to come. Maggie had tried adopting her own breezy come-and-go approach, leaving the apartment on invented reasons, criss-crossing the city on foot for hours, trying to make it hers, to map it onto her body so that maybe she could start feeling like she belonged here even if she couldn't feel she belonged with Daniel. Trying to give Daniel the chance to miss her. But leaving the apartment for any length of time required funds. And funds were a problem. A problem she planned to rectify today.

In her hand, her phone sang. It was time for her virtual date/meeting/beg-fest with her mom, and she wasn't ready. She'd planned to take extra care—if not dress her best, at least get dressed.

She took one final composing breath and accepted the video call. There was her red-eyed self on the screen. There was her mother, in her pearl studs and navy caftan.

"Sweetheart, are you all right?"

"Yes, just—you know." Maggie ran her fingers through her hair and laughed. "The morning got away from me. Daniel and I were . . ." She let that thought trail away and hoped the bed-head and negligee would speak their own story.

Lying to her mom was a bad sign. But she had no choice, because when she'd called her mom in that first euphoric week to tell her she was a married woman, her mom had been alarmed—*You've only known him in person for two weeks and you* married *him?*—and Maggie could not allow the judgers (her parents, Eve) to be right.

Her mother had flown to New York in October, ostensibly to visit her daughter in her new home and her husband during his Columbia teaching stint, but definitely to check that Maggie was still sane. Maggie and Daniel had gone out for dinner with her parents. It had been a good stretch with Daniel; even now there were good stretches, which was almost worse than constant disconnection because it kept her hoping and reinvesting. At dinner Daniel was attentive—talkative, even. Her dad was wowed by his medical degree and his address near the park, and even her mom had liked him well enough, but that didn't mean she thought Maggie should have married him.

Only Charmaine knew how much Maggie was struggling. Charmaine had also been a judger—she'd cried when Maggie told her about the wedding, saying she wished Maggie had called her before she did it—but Maggie needed at least one confidante, and she'd pretty quickly begun telling Charmaine the truth.

But she could make this marriage work. Daniel was grieving, and Maggie was pretty sure he was also clinically depressed. Both of these states were temporary and fixable. They just needed time.

And *Maggie* needed independence. Means to build a life of her own here that did not revolve around Daniel. Money.

She and her mom small-talked until the conversation circled from the green card to Maggie's shambles of a dissertation to her dire financial straits, and she asked the question straight out: "Would you be willing to help me get my trust money?"

"You mean—now?" Her mother looked perplexed.

"If I wasn't your daughter, wouldn't you and your colleagues be having closed-door discussions about how I wasn't cut out for academia? I'm never going to have that Ph.D., and I think we all just need to face that fact."

"Deciding not to pursue a career in academia is one thing," her mother said, "but quitting the dissertation when you're so close doesn't make sense."

"Continuing so long didn't make sense."

"Maggie." Never had her mother looked so disappointed. "You've been working toward this money for yourself and your career and your future. Now you want it for living expenses because you impulsively moved somewhere you can't legally work and married a brand-new widower you knew only via text? You do understand why I'd be worried about this."

"I believe in Daniel and me, okay? But we do have a few challenges, and it would help if me being broke wasn't one of them."

"If you really want to get the money now, you'll need to talk to your father." Her mother's lips tightened into a puckered oval. "He's right there in New York. He told me you keep canceling when he tries to see you."

"I'm reaching out to him next. I just hoped you could lay the groundwork for me."

Her mother shook her head. "Finish the revisions, defend your dissertation, get your Ph.D.—that's my advice. I know you've been through a lot, but from what I can see, my love, an inheritance magically landing in your bank account isn't the solution you truly need here."

Maggie nodded and said she had to be going, feeling the refusal as forcefully as if her mother had slammed her laptop in Maggie's face. She sat there for a long time afterward, in her unbrushed hair and negligee that had been so lovely when she spied it in the SoHo window that first week but was only pathetic when you were still wearing it at noon after what was supposed to be a grown-up conversation with the one person who had always loved you and now was cutting you adrift into the predictable consequences of your own choices.

Chapter 32

Eve

The morning after Karl's adventure center suggestion/demand, Eve woke alone in the bed. A note on the nightstand read *Working on the dining hall.* She stretched, still half asleep, her legs and arms spread-eagled to the four corners of the empty bed, then sat up, crossing her legs and brushing her fingers over the contours of each toe, smoothing her palms along the tops of her feet to her ankles. Up her legs, circling her knees, her powerful inner thighs and large, curvaceous belly. Her breasts were soft and sensitive, nipples darkening. Round shoulders. Throat. Lips. This body she had resented again and again, this female body she'd experienced, for most of her life, as a betrayal. And here it was, unveiled to her senses, beautiful and strong.

"We're strong," she whispered to the baby. "We can figure this out."

She got up and made herself a quick breakfast, then walked with Flora in the direction of Sam's. Walking was good for the baby and good for her birth preparation, according to Abby. She didn't take the road but bushwhacked along the lake, a route she'd never tried, unzipping her coat as she walked. The temperature had risen and the snow was already melting. Hints of a possible one-time trail started to appear, overgrown with saplings beginning to become trees. And then, not far from her house, a clearing. It sloped to the lake on the right, to a spot clear of cattails and trees. A place where a boat could put in.

Truth Landing.

She stood there and the painting materialized in front of her—the tranquil lake, the grassy bank. Not a summer scene like in the painting, but Eve still recognized it. The only thing missing was young Bernice, bold and shame-free as she reclined against her brawny arm.

Look at those arms. Those are brawny arms.

They're strong arms, Karl. They're capable arms.

The Truth Landing *woman is naked, but you can't mess with her, Karl. She's bare and open, but she isn't weak.*

Beside her, Flora let loose her excited, sound-the-alarm bark.

A wolf stood on the other side of the clearing, forty meters away. Grey coat matted, ears forward. Flora was set to bound ahead, but Eve grabbed her collar and pulled her back.

"Hush," she commanded under her breath, her heart rate spiking and her body poised to flee. Flora downgraded to an imploring whine. Eve stood stock-still, every one of her senses on alert, as the wolf eyed them across the distance. Eve was afraid, but she also felt drawn to the wolf, to her raw and worn and powerful animality, her solitary strength. Eve barely breathed as she watched, motionless. Finally the animal turned and loped into the bush, and Eve stayed where she was, certain she'd witnessed magic. She felt the urge to tear off all her clothes and recline naked right here in the snow, the *Truth Landing* woman incarnated.

When she got to Sam's, she told him she needed to use his office to take care of her own work today. He motioned her through the door, made her a cup of tea, and left her to it.

She still felt full of the wolf encounter, and she tried to channel the animal's power as she picked up the phone. Three hours later she'd forced herself through ten calls and sent off twice as many emails, approaching every wealthy client or supplier in her Stillcraft contact list whom she could stand the thought of speaking to who might want to invest in a retreat center.

They needed to see a formal business plan. They needed to see a clear return on investment. They weren't up for a gamble. Their funds were tied up. Three hours of fake-cheerful catch-up and over-optimistic pitching later, she was exhausted. She'd never been good at networking. She wasn't a salesperson. She was a maker. That was why she'd quit Stillcraft, because she wasn't making anymore. This part was supposed to be Maggie's job. Maggie could inspire anyone to sink their life's savings into a dubious venture. Look at how she'd done it to Eve.

If Maggie knew their tranquil space of retreat and renewal was in peril, wouldn't she want to do something? Wouldn't involving Maggie be better than losing the lodge?

But it wasn't just Maggie's money Eve needed. It was *Maggie*. Maggie's ideas, vision, enthusiasm, presence. Eve closed her eyes and allowed herself to imagine it. Maggie coming back to live at the lodge. Karl and Eve next door, in their house with their baby. Maybe Daniel—Maggie's husband, after all, whether Eve liked it or not—would leave his job and find work here; maybe he was ready for a fresh start. A big, happy family.

Because what was Maggie's offense, really, besides hurling herself into love? It was misguided, but it wasn't a crime. And what was Maggie supposed to have done—stayed here with Karl and Eve and their newly reignited relationship? How would that ever have worked?

The daydream dissolved in front of her. It wouldn't have worked then. It wouldn't work now. She missed Maggie constantly, but it was the missing of something that no longer existed.

Her email refreshed and the message preview flashed in front of her: No thanks, but good luck! She checked her bank account again. The numbers had not changed.

Eve returned from Sam's deflated, defeated—if she had any wolf energy in her, she was a bedraggled lone wolf, starved and badly in need of a pack. She stood silently in the doorway of the dining hall. Karl was on his knees, his right hand gripping the hammer, his arm tensing with each blow. The rotted floor she and Maggie had hacked through together, euphoric as they wielded the crowbars, was now almost fully replaced.

Karl leapt to his feet when he saw her, dropping the hammer. They stood there, Eve on the chipboard subfloor, Karl on the brand-new hardwood, several feet from each other. He crossed the floor to her and extended his hand.

"I have to sell," she said. "Either that or let the bank repossess."

He motioned her across the room to where a chair rested against the wall. He pressed her gently into the chair and stood before her. "No, you don't," he said.

"Yes. I do. I've looked at it every possible way. I'm stretched beyond the limit."

"This is what we'll do."

She opened her mouth to speak and he put one finger to her lips and shook his head.

"I've been thinking about this, so hear me out. Will you hear me out?"

She exhaled loudly. "Fine."

"We can start generating income with the lodge right away if we open as an outdoor adventure center this winter. The needs are so much simpler when people are coming to spend most of their time outside and the buildings themselves aren't the point. All anyone needs is a basic place to crash, and if it's a little rustic, who cares. We have three double-occupancy rooms that are livable. That's enough to get started. We don't need a chef cooking fancy meals in a fancy kitchen full-time. We don't need some lavish studio space. We don't need to hire anyone. You and I can do this alone, or I can do most of it while you focus on the baby. And she'll nap sometimes, right?"

"Let's hope."

"The point is, I think we can keep operation expenses minimal, and we can start bringing in revenue right away. We'll finish renovating gradually. Concentrate on one room at a time, do the work ourselves, and as we add more rooms we increase our capacity."

"It's December. You can't even take canoe trips out."

"Snowmobiling. ATVing. Ice fishing. Cross-country skiing and snowshoeing."

"I do not own, nor do I want to own, snowmobiles or ATVs, which are insanely expensive, by the way."

"Winter camping."

"Winter camping is for fools."

"There are plenty of fools worldwide. They'll come. Sam's open year-round, right?"

"Yeah, but barely. There's, like, one family there right now, and only because it's Christmas."

"We just have to market it right. I already know who to reach out to."

"I had some people of my own I was reaching out to today. I've already spoken to them. For the retreat center."

"Oh. Well—how'd it go?"

"Not awesome," she admitted. "But what you're describing sounds way too close to Labelle's Cabins. I don't want to poach Sam's clientele. A women's retreat center with art and wellness and mindfulness programs—*that's* completely different from Labelle's Cabins."

"Sure, but come on. A bunch of women *om*-ing all day? That's really not you. You *like* canoeing. You *like* camping. *This* is your kind of thing."

"It's still too close to Sam's," she said.

"I don't see it. He gets families and old-timers. This'll cater to the crowd in between. Active people, probably twenties to fifties, roughly, no kids—"

"*We'll* have a kid!"

"Okay, sure. Kids don't have to be banned or anything. But the point is, we're making it for people who really want to be *doing* something on vacation, having a great time pushing themselves, developing skills. In the summer we could groom some trails for mountain biking. Dirt bikes, maybe? Definitely fishing, since this used to be a fishing lodge, right?"

She called up an image of this room's future, teeming with sweaty guys in hiking boots playing drinking games, speakers blasting Top-40 radio, fishing tackle and crash helmets against the wall.

"We get a website up, we start promoting it, and we're ready to go," Karl said. "I've got online groups where I'm active, and they'll help spread the word. We'll grow slowly, but we can start growing *now*. It's so much more sensible. It's *doable*."

There was no way she was ever going to run a women's retreat center with Karl. Or on her own, for that matter. It was never going to happen.

But an outdoor adventure center. If they could make it different enough from Sam's . . .

She was so tired, so out of options and ideas, and she just needed this struggle to be over. Karl was right. She had to scale the vision way back, work with what she had, or lose the lodge.

He knelt down in front of her and laid one hand on her belly. She held her breath, waiting for the skittish pulling away. He held her gaze. He kept his hand there.

The *Truth Landing* woman looked out across her shoulder with her peaceful and accepting eyes. Her nakedness pure, a woman in the wild, a woman belonging to nothing but herself and the lake behind her, still and deep blue.

Slowly, Eve nodded her head. "Okay," she said. "Let's try it."

Karl followed her gaze. "And honestly," he said, "do you think we could move this painting somewhere else?"

Eve said, "I'll put her in one of the bedrooms."

That night, Eve joined Karl in the shower. He had closed the bathroom door, but she knocked lightly and nudged it open, then stood in the doorway for ten seconds, twenty. Karl's body was a silhouette through the sheer plastic shower curtain, and it jarred her with its unfamiliarity. When had she last seen him naked?

"Mind if I come in?" she asked.

"I'm almost done. But sure. I'll leave the water running."

She took off her clothes. The metal rings clanged along the rod as she swooped the curtain aside.

"Careful," he said. "Don't want you slipping in your delicate condition."

"Karl."

His body was almost too beautiful for reality, an overabundance of muscle and ripple, blondness and smile.

"I don't know if you realize this," Eve said, "but I have never been stronger in my life."

He stepped away to give her the water. She lathered her arms and her sides, the full breasts, the graceful bump protruding from her frame. The soap flowed down her body, white bubbles like a length of lace.

Karl was so close. A short step and he could be inside her.

She leveled her gaze at him, a frank invitation. "I love you," she said.

"I love you too," he said.

"Show me."

She waited for him and he approached, one step to meet her and then his mouth was on hers. She cupped his ass and pulled him nearer. Her breasts at his chest, her belly at his. He sucked his stomach in and it made a hollow where the contours of her belly could rest.

His mouth was hard and determined, aggressive swipes of his tongue. She opened her mouth to take it in, bit his lip and he bit back. His grip was tight at her shoulders. She pulled away enough to see his face, and his expression was resolute, like a person buckling down to a chore.

Their eyes locked and in the look that passed between them she understood two facts:

Karl was repulsed by her body.

He was desperate for her not to know this.

Eve pulled the curtain aside and tramped onto the bath mat. The impression of her foot remained in the plush fibers after she stepped off it. A film of soap covered her arms, and she seized a towel and wiped it off.

"How long?" she asked.

The water pounded down on Karl's head, streaming along his face and into his eyes. He jabbed his palm into the lever and the water stopped. She handed him a dry towel. He swabbed his face and pulled the towel tight around his waist. She felt him already as an entity apart from her.

"Since you started showing more, I guess."

That he didn't try to deny it was a simple, searing gift.

"I was already showing when we got back together."

"I know, but—not this much."

"On a scale from mild distaste to outright disgust, what are we dealing with here?"

He grasped the grey bathrobe on the back of the door. The robe was around him and the towel whisked off with the same modesty-preserving technique she'd once used changing into her bathing suit in Bushwhack Cabin.

"Don't make me say it," he said.

"Just tell me the truth."

The room was warm, steamy against her bare skin.

"It's not you. It's more . . . all the things happening to you."

"Those things *are* me, Karl. This body is me."

"I know, but—"

"So you're actually repulsed by *me*."

He opened the door, cool air rushing in. She followed him out into the living room.

"I looked it up." He turned to her on the braided rug, and she could see the effort as he made himself look into her face. "Trying to reassure myself I wasn't a complete jerk. And hoping it would go away. It's common, apparently—or at least it happens."

"Men knocking up women and ceasing to find them attractive. That happens, does it?"

"As a—not a condition, but it's a thing."

"Yeah, a thing called misogyny."

"No—"

"If it's because of the weight gain, you do know how problematic that is, right?"

"No, no, not that, it's more—the creepiness factor."

She did not know what to say.

"The way your body's been . . . taken over by an alien, almost," he said. "The fact that there's a person in there."

"Yes. *Our* baby."

"You have to admit it's kind of sci-fi. It's like we're not alone in the room anymore. Like we're being watched. And then the baby moving—I don't want to feel that when we're having sex. It's weird. Indecent, almost."

"Since when are you such a prude?" She was standing in the middle of the room, her hands resting on her naked thighs, her breasts replete and exposed. "I think it's beautiful. It's a complete circle. What do you think put this baby in here?"

"Believe me, I want to want you. I'm just saying how it feels."

"Is that everything? Anything else you need to tell me about how you're feeling about my pregnancy?"

He turned away and crossed to the bedroom. A drawer rasped open and she stood there, waiting, until he came out dressed in sweatpants and a T-shirt.

"Are you hungry?" he asked. "I feel like pancakes. What do you think—bedtime pancakes?"

He cracked eggs into a bowl. A swath of skin showed between waistband and T-shirt as he reached for the oil.

She stared at him.

"It's like you're turning into something else," he said, not looking at her. "You've been my lover and now you're becoming a mother. It's in a whole other category. It's not the category of people you have sex with."

"I'm not *your* mother."

"I didn't say it was rational."

He poured milk into the bowl and beat the batter in vigorous circles. He turned his back to her and clanked a skillet onto the stove. She felt outraged and incredulous but also ashamed, as though *she* had done something wrong.

"You know what?" Eve said. Karl was so horrified about a pregnancy *he* had caused? He didn't even know he'd caused two of them! Why was she protecting Karl from this information? Why was she keeping Maggie's secret for her? "You got Maggie pregnant too."

The gas burner clicked, trying to light, as Karl stood dumbfounded in front of the stove. Eve reached across him to flick the knob so the flame caught.

"If you're concerned suddenly about being a jerk, you should know that your other girlfriend—you know, the one you were seeing behind my back?—she got pregnant too. Only the egg implanted in her fallopian tube instead of her uterus, and it erupted and she almost died."

He was open-mouthed. Speechless.

"So that was lucky for you, wasn't it?" Eve said. "Because you didn't have to deal with how repulsive *her* pregnant body would have become."

"I got *both* of you pregnant?"

"With help from your stash of expired condoms, yes."

"Fuck."

"Yeah, Karl. Fuck."

"That's what she wouldn't tell me?"

"I guess you didn't feel like a safe space, for some reason." She stalked to the bedroom and pulled a purple maternity halter top over her head, tugged on a pair of stretchy pants, then returned to the kitchen.

Karl was still staring at nothing, thinking—what? Was he sad? Guilt-ridden? Relieved? It had to be relief. He'd just learned what a huge bullet he'd dodged. Two girlfriends expecting babies at basically the same time? How would he have handled *that*?

"Nobody told me," he said.

"Yeah, well, you were a little hard to reach at the time. Trust me, we tried."

Karl began ladling batter into the pan. Had he been half expecting *Eve* might miscarry, pretending to embrace his duty while hoping it would be short-lived?

She approached as far as the fridge and waited for him to look at her. "You say you're freaked out by my pregnant body, but I think it's the relationship. Parenthood. The whole deal."

He jiggled the spatula against the pan. "Didn't we just talk about this?"

"Yeah, and to be honest, you weren't that reassuring."

"I have some worries, sure. But so do you. Does anyone go into parenthood feeling ready?"

"This feels like more than that."

"I love you and I got you into this. I'm committed."

"You say that like someone heading to prison."

He flipped one thin pancake over. "It won't be prison, because I'll be running an outdoor adventure center."

She glared at him, pure fury flooding her body. In the skillet, oil sizzled and spat.

Chapter 33

Maggie

"There's still time to bail," Daniel said as he and Maggie arrived at the top step of Violet's best friend's Park Slope brownstone. "This might not be such a great idea."

"We're not bailing," Maggie said.

She was holding flowers purchased with money she couldn't spare, because that, evidently, was the kind of wife she was—the kind who needed her husband's dead wife's friends to think her kind and sophisticated and worthy of taking her place at a dinner party seven months after she'd died. Even if it meant throwing herself further on the financial mercy of a husband who preferred photos of another woman over photos of her.

Maggie reached for Daniel's hand. He squeezed her fingers lightly, then let go. She wiped her palm on her long wool coat and adjusted the skirt of her vintage red dress, bought in a thrift shop her first week here, paired for tonight with tights and boots and a little glittery jacket. The red was a bit audacious, but it was December and surely appropriate for a holiday dinner party?

The door swung open. A petite woman wearing a black shift dress and holding an enormous-bowled wineglass winged lightly into Daniel's arms, dabbing her mascara with one finger. Renata, the best friend.

"I'm sorry, we've been weeping already." The woman stood on tiptoe to kiss Daniel's cheek. "She would have so loved to be here," she whispered into his ear. "Happy Violet's Birthday."

Maggie stared at Daniel. "This is Violet's *birthday*?" she whispered as Renata reached through the door for a tissue on the hall table. "This is Violet's birthday *party*?"

Renata pivoted back to them, delicately blotting her eyes.

"How have you been?" asked Daniel, in a remarkable performance of a composed and communicative man.

"Oh, you know." Renata sighed. "Hardest months of my life, but I don't need to tell you that."

Daniel nodded.

Maggie took the opportunity to thrust her flowers forward. "I'm so sorry," she said. For your loss? For not being Violet? For coming to this party?

Renata wrinkled her nose. "You're not from the bakery? I didn't order flowers. I hope there wasn't a mix-up."

"No, I—"

She cast her eyes to Daniel for assistance, but a man had arrived at Renata's side, was drawing Daniel into a bear hug and leading him indoors with one beefy arm across Daniel's shoulders. "Daniel, how you been, man? Rough, I know it must be rough. I mean, we're all grieving, but *you* . . ."

"I'm Maggie," she said to Renata. "I'm Daniel's—"

Renata's eyes were wide and uncomprehending.

"I'm here with Daniel."

"Oh!"

"I'm really very sorry for your loss." She nudged the flowers in Renata's direction again.

"Did you . . . are you a family member of Daniel's, or . . . ?"

"I'm—I'm a friend of his sister's."

"Oh!" Maggie hoped Renata didn't know about the difficulties between Eve and Violet. But they were best friends—of course she did.

"I'll bring these in, then," Maggie said to the flowers. "Find a vase, maybe?"

"Oh, please don't. I'm allergic to daisies. If you wouldn't mind leaving them on the stoop. I do appreciate the thought."

"Oh. Well, no, of course, I'm sorry." She was so very sorry.

A tall man and a bird-boned redhead ascended the steps behind Maggie. Maggie dumped the bouquet beside a small statue of—Apollo? Zeus? maybe Hippocrates, these all being doctors—and slipped inside past the hostess into a wide entryway. Daniel had vanished. She added her coat to an overburdened rack and moved toward the living room. A man and a woman were seated on cushions at a low square coffee table, spreading soft cheese on crackers, looking at photos on a phone. The woman was crying. She was, like Renata, dressed in black.

She stood as Maggie entered the room. "Are you here with the cake?" She sniffled. "Renata will want it in the kitchen."

"No." Did she look like she was carrying a cake? Was there a cake box in her hand visible only to the eyes of persons with medical degrees? "I'm Maggie." She held out her hand.

"I'm Aya." Next-best friend, pediatrician. Married to Nigel, brain surgeon.

"If you'll excuse me." Maggie continued through the living room into a high-ceilinged kitchen with a six-burner range and more silver appliances than Maggie could identify. Daniel stood alone at a sideboard, pouring his own enormous-bowled glass of red wine.

"You haven't *told* them?" she whisper-snapped. The tears were tight in her throat. "You haven't told them you got married. They don't know I exist."

"I haven't been seeing people. I haven't been telling anyone anything."

In the dining room, visible through another doorway, a long table was set for seven. Renata was snatching up place cards—hand calligraphy, it looked like, though possibly just a nice font—and stuffing them into a drawer. Maggie turned away so she wouldn't see Renata bustling into the kitchen, lifting down an extra plate. She could hear the clink of cutlery as Renata returned with it to the dining room.

Maggie's hands trembled as she reached for a bottle of red. The wine sloshed into the bottom of a glass, and it was warm and bolstering against her tongue.

"Then you had better tell them now," she said.

She hitched her arm through Daniel's and pulled him back into the living room. Aya and Nigel were there, along with the bear-hug man and the couple who'd arrived on the doorstep after Maggie and Daniel, who must be Cicely, gynecology, married to Jeff, oncology. They were all older than Maggie. They were all wearing black.

Four couples, and half of one couple was now missing his complement; Maggie could be here with no one else, and they assumed she was from the fucking bakery?

Renata came in from rearranging the table settings.

Maggie swallowed more wine. "Now," she whispered to Daniel. "Introduce me *now*."

Put your arm around me is what she wanted to say. *Look at me tenderly. Claim me. Desire me again.*

Her heart was breaking.

"Everyone," Daniel said. "This is Maggie."

A chorus of hellos, hands extended and names offered. Maggie's smile was an impostor's, glued on from another person's face. She waited for more from Daniel, but he stood motionless at her side, staring straight ahead. He was not going to do it.

"Thanks for having me," she said to the room. "I realize it's awkward—I didn't know Violet, and I had no idea today was her birthday. I truly wasn't trying to crash anything. I've just been wanting to meet Daniel's friends, and—"

Aya's brow was furrowed, her mouth trying to smile.

Renata looked at Maggie with undisguised hostility.

"I'm sorry," Cicely said. "Who exactly are you?"

Maggie's breath caught. She said, "I'm with Daniel."

"Yeah, but—as *what*?"

Briefly, she considered lying.

"His wife," she said.

A gasp mushroomed across the room. Renata put her hands to her hips and stared unblinking at Maggie.

Maggie could no longer even smile. No dress in the world had ever been more red.

A full minute of blank stares passed—the men shuffling, tears springing visibly to Aya's eyes—before Renata's husband, Ivan, gave Daniel a half-hearted slap on the back. "Hey, congratulations, man," he said.

"How long ago?" Renata asked.

"September," Maggie mumbled.

Renata just stared.

"I guess there wasn't a wedding?" said Cicely. "Given the circumstances?"

Maggie's throat was clogged with unshed tears. Her sparkly jacket caught the light and she wished she could take it off, but showing skin in just the strappy dress would be worse.

The doorbell gonged through the house. Renata spun on a black pump and stalked across the room into the entryway.

"I'm here with the cake you ordered!" The cheery voice carried into the living room.

"If only," said Renata, "it had been you earlier."

She strode back through the living room a moment later, laden with a large box. "I have Violet's birthday cake," she said. "It's red velvet, which we all know was her favorite. The food is ready now, so get into the dining room."

She didn't look at Maggie again, but Maggie caught her eyes on Daniel, and the look she gave him brimmed with venom.

Maggie could imagine that these were nice people. Violet had been, by all accounts, a kind and compassionate person, and surely her closest friends would be the same. But they were not making an effort to be nice to *her.*

The dinner conversation centered on Violet's amazingness. The charity where she donated her skills. The counsel to friends in crisis. The *brain*—she was so smart, but she never lorded that over anyone. *You couldn't hate her*, Eve had told Maggie once. *That's what was maddening about her.*

Beside Maggie, Daniel was silent. Maggie was silent too. This was not a conversation she was equipped for.

"You know," Daniel said all of a sudden, "she wasn't a saint."

The clatter of cutlery ceased. Glasses paused mid-air.

"She was human," Daniel said. "She had faults. She was pretty disorganized, did you know that? Her dresser drawers were a mess. And in private, she could get really irritated—pissed off, even. Sometimes she resented being everyone's go-to. But when she wasn't letting that out, the perfection could be a bit much, don't you think? A little sanctimonious?"

"Oh, shut up, Daniel. You were smitten with Violet, and you were as smitten on the day she died as on the day you met," Cicely said.

"Well, dying. That was one thing she did wrong, wasn't it? Going out on that bike, her fucking rose-colored glasses. She never thought anything could go wrong. You'd think a doctor would know things can go wrong. We see that every day."

"Anger is a stage of grief," Aya said placatingly.

"Is it?" said Daniel. "Am I on schedule?"

Across the table from Maggie and Daniel, Renata's eyes were daggers. "I don't know what stage it is when you fall in love with someone else," she said sharply.

"Am I not grieving adequately for you, Renata?" Daniel dragged a hand down his face, as though trying to hold himself together. "My ripped-out, shredded mess of a heart isn't messy enough for you?"

"What was it, two minutes after she died? Or did you wait three?"

"Renata." Her husband laid a hand on her arm and Renata, half his size, flicked it away.

"Because I'm trying to put this picture together," Renata said. "I'm trying to understand. Did you and Maggie know each other before?"

"We met after, through my sister," said Daniel.

So much for the romantic wrong-number story.

"I miss her every minute of every day, Daniel. And here you are—"

"Don't make assumptions about where I am, Renata."

"You've clearly moved on, is what I'm saying."

"Violet and I were together for fifteen years," Daniel said. "We became who we were together. We dreamed the same dreams. We were inseparable. *I* miss her every minute of every day."

"It was definitely fast," Maggie squeaked. "Of course you're all thinking that. Because it's true. Neither of us denies that. But we were both in places in our lives where we were broken open, and we connected deeply because of that. We were there for each other."

"Maggie's Canadian," said Daniel. "Getting married was the only way she could stay. The legal part is just a technicality."

An uncomfortable ripple skimmed the table. Maggie turned to Daniel, her mouth open. She couldn't keep the tears back any longer. The upholstered dining chair she sat in was heavy, and she struggled to push it back and wriggle out of it. No one said a word as she fled to the kitchen. She braced herself against the counter and squatted, breathing deeply into the mahogany cupboards, trying to find her center.

Daniel entered the kitchen, opened a cupboard door, and pulled out a glass. He reached over her to switch the faucet on, filled it, and handed it to her.

Maggie raised herself slowly to standing. "A green card marriage?" she said. "Is that what you think we have?"

"That came out wrong," Daniel said. "I'm sorry."

She drank deeply from the glass, staring at him over the rim. She set it down on the counter. "That's not good enough," she said. "You don't get to treat me like garbage for months and humiliate me in front of your friends and then apologize like that fixes it."

"I'm really struggling, Maggie. I know I've been shit. I've let you down in every way possible, which only makes me feel more like shit."

"I don't need you to beat yourself up. I just need you to treat me decently and show up for *me* once in a while." She was aware of the open doorway and the table full of people through it, but after months of tiptoeing and mollifying and excuse-making, she was finally speaking, and she couldn't stop. "Do you know what I gave up to marry you? I gave up having an actual wedding. My parents—not there. My friends—not there. Charmaine! *Eve!* We could have had a beautiful wedding at Still Lake, maybe. A white dress. I gave it up. Flowers, veil, aisle. Engagement ring. Honeymoon. All of it. More *time* to bring Eve around, to get her support." She looked up at the hard line of his jaw, the dark hair curling at its edge, and willed him to return her gaze. When he did at last, tears glistened at his eyes.

"You know why?" Maggie whispered. "Not because of a green card. Because I *loved* you. And you loved me. So I didn't care about all those things. All I cared about was being with you."

He nodded. "I know. I wanted to be with you too. I did. I do."

"Your *sister*," Maggie continued. "I gave her *up*. Eve was my friend and my partner and my—my—" And now she was sobbing, a geyser of heartache. She had given up the life she and Eve were making at Still Lake. She had given up the retreat center. She had given up Eve's baby. In a flurry of impulsiveness and passion for this man who would now barely speak to her, she had given up Eve.

She had given up Eve.

It was too devastating to contemplate. She covered her face with her hands and slid down the cupboard door to the floor and cried.

"Maggie," Daniel said at last.

She opened her eyes and he reached out his hand. She grasped it and let him pull her to standing. He wrapped his arms around her and she stood inside them in Violet's best friend's kitchen beside Violet's red velvet birthday cake.

Perhaps Violet would have appreciated her red dress. Perhaps Maggie had got something right after all.

"We need to have this conversation," Daniel said. "But this might not be the time or place. Today is pretty huge for me. Maybe for now we could just get more wine and go back to this dinner? Would that be okay?"

"No," she said. "That would not be okay. None of this is okay."

She could see the friends through the doorway, and they were terribly close; everyone had heard everything.

She could not go back into that room.

She took the other exit from the kitchen, through the living room to the front door. The coats had disappeared, probably spirited to a bedroom, but she was not about to go hunting. Her sparkly jacket was completely inadequate to the weather, and her purse was still on the floor beside her dining chair, but at least she had her phone, and the doorman could let her in when she got home.

On the front stoop she grabbed her failed-gift bouquet and tucked it into the crook of her arm. She walked and walked through festive lit-up streets, a mess of cold limbs and tears, until finally she stopped to huddle in the shuttered doorway of a store. Park Slope to the Upper West Side was way too far on foot, even if she were dressed for it. She didn't want to spend money on an Uber, but she needed to get somewhere warm and safe as soon as humanly possible.

Her phone vibrated as she reached for it in her pocket. She turned it over to check the caller, determined not to pick up—Daniel should be coming after her right now, should have taken her home himself, not chosen his friends over his distraught wife and then tried to compensate with a phone call—but it wasn't Daniel. It was Eve.

Eve? Eve! She felt elated and nervous and relieved all at once.

"Eve," she breathed into her phone.

"Eve told me," said a male voice, deep and empathetic, a voice from another life.

Karl. Karl calling from Eve's landline.

"Oh."

"How are you?" he asked.

Oh, Karl. How am I? I am at rock bottom.

She crouched lower in the alcove beside the shop door, shielding as much of her body as possible from the cold. "Okay."

"I wanted to say—Eve told me. About the baby."

Oh.

"She said it was traumatic. You almost died."

Maggie's nose was dripping, a slimy wetness heading toward her lip.

"I wanted to say how sorry I am," Karl said.

Maggie wiped her nose on her jacket, the sequins scraping against her skin. She would need a hundred jackets, a thousand tissue boxes, to soak up all the sad, drippy moisture coming from her sad self.

"I had no idea," he said. "I'm so sorry you had to go through that alone. That you had to bear the brunt of it and I was—oblivious."

"I tried very hard to reach you at the time."

"I guess I was in Patagonia."

"I guess you were."

All she had wanted was to tell Karl about the baby. That had been a driving goal, once. What was it she'd thought he could do for her?

"Are you okay now?" he asked.

"You mean physically?"

"Yeah, I guess."

"I'll live."

"That's good."

"I should go now," she said, before he could ask how she was doing emotionally.

"Okay. Maggie?"

"Yeah?"

"I'm so sorry."

Was he sorry, did he really care, or was this call just another stop on his apology tour? And did it even matter to Maggie anymore? Eve, not Maggie, was the one stuck trying to build trust and create a real relationship with him now.

"Sure," she said.

"Take care."

"You take care too."

She was an ice block by the time a black Tesla arrived to pick her up. At least she'd achieved one thing in her relationship with Daniel, she decided as the car crossed the East River and she watched the lights of Manhattan grow clearer and closer: She really didn't care how Karl felt about her anymore.

Chapter 34

Eve

The night Eve learned that her partner was repulsed by her body, she left the house with Flora and ducked into the path between the trees. She could not remain anywhere in the vicinity of Karl, could not bear to place herself in his gaze, to witness his quick glance away and his body angling ever so subtly from hers.

She emerged from the path and gazed up at her lodge. No—her outdoor adventure center. Karl's outdoor adventure center.

The outdoor adventure center of the partner who was repulsed by her body.

She took the stairs to the dining hall. She pulled the *Truth Landing* woman off her perch and balanced her awkwardly against her hip as she wandered, without acknowledging her direction, into the main building, through the common room, up the stairs, until she stopped at Maggie's room.

It was unchanged. The same quilt covered the bed. Eve hadn't even stripped the sheets. She hadn't, in fact, even opened this door since the panicked day she'd hunted for Daniel and Maggie. She leaned now on the doorframe and took it in, then slipped her boots off and hauled herself onto the bed to reach up for the nail where the painting had first hung.

Truth Landing, the painting and the woman, baring her body and her essence so unapologetically. So fucking brazenly.

She turned away and crossed the room to the desk. The drawer squeaked as she opened it. Inside, a stack of file folders nestled against each other. She flipped the top folder open.

Maggie. Here, in these folders, was Maggie, living in this lodge room all along. Her handwriting. Her ideas. Her vision for the future they'd been creating together.

Eve rifled through the folders, breathing heavily through her nose, some emotion she couldn't name rising sharply in her chest. Maggie had done loads of work, more than Eve realized. There were printouts of sample retreat center websites, notes in the margins detailing ways they would be different. Frayed-edged pages torn from a notebook, names brainstormed, cost structures outlined, programs to offer and groups to market to, website copy, paragraphs describing their ideal customer. A page-long description of the retreat center, in language plain and evocative, beautiful. It described women caring for women, coming together where they'd been taught to compete or tear down, forming alliances to help each other bust out of unhelpful patterns and grow into the truest versions of themselves. Healing. Expanding. Transcending. Creating community. Becoming family.

For one brief moment Eve closed her eyes and allowed herself to feel what had been lost. This. This! It was everything she'd missed growing up and couldn't even acknowledge she needed as an adult—until Maggie. It was what Maggie had been to her. It was what Eve was learning she could be to others. Care and community—how she wanted that for herself. And oh, how she wanted it for her child.

And *she'd* pushed Maggie away. She'd been judgmental and angry—hurt and afraid too; afraid of getting left behind, being forsaken, being alone. So instead she'd forced Maggie to leave. *She'd* done that.

All Maggie had done was respect Eve's wishes and go.

Eve went downstairs to the common room to fetch the laptop she'd bought after Maggie left, hauled it into the bed with her, and opened FaceTime. She took a deep breath and pressed call.

"Eve," Daniel said. Just her name, but that one syllable conveyed all the complexity of apology and love and knowing that Eve felt herself.

"Are you okay?" she asked. Because she could also tell from that one syllable, from his sunken eyes and haggard face, that he wasn't.

"No," he said. "Not especially."

"It's Violet's birthday," Eve said. "Isn't it?"

"Yeah."

They sat together in the shittiness of that fact.

"Are *you* okay?" he asked.

She leaned back in the bed and closed her eyes.

"I'll take that as a no," Daniel said.

"How about Maggie?" Eve asked.

"No, I don't think she's doing great either."

"You don't know?"

"No, I know."

"Oh, Daniel. Where *are* you?"

"Renata and Ivan's guest room."

"Crap. It's that bad?

"It all got a lot more complicated once we tried to settle into normal life."

"Because normal life has Violet in it?"

"It's my fault. Maggie's trying hard. I'm just not capable. I can go to work, but that's about it. Work is a good distraction, actually, but at home—I can't get away from thinking about Violet. And she's not there. And I'm so fucking devastated about that."

"Daniel, do you need help?"

He laughed abruptly. "Yeah, probably."

"I mean for real."

"No. I mean, I guess I'm depressed. I guess this is what depression feels like?"

"You need to see a doctor," Eve said.

"I am a doctor."

"A psychiatric doctor."

"I just need time to get myself together. But I'm definitely failing Maggie, I can tell you that."

"In what way?"

"Every way."

Geez. Poor Maggie.

"I'm not glad to be right," she said.

"You might as well be. Then at least somebody's getting some happiness out of this marriage."

He was attempting humor, but the joke only felt sad and horrible. Eve *wasn't* glad. She wasn't glad for any of it.

"How's my niece?" Daniel asked.

"Thriving. I'm more worried about how she'll do once she's living outside my body."

"You're going to be a good mom."

She nodded dully. Then she spoke out loud the words she couldn't scrub from her thoughts: "Karl is repulsed by my body."

For a moment there was silence. Then Daniel exploded with "What the fuck?"

"Yeah. Let's just say he's at no risk of developing a pregnancy fetish." Her own flat attempt at humor.

"Oh, Evie. He *told* you this?"

"I dragged it out of him, but yeah."

"*See?* I warned you. He's an asshole."

"Maybe he is, I don't know." Tears pressed at her eyes. "But I can't afford to look too hard at that. My baby will be here in a month, maybe less. I won't be able to work. I'll have to take care of her—I *want* to, I want to be able to focus on her and immerse myself in that experience without stress. But right now all I have is stress. I need support and Karl is it. At least he's *here*. I already depend on him for all kinds of practical things, and I don't have an infant requiring non-stop care yet."

"You can pay people for help. You can get a nanny."

"No, I can't! Because I no longer have money, Daniel. I invested in this lodge with the understanding that Maggie would be here to help make it happen, *with* her money. And now Maggie is gone. And so is her money. And so is mine."

"She doesn't have that money. Just so you know."

"That's not—that's not the point. Sorry, this is coming out wrong. I've been upset with her, but I think I didn't want to see how much this is my fault. Her leaving. Because it *is*, isn't it?"

"I think you don't realize how harsh you can be sometimes."

"I don't know how to fix it. I think we pushed each other too far to come back from."

"She was pretty hurt when we left, but you could try reaching out to her. She's a forgiving person. But god, Eve . . ." Daniel's face crumpled in front of her. "I don't know if she'll ever be able to forgive *me*. I've been so awful to her."

For the rest of the call, Eve did her best to comfort her brother.

Eve and Flora spent the night in Maggie's room. Eve was awake for hours as usual, as though the baby was settled onto not just all of her essential organs but some button inside her that prevented sleep. She lay there, Flora snoozing beside her, and worried about Daniel, about Maggie, about money, about her relationship with Karl, about what kind of environment she was bringing her baby into.

Each time she almost succeeded in drifting off, her bladder nudged her up again.

Finally, she slept. When she woke, it was to ice pellets thrashing against the window. She pulled the quilt over her head and Flora nosed under the covers with her. They stayed cocooned there, Flora's head on Eve's chest, Eve caressing her silky ears, listening to the wind and the freezing rain.

A finger poked her side and the bed sagged under a new weight.

"You keep doing this," Karl said.

"What?" Eve said from inside her cocoon.

"Spending the night somewhere else without telling me."

She pulled the covers from her head. Karl was seated on the bed beside her, wet-haired and shining in a dripping puffer jacket.

Eve said, "Did you really think I was going to sleep beside you last night after what you told me?"

"I'm sorry. I never would have said any of that to you if you hadn't—you know, guessed. I never wanted you to know."

"Yeah, no shit."

"Eve. Forgive me. Please. I'm doing my very best."

She rolled over and buried her face in the pillow.

He cleared his throat. "So, I've come to fetch you for the nailing of the final board."

"What?" she mumbled into the pillow.

"On the dining hall floor. It's done. After this last piece."

The pillow was soft and squishy, perfectly formed around the contours of her face. "It's hardly the last piece that needs to be put in place in this lodge," she said.

"Come on, Eve. Pretend it's momentous. That floor was a disaster, right? It was rotted through. Now it's not. Symbolic."

"I appreciate your sentimentality, but I'm exhausted and it seems like we're in the middle of an ice storm."

"It's not far."

He gripped her hand and tugged. She felt heavy, heavier than the weight of this baby warranted.

Flora was already at Karl's heels. Eve got out of bed, slipped into her boots and coat, and followed.

In the common room she grabbed a newspaper off the table, holding it over her head. As she stepped outside, the wind whipped it from her hands and it somersaulted off into the air. Freezing rain pummeled her head and sluiced down the sides of her face and inside her collar. Everything was encased in ice: every tree and shrub, the ground, the sides of the buildings. Karl had spread ashes on the path to the dining hall, and he held tightly to Eve's arm as they inched forward. Beside them, Flora cowered, then leapt ahead to whine plaintively at the dining hall door. Karl threw it open and Eve ducked after him into the cover of the building.

The floor was smooth and gleaming, only one gap by the door awaiting the laying of the final piece.

Karl grinned at her. He shrugged out of his jacket and handed her a hammer. He fitted the length of hardwood into place. "Ready?"

She was shivering. She knelt down and aimed her hammer, and they pounded together.

"*Now*," he said, "we're ready for guests."

He was like a little boy, elated over his very large, very expensive toy.

"We still have zero financial wiggle room," Eve said. "We need people in here immediately—like tomorrow—and we also need to be really clear about all the ways this place is nothing like Sam's. I don't want any demographic overlap."

"I'll make a website today, then we can start marketing. To people Sam wouldn't even think about marketing to."

"*No* overlap."

"Yes, I get it! Don't worry."

"You're really going to put up a website in a day?"

"It'll be basic."

"We need pictures. I don't have any good ones, and we can't take them in this weather."

He crossed his arms. "Are you going to be like this with everything?"

"Like what?"

"Bringing up every single reason something won't work."

Another fierce blast of wind. The building groaned and Flora hunkered low to the floor, whimpering.

"You're not the one whose life's savings is on the line," Eve said.

"I'm aware of that, but maybe drum up a *little* optimism about our business, or else why are you even doing this?"

The way he said "our business"—she suddenly wanted to scream deep from her gut. It wasn't his business! It was hers. It was *supposed* to be hers and Maggie's, a restorative space they were building together to help other women become themselves—help them heal from the wounds inflicted by men like Karl!—and what the fuck was she doing now trying to make this place *with Karl?*

And *that*, she suddenly understood, was why she hadn't involved Karl in the loan application. Because this *was* her business. It wasn't his, and she had never, ever wanted it to be. It certainly wasn't a goddamn fucking dirt-bikes-and-snowmobiles *adventure center*.

And more than that, she hadn't wanted his name anywhere near her loan or her lodge because she didn't trust him. Because she didn't truly believe, deep down, that they would be together for long.

There was a tremendous crash. Flora yelped and Eve dove to the floor beside her. The floor—the walls—everything was shaking. Above them, glass shattered. It clanged to the floor and shards lanced the skin on Eve's hands and neck. Splintered wood and muddy snow sprayed the room. Eve hunched over her stomach and tucked her head between her knees, her eyes open and upturned as her mind grasped frantically at explanations. In the next instant, a tree crashed into the room, bare limbs tremoring from the impact, thunderous and affronted as it landed. Inches from her face, the crisp perfection of a branch coated in crystal, breathtakingly beautiful.

Something pricked her cheek. Something else scraped her arm. She lifted her head to look over the tree, and freezing rain pelted her face through a gulf in the ceiling. The floor was plastered with shredded wood and shingles, branches and mud and snow and water.

She could not stop screaming.

Karl climbed over the tree trunk toward her, soaked and mud-spattered but apparently unharmed. He gripped her shoulders with two hands and pulled her to him. Her teeth chattered. She splayed her hands across his wet back, ran them over his wet head, pulled twigs from his hair, words juddering from her. "Holy fuck, holy fuck, holy fuck, holy fuck." Her whole body was quaking.

"It didn't hit you?"

She shook her head. And then, "Flora!" Her eyes were huge with horror and her lungs heaving with the effort of screaming Flora's name. Surely Flora would be barking—but then, Eve couldn't hear anything over the wind and the clattering rain, all of it pounding down around them through the dining hall roof and its north wall, the roof and the wall that no longer existed.

Flora had been right beside her. Where was Flora?

She and Karl clambered along the length of the tree, digging through mud and sharp, icy snow, yelling, "Flora!"

Eve spied the chocolate-brown tail protruding from beneath a thick branch. She lunged for the branch, screaming at Karl to help her. She gripped the bark and heaved.

"You'll hurt yourself!" Karl leapt to the other side and they pulled together. It was too heavy.

"We need to saw it off," Karl said.

"Hurry!"

The door was blocked by the tree, but Karl scrabbled through the hole in the wall that the tree had made. Eve groped her way around the tree to get to Flora's head. The luminous eyes pleaded up at Eve. *Do something.*

Eve took Flora's front paws in her hands. "We'll get you out of here, baby, we'll get you out." She was only barely aware of her tears as she moaned along with Flora.

Karl returned with a hand saw and Eve cradled Flora's head against her thigh, murmuring to her while Karl sawed. Her head was fine, the tree had not pinned her head, she would be fine, she would be fine.

At last the limb was free and Karl lifted it off. Flora's right hind leg was broken; there was no way it wasn't.

"We need to get her to the vet," Eve shouted over the rain.

"Driving in this is too dangerous."

"We don't have any choice!" She couldn't tell the difference between rain and tears on her face.

Karl knelt beside her, framing her face with his hands and looking straight into her eyes. "Eve, she's going to be okay."

For one moment, Eve allowed herself to be calmed by Karl's certainty. "Not if she doesn't get immediate medical attention."

"I'll take her," he said.

"No. I need to. I can't leave her."

"Eve. If something happened to you—"

"I'll be careful."

"We'll go together. I'll drive. We'll take the Wrangler—it'll handle the conditions better."

Eve nodded. She stayed with Flora while Karl ran to the house to call the nearest emergency veterinary clinic, to fetch ice grips for their boots and spread a layer of ash on the driveway. Now that winter had arrived, they were parking their vehicles at the top of the hill, and he'd have to carry Flora all that way. As he lifted her gently into his arms, she yelped in obvious pain.

"I'll come back for you," Karl said to Eve. "Do not even try to get up the hill on your own."

She didn't argue. When he returned, he gave her his arm and they shuffled forward with careful footfalls. Every step felt precarious.

"She's going to be fine," Karl shouted over the rain as they inched up the hill. "A broken leg, but that'll heal."

Eve nodded grimly.

"And we can salvage the dining hall," Karl said. "It's just a setback. You have insurance, right?"

Eve inhaled sharply, stopping for one second as the rain lashed her face and snaked past her tightly tied hood, icy down her neck. She couldn't let go of Karl or she'd risk slipping back down the driveway. She wanted to push *him* down the driveway.

"You tell me," she shouted. "You said you would handle that! You said you had a guy."

"You said you were using the company Sam recommended."

"I said that was my original plan, but—you were going to speak to both of them, remember? Get quotes. Make the decision. Weren't you? *Didn't you?*"

He gripped her elbow and nudged them forward again. "Let's just focus on Flora right now."

"Oh my god, oh my god, oh my god, oh my god."

"Okay, don't panic. We can salvage this," he said again.

But something had broken in Eve when that tree crashed through her building and almost killed her dog. By the time they arrived at the Wrangler and she was settled in the back seat, caressing Flora's head in her lap while Karl navigated the icy road, she knew once and for all that none of this was salvageable.

"No," she whispered to Flora. *No.* She spoke it louder to Karl. "No. I'm done. With all of this."

Chapter 35

Maggie

There was freezing rain the night of the disastrous dinner party, a torrential racket that woke Maggie with its pounding against the bedroom window. The blankets on Daniel's side of the bed were undisturbed. She peered into the guest room—not there either—and checked her phone for messages. There were none. It was four in the morning.

She padded barefoot to the kitchen, past the bouquet of flowers she'd retrieved from Renata's front stoop when she left the party. She threw open the kitchen window and stepped over the low sill onto the fire escape. The freezing rain pierced her head, her face, her bare shoulders. In an instant she was soaked through.

"Enough," she said out loud to the night. "I have had enough."

Enough of Daniel, enough of the sham marriage. But also enough of herself. Enough of contorting herself to please another person. Enough of looking to someone else to make her feel valuable and loved when clearly no one but her was ever going to do it.

When she woke again two hours later, the rain had stopped and Daniel still wasn't there. She pulled on leggings, a hoodie, and a raincoat, found ten dollars in change on the dresser, shouldered her bag and her yoga mat, and left the apartment, holding on to the sides of buildings to keep from slipping on the ice. In her neighborhood wanderings she'd seen an early-morning pay-what-you-can yoga and meditation class. She could pay nothing. It was a direction and a purpose, and she needed direction and purpose because she was pretty sure she was done with the green card application. She needed community too, needed to be around other humans breathing and moving in sync with her. She needed sanctuary.

By the second half of the class she was crying. She would not have thought she had tears left. Seated in sukhasana on her mat, soothing music washing over her, the teacher's voice instructing, "Breathe out resentment, breathe in acceptance." The simple words repeated with each inhalation and exhalation, and she had so much to resent, and so much to accept, and it hit her all at once at the base of her spine.

Breathe out resentment. Eve's rejection, Karl's rejection, the wreck of her so-called marriage. Breathe in acceptance. *It has happened, I am here, I am beautiful and whole.*

Breathe out resentment. The ways Eve let her down and pushed her away, the loss of the beautiful life they'd been creating, the baby she might have helped raise, the future she'd thought she had but didn't. Breathe in acceptance. *It has happened, I am here, I am well.*

Breathe out resentment. *Her* baby, who she'd wanted and lost. Breathe in acceptance. *I am not a mother, I am here, I am well.*

Breathe out resentment. Her mother didn't approve of her life choices, Maggie was not getting the money she needed. Breathe in acceptance. *She loves me, she has always loved me, I'm not dependent on her affirmation. I am well.*

Breathe out resentment. She would never be the person her father wanted her to be. If his approval and love came at the price of becoming someone she was not, it was time to let go of her desire for his approval and love.

Each experience entered her and exited with the breath, and the tears flowed from her closed eyes, in, out, acceptance, acceptance, acceptance, *I am well.*

She felt cocooned inside this quiet room with other women who had braved the ice and come to share space and breath. She had not felt safer or more in tune with herself since she left her lodge room. She had not felt more held, more free to know and admit the truth.

She rolled up her yoga mat and retreated to the studio reception room in a silent flow with the others. She pulled her coat off its hook, then sat on a bench to tug on her socks and boots. When she reached for her phone, the once-familiar flash of Daniel's number lit the screen. She'd never attached his name to it, so in her contacts he remained the mystery person at the mystery number, arriving as though by divine benevolence to shepherd her through her sorrow, not the man who had chosen and so quickly disappointed her.

The text read: I'm sorry. I stayed the night at Renata and Ivan's. You don't deserve any of this. I've decided I need to start some kind of grief therapy or psychotherapy or maybe antidepressants. I hope you'll stick it out with me long enough for me to work on this and fix it.

Maggie stood. She knew immediately she couldn't do what he'd asked. If Daniel was going to get help, she would root for his healing—but she couldn't *be* his healing. Inside her new acceptance, she understood that. Trying to be hadn't worked.

And then: I get it if you don't want to talk to me right now. But I thought you'd want to know that there's bad news from Eve. The dining hall was wrecked in an ice storm. A tree crashed through the roof. Flora is hurt—one of her hind legs is broken, but she'll be ok.

Maggie felt like someone had taken a broomstick to the back of her knees.

Flora. The dining hall. The lodge. But mostly—*Flora?* The tears rose instantly to her eyes. *Oh my god, Flora.*

Maggie sank back onto the bench. Sweet-natured, companionable Flora. Flora, who knew what Maggie needed when she needed it, who had kept her company and made her feel that she would be all right. Flora, without whom Maggie was certain she would not have survived.

Poor Eve! Is she ok? Is the baby ok?

Maggie waited for further news as the dots pulsed on her screen, and then Daniel texted: All fine. Eve has decided to sell the lodge.

Slowly she rose from the bench, clicked the phone off, and dropped it into her bag. She took a stabilizing breath.

Flora is injured but will be all right. Eve is selling the lodge.

Breathe out resentment, breathe in acceptance.

Out on the street, the sun was already beginning to melt the ice into puddles on the sidewalk. Maggie set out uptown, away from the apartment. She kept going through hordes of noisy humanity, past bodegas and shoe repair shops and fruit markets festooned with holiday garlands and bright-red ornaments and lit-up plastic Santas. She crossed into Central Park, sat by the reservoir, and tried to imagine it into being Still Lake. Wider, longer, deeper, not overrun with dog walkers and joggers and nannies pushing strollers through the flooded concrete.

Flora was injured but would be fine. Eve was selling the lodge, and the retreat center would never happen, but it wasn't happening anyway because Maggie had left. Breathe in acceptance.

She stood and exited the park, walked all the way across to West End Avenue and the Hudson. Again, it was not Still Lake.

She'd zigzagged south and east, was nearing home, when she looked up and saw it: Stillcraft Designer Furniture. The name hit her like a warm wave. Stillcraft. Eve's Stillcraft. How had she not wandered down this particular block before?

She went in. The store was spare, simple. White walls, white floor, cozy and quiet, an oasis after the noise of the street. And against the white, wood.

A stocky man stood behind a counter but didn't approach her or ask if he could help. She set her palm flat against a table. The wood was an interlacing of blond and deep brown, grainy and knotted, its single leg a solid cube. The chair beside it was a scooped-out cradle, like sitting in a hollow log. A floor lamp was a three-legged triangle with a ball of light nestled atop it. A high stool, a low bed, a bookcase: They all looked half animate, as though they had walked out of the forest on their own and might come to life again at any moment. They looked like Still Lake.

Maggie was no craftsperson, but she recognized heart. This furniture had heart. You did not think up furniture like this without caring a great deal. About wood, about detail, about beauty, about the practical uses to which this beauty would be employed. About expressing something of yourself in the physical universe. You did not create furniture like this without being patently capable.

Eve had created Stillcraft. Surely, ice storm or not, she could create their retreat center without Maggie if she wanted to. Did she not want to? Was it only money? Did Eve need Maggie's money, or did she need Maggie? Did she want Maggie?

The feeling of refuge and communal support she'd had this morning at the yoga studio—that was what she'd wanted to create with the retreat center. That was the purpose and the vision. She still cared about it immensely. Was she really going to give it up without a fight?

Maggie beelined out of Stillcraft. In the café across the street, jazz collided with half a dozen conversations. She ordered tea, the cheapest item on the chalkboard menu, and chose an armchair in the corner. With her spiral notebook balanced across the arm of her chair, she hauled out her laptop and scrolled to the bottom of her files list. She pulled up the retreat center business plan, and it was all there: her vision. *Their* vision.

She stayed for four hours, writing as though she could never run out of words. She researched every question they would have to answer in order to move forward, and then she wrote the answers. For their *About* page, she wrote the story of how she and Eve met—two women coming together in a circumstance that should have divided them, supporting each other, hatching a dream for a beautiful place where other women could come together in support too. She refined her descriptions of their package offerings, adjusted prices, clarified a profit plan. Researched what the heck a profit plan was. She would need to speak with Eve to find out exactly how much money they were looking at for renovations, but she put in some placeholder estimates for now.

She googled *How much does it cost to fix a roof that a tree has crashed into?* The numbers varied wildly.

When she was long past justifying her presence on one cup of tea, she stood to gather her things and texted Daniel: When is she selling?

ASAP.

I can't let her sell.

I don't think it's up to you.

The three women waiting for takeout at the counter erupted into laughter, their heads bent together.

Maggie scanned Daniel's earlier texts, reviewing his promises, his request for her to wait by his side while he healed. She texted:

I need better, Daniel. I've let myself down by accepting this situation with you where I'm second-best.

I love you, came his answer at last. You're not second-best.

We both know I am.

It was the realest conversation they'd had since they married.

He went quiet then and she turned her phone off again, packed up her laptop, and left.

Daniel didn't come home that night either. The next day Maggie went back to the same café across from Stillcraft and bought the same cheap cup of tea. Every time she needed inspiration, she looked out the window at Stillcraft and breathed in the tangible proof of the excellence and beauty Eve had created once and could create again. Tree or no tree.

If Eve was out of money and out of options and selling immediately, Maggie did not have time to finish her dissertation, and her father would have to see that.

She finished the manifesto/provisional business plan, laid it out in a simple design program and saved it as a PDF. She messaged her father: Your apartment doesn't happen to have room for your favorite daughter for a night or two, does it?

Then she texted Daniel: Are you home?

He replied: Yes.

When Maggie arrived at the apartment, Daniel was sitting on the couch, watching a video on his phone, a plate of crackers and cheese in his lap. He put down the phone as she came in. She sat in the chair opposite him. She studied him, this tall, curly-haired man she did not know, this man she loved.

"I'm leaving," she said gently.

Daniel balanced a lump of cheese on a cracker, and it wobbled there. "I know," he said. "I know you can't stay here like this."

"I wish I hadn't used you as my escape route back in September instead of staying and facing the hard things I didn't want to face. But I can see now that I did."

He stared at her. She got up and moved beside him on the couch. He set the crackers on the coffee table and did not resist when she took his hand.

"If anyone used anyone," he said, "it was me using you."

"We were both needy and acting out of our need. Don't you think?"

"Me more than you. I had no business trying to be anything to anybody," he said. The look he gave her was deeply sad. "I'm so sorry."

"I know," she said. "But I'm leaving anyway. I need to see what I can be for myself. And you need to heal, whatever that looks like. I hope we can still be friends."

"I'll miss you," he said.

"Will you?"

He nodded.

"We'll text," she said, and he opened his arms and they embraced. In the end it was that simple. They released each other.

Maggie spent the night on her father's couch. They watched a Charlie Chaplin film and laughed and ate Chinese food together. He didn't ask for an explanation for her presence, but he was more tender than she'd ever seen him as he brought her a pillow and blanket, a washcloth and towel, lingering beside the couch and saying only, "I hope you're all right?"

"I am," she said. For the first time she thought maybe he *would* have been a loving caretaker after she lost the baby.

He had an early appointment the next morning, but she arranged to meet him in a café afterward, telling him she had business to discuss. He was there when she arrived, at a table near the front window, and he stood as she entered, waving one long arm to get her attention. Bespectacled and corduroy-jacketed, the picture of intellectual acuity.

She had come armed—with her business plan, already out of her bag and in her hand, with her clarity of direction. This was a business meeting, and she planned to conduct it with intention and empowerment. But as she held out her palm for a handshake, her father drew her into a hug, and her heart lurched as he held her against his own heart.

"You really are okay?" he asked. "I worried half the night. You haven't even told your mother what happened. She's in the dark as much as I am."

"I'm good," she said into his chest. "There've been some pretty big bumps this year, but I'm all right."

She pulled away and they sat down across from each other.

"I left Daniel," she said.

"I'm sorry to hear that." His eyes roamed the room and then he said, "Am I sorry?"

"No."

"All these months we were both here, and we've hardly seen each other."

"Are you hurt that I haven't been in touch more?"

He blinked. He seemed to consider for a moment. "Why, yes," he said, abruptly and with some surprise. "I believe I am."

"I'm sorry," she said. "I was caught up in my own vortex of—well, you don't want to hear it—but I didn't consider that maybe you'd *want* to hear from me. I thought it was just Mom pushing us to get together."

"Why wouldn't I want to hear from my own daughter?"

She laughed. "I've always been a bit much for you, Daddy-O." She'd started calling him that at around age sixteen, and it stuck for a full year despite the fact that he cringed every time she said it. Probably because he cringed.

He cringed now, but then smiled. "Daddy-O."

She pulled the business plan from her bag and set it on the table between them.

He gestured to a teapot. "I took the liberty," he said, and began to pour, eyeing the thick stack of bound pages. "Have you come with a script?"

"Kind of. There are a few things I want to say to you. You ready?"

"I do appreciate directness."

She laughed. He sure did. She wasn't sure she'd ever been direct with him in her life—even when she was trying to follow his straight line to respectability and security. She'd only ever brought him amorphous emotion and need, and it had only ever overwhelmed him.

"The first is that I understand how much you value higher education. I know it can open doors you've always wanted opened for me. I know it's been the backbone of your life. But I also feel that you made choices for me before you even met me—and you were so fixated on those choices, due to wanting the best for me, that you never quite saw the person I actually was. Does that seem like a fair assessment?"

He drew a microfiber cloth from his pocket, took off his glasses, and wiped them carefully. "If this is your experience," he said, "it's valid."

"Here's the second thing," Maggie said. "I'm not going to complete my Ph.D."

He opened his mouth to protest, but she put up her hand and he stayed silent.

"I'm not an academic," she continued. "I've known that for a while now. This degree just doesn't matter to me in the way something needs to matter to get me across the finish line." She pushed the business plan forward. "Here's what *is* important to me. This is my passion, and something I think I could be great at."

He flipped it open, his Adam's apple jumping as he looked from Maggie to the business plan and back to Maggie.

"I want you to read this," Maggie said. "With an open mind, as much you can. You might not understand all of it—there's some airy-fairy language in here you're not going to love—but I want you to look at it not through your eyes but through mine."

He blinked again. She'd never seen her father blink so much.

"Now, the final thing," Maggie said. "I'm sharing this document with you because you control my access to the funds you set up for me. I know you put conditions on those funds that you believed were in my best interest. But I'd like to have access to them now, without meeting your conditions, because this"—she nodded to the bound pages in his hand—"is what I need to do, what I can and will do, the way that I'll create *my* purpose and fulfillment in the world. I'm ready for it."

He shook his head with something Maggie thought almost approached respect. "I'll read every word," he said. "I promise."

"I'm heading back to Toronto now—I'll stay with Mom and spend some time with Charmaine over the holidays, but I do have a ticking clock on this. I don't know how long it'll take to transfer money once you've made your decision, but I'm hoping not long."

"I'll be home soon too. Will you be with us for Christmas?"

"Yes."

"Wonderful. I will prioritize this. I will read and consider as you've asked."

They ordered sandwiches, and they talked about his semester at Columbia, about the city, about an exhibit he'd recently visited and wished he could have taken her to. As they hugged goodbye, Maggie had a sudden realization.

"You love me," she said.

"Of course I love you," he said. "You're my daughter."

"Not because I'm your daughter. You love *me*. For me."

He stepped back and held her at arm's length. He nodded thoughtfully. "I would say that's a fair assessment."

Chapter 36

Eve

For two weeks, over Karl's protests, Eve slept with Flora in Maggie's room, and she worked—tirelessly and as one possessed—to sell the lodge. Now that she and Karl were over, animal instinct pressed her onward, driving her to get her affairs in order and to make her environment safe so that she could birth her baby. She could not birth her baby into a relationship riddled with mistrust, and she could not birth her baby into a financial and physical disaster. She needed not only to be free of Karl as anything more than a co-parent, she needed the missing roof, the damaged floor, the whole mess of the lodge to be someone else's problem.

Karl was still living in Eve's house. She wanted him to stay close at least through the first six weeks, while she recovered from childbirth, adapted to round-the-clock infant care, learned to breastfeed, tried to keep her own self fed and whole. He insisted he'd still be a hands-on father and would get a place nearby; he insisted she should live in her own house and he would stay in the lodge; he insisted she didn't have to create this distance between them at all. Most of all, he insisted that selling the lodge was a mistake.

He went to his parents' for Christmas. Eve had dinner at Sam's, then came home to put together a hospital bag. Karl still came with her to appointments with the midwife, he'd bought two car seats with her, one for each of their vehicles, he'd cut the remains of the fallen tree into firewood, stabilized the broken windows with two-by-fours, called the power company to inspect the wiring, but he was not going to help her sell the lodge. Fine. It wasn't his money draining into oblivion by the day. She didn't have time to get it ready to sell anyway. She was just selling it, without a realtor, in exactly the terrible shape it was in.

Flora was healing. Eve was grateful she was alive. Every day, she woke up grateful for that one thing.

Her for-sale listings had yielded only one response, but she'd worried that in the dead of winter, over the holidays, for a half-destroyed property requiring a total lifestyle commitment, she wouldn't draw any interest at all. The couple was arriving for a second viewing any minute.

Eve stood on a chair in the common room, draping fabric across a window to approximate a curtain, while Karl droned on about how wrong she was to sell the lodge.

She pressed her hands into her lower back. There was a dull ache in her abdomen.

"If these people are sensible enough to turn down this place," she said, "there is no one lining up behind them. And then you know what? I am fucked." She spoke through her teeth, lumbering down off the chair and shambling toward the door with both hands on her belly. Her stomach cramped, like menstrual pain, but sharper. *No.* She wasn't ready yet.

Through the window, Eve could see Geoffrey and Linda Watts climbing from their Ford Escape. Karl kept talking. The cramping passed, and Eve shuffled forward again. Just more practice contractions. She hoped. She'd been having them all week.

"Please go," Eve said to Karl. "I can't deal with you right now."

He gave her one last disappointed look and left through the side door.

Eve greeted her buyers—*Please, please be buyers*—and tried sending them off to explore on their own, but Linda insisted she come with them.

"We might have some questions for you," she said.

Eve forced a smile. Someone was tightening a vice around her middle.

Linda bounded up the stairs with her husband, chatting away. Eve followed more slowly, a step at a time.

Let me get through this hour, Baby. Let me get this deal sealed, and then you can be born.

"I keep seeing this room in my mind's eye," Linda said. She stopped in front of Maggie's room. "The potential is all here. We knock down this dividing wall and create one big honeymoon suite—I mean, huge. This'll be our money-maker."

No! Eve felt the word in her whole body, irrational. *You can't have Maggie's room!*

"You've already convinced me," Geoffrey said. He turned to Eve. "We'd like to make an offer."

"Contingent on an inspection, of course," said Linda.

Downstairs, a door thudded shut and footsteps approached the stairs. Anxiety scrabbled at Eve's chest. The last thing she needed was Karl's bad attitude coming in and sabotaging the sale.

"Would you excuse me a moment?" Eve said. She walked out and looked down into the common room.

In boots and a long wool coat, peering up the staircase at Eve, was Maggie.

Tears rose instantly in Eve's eyes. Her whole being flooded with relief. Maggie's mouth opened and they stood for what felt like minutes, staring at each other.

"Look at you," Maggie breathed at last, her eyes on Eve's belly, awe in her voice. "Oh, Eve. You are *beautiful*. And the baby—she's almost here!"

"*You're* here," Eve said, too stunned to do anything but state the obvious. She looked for traces of anger—in herself, in Maggie—but all that thrummed through her was hope. "Why are you here?"

Maggie fumbled with a thick stack of bound pages in her hand. "I heard you were selling," she said. She ascended to the second step. "I know it's presumptuous, but—I came to make an offer."

Eve's spine softened, as though some invisible weight had slid off her shoulders.

"I'm so sorry for taking off on you," Maggie said. "I'm sorry for taking off with Daniel. For not sticking to our commitments. I know I fucked you over."

I fucked you over too, Eve wanted to say, but there was another tightening in her belly and she backed against the wall, trying to keep herself steady.

"I know you might not want anything to do with me anymore," Maggie went on. "I know you might not be able to trust me again. And I know Karl's still in the picture. But I'm ready for this now. I'm ready if you are."

Eve shook her head, meaning *No, it's over with Karl*, but Maggie clearly thought she meant she wasn't ready to trust her, because she started paging fervently through her little book, a determined set to her mouth.

"Picture a lake," she called softly up the stairs, eyes flitting from the page to Eve's face, like she was delivering a sermon for one. "A calm Northern Ontario lake, deep and cold and fresh. This is Still Lake."

Eve exhaled through her mouth. She didn't have to picture it; it was right outside.

"Picture a woman in a painting, naked. A strong woman, not easily swayed. She owns her bareness. She isn't afraid of that vulnerability. She's powerful and she's open. This is the *Truth Landing* woman."

Eve closed her eyes and saw the woman in the painting, telling her she could do this, she had it in her, she was made for it.

Maggie stepped closer. "Picture two buildings—weathered, old, but recently renovated, retaining the charm of their history but in good repair. Rooms with high beds open onto a wraparound balcony. In the dining hall, women eat and talk, read, write, meditate, make music."

Linda and Geoffrey came out of Maggie's room and joined Eve on the landing. Eve had actually forgotten about them.

Maggie kept right on going, her voice rising the longer Eve was silent. "They sweat in the sauna, they swim in the lake, they hike the trails! They sleep! They recharge! Renew!"

The contraction passed and Eve stood up straight again.

Linda shot her a curious look. "What's going on?" she whispered.

The bizarreness of what was happening struck Eve, and she laughed, shrugging, as Maggie kept reading from her endearing little treatise like no one else was there and Linda and Geoffrey kept looking back and forth between Maggie and Eve, bewildered.

"They find a place in themselves to integrate their strength and their vulnerability," Maggie said. "Their doing and being. Their active selves and their receptive selves." She'd been ascending the stairs as she read, and she was now only three steps away. "They find a place in themselves to become whole. This is the Truth Landing Wilderness Retreat Center."

"That's quite poetic," Linda said, when Maggie stopped for breath. "I'm sorry, you are?"

"Eve's partner," Maggie said, still looking at Eve.

"Oh! We didn't realize."

"Eve." Maggie took one more step toward Eve, setting her booklet down on the stairs. "I will buy half the lodge. Or all of it, if that's what you need. There's enough for the repairs too. We can still do it. We'll write up a formal agreement this time. We'll do it right."

Linda's cheerful face turned wary. "We have cash too," she said. "I'm pretty sure we were here first?"

"You actually finished your dissertation?" Eve asked Maggie.

"I didn't. But I convinced my dad I'd found my true path."

Eve laughed. Of course she had. *Eve* had lost her hard-earned life's savings to this property, then driven herself to the edge of breakdown trying to raise money to save it, but all Maggie had to do was initiate a heart-to-heart with her dad, and here you go, wads of cash.

"The money is in my bank account right now," Maggie said.

"Would you mind explaining what's going on here?" Geoffrey said.

Maggie was looking up at Eve, her face expectant. She seemed changed, but only a little—more confident, more steady, but still Maggie.

Was Eve going to give up the most supportive friendship of her life, turn down the work and the future whose loss she'd felt like a death, refuse this community she'd longed to give her child? Was she going to keep protecting herself from what she most wanted, when Maggie was here and all Eve had to do was open herself up and say yes? If she and Maggie had a shot at this, she would forever regret not taking that shot.

Eve drew a breath, felt the old fear rise—and chose to let it go.

"I'm so sorry," Eve said to Geoffrey. "There's been a change of circumstance. The lodge is no longer for sale."

Maggie threw her hands in the air and whooped.

Linda gave Eve a look that managed to be equally mournful and accusing.

"We appreciate your interest!" Maggie called as Geoffrey and Linda turned heel, muttering as they stomped toward the door.

Maggie scampered the rest of the way up the stairs and threw her arms around Eve. Eve laughed and hugged her back. Maggie dropped to her knees so her hug encompassed the baby too, looking up at Eve with reverence.

"I can't believe how big she is. I can't believe how gorgeous you are!"

"I can't believe you're back," Eve said, just as the next wave rolled across her abdomen, stronger than any of the others. Still not pain exactly, but pressure, insistent and certain. In slow motion, Eve sank toward the stairs.

"Eve?" Maggie asked. "Are you okay?"

Eve breathed, long and slow, through an O in her mouth. The next wave of pressure rolled through her, quicker and harder than she expected.

"Let's get you to a bed," Maggie said.

Another wave—forget pressure, it was pain—and Eve arched her back and pressed the heels of her hands into her hips and stared into Maggie's face and thought, *Breathe, breathe, breathe.*

Maggie knelt beside her on the stairs. "Or—the hospital? Is this it? This is it, isn't it?"

A little rest, then Eve gripped Maggie's hand and gasped, "Thank god you didn't take any longer to get here."

Chapter 37

Maggie

Short, powerful grunts rumbled out of Eve, not desperate sounds but guttural and controlled. Maggie scooted to a lower step to place herself in Eve's line of vision.

"Listen, Eve. Can you tell me where Abby's phone number is? Do you have a bag you've packed for the hospital?"

Eve rose into a high kneel, grasping the staircase railing as she closed her eyes and growled. Maggie shuffled back to press her hands into the small of Eve's back.

"House," Eve said.

"Let's take you to my room so you're more comfortable. I'll run to the house and get your things." She didn't want Eve falling down the stairs while she was gone.

The contraction seemed to be over. Eve submitted to a slow, supported shuffle toward Maggie's room. Maggie reached for the water bottle in her bag, uncapped it, and held it to Eve's lips. Eve swallowed, water dribbling down her chin and onto the front of her sweater.

"Abby's number?" Maggie asked gently.

"On the fridge."

"Is Karl at the house?" Maggie asked.

Eve's hair clung to her temple in sweaty tendrils. "Who knows?" she said.

"You don't know where Karl is?"

Eve bent forward into a modified child's pose on the bedroom floor, her long back curved around her shapely, beautiful belly. She said, "Are you surprised?"

"I'll be as quick as I can," Maggie said. She planted a kiss on the top of Eve's curly head and leapt to her feet.

"Maggie," Eve said when Maggie reached the door.

"Yeah?"

"Don't waste time tracking down Karl."

Maggie flew. Down the stairs and outside, down the rickety exterior staircase covered with snow—not fixed yet, she noted as she ran—and across the wooded path to Eve's house.

"Karl!" she shouted as she threw open the door. The kitchen was neat, Eve's long dining table clear. She dashed into the bedroom, knocked and opened the bathroom door. No Karl.

She found Abby's number on the fridge and dialed. "It's happening fast," Maggie told her.

"Are you timing the contractions?"

"No, but they seem strong, and it was all of a sudden. I don't know what I'm doing. I didn't know I would be part of this."

"Just keep her comfortable and get her here. It's pretty rare for a first labor to progress quickly, but you're so far outside the city it's best to head in right away. I'll meet you at the hospital."

"What if—?"

"Just let her do what her body wants. Her body knows."

Maggie roved the house, throwing open cupboards, looking for a suitcase, a packed bag—surely Eve had made preparations? She grabbed a stack of towels from the linen closet, filled a water bottle, pulled a spare blanket off the bed, taking anything that could be useful on the drive in. Finally, in the bedroom closet, she found a duffel bag full of onesies, sleepers, tiny little diapers. She knelt on the floor with the bag, a soft yellow sleeper unfurled in her hands. She brought it to her face.

This yellow sleeper, these tiny diapers. A real live baby was coming, imminently.

Breathe in acceptance, breathe out resentment.

Breathe in courage, breathe out fear.

Eve was having a baby and Maggie was not. Eve was having a baby and Maggie was going to help her have it.

She stuffed the sleeper back into the duffel, snatched the bag up along with the other supplies, and made for the door. She'd wrenched it open with one hand and was maneuvering her awkward stash through it when she remembered Karl. She texted him from her own phone, then for good measure raced back to the cordless on the table and dialed him. Typically, it went to voicemail.

"Eve's in labor," she said after the tone. "Hurry." She pulled the phone from her ear, then brought it back. "By the way, this is Maggie."

When Maggie returned to her room at the lodge, Eve was squatting, one arm holding herself up against the bed, the other reaching down to tug at her pants.

"What's happening?" Maggie said.

"I can feel the baby there. Right there."

"Like—coming out right there?"

"Can you look?"

"Shouldn't we just—go?"

"I can't go if the baby's about to come out!"

Holy shit.

Maggie helped Eve tear her pants down past her hips and over each leg, then the same with a pair of black cotton underwear. She dashed to the bathroom to wash her hands. She should have gloves. She should have training. She should have a medical professional.

Maggie lay down on the floor to angle her head underneath Eve's body, trying to keep her expression calm. No biggie, just staring at Eve's vulva. Just looking for any signs of a human being coming out of it.

"I don't see a head," Maggie said. "Yet."

Eve felt between her legs. "It's right there," she said. "The head. I can feel it."

"What do you want to do?"

"Push."

Holy shit, holy shit, holy shit.

"Can't leave," Eve panted. "Not like this."

"Okay," said Maggie. "Okay."

Eve's eyes on her were anxious.

"I was at both of Charmaine's births," Maggie told her, doing her best to imply confidence and active participation, like there hadn't been midwives in charge while Maggie did nothing except cheerlead and hold Charmaine's hand. All she could think now was *Holy shit, holy shit.*

Footsteps pounded up the stairs, and Maggie leapt with irrational hope. Abby had intuited that she should come here instead of the hospital. She had teleported!

Karl burst through the door. He stopped just inside and took in Eve's naked bottom half, Maggie crouched beside her.

"What the hell's going on?"

Maggie cast a quick, protective glance at Eve. "Can you stay with Eve while I call Abby again?" she asked him.

"What are you even doing here?" Karl asked.

"Karl, go!" Eve barked. She was on her hands and knees and her eyes were closed; she was not in the same world as Karl and Maggie.

"All right. Karl, please go call Abby," Maggie said. "Ask her if she can come here instead of the hospital. Tell her Eve's already pushing."

"She's actually in labor?"

"She's beyond labor, she's delivering."

"Then this is insane." Karl barreled into the room, stopping just short of Eve and Maggie. "Eve, I'm taking you to the Wrangler. I'll carry you."

"Karl, please just go call Abby," Maggie said. "Eve won't make it to the hospital before the baby comes."

"So you guys are playing pioneers and having a baby in the lodge?"

Eve's face had closed down. She was somewhere deep inside herself and Maggie sensed it was important she be allowed to stay there. She clamped one hand on Karl's arm and propelled him back through the door.

"Eve needs us not to add to her stress right now, okay?" Maggie whispered. "She has to feel supported—not challenged."

"I'm calling 911."

"Thank you. 911 and Abby. My phone doesn't work here."

He looked back through the doorway. Eve had removed her sweater and bra and was naked now, squatting as she gripped a bedpost, a statuesque Venus of Willendorf in Maggie's lodge room. A *Truth Landing* woman in Maggie's lodge room.

Maggie's heart thumped in her throat.

"Look at her," Karl said. His body lengthened as he drew himself to his full height.

Maggie smiled. Yes. Look at her. Eve was a fucking goddess.

"I won't stand by and be party to this," Karl said, and that's when Maggie heard his disgust.

"To a woman giving birth?" Maggie guffawed.

For a moment they faced each other, a hundred unspoken words sparking. Then Karl strode back into the room toward Eve.

"Karl, she's *crowning*! If we leave, she'll have the baby in the car!" Maggie cried.

Karl stooped to gather Eve's scattered clothing, holding it out to her. "Eve, I need you to get dressed. We have to go *now*."

Eve didn't budge. Karl maneuvered the neck of the sweater over her head.

"She doesn't want to be moved!" Maggie cried as he began wrangling Eve's left arm into a sleeve.

Eve was a rock on the hardwood floor, eyes closed, breathing in deep, rumbling oohs. Maggie grabbed Karl's arm, trying to pull him away.

"You need to choose between Maggie and me," Karl said to Eve, "because I don't think we can be in the same room."

"An ultimatum is the last thing she needs right now!" Maggie said.

"Maggie." The word came from Eve as from a mountain, gravelly and commanding.

"What?" Karl and Maggie said together.

"I choose Maggie."

"You do?" Maggie said.

"Eve, honestly," Karl said, an edge of warning in his voice. "This isn't a time to mess around."

Eve still didn't open her eyes. Her voice was calm. "You're released. You don't want this. I don't want this with you. Maggie's here now. Just go."

Karl stepped backwards. His foot snagged on the duffel bag of baby things and he stumbled, then caught himself.

"*Maggie*," he said. "That's who you're choosing."

But Eve had closed back inside herself and did not respond.

Karl sent one withering glare at Maggie and strode from the room.

Maggie called after him, "But please call 911! And Abby!"

Chapter 38

Eve

Karl left and it was like a blockage removed from a pipe. Eve's muscles loosened, her vagina opened, and her water broke with a warm, wet plop against her thigh. She had no sense of passing time—had it been one hour or ten? She pushed and she pushed and she pushed, suspended in this altered state where the material world, where thought and intellect and language, were irrelevant. She reached down and the pads of her fingers touched wet whorls of hair against a soft skull.

Where was she? It seemed to be a low stool—Maggie had brought it up from somewhere and covered it with a towel. How long had she been on it? Maggie sat cross-legged at her feet. A blanket lay across Maggie's lap, ready to receive.

"It's coming," Eve said. She pushed again, she pushed again, and there was a sensation both horrible and wonderful—not pain, beyond pain; there was no word for what this was, this ferocious, productive, mind-altering, terrible state of being.

"The head!" Maggie cried. "The head is out. Oh, there's lots of dark hair! You're doing this, Eve, you're doing this."

Eve's whole body was damp. The fabric of the sweater around her neck felt alien on her skin. She whipped it off and it smacked against the floor. Maggie held the mirror and Eve was shocked at the scrunched-up face, little nose, eyelashes, mouth.

"Holy shit," Eve said. A human being was emerging from her body.

"Eve," Maggie said. "I don't know for sure, but it seems like you probably need to get the rest of the baby out now."

Eve nodded.

"Can you do that?"

She pushed. She pushed again. A release, a gush, a whoosh of slick flesh passing through her, and there she was, Eve could see her in Maggie's arms, her baby.

Maggie passed the bundle of limbs to Eve, and Eve's arms reached out of their own accord and gathered her baby to her. Slippery skin. Hands and feet, little bum nestled into the crook of Eve's elbow. A hearty cry. Eve sobbed.

"My baby, my baby," she heard herself saying, over and over, those two words such awe-inspiring fact, and even more so the reality of this skin on her skin, this body against hers—this person! Here was a person, and it had come from her body. Had she ever done a thing so amazing in her life?

Eve laughed. She bent and kissed the little forehead, the film of white vernix on the dark, wet curls plastered to the little head, and then she turned to Maggie and kissed her on the cheek. Maggie laughed, and Eve looked down at the being in her arms, crying now with a high-pitched, warbling wail, skin against the wrinkled, sagging skin of Eve's stomach.

Maggie had pulled her hair back into a disheveled ponytail, and wisps were coming loose at her ears. She grazed her pinky finger across Eve's baby's small red cheek. "Welcome to the world, little one," she said. She was crying too.

Eve gazed at Maggie in amazement. Everything was amazing, especially Maggie here with her in this lodge room on the other side of the most tremendous feat Eve had ever accomplished.

"Thank you," Eve said.

Maggie ducked her head and grinned. "You were incredible."

"There's honestly no way I could have done that without you."

"No?" Maggie was now smiling and crying at the same time.

"No."

"It was the scariest and most amazing thing *I've* ever done."

"Thank you," Eve said. "Thank you for being here."

Eve had spent all her strength; her legs were noodles, incapable of bearing weight. Maggie bolstered her from behind with an arm under each of Eve's arms, helping her clamber awkwardly into the bed while Eve hung on to the baby, still attached. Maggie covered them both with the quilt.

"There'll be a placenta coming," Eve said. Perverse cruelty, another thing to birth after all that, and it wasn't even her baby. "And you're going to need to cut the cord."

"Right. Let me go call for help, just in case it's not already on the way. I'll be quick."

Maggie dashed out, and Eve lifted her baby to her breast and the little mouth closed around her nipple and sucked. Her tiny face was crumpled and red, old-mannish and exquisite, and Eve watched it with tears falling unchecked down her cheeks.

When Maggie returned, Abby was beside her.

"I've never been more relieved to see a person in my life!" Maggie said.

"You win the first-birth speed award," Abby said. "My bet is you were in labor most of the day."

"I thought it was more practice contractions."

"The paramedics are downstairs," Abby said. "They got here the same time I did, but we might not need them. It looks like you two made a great team."

Abby clamped the cord and Maggie cut it. Abby was there to catch and examine the placenta, examine and weigh the baby, confirm that Eve was fine. Eve had a small first-degree tear that wouldn't require stitches.

After Abby's exam, Maggie climbed into the bed beside Eve and pressed her face into the baby's curling hair. "What will you name her?"

The baby's little jaw worked against Eve's nipple. Already a full person, already knowing what to do. Already taking what she needed.

"How does Elizabeth Violet Moretti sound? We could call her Lizzie for now. Is that cute?"

Maggie squeezed her hand. "It's beautiful, Eve. Daniel will be really moved."

The three of them lay on the bed together while Abby bustled in and out, bringing tea and checking Lizzie's latch. Eve and Lizzie skin to skin, Eve and Maggie soaking in each movement of Lizzie's lips, each small, quavering cry. She was a wonder. Nothing and no one in the universe had ever been so amazing, and Eve could not get over her.

At length Maggie asked, "So, can I be Auntie Maggie?"

"You might need to be *Mama* Maggie," Eve said, "because I just banished my co-parent."

Maggie's eyes teared up. She looked away, then back at Eve. "Really?"

"If you want to be?"

"Are you kidding? That would be the hugest gift in the world."

"I mean it."

"Why *did* you do that? Choose me over Karl?"

Eve slid her pinky onto Lizzie's palm, and her baby's fingers closed around it in a fist. "It was a no-brainer. You were here supporting me. Listening to me. Asking what I needed and doing your best to make it happen. Pretty much the opposite of Karl." She shrugged. "Also, I don't think I was using my brain. I was using my body."

"But I haven't always been here supporting you."

"Only because I was so angry and stubborn that I sent you away. But I've been devastated that it fell apart."

"I've been devastated too."

"You should be a midwife." Eve smiled. "You're a natural."

"I think I'll stick to—whatever it is I'm doing with my life."

"Opening a retreat center, obviously."

Maggie shook her head. "That discussion can wait."

"I think we're done talking," Eve said. "I think we're just doing it now."

Maggie sat up straight on the bed. "You're sure this is what you want?"

Eve laughed. "You heard Abby—we make a great team."

"You are high on hormones."

Eve had never loved anyone as much as she loved her baby, and she had never second-best loved anyone as much as she loved Maggie, and in fact she loved all of life and the world in this moment—even Karl, because without him she wouldn't have this baby—so she probably was high on hormones.

"Are you telling me that's not the best time to make life-altering decisions?"

Maggie cupped Lizzie's head with one hand. "It is a life-altering kind of day."

"You really have the money, right?"

"Yup."

"And you're staying this time."

"I have to." Maggie smiled, and Eve could see tears glistening in her eyes again. "I'm Mama Maggie."

Eve leaned down and inhaled the damp, fresh scent of her baby's head. When she turned back to Maggie, tears fell freely down Maggie's cheeks.

"I'm ready now," Maggie said. "I really am."

Eve said, "I'm ready too."

PART 4

8 years later

July

Chapter 39

Maggie

The sounds of the party reached Maggie from the balcony outside her room. An upbeat dance mix, the occasional cheer. The dining hall was lit up by a rotation of pink and green and purple LEDs, the patio dance floor swarming with bodies. Beyond the dining hall, more light glowed from the firepit, and she could just make out Still Lake under the full moon.

She'd retreated just for a minute to grab a Band-Aid. Lizzie had cut her toe dancing barefoot on the patio, exuberant, incautious, going all in as usual. The cut was small, didn't really need attention, but Maggie had wanted the excuse to come here—to her refuge of a room, to the place where it all started—for a second of sentimental acknowledgment.

There'd been plenty of acknowledgment already during this all-day fifth anniversary celebration of the Truth Landing Wilderness Retreat Center. In the speech Maggie and Eve gave together, in the music, skits, and toasts from their retreat partners and participants, in the song Lizzie had surprised her moms with, written by her with the support of one of their regular musician guests. But Maggie wanted just a moment of silence inside the festivities to remember and give thanks. For the retreat center. For the girl she was so lucky to be helping to raise. For Eve, her friend, her business partner, her platonic soulmate, her co-parent, the woman who had allowed her to become a mother. They'd given up trying to find definitions for what they were to each other, and they usually corrected people's assumptions with "No, just friends." Even though there was no "just" about it.

A knock sounded at the door, and Eve came in through the room and then out onto the balcony in the red maxi dress Maggie had talked her into—stunning, of course. Flora, now grey around her eyes and mouth, followed slowly behind her. Eve bumped her hip affectionately against Maggie as she joined her at the rail.

"Sorry," Maggie said. "I've got the Band-Aid, I was coming right back."

"Oh, she's fine," Eve said. "She's still dancing up a storm—with your dad, if you can believe it."

Maggie laughed. "He's obsessed."

"Did you see her getting him into downward dog this morning?"

"He will do anything she asks him to. *Anything*."

"He's wondering about spending his first year of retirement here, both he and your mom. He tell you that?"

"No!"

"Lizzie would be thrilled to have a set of grandparents nearby again, don't you think?" Both of Karl's parents had passed the previous year; they hadn't exactly been demonstrative or all that helpful, but they'd tried. Eve's parents and step-parents were more doting, coming to visit a couple of times a year, which was enough for Eve but not for Lizzie.

"She's a lot to keep up with, though," Maggie said.

"Yeah, well, she gets that from you."

Maggie grinned and pointed toward the party, certain the white blur was their daughter, whirling in the colored lights.

"Daniel's toast was beautiful," Maggie said. "He's so proud of you."

"And you."

"What do you think of his new girlfriend?" Maggie asked.

"What do *you* think?"

"I'm fine," Maggie said. "I want him to be happy, and I thought she was very sweet. He's been texting me about her, and she's exactly like he described. I'm excited for him."

"Karl's new girlfriend, on the other hand . . ."

They erupted into laughter together.

"I'm glad we decided not to invite them," Eve said.

"As long as she's good to Lizzie, that's all I care about," Maggie said.

"Oh, she won't last long if she isn't."

True. Karl was way too protective of Lizzie to put up with anything else. He was taking her to Peru for her ninth birthday, and the girlfriend had been vocally miffed about it being strictly a daddy-daughter trip. With any luck, she'd leave Karl over it. He was living in his parents' house now, still traveling occasionally with Vital Adventures, but Lizzie stayed with him every weekend he was home.

"This is nice," Eve said. "Think we could get away with not going back to our party?"

"Nope, we could not."

They called for Flora and ambled down the outside staircase, moving at her slowed-down pace. In the colored party lights, the dining hall looked like the court of a woodland fairy queen, Maggie decided. Or else just the most magical community hub—a place of renewal and possibility run by two friends, a girl, a dog, and a whole lot of others, coming together, choosing love and growth and hope and each other, again and again and again.

Lizzie's dark-brown hair was coming loose from the French braid crown Maggie had given her that morning, and her white dress had long since taken on grass stains. Her head was thrown back in laughter, her skirt hiked as she kicked her legs out. She was dancing with Daniel and Charmaine now, each of them taking turns imitating the other's moves.

Lizzie spotted Maggie and Eve, and she broke away from the patio, arms open as she flew toward them. "Come on, come on!" she cried. She grabbed each of their hands and pulled them onto the dance floor, a circle of three with Flora in the center. "There's so much fun happening here, and you don't want to miss it!"

ACKNOWLEDGMENTS

Thank you to Anena Hansen, who said, “I think the short story you just wrote is actually your next novel,” then cheered the first draft chapter by chapter as I wrote it, brainstormed innumerable story elements, and cared about these characters like they were her own. Thank you for being the Maggie to my Eve—my support and spurrer-on toward dreams, my partner in unpacking baggage and creating something else instead.

Thank you to Arielle Datz, my literary agent, who fell in love with this story and never stopped believing in it even when we had good reason to think no one else in the world ever would. Your faith and tireless effort are a huge part of the reason this is now a book. You told me it would happen one day, and look—it did!

Thank you to Sarah Jackson, my excellent editor at Random House Canada, who understood this story and asked the deep questions to guide it into all it could be. I’m so grateful to have worked on two books with you, and it does speed up the editorial process now that I know you’re basically always right. Also at Random House Canada, thank you to Sue Kuruvilla, Deirdre Molina, Polly Beel, Megan Costa, Erin Cooper, Catherine Abes, and Madison Hendricks. And thank you to my copyeditor, Sue Sumeraj, and my proofreader, Sarah Ratchford.

Thank you to Pippa White at Lake Union, who came on board our editorial ship at just the right time to tighten, elevate, and deepen the story in all the right places. Thank you for catching the vision and championing this book for US readers. Also at Lake Union, thank you to Carmen Johnson, Tree Abraham, Kimberly Glyder, Kathleen Lynch, Liz Gluck, Cheryl Weisman, Jaime Roberts, Caitlin Hansen, Rosanna Brockley, Brittany Morris, and Rachael Clark.

Thank you Rebecca Aldernet for allowing us to use your gorgeous artwork on the cover!

What We Found Instead went through many iterations on the way to finding itself. The following people read and gave feedback on some of those versions: Suzanne Alyssa Andrew, Julie Booker, Francine Brody, Laura Cameron, Kerry Clare, Dominic Farrell, Sarah Henstra (at least twice), Erika McDougall, Maria Meindl, Marja Reimer, Leah Reimer, and Richard Willis. Also Anena Hansen, 800 times. Thank you all for your generosity and insight.

Thank you to Heather Morrison for medical guidance (errors are entirely my own), as well as for excellent all-round support and cheerleading. Thank you extra specially to Sarah Henstra, Sarah Selecky, Kathryn Kuitenbrouwer, and Kelly Anderson for creative companionship on the journey.

Thank you to Sarah Selecky, Ryan Henderson, Leah Fae, and all the incredible writers I've been privileged to work with in my novel coaching programs at Sarah Selecky Writing School—for being constant sources of inspiration and awe, and for giving me the best non-writing work I've ever had.

Thank you to Richard Sheridan Willis for supporting my work on levels both practical and spiritual, for always having my back, and for making our life together possible. Thank you to Maia and Aphra for being the vibrant, insightful, incisive people you are, for caring about the cover and listening to my endless title considerations and being a bit proud of your mother. Thank you to Misty and Bean for sitting on my notebook when I'm trying to write. I love you all.

Thank you to my parents, Paul and Marilyn Reimer, and my siblings, Marja, Rebekah, Leah, John, and Mark, because I wouldn't be the writer I am if I hadn't started out life with you.

Thank you to the booksellers, festival organizers, librarians, podcast hosts, interviewers, reviewers, and others who supported *The Mother Act* and are such essential champions of books and writers.

Thank you to the Ontario Arts Council for supporting the writing of this book, and to Laurence Steven at Your Scrivener Press for recommending the manuscript for funding.

Bernice's lodge is inspired by the Sportsman's Lodge Wilderness Resort on Kukagami Lake, Ontario. I'm very glad I picked it for my wedding and stayed in what would become, in my imagination, Maggie's room.

I grew up "up north" (as people who aren't from there tend to call Northern Ontario) "in the bush" (as people who are from there tend to call the woods). The isolation, lakes, rivers, rocks, pines, birches, 40 below winters, and mosquito-outwitting strategies of this place will always be at the core of who I am. There probably aren't enough mosquitoes in *What We Found Instead.*

ABOUT THE AUTHOR

Photo © Leah Fae

Heidi Reimer is a novelist, a writing coach with Sarah Selecky Writing School, and the author of *The Mother Act*. Her writing explores the lives of women, usually those bent on breaking free of what they're given to create what they yearn for. She has published in *Chatelaine*, *The New Quarterly*, Literary Mama, Lit Hub, and in the anthologies *The M Word: Conversations About Motherhood* and *Body & Soul: Stories for Skeptics and Seekers*. Heidi grew up in the wilds of Northern Ontario and currently lives and writes in Brockville, Ontario. For more, visit www.heidireimer.com